PEACOCK IN JEOPARDY

'The lovely Leda told me you had a private view of the Peacock chain. Very striking, isn't it?' He turned to face her. 'Where does he keep it?'

She stared at Richard, her eyes so wide that the picture of him blurred.

'Richard, what are you thinking of? Not stealing the Peacock?'

'I am indeed thinking of stealing the Peacock. I have been trying to do just that for nearly a month, and a pretty penny it has cost me so far, too.'

'But it is well known as the Koh-i-Noor. You could never sell it!'

'I wouldn't dream of selling it. It has other values. "Who wears the Peacock, holds the throne". Haven't you heard that? I know someone who would give a lot for the Peacock chain. Where is the key kept, Sarah?'

'He has it – Sher Khan.'

'What, all the time? No safe hiding place confided to you?'

'No, Richard, no. I have no idea where it is kept. Oh for God's sake, stop!'

'The Peacock chain,' he said softly, 'the fabulous Peacock. I can pick up a lot of the pieces if I get hold of that . . .'

Peacock in Jeopardy

Katherine Gordon

CORONET BOOKS
Hodder and Stoughton

Copyright © 1982 by Katherine Gordon

First published in Great Britain
1982 by Hodder & Stoughton Ltd

Coronet edition 1984

British Library C.I.P.

Gordon, Katherine
   Peacock in jeopardy.
   I. Title
   823'.914[F]   PR6057.069

ISBN 0-340-35480-1

Printed and bound in Great Britain for
Hodder and Stoughton Paperbacks, a
division of Hodder and Stoughton Ltd.,
Mill Road, Dunton Green, Sevenoaks,
Kent (Editorial Office: 47 Bedford
Square, London, WC1 3DP) by
Richard Clay (The Chaucer Press) Ltd,
Bungay, Suffolk

'Were we not granted dreams to weave into the fabric of reality, how poor and fragile a thing life would be.'

To the memory of the valley and its Ruler, and to Eve, who encouraged me to write the story.

The first Ruler of Lambagh State had no children. He was killed in 1857 and his heir, Sher Khan, his nephew, became the Ruler.

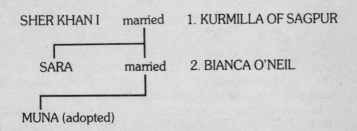

SHER KHAN I   married   1. KURMILLA OF SAGPUR

SARA   married   2. BIANCA O'NEIL

MUNA (adopted)

SHER KHAN I had no children by BIANCA. His nephew, KASSIM KHAN, son of his eldest sister MUMTAZ BEGUM and an English officer, became his heir.

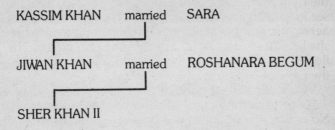

KASSIM KHAN   married   SARA

JIWAN KHAN   married   ROSHANARA BEGUM

SHER KHAN II

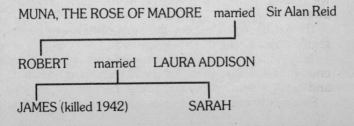

MUNA, THE ROSE OF MADORE   married   Sir Alan Reid

ROBERT   married   LAURA ADDISON

JAMES (killed 1942)   SARAH

1

The train rushed across the wide Indian plains, a long scarf of sparks blowing back from the engine.

In the carriages people slept, or sat wakeful, watching the night go by, each compartment a little isolated world, hurtling along through the night.

Presently, the train left the plains and began to climb, shuddering and clanking, pausing as the gradients grew steeper, and then jerking into movement again. The low hills gave way to rocky cliffs and the mountains came closer, shutting out all but a narrow strip of sky.

The sharp hissing of steam and the jerky movement of the train woke Sarah Longman and she sat up, trying to see her watch, but afraid to put on the light because of her sleeping children. She was fumbling for a torch when she heard her Ayah, who was sleeping on a quilt on the floor of the compartment, begin to stir. Sarah leaned over the edge of her berth and whispered:

'Ayah, are you all right?'

'Yes, but as wet as a fish. The ice box has leaked again. No doubt my old bones will be fevered tomorrow.'

'Oh, Ayah – now, you sleep up here, on my berth. I cannot sleep. We must be getting near Gurdwara, where we change trains, so I will sit in the chair and stay awake.'

The Ayah, wringing out the ends of her sari, barely seen in the dim light, shook her head.

'Nay, child. Do you lie back, and rest. I have slept enough. I will change my sari, and then sit in the chair, and I will waken you in good time. Sleep now.'

Sarah did not argue with her. This was the voice that

had ruled all her childhood days. Ayah had been her nurse until she was seven and had been taken to England to school. The old woman had been her maid when she came back, grown up, and had stayed with her ever since, companion, servant, nurse to her children, and a beloved part of the family.

Lying back, Sarah checked off the list of things that had to be moved from this compartment to a compartment in a carriage on the other train at Gurdwara. She could see the list whenever she shut her eyes. Four bedding rolls, the Ayah's rug-covered bundle, four basins with leather covers containing their toilet articles, the leaking ice box, full of bottles of milk and drinking water, the picnic basket, four suitcases, the children's toy basket, her beauty box, Julia's beauty box, the dog basket, the parrot in his cage, David's push-chair, and a covered bucket. Then there was the stuff in the guard's van. She decided to unload the luggage in the compartment first, leave Julia, her young sister-in-law, guarding it, and then go and get the trunks and boxes from the guard's van. Pyari Lal, the young bearer, would have to stay with Julia. Julia on her first trip to India was still so beglamoured and astonished by practically everything that happened that she could not be trusted to cope with all – or, indeed, *any* – of the organisation that went into a long train journey with several changes from one part of India to another. Sarah made a face at herself. She was being less than fair to Julia, and had not in fact allowed her to help in any way, although Julia had asked several times to be allowed to lighten Sarah's load a little bit.

In the dark, it seemed this journey was endless. There was another change of trains after Gurdwara, and another day's journey after that, before they reached Madore, where Richard, Sarah's husband, and his regiment were stationed, though for how long no one seemed to know. Sarah vowed to herself that no matter where Richard was sent, she was going to stay in Madore for at least six months for the children's sake. This gallivanting up and down the length of India was not good

8

for them. Penelope looked like the ghost of the plump rosy little girl who had arrived in India only a month before, and even David, so robust and cheerful, was becoming pale and querulous.

Her thoughts were sharply broken as the train shuddered and came to a noisy, jolting halt. There was no platform, and no lights outside, so this was obviously another stop to check the lines. There had been many derailments on the track in this part of the country, and the drivers of the trains were careful and nervous.

Sarah let down the window beside her, and leaned out into the darkness. Far ahead she could see lanterns being waved, and torches sending swathes of light along the ground. The air felt fresh and cool, and as her eyes grew used to the darkness she could see the outlines of trees and rocks. It was desolate, empty – there was no sign of house or cultivated fields. Sarah sat, leaning out, enjoying the fresh air, the stillness, and the lack of noise after the swinging stuffiness of the train.

Julia's voice from the upper berth roused her. The girl's voice was frightened, and Sarah turned quickly to reassure her.

'I do not know what is happening, Julia, but I think it is only a stop to check the lines – you know, the rails.'

'Goodness, they keep checking them. This journey will end one day I suppose?'

'The way things are going, I doubt it. I see us endlessly clanking over India, stopping every two hours to change trains, for the rest of our lives –'

'Oh, *don't* talk like that, Sarah – I wish –'

What Julia wished was drowned in a rising clamour outside. Sarah leaned out of the window again, listening, and watching the lanterns bobbing down the train, and then sat back.

'You are perfectly right. I shouldn't say things like that. This time I fear we really are stuck. The rails are up. I suppose some of our disaffected Congress friends have been working on it. Very lucky that the engine driver saw what had happened before we ran on to it.'

She heard Julia draw in her breath and wished that her sister-in-law had had a gentler introduction to travel in India – or better still, that she would relax and take things a little more lightly. The girl sounded as if she might burst into frightened tears. To have to soothe her and calm the children, who were now both awake – it all seemed too much. But Ayah had things well in hand.

'If the Miss Sahib will come down from her berth and take her seat beside Penelope baba, it will be more better, and the little one will not be afraid. I will take David baba, and we will hear the story of the elephant who lived in a palace in the hills. Listen now –'

Julia climbed down, glad of something to do. She sat cross-legged on the foot of the children's berth, and Penelope, only half listening to Ayah's story, crawled tousleheaded to sit nested in Julia's arms, her wide eyes staring round the compartment, looking for Hans, the dachshund, and Bonnie Prince Charlie. Bonnie Prince Charlie, the parrot, was still fast asleep in his cage, his slender green body perched on one foot, his head tucked safely under his wing. Comforted, Penelope's eyes began to close, and Ayah's voice, telling of the wonderful elephant, grew quieter and quieter.

Sarah leaned out of the window again, in time to see the guard coming towards their carriage, his lantern held high.

'All passengers to leave the train, please,' he announced. 'Oh, *no*.' Sarah's mind reeled at the thought of what lay before her. 'But yes, Memsahib. And now, at once, immediately, if you please. Rail is up, and we cannot proceed until repairs carried out. Meantime, up train from Nilgai is soon coming. Perhaps not seeing signal in time, who is telling? Then more better, if hitting this train, that train is empty. So, better if Memsahib is getting out with small family, and sitting where I am showing. Only for very *short* time.'

Sarah sighed and turned back to her family. 'We move out.'

Over a spate of questions she explained why and,

unlocking the door, asked the guard to send Pyari Lal to help them. Ayah, clutching David, climbed out first, followed by Julia with Penelope. Sarah, handing down baskets and bundles requested by Ayah, saw that the old woman had already collected two coolies to carry the things. With Hans the dachshund struggling in her arms, Sarah clambered down, deciding that the parrot would have to stay where he was. But her daughter had other ideas. 'What about the bonnie bird?' Penelope demanded.

Sarah climbed up again and brought down the fluttering bird in his cage, and pulled along by Hans, who had been cooped up in railway carriages for nearly four days and was delighted to get out, she followed the guard and her family a little way up the slope of the hill. There the guard left them, seated among the rocks, their baskets and bundles around them, with his lantern, firmly appropriated by Ayah, to give them light.

All down the train similar evacuations were taking place, but Sarah knew that they were the only European family travelling.

The lantern light made a little golden island in the sea of darkness. Pyari Lal was collecting thorn twigs for a fire. Ayah was lighting the primus stove.

'Tea is good for us all now, I think,' she said. And added with an appallingly dissolute leer, 'Also little little brandy – yes?'

Julia looked at her, her underlip caught between her teeth, her eyes wide. This was like no children's nanny or indeed any other kind of servant she had ever had anything to do with.

'Sarah, I know she's a very good old lady, and she has been with you for ages – but right now, this minute, she looks like – like – well, a sort of rather drunken witch. Do you think she *does* drink?'

Ayah, who understood every word, stared balefully at Julia and turned away. Sarah put a soothing hand on her arm.

'Certainly she drinks. So do I. And so will you in a

11

minute. But Ayah is a sober witch, aren't you, Ayah? She knows all sorts of magic spells – and she can tell fortunes, and stories, and make you better when you are ill and, as far as my family are concerned, she is the most important person in it. She is older than the hills and younger than the smallest child – and she speaks the most beautiful English –'

While Julia was digesting that, Ayah went on with her tea-making. She put a large tot of brandy into Sarah's mug of tea, and handed it to her with a flourish. Julia got plain tea, without very much sugar in it, and felt suitably humbled.

Sipping the hot tea and brandy, Sarah felt more relaxed and happy than she had for months. If only life could be lived simply, like this, always. Here, under her eyes, was everything she loved. The two children sitting up on a bedding roll, drinking warm milk, the lantern light throwing a rosy glow on their faces. The Ayah, crouching beside them, was making herself some pan, spreading the green pan leaf with a mixture of spices and lime, before folding it and popping the little green triangle into her mouth. Presently she would retire discreetly to spit out the red juice that discoloured her teeth and made her smile so sinister. Sarah thought of all the many times she had watched the slender wrinkled hands folding the pan leaves. Penelope, when she grew up, would have the same memories, and so would David. But would they be lucky enough to come back to India to live and work? It seemed very unlikely. Looking at Penelope in the lamplight, bright-eyed and as perfect as a little girl could be, marriage for her seemed beyond the edge of the foreseeable future. Yet it was only yesterday, only the day before yesterday that she herself was Penelope, seated drinking from that same silver mug, on some trek with her father and mother. Caught in the circle of lamplight, today became yesterday, was one with tomorrow. David was not her beloved little son, he was her own brother, safe and alive again, her father and mother were somewhere close by, and all the years from childhood to the present were blurring – were gone.

Julia's voice broke into her dreaming thoughts, and time settled back into the present. With her eyes full of tears, Sarah looked speechlessly at Julia.

'Sarah! *What* is it?' . . .

Julia broke off her question and looked away. Better not to enquire what was wrong with Sarah. Julia was aware of her loyalties and not sure enough of her facts to want to look too closely at Sarah's troubles. So she only said, after a pause, 'How long do you suppose we'll be here?'

Sarah's voice, when she answered, was steady. 'Heaven knows. Hours, I should think. But it is very pleasant. I was getting terribly tired of that train.'

'Yes – yes, so was I. But –'

Julia sounded and felt exasperated. This wonderful trip to India, promised to her as soon as the war was over, was not turning out to be as wonderful as it had sounded.

In fact, it had started to go wrong as soon as Sarah and Richard arrived in England on their leave. Sarah had looked strained and ill, and Richard had been closeted with his father and mother for hours at a time. Then it had looked as if Julia was not going to be allowed to go at all. Her mother had said, with her face screwed into a worried frown, 'Later perhaps, Julie dear – not yet. Things are not too stable out there just now.'

'Things' had obviously meant Sarah and Richard. Nothing seemed very stable between them, Julia had very soon realised that. She compared the beautiful laughing girl who had been Sarah at her wedding to Richard, with the cold, controlled stranger Sarah had become, and wondered what had happened. Questioned, her mother blamed everything on what she called Sarah's 'unfortunate background'. All Julia knew about Sarah's background was that her family had been connected with India ever since the days of the East India Company and that her grandmother on her father's side of the family had been an Indian girl of great beauty and riches. Julia

13

was unable to agree with her mother's views about Sarah's background being unfortunate. She thought it terribly romantic and longed to hear all about it from Sarah.

But Sarah would not talk about her grandmother at all. Julia guessed why her sister-in-law had become so shut away and cold and aloof. Julia's mother was not the most tactful woman, and Julia could imagine the little talks that her mother and Sarah had had when Sarah came back from India, sick and, it appeared, in disgrace over some other man. She knew Sarah had asked Richard to divorce her, but that he had refused. Julia could not imagine how Sarah, married to her adored brother, could have looked at another man, but did not attempt to judge her beautiful sister-in-law. She found her enchanting, and longed to know all about her, and be her friend. Sarah avoided her as much as possible and certainly offered her no confidences or friendship. Julia could not have guessed how much her mother had hurt Sarah.

'Sarah dear,' (Mrs Longman always added 'dear' to everyone's name) 'Sarah dear – one thing I do ask of you, if I let my little Julia go off with you. Just remember how young she is. Stupidly, I suppose, I have sheltered her from everything unpleasant in life. I am sure, that being a woman of – well, shall we say, Sarah dear, a woman of some experience, you are probably less easily shocked than a young girl would be by certain things. Will you promise me to try and keep my little girl from seeing too much of the seamy side of life? She is so innocent and impressionable –'

Sarah, aged twenty-five, decided rightly that the seamy side of life would refer to her entire life in Mrs Longman's eyes. Later that same day she overheard her mother-in-law saying to her husband, 'I am not at all colour conscious, Jack. But I cannot help feeling that bad blood, white *or* black, will out. And the – er – *coloured* side of that girl's family – well, we do know that her father's mother was, after all –.' Black! Sarah could not forget that, or forgive the rest of the sentence. She seemed to

14

grow an icy shell, and no one could reach her through it except her own children.

So Julia never got close to her sister-in-law, and both girls inwardly regretted this.

Mrs Longman was finally overruled, and Julia had been allowed to go to India with Richard and Sarah when Richard's leave ended.

The voyage had been a terrible disappointment. No dancing, no changing for dinner, no romantic gazing at the moon with handsome young men. Wartime restrictions had not yet been lifted. Sarah and Julia and the children had been crammed into a dormitory type of cabin with ten other women and five children. The bunks had been in three tiers along the walls, and there had been only three portholes.

There had been very few young men on the ship, and those few had shown more interest in the married women than they had in Julia. Sarah! Sarah had treated everybody, men and women alike, with a sort of burning disdain. She spent all her time with her children, and when they were asleep she had walked alone round the deck, with a furious impatient stride, as if she was trying to escape from something. She had snubbed all Julia's efforts to be friendly, and Julia had eventually spent most of her time playing bad bridge and walking the decks with various elderly admirers of her youth and her silvery beauty.

Their arrival in Bombay had at least promised more freedom and entertainment, but then Richard had been transferred up country immediately and had gone off, leaving them to follow him half across India in various slow trains. And now – this. Julia sighed heavily, and turned to look into the fire that Pyari Lal was lighting, and dreamed of how things might have been.

Sarah knew exactly what she was thinking, but for the moment could find nothing to say to her. She was a constant reminder of Richard, even her voice was a feminine version of his, and Sarah could hardly bear to look at her. The Longman stamp. The children had it too, but somehow that did not matter because they were hers as well. Penelope had her father's eyes, fringed in thick black lashes, and her hair had the same golden fairness; and although David was dark, like herself, his features were all Longman, from the firm chin to the brilliant blue eyes. They were beautiful children –

'And as good as gold,' said Sarah, finishing her thoughts aloud, and getting up and gathering David into her arms to kiss him until he squeaked with delight.

'And me – and me, Mummy,' Penelope cried jealously, and was kissed and hugged in her turn, nearly strangling her mother as she hugged back.

'And now to sleep, until we have to carry you back to the train. Down you go; count the stars, and you'll be off before you know it.'

It was true. Counting stars and the crackling of the fire were an irresistible lullaby. Both children were asleep before Sarah had finished her second cup of tea.

2

The fire was dying, and both Julia and the children were asleep when the train from Nilgai came to a halt just behind their train. Soon lanterns were flickering along the carriages, and all the passengers were getting out and climbing up the hill as they had done. It was too dark to see if there were any English people among them.

Seeing the other train cleared of its passengers made Sarah certain that they were in for a long wait. She was relieved to see that Julia was asleep, so that no questions would have to be answered. She sat thinking and remembering other journeys, and the hillside began to settle into silence as the newcomers either fell asleep, or gave themselves up to patient waiting, with the easy acceptance of the East.

Sarah's own eyes were growing heavy when a man moved up through the shadows and bent over her.

'Mrs Longman? My name is Lawton. The guard said that you were up here with your family. I just want to tell you –'

His voice was drowned in the crackle of gunfire somewhere close to the train.

'What on earth – ?' Sarah was on her feet and diving for the children, and so was the Ayah.

'Get down, you little idiot – sorry, but you must keep down. I came to warn you there is a small party of dacoits attacking the train. They thought it was unguarded. We are dealing with them, and I doubt if the shooting will last very long, but I would like you to keep down and move round a bit behind those rocks. I must go, but as soon as things quieten down I'll come back again. Don't

17

worry – just keep down, and for God's sake don't come anywhere near the trains until I come back.'

He went off rapidly down the hill and out of sight. Ayah was already behind the rocks, the children still sleeping peacefully beside her. Pyari Lal had killed the last of the fire by throwing earth on it and the lantern was out.

Julia, who had woken with a start, had moved quickly when Sarah told her to. Sarah joined her behind the rocks, with the parrot and Hans, who did not care for gunfire and was whining. Sarah, crouching uncomfortably behind a rock, tried to see what was happening, but apart from sporadic bursts of firing and a great deal of shouting, she could see nothing except degrees of darkness – all the lanterns and torches were out.

Julia said miserably, 'Sarah, I think I am going to be sick.' Poor girl – she was trembling, and her hand was clammy when Sarah took it firmly in hers.

'Oh, poor Julie! Listen, I'm going to get the brandy, and we'll both have a quick swallow – it is only because it is happening in the dark that it seems so bad. It will all be over in a minute or two, and we'll go back on to the train as if nothing had happened, and it will be a good dinner-table story.'

She wriggled round the rock and returned with the brandy bottle, putting it to Julia's mouth and making sure that the girl took a large swallow. Julia choked, but she was not sick, and she sounded stronger when she spoke.

'Sarah, you are so brave. *How* can you not be frightened? I'm terrified! This is far more frightening than the bombing at home.'

'Only because it is happening in strange surroundings. After a bit, you will be taking this sort of thing for granted.'

'For heaven's sake, don't tell me this is going to happen every five minutes?'

'Of course not. But this is India, and there are dacoits and goondas and disaffected political groups – and

18

snakes, for that matter, though they are not quite so noisy.'

'Well, I still don't know how you can be so calm – did you say snakes? There, you see, you are laughing. You are completely unafraid.'

Completely unafraid, thought Sarah, conscious of the sick chill in her body, of the panic that was making her hand shake and slip on the bottle. She could think of no reason at all for being calm and unafraid.

'Well,' slowly she found words. 'Well, I suppose I know that there is nothing to worry about. That train that pulled up behind us is a troop train, and we are now protected by soldiery. The dacoits couldn't have chosen a worse time for themselves.'

But supposing I am wrong, she thought. Supposing the dacoits are stronger than the troops and better armed. Supposing it *wasn't* a troop train but just a few men coming back from leave and they cannot hold the dacoits – what happens then to my children, and to Julia – and to me. She fought down the blind panic that was almost overcoming her and took a quick swig of the brandy herself. Was this night going to be her punishment, were the children to be victims because of her lack of morals, her inherited loose nature? Did the Christian God who said, 'Suffer little children to come unto me', and was gentle to the woman taken in adultery, also punish blindly the innocent and the guilty, because he hated sin? There were no answers to these questions, no one could answer for this strange triple God, and so there was always a risk for the people a sinner loved – in life, and in death, always the threat of punishment through the pain of the beloved.

A great burst of shooting, a scream, and then shouts, more shooting and a long, long silence. Hans barked briefly and was clouted, and they sat listening. Presently Sarah heard footsteps and quietly took up the pistol Pyari Lal had put beside her. Torch in one hand, and pistol in the other, she waited tensely as the footsteps came closer and closer – noisy, confident footsteps. With

19

a sigh she relaxed, put on the torch, and to Julia's complete mystification, said with a laugh: 'Ah – the U.S. Cavalry, as usual in the nick of time,' and getting up, walked out to meet the newcomer.

'Digby Lawton here, Mrs Longman. All over, including the shouting. They ran off as I thought they would, but we got four of them.'

'Any of your men hurt?' asked Sarah, putting down her torch so that she could have both hands free. The Colt .32 was a brute to unload. Pyari Lal had already lit the lantern, and they all stood in the yellow light, looking at each other.

'Yes. My subedar got nicked on the shoulder, and a civilian got himself killed. Those dacoits were very well armed. However – look, please give me that pistol – give it to me, I'll unload it for you, you're going to shoot your own feet off in a minute!'

Sarah, furious with her shaking hands, gave him the pistol, and he unloaded it neatly and handed it back.

'Any more of you carrying dangerous weapons?' His enquiry was anxious.

'No, that is our only defence – thank you. Now I suppose we re-mount our train, do we?'

'Yes. The guard would like you to check your things in the van. I'll take you down. Perhaps the rest of your party could put themselves back in your compartment?'

His raised eyebrows above smiling blue eyes turned from the Ayah and the children to Julia, who was frankly staring at him. Sarah quickly introduced him and, giving instructions to Ayah, took her handbag and prepared to follow Digby Lawton down the hill.

'I won't be long, Julia. Will you be all right? Ayah knows the compartment. Do you think you can manage?'

'Yes, of course. Ayah will tell me what to do, won't you, Ayah?'

She wished she could go off down the hill with the handsome Major Lawton, but realised that she would be worse than useless about the luggage in the guard's van.

She had never seen anyone travel with so much luggage. She watched the torch beam wind down the hill, resting her hand on the parrot's cage. Bonnie Prince Charlie had had a trying night. He stretched up a bright-eyed green head, red beak at the ready, and nipped the hand that was so temptingly close. Not a hard nip. Just enough to make Julia jump.

'Oh – oh, the *last* straw. You evil little green bird!'

Bonnie Prince Charlie shook his feathers and snapped his bill at her, making her jump again, and Penelope's laughter and Ayah's cackle followed Sarah down the hill.

She was glad to be doing something. The dark hillside seemed haunted with her own fears. She kept close to her companion until they got to the circle of light outside the guard's van. There the dead man lay on a stretcher, his young face uncovered, his eyes staring up at the stars he would never see again. Sarah stopped beside him and pulled up a fold of the grey blanket he had been wrapped in and covered his face. The wounded subedar was sitting on the ground nearby. Someone had already packed his shoulder with a field dressing and bandaged it neatly with a khaki puggaree. There was nothing Sarah could do for him except offer him a drink from her flask of brandy and a cigarette, both of which he accepted with alacrity.

'Hamid, you will never be accepted into Paradise, drinking spirits as if it was water!' Hamid grinned at his officer, and pulled on his cigarette with a flourish.

'Speaking as a non-Muslim, I could use a slug of that myself, Mrs Longman.'

Seen in the lights from the train, Digby looked younger than he had sounded, certainly very young to be a major. He was not much taller than Sarah herself, but he was very broad, with blue eyes which turned hopefully to the flask Sarah was holding. She surrendered it to him.

'But of course – do have it. I brought two bottles of brandy with us for the journey and some whisky, and with luck we should get to Madore before we finish all that!'

'Madore! You are on your way there? So are we. We were due to change on to your train at Jalkote, but now we are being hitched on here. This drink is saving my life. I've been travelling for a week, and although I laid in a good stock of beer for the journey, the 6th Battalion were at Nindhal station when we went through and we had rather a party on the platform. Do you know any of the 6th?'

Sarah, taking a deep steadying breath, said that she knew the 6th quite well. She turned to the guard and checked her list with him, hoping that this break in the conversation would change the subject. But when the guard had satisfied himself that all her luggage was intact Digby went back to the original conversation.

'It was James Lincoln who helped to finish my beer – and of course the splendid Bruce – you know Bruce Whigmore?'

Sarah turned to him, her face clear in the light from the van. Her voice was cold, and her eyes very bright.

'If you know my name, you know of course that I know Bruce. Know him very well in fact. Let us not be silly –'

Digby stared at her, and she glared back, frowning, her eyes hard.

'Oh, *God*,' said Digby suddenly, 'Longman – you are Sarah Longman –'

'Yes. I am Sarah Longman. Didn't you know?'

'No. You won't believe me, but I didn't. I've only just got back to India. I was in Burma – or didn't *you* know?'

'The next thing is, you'll be reminding me that there has been a war.' Sarah spoke lightly enough now. 'In any case, it really doesn't matter whether you know all the local scandal yet or not.'

'But it does – I would not have been so clumsy! Here, hang on, are you all right?'

Sarah, sick and dizzy, could not answer. He put the brandy flask to her mouth, his arm behind her shoulders. The brandy burned her throat, the world steadied, and she came back from the edge of whirling darkness to his anxious face.

'I'm all right now – so sorry to be stupid. I'm terribly tired. I've been travelling a long time too.'

She took another swallow of brandy, and Digby tightened his arm which was still round her.

'I'm going to carry you back to your compartment and get you lying down.'

Sarah shook her head. Carried down the length of the train? Julia would be horrified, and the children frightened to death.

'Oh, no – I'm perfectly all right now – I can walk.'

She took two steps outside the circle of light and was immediately desperately sick. His hand was firm on her head, and when she had finished and was leaning against him, completely exhausted, he pushed a big clean handkerchief into her hand, and then picked her up and turned towards the train.

'I am going to put you in my compartment. It is just here, and when you are settled I will go and check up on your family. We shall be moving very shortly and I do not think you are fit enough for a run to the end of the train.'

Shaky, dizzy, and feeling that she might be sick again at any moment, Sarah could not argue with him.

Presently she was lying on his berth, which his servant had already made up. A basin and towel were beside her. This thoughtful touch made her smile, and she began to feel better, but as soon as she tried to sit up the dizzy nausea was back. She had to lie still, with her eyes closed, and so lying, she fell asleep at last.

She woke to the rattle and sway of the moving train, feeling much better, but was immediately very worried about Julia and the children. Julia would be in a desperate state, although Ayah was capable of convoying the whole expedition to China if need be. Sarah sat up, to see dawn lightening the windows to grey squares and Digby Lawton watching her from a chair beside the berth.

'Better?'

She nodded and put a hand up to her disordered hair.

'Yes, thank you. Thank you very much. But Julia – my sister-in-law – did she get on board all right? She must be terribly worried.'

A vision of Julia and the children marooned on the lonely hillside made her catch her breath and whitened her face.

'For heaven's sake lie down. Of course they got on. Your sister-in-law was cackling a bit – for one so young she does seem to get into a state very easily. I calmed her, helped by that wonderful old beldame of yours, and I told them I would take you back, provided you were better, as soon as we get to Gurdwara. Both the children were asleep. Your sister-in-law gave me a cold eye. I think she suspects that we arranged this between us – the hold-up and all, including dacoits, so that we could satisfy our wild lusts.'

'Quite possibly she thinks just that,' Sarah spoke drily.

Digby, looking at her downcast eyes, said, 'Oh, don't be ridiculous. I was only joking. You make me feel that I am constantly offending you. Please don't. I do not mean to hurt you in any way.'

Sarah looked up at him. 'I'm sorry. Don't pay any attention to me. I am so grateful to you for helping Julia. She hasn't been away from home before, and this journey has not been a very good beginning to her time in India. That is why she seems so fraught.'

'Oh, I see. But one thing I *did not* understand. She seems to think I am doing an attachment to some American Cavalry regiment – asked me, for God's sake, if we had horses with us. Well, I am delighted to have made you laugh, but I do not understand at all. Horses! Is she given to hallucinations?' Sarah, still laughing, shook her head.

'Oh no, poor Julia. It was all that banging and loud cries and then you arriving victorious out of the night, in the nick of time as it were, and I made a silly remark about the U.S. Cavalry. I confused her.'

'Yes, I see where you might have confused her. It all

seems terribly unclear to me too. Sometime you must explain it to me.'

'I will. *And* to Julia. May I go and wash?'

'Of course. There is a clean towel in there all ready for you, and a brand new toothbrush.'

'Oh, thank you – and could I borrow your comb? I am afraid this is my wrong handbag.'

'Your *wrong* handbag?' said Digby politely, bringing out a pocket comb.

'Yes. This is the bag that is full of tickets and papers about my luggage and the dog ticket and the ticket for the parrot. There isn't room for anything else.'

'No, I can imagine there wouldn't be,' said Digby, eyeing the bulging bag, and opened the bathroom door for her.

Standing shakily in the little swaying bathroom, Sarah splashed her face with cold water, thinking how very kind Digby was. She wished that she had some make-up with her, but she had not, so there was nothing she could do to improve her appearance. She combed her long hair with his comb and then twisted it up into a coil on top of her head. Her face stared back at her from the glass, thin, shadowed, and pale. She pulled a face at her reflection and, opening the door, went back into the compartment.

Digby had a thermos of coffee and some fruit, and they talked quietly as they ate and drank. It all seemed easy and relaxed but Sarah was conscious of tension and his eyes were speculative as he watched her. She could eat very little, but drank coffee thirstily, holding out her cup for more. When she had finished he put the things away in a basket as neatly as a woman, refusing her offer of help. Then he lit a cigarette for her and one for himself.

'You are feeling better, I hope. You look better. You looked ghastly earlier.'

'Thanks very much.'

'No, really. You looked terribly ill in fact. What is it? Have you been ill, or have you been having too many farewell parties, beating it up too much?'

There was no impertinence in his question, but that

made it no easier to answer him. Finally she said, 'No, I can promise you I have not been beating it up. Nor have I been ill – well, not since last year. I've been back to England since then and should look blooming.'

'Well, you don't, frankly.'

'We had a fearful voyage back and, apart from two weeks in Bombay, we've been travelling ever since. These train journeys are not funny; I expect I am over-tired.' You know what is wrong with me, she thought bitterly, you have heard all the scandal, you know all about me. I know you do. So why torment me with questions?

Watching her, he was thinking that of all the girl-friends Bruce Whigmore had made notorious, this was the most unlikely. Not Bruce's type at all; he usually chose his companions for their more obvious charms, and Digby recalled a stunning series of redheads and blondes. This girl was a very different type, beautiful, dark – those long oriental eyes came from the grand-mother he supposed, and the high, almost too noticeable cheekbones – and she was terribly thin. He remembered the story of the Longman marriage. India was a small place where scandal was concerned. But the stories had all been cooked up by bored nobodies. The old India hands, both civil and army, had seen nothing strange in this girl marrying into the Indian Army. Her family had been connected with India in one way or another for three generations and the fact that one of her grand-fathers had married an Indian girl was not a matter for surprise. There had been stories about that marriage, old scandals, but the girl had brought a fortune with her, and the stories had died for lack of material to feed on. Sarah's grandfather had taken his Indian bride and her fortune straight back to England. No, the real scandals had started later, after Sarah's marriage to Richard Long-man. Bruce Whigmore as a constant escort was automati-cally cause for scandal.

He studied her, wondering what could possibly make someone like her, with apparently everything she could ask for in life, go off the rails with an obvious womaniser like Bruce. Digby did not know her husband very well, but he seemed a decent enough type and must be a kind and loving husband, for after all the talk and excitement last year here she was, still safely married and returning to her husband. Looking at her, two things occurred to him. The first was that she must have been most bitterly hurt by all the gossip that had attended her affair and its ending. The second was that she was the kind of woman a man might be very glad to keep, the sort of woman a man might find himself unable to give up.

She turned her head, flushed, and said in a voice that was as hard and cold as crystal, 'Well? What are you thinking?'

'Thinking? I was thinking – I was wondering –' Digby, caught off-guard, flushed in his turn and they both became silent. Then Sarah said quietly, 'How long will you be in Madore?'

It was a sudden change of subject, but welcome to them both. They talked about Madore and the mountains round it.

'I am longing for my first leave. I shall go on trek up to Gilgit, I hope, and then try some of those valleys round Kashmir. I believe that is wonderful country, those valleys that lead down to Kashmir. The fair weather road is only open for a short time in the summer but I would like to do a proper trek.'

'Yes, I know what you mean. I would love to go on trek again.' Her voice was wistful, her eyes dreamed, as she thought back into the past.

Towering snow ranges, deep green valleys, were clear in her mind's eye. The friendly village lights at footsore evening, the amazing dawns when the snows turned from blue to leaping crimson and then to blazing white. The air of those happy, free journeys blew for an instant in the rocking dusty compartment, and then the present was back, the vision gone, and she stared at Digby, all her composure broken, her face convulsing to ugliness with her effort to refrain from weeping. He jumped up

27

and bent over her.

'My dear girl, what on earth is wrong? Are you in pain? Tell me!' She wept like a child weeps, with abandon and no grace. As the paroxysm passed he gave her his handkerchief and looked at her narrowly.

'You are not now about to be sick again, are you?'

She shook her head, the anxious enquiry made her laugh, the laughter of near hysteria; he heard the wild note in her voice and admired the tremendous effort she exerted to control herself. When she looked at him with drowned eyes and apologised he longed to put his arms round her suddenly, and was surprised to find how hard it was not to touch her.

'Look, I do not know what is wrong, but if it would help to talk to me, well, I am a good listener.'

The carriage rattled and swayed, trees and rocks and hills rushed past and were gone, they were shut away in a small intimate world, a time and place of their own. It would be so easy to talk – but about what? What could she tell a strange man, even in the face of this sudden intimacy that had grown up between them, born of the shooting, the relief of safety and the enforced isolation? She imagined herself telling her story, speaking of her unhappy affair, speaking of her fears of the future, her total disillusion with her marriage. No. There was nothing that she could tell this man, however kind he seemed. She sat, looking utterly lost and miserable, forced to speak in the end because he so obviously expected her to say something.

'All that is wrong with me is the aftermath of a fright and a long railway journey.'

'Really.' He looked disbelieving, and after a few minutes spent looking out of the window, turned back to her to say quietly,

'I did hear gossip, it would be stupid of me to pretend I didn't. But it is all over now, so shed no more tears. Don't let malicious tongues hurt you. And certainly don't weep over Bruce Whigmore. He is a charming chap, but not worth a single tear – half the women in India have been

28

in love with him at one time or another. Another thing – girls who are beautiful always suffer from the tongues of envious onlookers. So no more tears?'

'No more tears.' She smiled at him, thinking that he was a very kind young man, but what a splendid black and white world he lived in! He might have heard some of the gossip, but obviously not all of it. As for Bruce – well, she had fallen in love with him, certainly. But if it had not been Bruce it would have been someone else. Sitting there, in the rocking train, she recalled clearly the morning when she had decided to take a lover.

It had been a cool grey morning, during the short rains, when she was checking the baby clothes from the cedar chest on the verandah of the house in Madras. The bearer had come and said that a memsahib wanted to speak to her – not a memsahib that was known to her. Sarah, feeling lumpy and plain in her last two months of pregnancy, had almost sent out to say that she was not at home, but she had instead ordered coffee and told the bearer to bring the visitor on to the verandah, and had thus brought the final disaster to her marriage.

The woman had been pretty in spite of her advanced pregnancy. Her blue eyes had widened when she saw Sarah, smocked and unwieldy, coming to meet her, and she had looked as if she wanted to turn and go away again. 'Snap!' said Sarah, smiling at her. 'Aren't we a lucky pair? When are you having yours?'

She remembered how the girl had first stared at her and had then burst into tears.

Two hours later, Sarah saw her out and went back on trembling legs to sit and stare at the neat piles of baby clothes, saved from Penelope's babyhood, and now to be used for her next baby. Mechanically she went on sorting and folding, and when Ayah brought Penelope back from her walk the clothes were there, all ready to be aired and put into the new cupboard in the nursery. Richard, confronted later, took refuge in bluster and accusations of his own. 'You are a cold uninteresting woman in bed, Sarah. Where all that hot-blooded expertise you people are supposed to have has gone in your case, I cannot imagine. It certainly didn't last long, did it?'

'"You people"? What do you mean, Richard, by "you people"?'

'You are, after all, darling, rather more than a little touched with the famous tar brush, don't you remember? And from all one heard, your father's mamma was by no means a cold fish. But you are. I was literally driven into Beryl's arms. However, don't let's make a stupid fuss about all this. She probably only came round because I haven't paid her off. I promised her a thousand, but I am a little short –'

'Don't distress yourself, Richard. I have already given her a cheque.'

His calm dismissal of the whole affair, his attitude in general, appalled Sarah. Later, his accusations of her frigidity cankered. 'Very well,' she thought, staring at her husband's handsome face. 'Let me get out of these loathsome smocks, and then we shall see.'

Bruce Whigmore was opportune and altogether charming. Sarah, tasting physical pleasure for the first time in her life, thought herself madly in love, and also thought how fortunate that everything was working out so well. Bruce was delightful with the children; Penelope adored him and David was too young to be distressed by anything. Richard would be free to marry a woman more suited to him, and she would marry Bruce and be blissfully happy. It did not matter when she found that she was pregnant by Bruce – it just seemed to make it all more perfect.

The fall from this cloud-cuckoo-land was very hard. Bruce Whigmore, that charming confirmed lover of many women, received the news that she was pregnant and had asked Richard for a divorce with stark horror and astonishment. Richard, instead of being overjoyed at the news that she wanted a divorce, went into a blind rage and told her that if he divorced her, she would most certainly never see her children again. Her beloved father, when she wrote and told him, wrote back a sharp condemnation of her behaviour, telling her in effect that she must pull herself together and behave herself. Meantime the Cantonment wives sharpened their tongues and sat back to watch the drama unfold.

One of the hardest things to swallow was the 'I told you so' look that even her friends wore when Bruce Whigmore stopped calling, and she began to realise that Richard had told most of them his version of the story and they had preferred, perhaps naturally, to take his side; and every day, within her, growing and living, was the baby. In the end Richard guessed and issued his ultimatum.

The Ayah had found a woman in the bazaar and after an hour of agony Sarah saw her child, her child that could have been, carried quietly away in a bloodstained newspaper. She had very nearly died and the army doctor, called in, had fortunately been skilful enough to save her life, but there would never be any more children.

What story Richard had told his parents she had no idea. 'Sarah had a bad go of malaria, very ill, nerves affected, went a trifle odd and had an affair –' It had probably gone something like that. It did not matter really. His parents treated her with wary civility, but this was nothing new. Mrs Longman had never liked her, nor approved of her marrying Richard. Looking back, Sarah realised that she would never have attracted Richard at all if it had not been for her money.

Her wealth, which was considerable, had come to her from her Indian grandmother. A strange will her grandmother had made; she had left everything to her first grand-daughter, on one condition. The girl was to be called Sarah. She had died before her son, Sarah's father, was married, but when his daughter was born she had been called an anglicised version of Sara and had come into her inheritance on her seventeenth birthday. Her parents, people of means in any case, had taught her to look on money as something one took for granted, something that made life easier. She had never thought of it as a weapon, as power. Now she thought sadly that there had been no need for that horrible bazaar abortion. Richard, threatened with the loss of all that her money brought him, would have made no trouble. How could she have been so foolish? Then, in her heart, something told her that for her, money was not a thing to bargain with. She could never have used it to threaten Richard – or could she?

She came back from her thought journey into the past to find Digby leaning forward speaking to her.

'Come back, Sarah. You've been gone a long time. Don't look so sad. No more tears – remember?'

'No. No more.' She smiled her bittersweet smile, and went into the bathroom to bathe her eyes, and then came back to get his comb to do her hair again. He watched her as she combed it and coiled it up again, completely unselfconscious, her arms raised, the big tortoise-shell pin nipped between her teeth. She was very attractive, balancing like a dancer against the movement of the train. For the first time since they had met, Digby had time to look at her as a woman, and knew just how attractive she could be. Strung like a stretched wire, tearstained and desolate with a grief he did not understand, she was, no doubt about it, one of the most attractive girls he had come across for some time. He did not blame Bruce Whigmore at all, and in fact envied him. Her hair up to her satisfaction, she sat down opposite him.

'Do you feel better now?'

'Yes, thank you, I feel fine.' She did not apologise, she said nothing more, and they sat in silence until the train drew into Gurdwara and he helped her down and said, 'The Madore train must be in. It is over the bridge, I'm afraid, but I'll collect some of my men and we'll get your stuff carried over for you.'

Sarah thanked him with an upward look, and Digby, who had been holding her arm, took his hand away as if he had been stung, astonished at himself, relieved that she seemed to notice nothing. They hurried together down the platform, threading their way through the hundreds of travellers and the tea and garland sellers, the pan and cigarette sellers, the crowded sweet stalls and the men selling hot food. She moved ahead of him, walking swiftly, with a grace of movement that held his eyes, so that when they reached her compartment he almost blundered into her because he was not looking where he was going at all.

3

Julia had made no attempt to move away from their compartment, but she and the Ayah and Pyari Lal had everything packed and ready, and as soon as Sarah and Digby came up, the children were lifted out and taken charge of by an enormous Punjabi sepoy, while another sepoy heaved out all the luggage and Ayah supervised. Digby watched the pile of luggage grow with the superior expression of a bachelor who travels with one neat bed roll, a suitcase and a covered basin for his shaving kit.

'If I hadn't known that he was a bachelor, I would know now, seeing his face,' thought Sarah. She said with dignity, 'As you will remember there are some trunks and things in the van too, and David's push-chair and one or two rug bundles.'

'Good grief – yes, of course. How you have managed all this alone, I do not know. Here, Esoof Khan, go down to the guard's van and get the rest of the Memsahib's trunks.'

As they finally set off down the platform, Julia, vastly relieved to have Sarah safely back with her, was able to enjoy the sight of the cavalcade. It was so strange to find herself in this group of people. What an odd collection! She tried to imagine them all walking down a platform on an English railway station, and failed. First, an old woman, swathed in a white sari which was miraculously clean, carrying a small boy; then an enormous Indian soldier, carrying a little blonde girl, followed by a British officer carrying a domed and ornamental cage in which a green parrot shrieked continuously. Another Indian sepoy carried a basket full of bottles and a tea-tray, and a coolie carried a bedding roll and pushed a pram which contained a large teddy bear, a roll of lavatory paper and two small chamber pots. This was followed by several coolies pushing a cart piled with bedding rolls, tin boxes, rug bundles and a small commode painted pale blue. Far in the rear struggled Pyari Lal, attempting to control the frenzied leapings of Hans.

Sarah, a list in her hand, checked off the luggage as it was carried past. She took Hans from Pyari Lal and told him to take the parrot from Digby who was looking very embarrassed by his shrieking burden.

Compared to the others, this change had been made so easy. Sarah and her family were settled into their compartment in half the time it had taken them to change trains alone. Her thanks were quietly spoken, but Digby could see how grateful she was, and was glad – at least this was one burden he had been able to raise from her shoulders!

Julia said, 'Oh, how much better this change was! The change at Dorunda was terrible for Sarah; she had to rush about alone, chivvying the coolies – I was useless to her. This has been wonderful – so *quick*.'

'Good. It is very good practice for my men. Now let's get everything out and time them, and see if they can do it even more quickly,' said Digby, leaning in the door. Julia stared at him, her blue eyes round with horror. Only Sarah's laughter saved her from saying 'Oh, *no* – why?'

They arranged to meet in his compartment, two carriages away, for a pre-dinner drink. 'The train stops at about 7 p.m. at Kumbh. That should be about right – yes?' Digby went off then, leaving them to settle in for the day.

The family's compartment soon looked exactly like the previous one. The children were settled on one bottom berth, Penelope with a drawing-book and lots of coloured crayons, David with his beloved bear Bluebell, whose eyes he was systematically trying to remove. A

35

zinc bath full of ice was on the floor, with bottles of soda water and milk and orange juice lying in it. Julia sat on her berth, cross-legged, and read *Gone With the Wind*. Sarah sat on the large cane chair with Hans on her lap, and looked out of the window. The Ayah was washing some of the children's clothes in the bathroom. The chink and tinkle of her bracelets came clearly through the noises of the train, and the whirring of the electric fan, like the sound of little bells.

Sarah felt as if she was convalescing from a serious illness. Her thoughts were scattered, and she felt weak and full of lassitude. She did not want to think, or move; she wanted to sit, endlessly, in the moving train, with no past and no future and nothing to do. Just the safe small present in this little moving house.

When the Ayah came out of the bathroom, Sarah roused herself, turned from the window and asked, 'Ayah, where did that zinc bath come from? Where is the ice box?'

'Huh,' said Ayah, 'that ice box was no good. So I gave it to the station-master at Gurdwara, and he gave me the bath from the Ladies' Retiring Room. It is a good, small bath, it does not leak, and it will be of great use to us for many years.' What the station-master would do with the leaking ice box did not appear to worry Ayah – or indeed Sarah, thought Julia, diverted from her book.

'That – isn't that government property?' she asked Sarah. Sarah nodded. The Ayah nodded too.

'Yes. Property of the Sircar. So who has a better right to it than my memsahib?' This seemed to settle the matter. With a smile to Julia, Sarah went back to her window watching, and after a short struggle Julia managed to reabsorb herself into Scarlett O'Hara's adventures, which were begining to look a little tame.

The day wore on to evening, the children growing hot and tired and bored. Ayah and Sarah fed them, bathed them and put them to bed, Penelope lying so that she could watch Bonnie Prince Charlie preening his feathers into place before he fell asleep. Sarah and Julia washed and changed and were ready when the train clanked to a noisy stop. Julia, in a fresh cotton frock, eyed Sarah's clean khaki shirt and trousers with envy. 'You look so smart in those,' she said. 'But it is no good. I cannot wear them. My figure is all wrong for trousers.' Privately, she thought Sarah was much too thin. She viewed her own rounded little body with hopeful favour. Her mother had always assured her that men liked womanly women.

Sarah could read her thoughts easily. She smiled as she said, 'You look very good. Let's go. The train will only stop here for seven minutes, or so that guard is shouting.'

They hurried down the platform, clutching their bottles, and met Digby coming to find them. Julia thought he looked very handsome, and smiled a welcome, which he did not see. He was looking over her head at Sarah, who did not smile, but who said, as if in answer to a question, 'Yes, thank you, I feel better. Almost cured in fact. The American Cavalry to the rescue again.' Julia raised her eyebrows to herself. What Sarah was talking about she could not fathom. She resolved to question her sister-in-law closely about Digby's American connections.

4

They sat in Digby's compartment until long after sunset, sipping their cold drinks and watching the landscape rolling past, the sky fading from pale lemon to darkness, with no intervening twilight. Conversation was light and easy. Julia was content to sit watching and listening. Digby did most of the talking – Sarah barely spoke. She sat in a corner of the berth, her head leaning back, looking out of the window until it was too dark to see anything but her own reflection staring at her, then she turned back to them in the closeness of the little compartment. She seemed happier and less strained than Julia had seen her for a long time. She thought how beautiful Sarah looked when she was relaxed, but saw beneath the beauty the thinness, and the pallor. Her thoughts wandered as she watched the other two. Digby, leaning forward towards Sarah, seemed as if he was unconscious of any other presence in the compartment. Julia's eyebrows rose again – so Sarah was a heartbreaker, a woman men were fascinated by, like Scarlett in that book. Apparently opulent figures were not all that important. But Julia did not have time to feel left out. Every time Sarah spoke she included Julia in the conversation, and Digby, as if warned, turned to her too. She suddenly felt secure in their company, they really wanted her there too. Julia rested content, enjoying every moment.

The mood lasted for the rest of the evening. They all had dinner together at Dholpore, where the train stopped for two and a half hours. The dining room in the station restaurant had stayed frozen in the world of 1904, with oil lamps on tall stands, and potted palms in the corners of the room and a punka creaking and flapping above their heads. They ate very hot chicken curry, and with it drank, at Digby's insistence, very cold champagne. 'But how on earth do they get it so cold, so quickly?' Julia marvelled

Sarah guessed that Digby had telegraphed ahead. 'Very extravagant,' she said.

'Well, I think we should celebrate. I thought I was going to have a fearfully boring journey, and instead I've got youth and beauty dining with me – youth and beauty twice repeated,' he added, as both girls turned with questioning faces.

The bearer in charge of the restaurant was a tall old man who wore his ragged white uniform with an air, and who was obviously delighted to be waiting on them. Digby noticed the badge on his turban and asked him about it.

'It is the crest of Colonel Bathurst Sahib. I went to Mesopotamia with him in the great war. I started work in the house of his mother as a masalchi. Then, when I was a young man, and the Colonel Sahib came to join his regiment, I became his servant, staying even after his marriage. When he went with his regiment to Mespot I went too. After he was killed, his memsahib, who bore him no children, went to England, and I went to work for Captain Campbell-Scott Sahib. He was killed in the Frontier campaign of 1929 and I took work with Colonel Kirkland sahib, who was killed in Burma. Now, I being old, and without heart, have taken government service here, and will get a pension from the Railway. But I keep the crest of my first sahib, for his family was as my family, and if he had had a son or a daughter, I would not be working for anyone else.' He sighed, refilled all their glasses, and retired to stand behind a screen at the door.

'Poor old devil. He'd drop all this, including the pension, tomorrow, to work for an English family if he could. The most faithful person in the world, the old Indian servant. God knows what will happen to them when we go.'

At his words, a shadow fell over them, the shadow of change, unbelievable change. It brooded darkly over India in that year of 1946; no one was sure of the future any longer. Sarah, watching the bubbles in her glass rise and break, thought, And what is going to happen to us all if – or when – we go? India was not going to be easily torn out of the hearts of the people who loved her, and India would miss her British guardians. The two nations were bound together with so many ties that other nations, watching the breaking up of an empire with greedy eyes, could never understand. And what about my own special people – the tar-brushed ones, the mixtures, the despised Eurasians – what choice would they have?

Digby, watching her sad thoughtful face, leaned close to say, 'Sarah, those who really love India, who belong to her in so many ways, they can never lose her. They can always come back, and there will always be a welcome. The people never change towards their friends, nor does the country.'

Digby was speaking as an Englishman who loved India, but who had never visualised spending his whole life there. Always, in his mind, had been the thought of eventual retirement to his own country, where, with nostalgia, he would dream of the old days, of pig-sticking and shooting, and dust drifting over parade grounds, dreaming of hot sun and dark friendly faces while he tended his roses or played a round of golf in the green dampness of the English countryside. Sarah thought of India as her own, her only home, the place where she wished to live and die. She looked at his kind face and knew that they had no thoughts in common where India was concerned. But she smiled brilliantly at him and said, 'Digby, you must be a wizard – how did you know what I was thinking?'

'Easy. I was thinking it too.'

Sarah looked at him for a minute, thinking sadly that he could not have been more wrong. But as she looked at him, she saw how attractive he was, and at once looked away. The wine that had sharpened her fears about India and the future had also lowered her guard. Her straight look at him had been misinterpreted, and had been answered by his aroused eyes. They had looked at each other, both attracted by what they saw, but Sarah turned firmly from the question in his eyes, and Julia, busy renewing her lipstick, did not notice the silence that had fallen. She held her compact out to Sarah. 'Do you want this, Sarah?' Sarah shook her head with a smile. 'No, thank you, sweetie. I'm too full of food and drink to bother. One of us looking beautiful is enough.'

But you, thought Digby, you, my strange girl, look beautiful even when you have just been sick. And that is not every woman's time for looking beautiful. He lifted his glass in a private toast to all beautiful women who didn't use powder and lipstick in public, and Sarah smiled at him, and he caught her smiling glance and could not look away from her. Too long in the jungle, too long in the war, too long without seeing a white woman, oh, too long away from love and all its enchantments – Digby's thoughts were utterly confused, and he only managed to lower his eyes when the old bearer came up to speak to him.

'Sahib, there is one Pyari Lal outside who would speak with the Memsahib. It seems that the Ayah of the Memsahib is attempting to stop someone from entering the compartment.'

'Oh, *dear*,' Sarah got up quickly. 'Now what disaster?' She went out, followed by Julia and Digby, both still holding their glasses.

At the door of their compartment a small crowd had gathered round the Ayah and an elderly Indian wearing a little round black cap and a spotless white shirt and dhoti. As Sarah and the others came up, they heard the Ayah say firmly, 'Nay. There is no room here. Go thou and find another place. My children sleep, and you must not disturb them. Also –' What else the Ayah was going to say they did not hear. The combined effect of her words and their arrival appeared to madden the man. He fairly screamed at them.

'Ho! I am entering this compartment. I am mounting in *now*. I am buying first-class ticket and having every right of individual in free country to travel anywhere I wish!'

Sarah's calm voice stopped him in midflow. 'But certainly, go in. Ayah, open the door at once. There is not very much room, but this gentleman wishes to share our compartment for his journey. All I ask, sir, is that you get in quietly. My children are asleep, and they are very tired. Also, the dog –'

Digby, listening to her aghast, said, 'But Sarah – Mrs Longman – you cannot possibly have this fellow spending the night in there!'

The man, who had been visibly surprised by Sarah's ready acquiescence and disconcerted by the mention of a dog, rushed into speech again at this unfortunate interruption.

'This fellow? This *fellow*? Who you are calling this "fellow"? I am Visanji Harbhanji, member of People's Assembly, and I demand use of one berth in this compartment. I am holding first-class ticket, and no other first-class compartment available on train. I instantly demand to enter.'

Sarah answered him quietly again. 'Of course you can travel with us, Mr Visanji. We are all women and children in this compartment, you understand.' She was not allowed to finish.

Digby was now trying to be soothing. 'Look, old fellow – you wouldn't want one of us breaking in on your women, if they were travelling alone.' The word 'fellow' had a disastrous effect on Mr Visanji. He visibly swelled.

'Do *not* refer to me as "fellow". I am educated man of distinction, graduate of University in Bombay, and I am telling you, I am climbing in this carriage. My wife, or other female dependents, would not be interfered with by you, on account she, or they, do not travel alone. Only dissolute painted British women travelling length and breadth of country without guardian husband or relative of male type. So –'

'So I am going to punch you on the nose, you vile little –'

'Oh, Digby, *no*!' said Sarah, under her breath.

Mr Visanji had begun to scream in real earnest now, yelling for the guard, the station-master and the police.

'Assault! I am being assaulted!' he shrieked. 'Guard, do your duty, free citizen of India is being prevented with violence from travelling on train by brutal Britisher. I demand—' From within the compartment, Hans' frenzied barking drowned even Mr Visanji's voice. Sarah had the door of the compartment open.

'Get in,' she said to the staring Julia. 'Quickly. And gag Hans.' Julia climbed in, and blessed silence fell. 'Now, Mr Visanji,' Sarah's voice was still quiet, but as cold as iced steel. 'Now. I am travelling with my sister-in-law, a young unmarried girl, and my children, and my woman servant. You have accused me, by implication, and in front of witnesses, of being dissolute. I shall write to my solicitor, Mr Bannerjee of City House, Malabar Street, Bombay – no doubt he is known to you – and you will hear from him in due course. I have already noted your address from this label on your suitcase. I will ask two of these gentlemen, who have heard all you said, if they are willing to be witnesses for me.' She looked enquiringly at the station-master, and at a tall Sikh who was standing near Digby.

The station-master smiled and nodded, the Sikh took out his wallet and gave her a card, saying, 'Certainly, Madame. This is a very rude fellow.' He then winked evilly at Digby, and stood back, ignoring a murderous glare from Mr Visanji.

'Thank you both,' said Sarah. 'Also, there is the guard of the train, and Major Lawton who heard you. If you still wish to travel in my reserved compartment, please put your luggage in now, and let us all get in, as we are very tired and want to settle for the night before the train starts.' Her cold level voice and determined manner had quietened the little man, but he was equally determined. He gestured to the coolies standing round enjoying the show, and his luggage was piled into the compartment. Then he himself clambered in, with much display of bony legs in his dhoti, and then Sarah, followed by Digby who said in answer to her raised eyebrows, 'I demand to travel in here too. I have a first-class warrant and am travelling in a second-class coupé. So there.'

Mr Visanji seated himself in one of the two chairs, and sat glaring round the carriage. Julia and Sarah both sat on Julia's berth, and Digby took the other chair. Hans growled almost continuously, and Bonnie Prince Charlie, disturbed by all the noise, shrieked raucously and said something in Urdu that was fortunately inaudible. Mr Visanji shifted nervously. Digby looked around him. 'We could have a game of Happy Families,' he suggested. 'Or perhaps Animal Grab would be more suitable?' Sarah frowned at him sternly; with Julia she was struggling with suppressed laughter.

David had wakened and was regarding the interloper with deep interest. He tried an experimental smile, but Mr Visanji's face was wooden. David then opened his mouth and howled, and Ayah hurried to him clicking her tongue. 'Hai – there, my princeling, do not look at him, he has a heart of stone, coming in and waking my little one. Sleep, heart's love, sleep, and do not heed him. Ayah will not let him harm you, not a finger shall he lay on you, my love.' Mr Visanji stirred uneasily, and the light glinted on his glasses, so that David howled properly, really frightened by the two round moons. Sarah went over to help to quieten him, and his yells dropped to sobs, which sounded more heartbroken than they were.

'Nay, child – do not weep. I will not harm thee. See, here is something for thee to look at.' A transformed Mr Visanji was holding out a large steel watch on a chain.

David's sobbing stopped altogether, and Sarah smiled at Mr Visanji, saying in Urdu, 'My thanks. It is seen that you have children of your own. Little ones are easily frightened by strangers, but soon forget.'

'That is so. I have four grandsons, children of my son.

The youngest is the age of thy son.' He broke off to look keenly at Sarah. 'Thou speakest Urdu well. Art thou indeed an Englishwoman?'

Sarah answered his question obliquely. 'I was born here, and even when they sent me back to England to school I did not forget Urdu – my first language.'

'Indeed, thou speakest well. If my eyes were closed, I would think it was a woman of my own country speaking. Most English people speak from their stomachs, I think.'

Ayah glared at him. There was no slackening in the hostility with which she regarded him, even though David had fallen asleep again, having relieved his feelings by crying.

Digby and Julia kept their faces turned away. The change in Mr Visanji was ludicrous. He began to collect his luggage, calling out of the window at a passing coolie.

'There is no reason for you to leave, Mr Visanji, now that we are all friends.'

'No, no, Lady Sahib. We are indeed all friends here now. I do not stay to inconvenience you, like some –' he paused to glare at Digby. 'Discourteous,' he muttered, 'discourteous, causing rage, which obscures reason. I regret that I was offensive to you. Of course all English ladies are not of dissolute type. Indeed, I would not believe you to be English, you have the gentle wisdom and manners of the high-born ladies of my country.'

On this handsome admission he left them, in a flurry of bows and smiles to Sarah. As he went, a bottle of champagne and three glasses were handed in by the old bearer from the restaurant. 'Because the Major Sahib has paid and has not drunk. The glasses can be given to the guard, he will return them to me on next trip.'

'For goodness sake, Digby, put up the window shades, or we really will look dissolute.' Sarah leaned back against the corner of the berth with an exhausted laugh. 'What an evening – what a journey! Oh, Digby, imagine the headlines if you had thumped him! "Indian civilian brutally beaten by drunken British officer, while attempting to board train".'

'I am *not* drunk! But I have an uneasy feeling that you could have managed better without me – I was of no assistance.'

'Digby, nonsense, you were great moral support. But he was quite a nice man really – just the usual chip on the shoulder.'

'I thought he was *horrible*,' said Julia. 'He said I had a painted face, and there he was in that extraordinary skirt thing, and pink suspenders, and purple socks!' Their laughter was carefree, but the Ayah was still furious. That her family should be subjected to such treatment!

'Verily the Colonel Sahib should travel with you,' she murmured to Sarah.

'God forbid, and heaven forfend,' said Sarah in English.

'What did you say, Sarah? It sounded like a prayer. Were you praying?'

'Yes, Julie, praying fervently that nothing more will go wrong.'

Digby, who had heard what the Ayah had said, and Sarah's reply, wondered again what sort of a man Richard Longman was, and what was holding the marriage together at all.

Presently the bottle was finished, and at the next stop Digby got out to go to his own compartment for the night. Sarah strolled with him, taking Hans for his final walk. They were due in Madore at ten the next morning.

'I suppose you will be going into Piri's Hotel?' Sarah shook her head. 'I wouldn't know where we are going.'

'Well, I expect you will. But I should try and get out of there as soon as possible. Piri's is pretty awful. However, your husband has probably got everything under control.'

Sarah said nothing. She doubted that Richard had done anything other than just book them into the hotel – if that. The shadow of her doubt showed on her face, and Digby saw, and thought how joyless her relationship with her husband seemed to be. And yet she was still married to him, was joining him, there must be something right with the marriage. Looking at her he thought again that she was a woman that a man might want to keep at all costs, considering himself lucky to have her. 'Lawton, you are a fool, and slightly drink taken,' he told himself, staring down at her, not seeing that they had arrived at his compartment. Then he walked back with her.

'This *could* go on all night,' said Sarah, 'but fortunately the train is about to move. Good night, Digby, sleep well – and thank you – thank you for everything.'

5

Digby did not sleep well. His pillow smelled faintly of – what? Sandalwood? Jasmine? It was evocative. A tall slim figure arranged her hair in front of his mirror, some-body sobbed heartbrokenly in his dreams, and he spent most of the night sitting up, smoking and thinking.

Sarah herself slept dreamlessly and deeply for the first time for months. She woke refreshed and rested.

'Must have been all that champagne,' she said cheer-fully to Julia, as she brushed and coiled her hair. Julia, wrestling with the lock of her suitcase, began to laugh helplessly.

'What, Julie?'

'Oh Sarah, it is still the funniest part of last night. Digby about to hit that little man, trying to protect us against the charge of being dissolute. I do like him, Sarah, I think he's sweet.'

Sarah nodded. 'Yes. The kind and handsome Digby. He nearly landed us all in jug. But he is charming, and honest and really kind. All the virtues it appears. Could eventually be terribly boring. For goodness sake, Julie, let me open that suitcase for you, you'll break all your nails.'

'Oh, no – don't, don't open it! I've only just got it closed.'

The Ayah, restored to good humour at last by their morning laughter and the fact that the journey was almost over, beamed at them and crooned happily to herself as she struggled to wash David's face. Penelope, ready dressed in very short blue shorts and a blue tee-shirt, was hopping from window to window, singing a wordless chant.

'How lovely to be a child, and always feel like this,' said Julia, capturing her niece to kiss her.

'Yes – *how* lovely,' said Sarah quietly.

Now what have I said, thought Julia, as she saw the familiar shadow slip over Sarah's face, taking all the youth and happiness with it. Really, Sarah was not the easiest person to talk to sometimes.

The train snorted into Madore at exactly 10 a.m. The platform was crowded with troops, both British and Indian, as well as ordinary travellers. Julia, hanging out of the window, said 'Oh dear, I haven't seen Richard yet. Not anywhere. Sarah, do you think he has been moved already?'

'Could be – but I doubt it. He is probably on his way here. Let us get the stuff out anyway.' If I know Richard, she thought, he will stroll up as soon as the luggage is all out of the carriage and the van and all the difficult part sorted out. She took up her handbag, and started for the guard's van, her mouth already settling into a firm re-signed line. Just as she got to the van, Digby caught up with her.

'Good morning. Still hauling out the household goods?' His cheerful voice, and the way in which he took over the removal of her baggage, shook Sarah's hard-held composure. Digby said quickly, 'Richard not here? Don't worry, he may have been sent to Ratna, there was a bother there not long ago. He probably deputed some feckless youngsters to meet you, and they have over-slept.' Sarah did not reply and the quality of her silence made him look closely at her and then turn away.

When the luggage was loaded on to the handcarts and the procession ready to move, Digby went to Sarah and told her he would have to leave her. 'I'm awfully sorry. But as soon as I can get hold of a telephone I'll ring HQ and find out where your husband is. Sure you'll be able to get yourself and all this to Piri's? Right, I'll drop into the club this evening. If Richard has been sent to Ratna, perhaps you and Julia will dine with me?'

49

Sarah thanked him, and watched him go off to join his men, but her eyes were registering nothing. All her being was strained to snapping point, waiting for something she knew was going to happen. Almost as her brain formed the thought '*Now*', she heard Penelope's high squeal of excitement, and Julia saying 'Oh, Richard, *Richard*, here we are – Sarah, look, here is Richard at last –' and turned to find him at her elbow, his uniform immaculate, his cap at just the right angle, his blue eyes smiling lazily, like his mouth under the clipped golden moustache.

'But he's just the same – no change. Why did I think he would be different? There is no difference in him at all,' thought Sarah childishly, and wondered why the thought of change in Richard had crossed her mind. Was it because she knew, deep inside her, that she had changed? She turned her cheek to his kiss, and shook hands with the Subedar Major who had come with him, and saw Kullunder Khan, her cook, smiling a welcome. It was suddenly very clear to her that these welcoming dark faces were closer to her heart than the splendidly handsome face of her husband.

Driving through the crowded narrow streets in Richard's jeep, he told her that he had booked rooms for them, as she had known he would have done, in Piri's Hotel. 'It is pretty awful there, but you will be able to look round you tomorrow and find something better. Go and see the Station Staff Officer. I'll send some kind of transport – probably a jeep, families are allowed to use them now that the war is over. I'll send the transport at about nine in the morning.'

Sarah did not really see the streets through which they drove. When Julia or Penelope spoke, she answered, but the only voice that really registered with her was Richard's voice. All the tones of that voice were known and were unchanged – but surely this time she must find something to hold on to within their marriage, something that would make her feel that she had done right to return. Surely, if she tried, she would find in her husband a man that she could make happy and content. She looked at the handsome officer beside her, driving the jeep so easily, and her heart felt physically heavy, as if a stone had lodged in her breast. It was early in the day, but already the shadows of the coming night seemed to be gathering round her. As she thought this, Richard put out a possessive hand to her knee and gripped it bruisingly.

'Still as bony as an underfed chicken. Sarah, we'll have to do something about you. Has she been eating and resting properly, Julie?'

Eating? *Resting*? Julia, with the ten-day journey still fresh in her mind, could find no sensible answer that fitted, but looked at her brother in amazement. Was he joking? He must have been, because Sarah had choked with laughter. In fact, Sarah had difficulty in stopping her laughter. She saw Richard's sidelong glance at her becoming a frown, but the look on Julia's face had been so funny – and how typical of Richard, that question! Also, how typical of Richard to frown at her laughter. It would never do for Mrs Richard Longman, the Colonel's lady, to arrive at the hotel in fits of hysterical laughter. She managed to control herself as they drew up outside Piri's Hotel. This was a large, ramshackle building, the whitewash flaking leprously off the walls, bushes and marigolds jostling each other in dusty profusion in the garden and no one in sight to carry the luggage.

Richard did not get out. It seemed that he had to go back to battalion headquarters at once. He sat calmly behind the wheel, while his driver helped Kullunder Khan and Pyari Lal to off-load the luggage, his only comment being, 'I see you've still got that – that *delightful* bonnie bird, Sarah,' when the parrot and his cage were lifted out.

Penelope was charmed that her father had noticed her pet. 'Poor Prince Charlie did not like the journey, Father. Not one little bit, he didn't.'

'No, I'm sure he wouldn't have liked it, poppet. Might have been better to have left him behind, and saved him

51

all the trouble. Never mind,' he said, to Penelope's suddenly suffused eyes, 'of course he had to come. And the journey is all over now. So he can settle down again, as soon as Mummy has found us all a lovely house. Sarah, have you got this lot off yet? Good. I'll be back in time for a drink before dinner. Goodbye till then – be good, all of you.' The jeep was gone, leaving Penelope on the verge of tears and a second jeep full of baggage which took a long time to unload with only the driver and Pyari Lal to do the work. For some reason Kullunder Khan had gone back with Richard. As Sarah bent to the task of comforting her little daughter, the mountain of baggage grew.

'Where on earth are we going to put it all, Sarah?' said Julia.

Sarah shook her head, and pulled her mouth into a wry grimace. 'God knows.'

The full horror of their accommodation broke on them after they had signed a fly-spotted and damp-stained visitors' book.

The rooms were dark, airless and gloomy, and widely scattered. The children were miles away from the bedroom Sarah was to share with Richard, and Julia's room was on the other side of the hotel, in a sort of annexe.

As she organised the arrangement of the luggage, Sarah played with the idea of having both children put into her bedroom, and then rejected the plan as likely to have unpleasant repercussions. She finally compromised by asking the manageress to put the children's beds on the verandah outside her room. It was flyscreened and large, and at least they would be near her and have plenty of fresh air.

'Of course, as you wish, Mrs Longman. But they are in such a *sweet* room – they will be quite safe even if not very close to you, this is a respectable family-type hotel, you know.' The manageress, brunette and flamboyant with lipstick, rouge, and breasts like gun-turrets, was inclined to take offence. Sarah soothed her, but was adamant about the children's beds being put on her verandah.

Five minutes later Julia, flushed and ruffled, arrived in

Sarah's bedroom and asked if she could sleep on the verandah too. 'There is a very odd man in the room next to mine. He is wearing a vest and underpants, and keeps knocking on my door to ask if he can help me unpack. He could be drunk –'

'He could well be drunk. We'll find somewhere else to live as soon as possible. Could you manage on a camp bed, Julia? I'll have it put on the verandah, but I simply dare not ask La Manageressa to have any more beds moved, I don't feel up to facing her so soon after the last struggle.'

Julia, having seen the manageress, sympathised deeply. 'I'll sleep on the floor rather than even speak to her,' she vowed. Sarah told Ayah, and the camp bed was unearthed and set up.

6

Richard had not returned by seven that evening. Julia was in her bath and when Sarah looked round the door to say she was going out for a little while to start things moving towards finding somewhere else to live, she was only too glad that Sarah should go. 'Anywhere at all,' she begged, 'any old shack – just away from here, Sarah.'

Sarah sent Pyari Lal for a tonga and when it came, bells jangling and wheels crunching up the drive, she perched herself on the hard back seat and set off for the club. As she jogged along the mall in the last of the evening light she thought to herself, I did not tell a lie, Digby will certainly help me to find a bungalow. But that isn't why I'm going to the club. I'm going there because I simply can't bear not to see someone male and human who likes me, and whom I like. As if I have to touch him for luck and courage.

As the tonga turned in at the club gates she had a private bet with herself that Digby would be waiting on the verandah, and paid the tonga walla before they stopped, to forestall Digby paying him. As the driver was pulling his skinny horse to a halt, Digby stepped off the club verandah and came to help her down. 'I have paid him, Digby,' said Sarah, pleased with her strategy, and turned to walk into the club.

'Wouldn't you rather sit out in the garden? It is cooler and quieter – the bar is full of everyone, and I will not be able to hear a word you say.'

Sarah looked up at him. His back was to the light and she could not see his expression, but he could see her face clearly.

'By God – she knows!' he thought, and followed her as she walked into the garden, wishing that he had chosen to meet her in the hotel, or anywhere rather than the club. Richard Longman, on his wife's first night back, was entertaining a girl, rather conspicuously, in the bar. Digby had seen them as soon as he arrived that evening, sitting close together with a bottle of champagne in an ice bucket on the bar in front of them. At first he had thought it was a reunion celebration, and that the girl with dark hair spilling over her shoulders was Sarah. He had been shocked to find himself mistaken. Now he sat silent, after ordering their drinks, and waited for Sarah to say something. When she did speak, she said something quite unexpected.

'That hotel is ghastly, Digby. We must get out of it tomorrow at the latest, even if it means sleeping in a tent or going back to Bombay. I'm afraid to eat or drink anything there and the children are going to get awfully tired of Bovril and tinned milk and rusks and boiled eggs – which are all that we can cook on the primus in the bedroom. Even the eggs I ordered for their supper were bad. Julia's been frightened by a drunk, and I suspect the drains. Can you help us? Do you know that Station Staff Officer? Is he nice?'

'As a matter of fact, I think he is very pleasant, but whether he will be able to find you anywhere else to live is another matter. Madore is bursting at the seams – two British regiments and three Indian battalions. I'll see what I can do tomorrow. I wish I had a bungalow, but of course all the bachelors are under canvas. I'm sharing a tent with an old friend, Alastair Crombie. I'd like you to meet him.' Sarah wasn't really listening, he thought. She looked blankly at him, finished her drink and stood up.

'Digby – thank you for my drink. I must go. I only came to tell you I couldn't come and have dinner.'

'I'm sorry – but perhaps tomorrow night? Let me take you back.' He could not imagine that Richard was going to take his girlfriend to the hotel, to dine with his wife and family, even if it was obvious that Sarah knew all about the affair and condoned it. She was certainly taking it very calmly. He had a sudden and horrible thought – was this a way of life for her, living with a chronically unfaithful husband? That would explain everything, including Bruce Whigmore.

Sarah spoke very little on the way back to the hotel and he felt her unhappiness and fatigue as if it was his own. He thought bitterly of how happy and relaxed she had been the night before, on the train – at least she had had that respite. Just before they got to the hotel she spoke to him. 'Thank you for being so kind. It makes a difference to have someone to complain to!' He found nothing to say, except, as they stopped outside Piri's, 'Try and get some sleep tonight, won't you?' Her laughter in answer was harsh and the note of hysteria in it shocked him.

'Oh, yes – I'll try.' She stopped laughing and, looking straight at him, said, 'Thank you for keeping me out of that bar tonight. Don't look so desperate, Digby. I'm tired and cross, that's all. I'll be fine as soon as we get out of here. So stop looking so worried. Good night, and bless you.'

But Digby did worry. He climbed back into his jeep and drove off, feeling that he should be staying to look after her. He looked back to wave but she was not there, she had gone straight in.

Richard did not arrive until nearly half past nine that evening. Sarah and Julia were having a drink on the verandah outside the dining room.

'Hello, girls,' he greeted them. 'You look melancholy. Let us have a bottle and cheer everything up – what do you say to that?'

'I'll say no,' said Sarah. 'I'm drinking whisky.'

'And I say no, too,' said Julia. 'I am drinking whisky. And I don't think you'll cheer the dining-room staff up by having a bottle. They've been out twice to tell us that dinner is off at ten. I think it is boiled crocodile. It smells like that anyway.'

'What a delicious thought, Julia. I haven't had that for ages.' But Julia was not at all amused. 'Absolutely nothing to laugh about, Richard. This is the most awful place. You must get us out at once!'

'Yes, well, Sarah is seeing about that tomorrow, aren't you, Sarah?'

'And what about you. Are you seeing about it too?'

Sarah, watching them wrangle together, thought how alike they were – in looks, anyway. Richard's golden fairness was transmuted, in Julia, to palest silver; she was a moonlit copy of his colouring, her eyes a softer blue. But so far, she had shown herself to be completely genuine. At the moment she was losing her temper with her brother.

'Aren't *you* going to do *any*thing to help?'

'My dear child! I'm not on leave you know! The battalion is on standby for a move to Ratna. I have an idiot boy as an adjutant and therefore have to do more myself. Everything is in an uproar, it always is at this time of year – an open season for riots of all sorts.' Richard was leaning back, relaxed and smiling at them both, ignoring Julia's implied criticism. The bearer brought him a drink, and he raised his glass to Sarah, his blue eyes glinting with laughter.

'You do look a happy pair! We must have a bottle or two and cheer you up – all right, Julie, we'll have our bottles with our dinner. After all, this is a reunion celebration – or is it?'

How handsome he is, thought Sarah, quite fantastic, all that in one face – blue eyes, firm chin, blond hair above a face that would make any woman look at him twice, and then again. But not I – not now, alas. If only I had seen past those smiling blue eyes, how much better for all of us. Richard broke into her thoughts.

'Sarah, you look like a private funeral – for heaven's sake!' He looked from one to the other of the girls with the air of a man who was about to become very irritable.

Julia also thought her brother handsome and charming, but she was tired and cross and could not help comparing the ease and gaiety of the previous evening, on the train, with their present surroundings. Now too,

57

as on the night before, Sarah scarcely spoke, but how different was her silence this time! The tension of her slim body was painfully obvious, her face had sharpened, and she looked skinny and plain.

Richard enjoyed himself. He talked almost without stopping, ordering wine with their dinner and laughing at what he described as their melancholia. Julia wondered if he was a little drunk, and she saw Sarah glance quickly at him as his voice rose louder. Dinner was not a pleasant meal. The wine was not cold, but the food was and floated in grease. Richard made no attempt on the food. He tasted his wine, made a face, and ordered a double whisky, leaving the girls to struggle with the wine. Sarah tasted hers, shook her head firmly and beckoned to the wine waiter. 'Take this away – and bring me a whisky and soda. Julia? Same? Yes – one for the Miss Sahib, too. Put this unopened bottle on ice – we will try it tomorrow. It will probably be less poisonous if it is as least cold. We won't be able to taste it at any rate.' She faced Richard's raised eyebrows without saying anything, her own face as hard and set as a painted mask.

Richard shrugged. 'Dear me, you've got very fussy, darling, suddenly – Still, as you like.' He sat smoking as they ate, and as Sarah finished her whisky he signalled to the wine waiter to bring her another. To Julia's surprise, Sarah accepted another drink and Richard leaned forward and toasted her. 'To us, darling – to us, and our continuing happiness.'

His glance locked with Sarah's, then she looked deliberately away from him and downed her drink in one long swallow, before she got up, saying, 'It has been quite a day. I think we should go to bed.'

Richard pulled her chair back for her, saying, 'But indeed – what an excellent idea.'

He had not been into the bedroom before dinner so had not seen the new arrangements, with Julia's camp bed and the children's beds crowding the verandah outside. 'What the devil? I booked three bedrooms!'

Sarah swiftly explained, and added with difficulty,

conscious of Julia undressing on the other side of the thin plywood door of the bathroom, 'It is only until we get somewhere of our own, Richard. Do understand, Julia was nervous, and I couldn't have the children so far away.'

'Well, hell, the Ayah could have slept with the children, couldn't she? As for Julia being nervous, what nonsense! This is a bit much. I haven't seen you for weeks, and now –' He paused, staring at her.

'You wouldn't have arranged this purposely, would you, my darling froggy wife – we're not going through the ice age again, are we?' Sarah turned away, but he went over to her and firmly took her into his arms and forced her to meet his kisses, saying between each bruising kiss, 'Are we? Are we?' until she replied,

'No, no, of course not,' her voice muffled and shaking. 'Please let me go now – I'm so desperately tired.' Her face was so white and her voice so faint, that after another searching glance, he released her and went over to the dressing-table, where he smoothed back his hair and then took out a cigarette. Sarah sat on the bed watching him. She was faint and sick, and when he turned towards her she felt her whole body clench itself together, and was afraid she had visibly flinched. But he did not appear to notice anything and sat down beside her, a carelessly possessive arm round her shoulders, while he studied her, his eyes half closed against the smoke from his cigarette. Or was it to hide his thoughts from her? Sarah looked away from his eyes, and held herself rigid within his arm. All she longed for was to lie down and be alone. Richard finally said, 'You are far too thin, you know – you've lost all your looks, Sarah. You must do something about yourself. Now that Julia is here, let her take some of the weight of the children off you. We'll have to do quite a lot of entertaining eventually, if things go as I think they will. Get a decent bungalow out of that old fool of an S.S.O., and for God's sake get some colour into your face, and some flesh on your bones. You've never looked so ghastly, not even just after –'

Her convulsive movement stopped him for a second,

and his mouth straightened into a hard line, but then he went on speaking. '*As* I was saying – you haven't looked fit for a long time. So just pull yourself together, there's a good girl. I'm going to need a wife to live with me, not a skeleton with hair.' He stubbed out his cigarette, and stood up. 'Well – I must be off. Oh? Didn't you realise? I'm sleeping out at Namkum with the battalion. We're on standby. I'll come in tomorrow, and possibly I'll be able to spend next weekend with you. Don't forget, a jeep will be here at nine tomorrow morning. Good night, my beautiful bony one. I'll look forward to the weekend, and a less cluttered bedroom – yes?'

When Julia came in from her bath Sarah was still sitting on the end of her bed and Richard had gone.

'He's *gone*?' said Julia in amazement.

Sarah nodded. 'He's gone, thank God.'

'Oh, Sarah, that's not very kind. After all, he is my brother, and your husband –'

'What a lot of people that makes him seem. Go to bed, Julie, and stop looking like a reproving angel. Listen, if you hear anything in the night – no, what am I thinking about! You'll all sleep in here now, of course. Give me a hand with the children's beds, please.'

Julia was glad that they were all together. She found the hotel strange and sinister in the dark, and did not sleep very well. But as often as she woke during the night, she saw Sarah sleeping as solidly as the children. In fact, so still did she lie that Julia got out of bed and bent over her, and even the light of the torch shining on her face did not waken Sarah. She is worn out, thought Julia getting back into her bed. Worn out, and not surprising. I shall speak to Richard. I think he is being very odd. He doesn't take any responsibility at all.

Julia finally fell asleep, convinced that unaccompanied travelling up and down India was too much for a delicate person like Sarah.

She said so to Sarah the next morning as they sat in their beds drinking their early morning tea. But Sarah laughed at her.

'Goodness, Julie, every Indian Army wife is used to taking her house on her back and setting off alone! The men never travel with their families – or hardly ever. They can't. They have to travel with their battalions. In my grandmother's day, they followed after their men in horse-drawn vehicles, and had their luggage in bullock carts. Some of their journeys took two or three months, and they would arrive sometimes and find that their husbands had died of cholera or heatstroke before they got to their destination.'

'It must be strange to be third generation India,' said Julia. 'Do you often take the same routes that your grandmother took?' She stopped, her underlip caught in her teeth. Sarah never spoke of her parents or of her grandparents. This was the first time. What an unfortunate question! If only it did not make Sarah retreat into her shell again. But Sarah, for once, went on talking.

'Yes, often. Only more quickly, and more comfortably. I have twice lived in my grandmother's old bungalows, once in Meerut, and once in Lahore, and I was once in a dak bungalow where the old cook remembered the burrah Sahib Adson – Addison was a difficult name for a lot of the servants, and my grandmother got quite used to being called Adson Lady Sahib. Kullunder Khan is the son of my father's bearer. Ayah looked after us when we were children, in fact she was with my mother when I was born. So it goes on. One of the things I have always loved about India, nothing changes, and everyone knows you –' And knows all about you too, she thought to herself, and her face clouded. Julia wanted to ask, 'But what about your other grandmother, your father's mother. Please tell me about her?' – but Sarah's clouded face did not encourage further questioning. Julia longed to hear about that legendary lady, the beautiful Rose of Madore, the Lady Muna. But she had never been mentioned by Sarah.

The children's voices outside took the frown from Sarah's face.

'Here comes the fourth generation back from their

walk. Ayah is pregnant with news, I can see.'

Ayah was, indeed, full of news. The children clambered on to Sarah's bed and Ayah sat on the floor and began to talk.

'There is a house that will be good for us. It is an old house, out by the Rama Tank. The house is large and empty, and has a very big garden. You must go and see it first, before you go to the officer sahib in charge of housing, and tell him that it is the house you want.' She straightened her sari with a pleased flick that set all her bracelets tinkling and ringing.

'The son of my younger sister is the head servant there. I met him on the road this morning, having sent Pyari Lal to find him last night. It is a very old house, and very beautiful. No one has been allowed to live in it for many years. It belongs to the Ruler of Lambagh.'

There was a sudden charged silence as Sarah looked at the Ayah, a silence that grew. Sarah broke it at last by saying slowly,

'The old Madoremahal?'

'Nay. The Ruler lives in what was left of that. This is the house that the old Ruler built for his wife, the Begum Bianca. You must have gone there as a child? You do not remember? It does not matter. It is for you. It is yours.'

Having said this, the Ayah got up and went off to organise their breakfasts in their rooms. Sarah nodded to Julia's raised eyebrows, and said in a strange, absent voice,

'Well, we have a house. An old and beautiful house, just waiting for us.'

Julia was dying of curiosity, but something in Sarah's voice stopped all her questions. All she said was 'Sarah, do you mean it?'

'Yes. Get dressed quickly and we'll go and see it as soon as you have had your breakfast. I do not want any, I will just have some more tea.' In spite of her solid sleep, Sarah looked pale and drawn. Catching Julia looking at her anxiously, she made a face at her and said, 'Next time I drink large quantities of whisky before dinner, please stop me. I have a splendid hangover. Don't worry, tea and fresh air will work wonders. Just think, we may be out of this place very soon.'

7

Driving through Madore, they both fell in love with the place. It was a semi-hill station, which meant that the weather was hot in summer, but not the burning impossible heat of the real plains, and in the winter it was cool enough for fires. In the distance were the foothills of the Himalayas, hazed and blue.

They left the Cantonments and drove through the native city, which still had remnants of its old red walls standing. The streets were narrow and winding, and as the harvest was in, the flat roofs of the houses were covered with chillies and corn cobs and pumpkins drying in the sun, a chessboard of scarlet and gold and. orange. The people looked cheerful and friendly; the women were brightly dressed in long full skirts and small tight bodices, and went unveiled, their heads covered by light cotton scarves. 'They walk like queens in a coronation procession – look at that girl with the brass pot on her head!'

'These women are famous all over India for their beauty and intelligence. A great many of the famous dancers and courtesans came from this part of India. I'm not surprised, I haven't seen an ugly woman yet. The men don't look quite so friendly, do they? But of course, there is an awful lot of unrest and disturbance going on. As long as the women are going about the streets, we are all right. But if you ever see a street with no women in it, Julia, get home as fast as you can. It nearly always means trouble is coming.' Sarah stopped the jeep to buy a great handful of pink roses, and the girl who sold them suddenly threw a string of jasmine round her neck – a good luck gift to the first buyer of the day. 'There, isn't that a good omen?' said Sarah, while Julia buried her face in the roses. 'They *smell* like roses,' she said. 'I know that sounds mad, but nothing smells quite the same out here.'

Rama Tank was in fact a very large artificial lake. There was a small island in the lake, on which was a white temple. At one end of the lake was the house they had come to see, surrounded by a wall made of rough rocks, with a carved wooden gate. The wall did not hide the house which was built on high ground, sloping down to the gardens and the lake shore. Looking up at the house, Sarah had the feeling that she had at last come to a place where she had longed to be, somewhere she had waited for all her life. Julia, also looking up, said breathlessly, 'Sarah, it is too good to be true. We'll never live in that house – look, it is too perfect, a palace with balconies!'

Sarah laughed at her. 'Come on, let us go and see if it has other more necessary things than balconies.'

The garden was neglected, overgrown and tangled with roses and jasmine and bricked paths that were almost hidden under the uncut grass and weeds. It seemed to brood in the sun, a beautiful sleeping garden, waiting to be cleared and discovered.

An elderly man came out to meet them, tall and thin, salaaming deeply, his smile as gentle as the sun on the lake. He seemed to take it for granted that they were coming into the house, and said that the garden was being cleared and made ready for them. 'I am Dip Chand, your servant, Khanum.'

'Your mother was the sister of my Ayah?' The man nodded.

'Yes, Khanum. She said this morning that you had come to Madore and that you would come here. The house is open for you to see.'

'The house belongs to the Ruler of Lambagh? How can I find him, Dip Chand? I must have his permission to see the house, and also make certain that he is willing to allow me to live in the house, before I go to the Officer in charge of Housing in the Cantonments.'

Dip Chand shook his head. 'This house, the Ranighar, is outside the Cantonment area, Khanum. This part of Madore is in fact in Lambagh State. So the Ruler has sole right over the house. If you and the Miss Sahiba will sit here beside the lake, and wait a little, the Ruler will be here very soon. He comes today to pay me the wages for the house servants. I will bring tea, and you can enjoy the lake for only a short time before he comes. He will be pleased that you are here, Khanum. We are all honoured and happy to know that you are here at last.'

'Well!' Julia watched the man walk away and turned to Sarah. 'What a welcome! He seemed to know you, Sarah. Have you been here before?'

'I was brought here once I think, by my father, but I cannot remember it – I must have been two at the most! But don't forget, he is Ayah's nephew.'

'Oh yes, of course, part of the family!'

Sarah nodded slowly, her eyes on the lake. 'Yes. You could say that. Part of the family. Well, once we have seen the Ruler, we will go straight to the S.S.O.'

'What do you think he will say?'

'He will think it is too far out of course. But as it is outside his area, there is not very much that he can say. If he won't take it on hirings, I shall just rent it myself.'

Julia had never got used to Sarah's wealth, or her cavalier attitude to it. Now she looked at the long fingers, ringless except for a wedding ring, at the khaki drill trousers and cotton shirt, and thought of the journey this girl so little older than herself had organised and said thoughtfully,

'But of course, even with money there is no other way of travelling in India, is there? It just is uncomfortable.'

Sarah stared at her. 'What a very confusing statement, Julia. What tangent have you gone off on?'

But Julia, realising that her thoughts were going to be impossible to explain to a girl who had a great deal of money and yet seemed to ignore it, waved a hand round her and said, 'I don't know what I am talking about. I am too excited to make sense. This is a very uncomfortable bench, but Sarah, look at the carving on it! Peacocks and tigers and heaven knows what! Look at the reflection of the temple on the lake! How long has this house been here? How old is the temple?'

The voice that answered was not Sarah's.

'The house was built in 1890. The shrine – oh, I think the shrine was built about 1536. It is very old. I am sorry the bench is uncomfortable – I will ensure that something is done about that.'

Sarah and Julia turned like puppets pulled by one string. The man smiling at them was tall and, by any standards, fantastically handsome. He wore breeches and boots and silk shirt, and a brilliant emerald green turban. His eyes were a very light blue, and he looked like a tanned Englishman. Both girls stared at him, and his smile broadened.

'I regret; did I startle you? Dip Chand said that you wanted to see me.' So this was the Ruler of Lambagh State. Oh, my sweet life, thought Sarah, did you startle us? You must startle every female you meet right out of her senses. She smiled, and held out her hand.

'Nawab Sahib? You only startled us because we were so busy discussing our chances of renting this lovely place. Do you think we could rent it from you for six months? I am Sarah Longman, and my husband is Colonel Longman, he is stationed in Madore Cantonments with the 1st/12th Garwaris. This is my sister-in-law, Miss Longman.'

The Nawab took Sarah's hand and to Julia's astonishment first kissed it, and then raised it to his forehead. 'Welcome to your house, Khanum.' His eyes were as full of welcome as his voice. Then it was Julia's turn, but to her great disappointment he only smiled at her and shook her hand firmly. He then sat down beside them and said, 'I am so happy that you have come at last. The house will be ready for you by this evening.'

Julia gasped. 'This evening! I don't believe it. Sarah,

will it truly happen?'

'Julie, you are not to say things like that. Of course it will happen!' She turned to the Nawab and nodded at him. 'You see, my sister-in-law thinks this place is too beautiful, that it is too much of a dream, so it will not come true that we live here.' The Nawab smiled.

'So you think it is beautiful? It was built to please a very beautiful woman. The Begum Bianca. Her father was Comptroller of my great great grandfather's household, and Military Adviser to the Tinpahari States, of which Lambagh is the chief state. Bianca was fifteen when my great grandfather met her, fell in love with her and carried her off to Lambagh. He married her there. There was very little opposition to the marriage, although I think her mother would have opposed it. But her father and mother could not raise any objections. They were both killed in Madore the night that the couple eloped.' He looked away, over the lake to the distant blue mountains beyond.

'It was a bad year, 1857. If Bianca and my great grandfather had not gone, they would have been killed in the massacre of Madore, too. But they were saved. She lived to be very old. She used to sit here, looking at the lake and the water-birds, and this was where I said goodbye to her the day I went to England to start my schooling. She was very beautiful even then. I never saw her again. She died soon after I left. I loved her very much,' said the Ruler with a charming simplicity.

He paused, and then said, 'Are you afraid of ghosts? It is a gentle ghost. The servants say that the Begum Bianca is still here, and my great grandfather also.' He shrugged. 'Could be true – or it could be smoke on a winter's night. Who knows?'

A flock of pigeons rose from behind the house, and mounted into the air with a flash and flutter of white feathers. The enchantment of the place grew with every minute that they sat there. Sarah felt that she was breaking a spell when she spoke.

'I cannot bear to leave, but we must go and see the

Station Staff Officer now. Where can I contact you, Nawab Sahib?'

'I shall be here tomorrow at half past nine. Can you come then? We could have a drink perhaps, and I will show you the house properly.'

The invitation obviously did not include Julia. She felt keen disappointment, but if it meant that they would eventually live in this beautiful place, then she felt it was worth forgoing drinks – good heavens, drinks at half past nine in the morning! Even with a Nawab! Sarah, however, said firmly, 'Very well, we will both be here, Nawab Sahib. I must tell you, that if the station staff officer refuses to take this house on hirings, I propose to ignore him and take the house myself. I would be grateful if you would tell me how much you want each month in rent.'

'I will tell you about the rent tomorrow. But I do not think you will have any trouble with Major Sperry. He is a very harassed man, and accommodation is very short in the Cantonment area. I think he will be glad that you do not wish to have a bungalow within a stone's throw of the club and the officers' shop! Well, then, Khanum, until tomorrow.' He bowed, taking Sarah's hand to his lips again, bowed to Julia, and walked back up to the house, calling to Dip Chand as he went.

'He is fantastically good-looking, isn't he, Sarah – *what* did he call you?'

'Call me? Oh, Khanum, it means rather more than lady. Yes, he is a handsome character. In fact, he is beautiful. Everything fits so well, he moves like a panther. No Englishman could bow like that and, in fact, no Indian either. But mix the two bloods, and you get something like the Nawab – a dangerous, beautiful animal.'

'Dangerous? Heavens, how do you mean?'

'Oh, just dangerous. Come on, we must compose our speech to Major Sperry – that harassed man!'

Following Sarah, Julia suddenly thought, 'So that is why *you* move so beautifully. The mixed blood. I wish I knew more about you –' and remembering the Nawab's greeting to Sarah, and his words, 'Welcome to your house, Khanum,' was more than ever consumed with curiosity.

8

Major Sperry, the Station Staff Officer, was a small fat man with a worried expression and thick glasses, through which he peered at Sarah thankfully when she said that she was prepared to live outside the Cantonments. 'Splendid, Mrs Longman, splendid. One thing, though – there will not be any transport for you. Not more than once a month. Of course, if your husband were going to live there too, I do not quite see how he would manage, but as he has to live with his battalion for the next few months, we don't have to worry about that. Things may loosen up a bit re transport. We'll have to see.'

So Richard had been telling the truth for once, he did have to live under canvas. Sarah rejoined Julia in the jeep. 'Well, that is done, and I wish we could move tonight. But never mind, Julie, we'll have a splendid evening at the club with Digby and his friend. The food couldn't be any worse than it is in the hotel, and the company will be considerably better.'

They found a note from Richard waiting for them when they got back. 'Hope you've managed to find something. Will not be seeing you tonight, on duty.' So, thought Sarah, letting the scrawled paper slip through her long fingers to the floor, it will be a foursome – and thank God for that. Aloud she said, 'Richard can't come at all today. He enquires if we have found a house. Well, we have, but I do not think he will approve of it, Julia. Too far away from everything.'

'Well then, he'll have to put up with it, won't he!' She was flushed with anger, a most unusual thing in the gentle Julia.

'Sweetie, don't be upset – we're almost in the house. Now, let's drink that awful bottle of wine I had put on ice last night – at least it will be properly cold this time.' Julia's ruffled feelings soothed, they had lunch and then spent the afternoon washing their hair, the Ayah ironing various evening dresses and crumpled shirts, while Julia made up her mind what to wear.

As the tonga jingled towards the club that evening, Sarah wondered if it was wise to bring Julia without first warning her that she might see her brother in unexpected company. Then she shrugged the thought away. Julia probably would not believe her, it would be better really to let her find out for herself. In any case Richard was unlikely to be in the club two nights running.

The bar was almost empty when they went in. 'I think we must be early. Let us wait for them in the garden, Julie. This is rather depressing.'

She led the way into the garden, and chose the same table at which she had sat with Digby the night before. She ordered drinks, and they were just taking their first swallows when Digby drove in. He looked round, saw them and came over, followed by another young man. 'I called at the hotel,' he told Sarah when introductions were over and they were sitting with their drinks. 'I hoped I would be in time to collect you so that you didn't have to rattle down here in another of those broken-down chariots. The Ayah told me that you'd gone. She also told me that you've got a house – and that it is a long way out, but not too far to visit – a positive mine of useful news, she was.' While Sarah was telling him about the house he watched her face, only half-hearing what she was saying. He had had a wretched night; her face and voice had come between him and his sleep and his work, and he knew, unhappily, that he was very deeply attracted to her. Attracted! Like a moth to a lamp, like a needle to a magnet. Digby had had many affairs since he grew up – India was full of bored women and Digby was very attractive, with his tremendous vitality and strength and his great good humour. A kind man, he took his love affairs lightly, and had always managed to slide gracefully out once they were over, without hurting anyone too much.

But now he found that he was thinking of Sarah all the time. She seemed to have taken hold of him mentally as well as physically, and as they sat talking round the table a wave of such fierce desire seized him that he was afraid the heat and passion in his body would be plain to everyone. Sarah, turning to speak to him, met his eyes, broke off what she was saying, put her hand out blindly for her glass and knocked it over. Then he was able to look away from her and get up.

'I'll go and order another round – and then I think we should be getting back.' He could not endure to sit beside her any longer.

There was a storm of protest. Alastair Crombie had just come down from the jungles of Tepoli and, after weeks of sitting in that dark, dangerous, steamy bamboo forest, felt like feminine company and gaiety. 'You must be out of your mind, Digby! What on earth do you mean, time for us to be getting back? I've sent the driver off to have his food and he certainly won't be back here much before half past ten. I thought we had asked Sarah and Julia to have dinner with us? For God's sake, sit down, old boy, and stop looking harried.'

Julia, to whom he had been paying outrageous compliments, added her plea. 'Oh, do stay, Sarah, please. I thought we were going to have dinner here – you said we would – and Major Crombie has just been telling me all about how they took the Jap surrender at Imphal, and he hasn't finished the story.' She looked pleadingly at Sarah. This was the India she had imagined, handsome young men, music in the background, dinner in a scented garden.

Meantime, Digby was talking to Alastair. 'The Jap surrender in Imphal, is it, Sir Alastair? No doubt you took it singlehanded, though how the hell you got to Imphal in time from where you were –'

73

Alastair made a rude gesture at him, apologised, and then said firmly, 'Right. That settles it. Just for that, I'm going to stay and give both these beautiful creatures dinner, and you can do a quickstep all the way back to Namkum – and I hope you enjoy it.'

Sarah looked very pale and withdrawn and Julia thought she was going to change her mind and insist on going back to the hotel. What on earth could have gone wrong? But Sarah said nothing. She looked up at Digby standing beside her, and he sat down as suddenly as if his legs had been cut off. 'Oh, *no*,' said Alastair to himself. 'So that's it. Poor old Digby, he's taking it hard for once.' He promptly turned to Julia and busied himself in so engaging her attention that the other two were virtually alone.

They did not speak to each other but presently Digby turned to her and, taking her glass, poured half his drink into it. He raised his glass to her as she smiled her thanks. To him, it was as if two lovers, long parted, had met again. Her smile seemed to him to be so heartbreakingly happy that he could not bear it. He put his glass down and stood up. 'Come and help me order dinner,' he said.

They walked into the shadows of the trees and stopped. Digby spoke first. 'Sarah –.' Her hair, her body, a slight movement of the air as she turned to him filled his nostrils with her scent. He said no more, but took her into his arms.

'"This is so *sudden*" is what I should say,' said Sarah shakily, a few minutes later, and his voice was as uneven as hers when he said,

'Yes – as sudden as an earthquake or a typhoon – or any other act of God. Don't talk.'

She held him off at last, her face transfigured, laughing, lovely, the long eyes glowing as she looked at him. 'Digby – wait, stop, you *are* like an act of God. We must go and order dinner – behave – oh lord, now look.' Her long heavy hair fell forward round her shoulders as she bent to look for the big tortoise-shell pin that he

74

remembered in her hands on the train. He stooped too, found the pin, and gave it to her, his hands tangling with hers, it seemed, of their own volition. He remembered how she had stood thus on the train, pinning up her hair. He caught her hand and they went off to order dinner.

The evening went too fast for Julia. Sarah led the party, turning the whole affair into something special; a sort of wild gaiety seemed to come from her, she insisted on dancing after their dinner, but not inside. 'We'll dance in the garden – we can hear the music – it is much nicer than dancing on that awful chalk they put down on the floor to make it slippery.' In and out of the shadows they moved, the scent of flowers all about them, the music sounding better at a distance. Heads close, kind shadows. Did Digby kiss Sarah? As Julia wondered, she forgot, for Alastair kissed her – and then held her away from him to look at her.

'Tell me something, Julia – how old are you?'

'Twenty – why?'

'Because that was your first kiss, wasn't it?'

Julia's indignant denial died on her lips as she looked at him.

He nodded. 'I know. And as far as I am concerned that was my first kiss too. We'll remember tonight –'

Too soon, Sarah called that it was time to go. Alastair arranged to take Julia riding the next morning. Digby asked if Sarah had transport to get her out to the new house.

'No – come to think of it, I haven't.'

'Well, I'm free tomorrow, I'll drop you there and come back for you if you like. I want to look round the plains outside Madore because we'll no doubt have to do some manoeuvres shortly to stop our chaps dying of boredom, and I think I can fill in two hours looking round.'

Sarah thanked him and, as it was so late, accepted his offer of a lift back to the hotel. The driver, asleep in the front of the jeep, sprang to attention as they came up. The two girls and Alastair sat in the back and Alastair sang 'Goodnight Sweetheart' all the way down the sleeping mall, until as they approached the lights of Piri's Julia begged him to stop, in case the manageress came out and ate them. Alastair obliged by dropping his voice to a growling whisper, and the two girls fled inside, and were relieved to meet no one.

'Wasn't that a heavenly evening, Sarah?'

'Yes, and I hope the first of many for you, Julie. Now, for heaven's sake, let us go to sleep. There is so much to do tomorrow, and Alastair is picking you up at half past six. Do you know what time it is? After midnight! Good night – sleep well.'

9

Digby arrived the next morning as she was finishing her breakfast, rather late as she had waited for Julia. Julia was full of how lovely it had been to ride again, and looked very happy and pretty, pouring out coffee for Alastair and coming out to the hotel steps to wave Digby and Sarah off.

'Poor Julia, this is the first fun she has had since she came out here.'

'We'll see that she has a wonderful time from now on,' promised Digby. 'There is so much to do here – lovely riding country, wonderful picnic places up in the hills, dancing every Tuesday to the club gramophone – and of course, plenty of pools and lakes to swim in. I think we shall all enjoy ourselves.' His casual voice, his careful avoidance of looking at her face, were the result of a long, wakeful night. Out of all his sleepless thinking had come the determination that, whatever happened, he was not going to add to Sarah's problems by presenting her with his heart and undying affections. Alastair, rising early to set off on his ride, found him awake, and they had, as old friends, talked together. Alastair had thought how sad it was that Digby should find that the only thing he could do for the woman he loved was to avoid showing his love. But now, sitting beside Sarah, watching her leaning back, relaxed and happy, Digby felt he was being rewarded.

It was a beautiful morning; the gold mhor trees on each side of the road were in full bloom, and the range of blue mountains ahead seemed near enough to touch. 'Digby, this is so beautiful – do you think sixteen miles is too far out?'

If I were your husband it would be, my girl, he thought, but said, 'It is a long way, but transport is easing up now, and I think if you hadn't found this house you would probably have been stuck in that hotel. Or you might have had to go into one of those one-storey blocks they are building to the west of the city – awful poky little places in straight lines, no gardens at all. No, Sarah, I think you've done well.'

They came to the carved gate in the high wall and Digby was about to get out and open it when Dip Chand appeared and swung the gate back and Digby, looking in, said, 'What a beautiful place! I'll go and have a look at the countryside with a view to both manoeuvres and future rides. I'll come back and pick you up in about two hours.'

The Nawab was waiting for her on the verandah. 'Ah, Khanum – you came alone after all. Good. Shall we go down and sit by the lake? Would you like that?' She nodded, with an exclamation of pleasure when she saw the cushioned chairs and the small tables that had been carried down to the shore. She followed him down to the water's edge, and wondered fleetingly how Kullunder Khan was going to fit in with Dip Chand, who was obviously a very well-trained servant too. But she put everything out of her mind as the Nawab pulled out a chair for her, and she sat down facing the lake.

The water was as still as a mirror and reflected the trees and rocks and the mountains clearly. A flight of green parrots flew screaming from the mango trees nearby and Sarah could hear pigeons murmuring and the crackle and spit of a thorn fire as the weeds and rubbish cleared from the garden were burned. She turned to her companion and said with a smile, 'I cannot believe this place is real. It is a dream, and I shall wake up and find myself back in that horrid hotel.'

'But I am here, and I am real flesh and blood – see –' He bent forward and took her hand in both his. It was only a momentary touch, he held her hand for only a second, but Sarah felt her fingers tingling as if she had put her hand too near a fire. 'See?' continued the Nawab. 'You are also alive and awake, and sitting here.'

'Yes. Yes, I am –'.

'Yes. Now you do not feel you are dreaming.' The Nawab nodded at her, as if he knew how her hand held the impression of his touch.

'You see, you feel this place is a dream because of course you have heard of it before. Were you never brought here as a child?'

'Perhaps as a baby, but not after that. When my father left Lambagh State we did not come often to Madore – or at least, I do not remember coming.'

'And yet this is the town which your father's mother made famous just by her name alone – the beautiful Muna, the Rose of Madore.'

'She was not mentioned very often, once I was sent back to school and lived with my other grandmother, my mother's mother. I never saw Muna, of course. She died when my father was quite young.'

'Yes. Poor beautiful Muna, dying so far away from all her friends and the people who truly loved her. You are very like her, you know.' Sarah nodded, her eyes looking away from his.

'Yes. I have been told that I am like her.'

'She is revered in our state, and for her sake all her family are honoured. We owe Munabhen more than we can ever repay. You know the stories, of course.'

Sarah shook her head. 'I have heard a little, but only from my Ayah. I know practically nothing about the famous Muna.' Except that whatever happened, it was foolish to talk about her because it always annoyed my Grandmother Addison, and even my own mother is never very anxious to talk about her, thought Sarah. In this beautiful place it seemed so natural to speak about the past and her lovely ancestor. The Nawab was shaking his head.

'You know so little about your own father's mother! Wah! Well, one day I shall give myself the pleasure of telling you her story. Very soon, I hope.'

A little breeze had risen, stirring the waters of the lake so that all the reflections trembled and ran together. Dip Chand was suddenly beside them with silver goblets, and a sweating bottle in a silver ice bucket. The champagne was deliciously cold, the little cheese puffs were smoking hot, and there was brown bread cut very thin and rolled round asparagus.

'Oh, luxury! Luxury is lovely!'

The Nawab laughed at her. 'For you, luxury is essential. You are a woman who should be wrapped in luxury and given everything you want, because you have the gift of enjoyment. It would be a pleasure to give you anything in the world.'

Sarah laughed with him, but could not meet the eyes that looked so directly at her. She finished her drink rather quickly and suggested that they should go back to the house. As they went from one beautiful room to another she saw several women, bright as parakeets in their swaying full skirts as they swept and polished and dusted.

'There is also some furniture that belongs in this house – I will send it over for you, but you will need more, I think. Alla Ditta, in Commercial Street, is the best man from whom to hire furniture. I shall leave a message with him, to say that whatever you choose is to be cleaned and out here by this evening. You could, if you wish, sleep here tonight.'

'I do wish. In fact, we will sleep here tonight. Thank you, Nawab Sahib, not only for the lovely drink, but for making everything so easy for me.'

'But of course – for a beautiful woman, everything should be easy. For yourself, Munabhen's granddaughter, nothing is too much. How many years have you, Khanum?' His question was as direct as a child's.

'I have – I mean, I am twenty-five.'

'Ah. You are no longer a child. You are a woman. That is good. You have children?'

'Yes – two. A daughter and a son.'

'May he be happy and fortunate, and may the girl have your beauty and good health. Tell me, Khanum, will Colonel Longman sleep here and go in to the Cantonments each day? It is a long way. I only ask these things in order that I may make all easy for you.'

'No. My husband must stay in the camp. But,' she added, something in the Nawab's expression making it necessary, 'he will come here for weekends.'

'Ah – thus. Well, then, I will not make arrangements for any transport for him. Transport is difficult these days. Another thing – there is no telephone in this house, but there is one in my house. If you need to telephone, you have only to send Dip Chand with a message and I will telephone for you. I am only on the other side of the lake. That white building you can see through the trees. It is an easy ride, if you wish another view of the lake, or there is a boat. A different view of anywhere is always interesting.'

He was looking over the lake as he spoke, his pose was still relaxed and easy, but something in his voice made Sarah turn her head to look at him, and as she turned so did he and she looked for a moment straight into his eyes, strange eyes, pale blue, and fixed on her face with a concentration that made her feel trapped. She moved her head in unconscious negation, and the Nawab turned his eyes on to the lake and began to speak of arrangements for moving her furniture. Sarah was relieved to hear Digby's jeep arrive, and presently he was brought out to them by Dip Chand. The Nawab was a charming host. Off with the hunting tiger, on with the civilised man, thought Sarah, watching him.

They stayed a little while longer and then left. 'Because if I do not go now, I will not be ready in time to move in today –'

The Ruler watched them leave, smiling his farewells, his blue eyes not quite as friendly as his smile when he said goodbye to Digby. 'Sarah,' said Digby above the noise of the jeep, 'do you know much about that man?'

'He's the Ruler of Lambagh – you know, that small hill

State right up in the mountains, beyond Jindbagh State. There used to be an enormous palace, the Madoremahal, but it was badly damaged some time towards the end of the nineteenth century. I think he lives in the remnants of it.'

'Yes, of course I know. He's the son of that very wealthy Nawab who killed himself and his wife in an air crash, flying his own plane. But there's something else – I heard something about him, some rumour, and I cannot remember what it was – something political, I think. I'll ask Dick Llewellyn, he'll know. His people have been connected with the hill states for years.'

For some reason Digby did not care for the Nawab. He looked at Sarah. 'Sarah, you like that house, don't you? In spite of a rather terrifying landlord?'

'Oh, the landlord does not worry me at all – and I love the place.'

Digby, still feeling vaguely uneasy, said, 'Oh well, thank God you are getting yourselves out of that dump Piri's. I cannot bear you being there.' His tone was proprietary.

Sarah, feeling that speech was better than silence for once, said quickly, 'Well, it won't be long now. Heaven knows what the manageress will think when we start loading all our stuff into your transport. A mass elopement, no doubt. Digby, you are good to get mixed up in all this.'

'You'll never know how good I am,' said Digby with deep feeling, and Sarah said no more. Her heart grew heavy, the light-hearted joy of the morning left her. There is nothing here for Digby, she thought sadly, and nothing for me. I must send this man away before I hurt him. Because there is nothing here for either of us that will not cause us pain.

10

Julia was waiting for them, with John Collins ready in big frosted tumblers. She thrust the drinks into their hands before they had time to sit down, and began to beg for news.

'Here, steady on, young woman. We are exhausted. Having kindly made these drinks, please give us a chance to drink them.'

'Oh, *Digby* –' even in the midst of her exasperated curiosity, Julia noticed the way Digby looked at Sarah, but in her anxiety to hear the news of their morning she pushed all other thoughts aside. Sarah took pity on her as Digby buried his face in his drink.

'We move in today, Julia. This very afternoon!'

With a shriek that brought Ayah out of the bedroom at a run, Julia whirled down the verandah to where Penelope was playing and, seizing her, waltzed back, singing, 'We're going to a beautiful house, my lark. We're moving there before it gets dark. Oh lucky me and lucky you. And lucky David and Bonnie Prince Charlie and Hans too!' Penelope's happy shrieks were a shrill accompaniment to this song. Sarah put her hands over her ears as Hans joined in with excited barking.

'Well, really, I like to see people enjoying themselves, but Mr Wisbeck is in his room, feeling under the weather, and he might find all the noise troublesome.' The manageress stood on the verandah, her mouth a tight scarlet line of disapproval. Julia made an appalled face at Sarah and vanished with Penelope into the bedroom.

Sarah said quietly, 'I am so sorry. But we will not be disturbing you for very much longer, in any case, as we are moving this afternoon.'

Disapproval became anger. 'Really? Already you have found a house? I understood from Colonel Longman that he wanted these rooms for at least a month. My brother is going to be very put out, I must say. We have refused many many people in order to keep these rooms for you – and right at the height of the season also.'

'Well, I do not suppose you will have any trouble filling the rooms when we go. There is no other hotel, is there? However, if Colonel Longman took the rooms for a month we will pay you for a month in any case – unless of course Colonel Longman paid in advance. Just let me know.'

'Well! Such insults! How would I ask for money, if it had already been paid? Nothing did the Colonel pay me, I kept the rooms out of goodwill for him. He is an old friend of mine, many times he is coming here before you came, to have a drink and a chat with me.'

Sarah's mouth twitched. 'Yes, I can imagine he might enjoy a drink and a – was it a *chat* you said? Yes, I am sure he would have done that. Well, just give me a bill. I'll pay for everything, drinks and chats included, before I leave.' She looked at the other woman with a cool clinical gaze that finally made the manageress lower her eyes, toss her head to set her gold earrings leaping, and leave without another word.

Digby, who had been standing beside Sarah's chair throughout this interview, drew a long breath. 'Sarah, I do not know how you cope! She was routed in disorder and you hardly said a word. What a vile woman!'

Sarah shook her head. 'Shush. Not in front of the children. Julie, you can come out now, she's gone. Can you be ready to leave by three?' Julia rushed off to pack, Digby went away to organise transport, Penelope unhooked Prince Charlie's cage and put it in a prominent position, so that everyone fell over it, and the air was rent with Bonnie Prince Charlie's furious shrieks. But the manageress did not return.

Digby came back to the hotel promptly at three. He

had commandeered two jeeps and six sepoys. It took nearly half an hour to load the two jeeps. One was already half full of furniture, small pieces chosen from the furniture store by Sarah and brought back to the hotel in a horse-drawn cart.

Ayah and David were put into the front seat of the second jeep, and four of the sepoys clung on in the back. Pyari Lal, Hans and the parrot would have to be collected on a second trip. Sarah and Julia sat on top of the luggage in the first jeep, and Digby sat beside the driver with Penelope, speechless with excitement, on his lap.

They looked back as they turned out of the hotel drive, and saw the manageress glaring balefully after them as they bumped off. 'Do you think she'll *eat* Pyari Lal before we get back to rescue him? With Hans and the parrot for afters?'

'Julie! What a horrible thought. She did look as though she could though, didn't she?'

'She looked as if she had. All that thick red lipstick painted round her thin mouth to make it look voluptuous, and those pointy teeth. Do you suppose she files them?'

'Be quiet, both of you, you horrible girls. You are upsetting the lady on my lap. How you can even think about that beastly woman?'

Julia raised her eyebrows at Sarah. Digby's voice had sounded raw with irritation. But Sarah put her hand gently on his shoulder. 'Don't let anything about that woman worry you, Digby. It doesn't worry me. We've left her behind now, she can't touch our lives again.' He turned to meet her steady eyes and for a moment they looked at each other, sharing the pleasure of leaving unpleasantness behind them. He admired her courage and ability to live with what he was beginning to realise was an almost impossible situation. Seeing her there, bumping along, surrounded by her possessions, one hand steadying a bundle of rugs and cushions, the other stretched out to hold his shoulder, he wondered why she stayed with her husband – and turned away so that she would not see his eyes.

He comforted Penelope. 'No one is going to eat Bonnie Prince Charlie, I promise you – don't listen to your aunt, she was only teasing. No one ever eats parrots. Their feathers get in the way.'

'Are you certain sure?' asked Penelope, peering mis-trustfully into his eyes.

'Yes, I am certain sure. Move a little bit further back, my darling Penelope, you are making me squint. Look, there's the gate of the house – we are almost there.'

The house welcomed them. It was not only the smiling salaaming welcome of old Dip Chand and the four women servants on the verandah. It was a feeling in the large beautiful rooms, an atmosphere. This house had welcomed few people down the years. Now something seemed to say, 'You have come at last, you are welcome, you are at home. Enter, live and be happy.'

Even the youngest members of the party felt it. 'This is a beauty house, Mummy,' said Penelope, beaming over the shoulder of one of the women servants who was bearing her off. She went without protest, bright-eyed with excitement, to see, 'The rooms of the babalog. Come, there are many things for little people here –.'

'Those two are going to get desperately spoiled,' said Sarah, watching the entourage go upstairs.

Julia had started to explore. 'Oh, Sarah – look! Look at the peacocks! There are peacocks everywhere – no, not live ones but carved over that door, and on the panels, and embroidered on the screens, and there is a big silver one there. Look.' 'Yes, well, there would be. They are the emblem of Lambagh State, you know?'

'No, I didn't know. They are carved on the newel posts of the stairs, too. Oh, Sarah, think of it, a real house, and going upstairs to bed –.'

'With or without peacocks?' asked Sarah. Julia's eyes were as brightly excited as Penelope's and Sarah felt as if she had three children, one of them just a little older than the other two. There was a kindness in her heart for this young excited Julia as she watched her rush upstairs.

She turned, smiling, to Digby who said, his voice

barely audible, 'You are so lovely.'

Sarah's laughing disclaimer died into silence as she saw his expression. Then, frowning, she managed to say, 'Digby, don't feel like this. You must not, it is quite pointless. Don't be serious, Digby, please.'

What he was going to say was interrupted by the sound of a jeep being driven rapidly up the curving drive. 'Who on earth? Perhaps it is the S.S.O. checking on the house, but he is driving like a maniac –'

The jeep did not slacken speed, but continued on down the road that led to the lake. The two on the verandah had a clear view of the driver and recognised him at once.

'Richard!' said Sarah in amazement. 'But what is he doing here, at this time? And where is he going?'

They saw the dust cloud raised by the jeep roll on down the road around the lake, towards the Nawab's house. Sarah watched the jeep and the birds rising disturbed from the lake, and thought how like Richard it was to arrive in a place and by his arrival destroy peace. Digby saw the shadow on her face and cursed himself and Richard impartially. If his love was going to give her nothing but added worry, then he must keep it to himself. As for her husband, 'Perhaps he thinks you are living over there?'

'No. I sent a note saying I had taken Lambagh House – this place. It really doesn't matter, you know.'

Julia was calling to them to come upstairs. They said nothing more about Richard's presence. Unspoken between them was the determination that nothing must spoil this arrival in the house. They followed Julia round the rooms, high-ceilinged and cool. 'Sarah, look, *look* at the furniture! I've got everything to match, all green and gold, even the bed is lacquered green and has a gold peacock-embroidered brocade cover. And you've got a bed as big as a house, and your walls are painted, and – oh, look, come and see –' She led them into the room the women had said was for the lady. It was like a jewel box, so beautiful were the colours in the Mogul paintings on the wall panels. Polo matches, hunting scenes, and lovers in forest glades; delicate brush-work and clear glowing colours, gleaming with touches of gold paint. Wide windows opened on a view of the garden and the balcony, with its long chairs and small painted tables, looked over the lake to the Nawab's white house and the blue mountains beyond.

'We'll have our early morning tea here together, Sarah,' said Julia with satisfaction, and they turned back into the room. Digby remained on the balcony, staring out over the lake and not hearing a word the two girls were saying as they admired the panels and the heavy silk curtains. He could not bear to be so close to Sarah and the great carved and painted bed without taking her in his arms. While he stood there, he slowly became aware of what he could see. He saw Richard's jeep parked outside the Nawab's house, and presently saw Richard himself come out of the house and drive off as rapidly as he had come. He heard the roar of the jeep draw near and then die away again. So Colonal Longman was not visiting his family today. He found difficulty in thinking of Richard calmly. Damn the fellow. Had he loved and valued his wife there would have been no opening in her life for outsiders such as himself. And how much better for me, thought Digby miserably and then, turning to leave, he saw Sarah standing against the bed talking to Julia and knew his thoughts to be false. Whatever happened, or did not happen, he could not bear to have missed meeting and loving her.

This time Julia had heard the jeep and rushed to the balcony and saw Richard go past. 'But that was Richard – and he didn't even come in to see how we are getting on!'

'Never mind, sweetie – he's terribly busy. Come and see the garden, and then we'll have a quiet drink to celebrate the move. Good idea?'

'Oh yes, Sarah. Can we drink outside? If we wait a few minutes it will be sunset and – well, in fact, Alastair said he just might be able to get away from Namkum early, and would look in.'

Julia turned pink as they both looked at her and then at the sky, which was also flushed with the afterglow of the sunset. The sun had already set. They both continued to look at Julia, Sarah with raised eyebrows and her mouth quivering to a smile, as Digby said, 'Well, *really* Julia! Sunset, indeed! The sun set about twenty minutes ago, and anyway if Alastair can seize transport so easily, why didn't you trap him into this exodus and then he could have brought poor Pyari Lal and all the rest of the ark?'

'Poor Pyari Lal and the ark are already here. I can hear the screams of Bonnie Prince Charlie, Hans barking and Ayah raging at Pyari Lal because he has broken Penelope's tooth mug. Stop teasing Julia, Digby, of course we'll wait for Alastair. Come and look at the garden, I think Dip Chand has chairs out there already.'

They sat late under the trees and watched the birds settle for the night and fires blossom in the village at the far end of the lake. There were lights in the Nawab's house, each light duplicated in the water. Alastair had brought two enormous bouquets of red roses for the girls. Watching Sarah bury her face in their crimson sweetness, Digby felt a flash of jealousy. Why hadn't he thought of flowers? He felt he wanted to do everything for Sarah, be everything to her. He sat opposite her and tried to discipline his eyes from her face and the rich swell of her breasts. How could a girl so thin have such beautiful breasts? He found his eyes and his feelings were both getting out of hand and sat half turned away from her, taking no part in the conversation, while the others made plans for the next day. Julia was riding with Alastair and it was arranged that he should stay to lunch when he brought her back.

'Digby, can you come too? Do – and then we can have a lazy afternoon. We could swim, or just sit. I won't do anything in the morning, except unpack. This house obviously runs itself.'

It seemed that she was right. With no orders given, lamps had been brought out, champagne clinking in an ice bucket, and Dip Chand had taken up a position out of hearing but in sight, and was at their elbows with a bottle at the first sign of an empty glass.

'This is so *heavenly*!' Julia, with thrown back head, was drinking the last of her champagne. 'But where is all this coming from, Sarah?' Her glass had been refilled immediately.

'I had one bottle on ice, because I thought we'd celebrate – but it does seem to have no bottom.'

'I brought three more out with me,' said Digby gruffly. 'So there is no mystery.' He met Sarah's eyes and saw her flush under his direct gaze, and felt better and more cheerful. He was sure she was not indifferent to him – he was sure her hand shook as she put her glass down. If only the other two were not here, what a setting for love this was! As if all were of the same mind, they turned and looked at the lake, silver and shadowed in the shifting cloud-swept moonlight. Somewhere a night bird called, and there was a light wind rustling in the reeds at the edge of the water.

Digby finished his glass and stood up, breaking a moment he could no longer endure. 'Time to go, Alastair. I sent my exhausted transport away, so I will come with you.'

Driving back to the camp he held the picture of Sarah standing on the verandah, her hair gleaming in the lamplight, waving goodbye.

Alastair broke into his thoughts. 'The doughty Colonel doesn't seem to do much for his family.'

'No,' said Digby. 'He was apparently on duty.'

'Yes, well, we all know that one. However, he did go and look in on you I take it?'

'Look in? Certainly not, he didn't come near us.'

'But I met him, just outside the camp, on his way back.'

'Oh, yes, he came out here, and went on past to the Rajaghar. Didn't even slow down at the gate on his way by.'

'He was driving like the clappers when I saw him.'

'On duty, no doubt.'

'Digby, what is the form? She seems such a charmer. I take it she knows what is happening?'

'Damned if I know. But if it comes to that, what *is* happening? I don't know anything, apart from the usual Cantonment gossip.' Digby did not want to go on discussing Sarah's affairs. But Alastair felt differently. He was worried about Digby, and continued to speak in spite of the withdrawal he could feel Digby trying to make.

'There is certainly enough Cantonment gossip to fill two large books. But it is not just gossip. He is living with some girl. She is actually set up in one of those old bungalows near Namkum which are condemned, so they are not on the army hirings. Richard had the place mended at his own expense and she's living there, plus a houseful of servants – including the cook, who is a friend of my orderly and wants to leave – he's not happy with the set-up.' Digby stared at his friend, astonished.

'For God's sake, is that true? Longman will never get away with that, surely?' The scandal for Sarah and the children, and the unhappiness he saw coming to her, were Digby's first thoughts. Afterwards, more selfishly, he wondered if this could be to his advantage – if she found out, and divorced Richard, she would be free. He was both ashamed and yet made happy by the thought of her needing him, turning to him.

Again, Alastair broke into his train of thought. 'I am sorry, Digby, that she is tied to such a bastard. She seems to be, as I said, a charmer in every way. But – well, *not* my business, but how deeply in are you?'

Digby looked at the kind embarrassed face of his friend, his oldest friend, and said firmly, 'I am, as you put it, very deeply in. Alastair, I love her very much, in every way, and truthfully, I have never felt so permanently involved before.'

Alastair sighed and frowned, and said, 'Well, that is straight enough. But Digby, you couldn't have picked a more tricky set-up – and not only because of her husband. You know her story, don't you?'

'There isn't a beautiful woman in the world of the

Cantonments that hasn't had some fearful story told about her.'

'No, I don't mean that kind of story. Digby, she is a half-caste, you know.'

'She is the daughter of an Anglo-Indian – her grandmother was a wealthy Indian girl who married a Colonel Reid. That does not make her a half-caste – you are making her sound like a railway institute girl. Stop being so stupid, Alastair. Frankly, I don't care if she is entirely black, or red or yellow. She is the most delightful person I have ever met, and if she can get free from her horrible husband I shall marry her, if she'll have me – and leave the army should it come to that.'

'It isn't as simple as that. Richard Longman hasn't a penny. The money is all Sarah's, inherited from that famous grandmother. Richard is not going to be easy to detach from that money – it's a great deal of money. So that filthy fellow will fight like a stag to hang on to his wife.'

'You've certainly used your ears to some purpose since you came to Madore,' said Digby unpleasantly. But Alastair shook his head.

'No. I didn't hear all this in Madore. My mother was at school with Sarah's mother, and they have remained great friends. She remembers all the hoo-ha when Laura Addison married Robert Reid. Robert was in the State Forces in Lambagh, and as far as Laura's family were concerned, he was a half-caste. It caused a terrible fuss. I met Laura, and I do not think that she cared for India. She took the children home to England as soon as she could. The boy, James, was charming. He went into the Gurkhas, after doing his British attachment, and was killed early in the war. Sarah married Richard, and you know all about *that*. Digby, you are going to run into trouble all round; but I can see that you are just going to tell me to mind my own business again. Very well. You know that I am on your side in everything, but I think you are making a terrible mistake here. I don't think that Sarah is for you —' He stopped, looking at his friend's determined face. Digby was not even listening to him.

They drove the rest of the way in silence. As they passed the first encampment, Alastair pointed at a small bungalow. Lights blazed from the windows, and a gramophone was blaring. To Digby's enquiring stare, Alastair said, 'That is the Colonel's home from home.'

Digby thought of the beautiful, peaceful house he had just left, and of Sarah's quiet voice speaking in the shadows on the edge of the lake. The contrast was great. There was no happiness in her marriage, of that he was now certain. He would take her away from it, make her love him. Alastair spoke again.

'Digby, I say again. Not for you. Don't get entangled.'

'It is for me. And I am, as you call it, entangled.' Silence fell between them again, until they arrived at their own camp.

11

Sarah lay in the big carved bed and thought about the day, which seemed to have been as long as two days. But how much harder it would have been without Digby! She knew that they could not have moved without his help. He was so kind, so thoughtful of them all. The hard coldness she had built into herself as a protection seemed to melt a little more each time she met him. It would be so easy to let herself go, turn to the desire she had seen in his eyes, find warmth and the security of love in him. But she must not. Her episode with Bruce had taught her a bitter lasting lesson. There was no security in love really. She turned restlessly on her pillow. The room she lay in did not help her, with the beautiful painted lovers seeming to move together in the lamplight and the scent of flowers blowing in from the garden. This is a room for love, thought Sarah, tossing in the big bed. It had been the Begum Bianca's room, and here she must have welcomed her adored husband. What hours of happiness this whole house must have seen, and this room must have been the heart of it. She thought of all the ease and relaxation and companionship that she was sure could be found in a happy marriage. How much she had expected to find in her marriage and, sadly, how little she had found!

Her thoughts, because she was overtired, were crystal clear. She seemed to see all the parts of her life with Richard as a time of uncertainty and unhappiness, from the beginning. She had had such a short time of security. She remembered with shame her attempts to retain Richard's interest when she had first seen his attentions engaged with other women. She recalled him using so easily, to so many others, all the charm that she had thought was reserved for her. All the special tones of voice, the deep glances and secret smiles that had once so delighted her, were soon a devalued coinage of love, and she had passed from jealousy to pain, and then to complete indifference. Bruce, she knew now, was merely the object on which her neglected loving tried to spend itself – and so she came back to the same sad thoughts, the ending of love, the sordid disaster of a dying affair. She was back to the thought of Digby, and the knowledge that there was no place in her life for another lover – nor could she face the thought of hurting him.

It was time to stop thinking and sleep. She opened her little jewelled pill box, preparing to kill thought for the night by taking a sleeping pill.

The curtains over the door to the balcony parted and a slender figure slipped through. A glass of fruit juice was handed to Sarah and a soft voice asked if it was sweet enough. Sarah, whose voice had left her completely, nodded, and the woman drew the curtains closed again and stood waiting while Sarah swallowed her pill, and then, taking the glass, she stepped back through the curtains as silently as she had come, and Sarah was left wondering if she was the spirit of some former serving-woman or a real flesh and blood servant. Her thoughts blurred, she put out her lamp and fell into a deep drugged sleep. All night she heard a voice speaking her name, and a man's face haunted her dreams – but it was not Digby's voice which called, nor Digby's face she saw.

She woke to the sound of curtains being pulled back and found a tea-tray on the table beside her bed. The girl holding her dressing-gown out to her was certainly flesh and blood, and very beautiful. Sarah was asked what time she would like her bath, and what clothes she would wear, and then left to drink her tea.

The morning was beautiful. Dew sparkled on green grass, the Nawab's white house had a polish and glitter as if it was made of marble, reflections in the lake were broken by swooping birds – kingfishers and flights of green parakeets. Sarah went out on to the balcony and could not look enough. She took her tea-tray out and sat there, absorbing the peace and beauty, and when Julia found her she was asleep, head thrown back against the cushions, her dark hair down on her shoulders.

She is beautiful, thought Julia. Beautiful, and strange and distant – and I like her more every day. I wish I knew what was wrong between her and Richard – it can't all be her fault – Richard's behaviour was making it hard for Julia to see him as blameless. He had done nothing to help in the move and had not even been to see them although he had actually driven as far as the Nawab's house. Most odd and unfriendly. Julia sat looking at her sister-in-law for a little while longer and then crept away, disappointed not to have had her planned Chota Hazari party.

She had finished her bath and was almost dressed when Sarah tapped at her door and came in. 'Oh, Julie, how awful of me! I fell asleep again. Come and have breakfast with me on the balcony. There are so many willing servants, longing to wait on us, that I feel it would be mean to refuse any service.'

'I know. I've got my own woman, and Ayah is in heaven – she's got two under-Ayahs to harry. Sarah, who pays for all these people?'

'I'll have to find out. But let us have a glorious fetch-and-carry breakfast first.' Sarah, in her white cotton dressing-gown, with her hair still loose, looked rested and relaxed and, over their iced pawpaw and toast and coffee, they were more at ease together than they had ever been.

When Alastair arrived to collect Julia she was waiting for him in the garden. As they drove off he sighed deeply and said, 'Aren't Digby and I lucky? Are you happy, my pretty Julia?'

Although she felt she should disapprove of her sister-in-law's name being linked by implication with Digby, Julia could not turn away from Alastair's smiling admiration. Am I happy? she thought, and gave him the expected and true answer. 'Yes – very happy.' He smiled more broadly and took her hand and held it closely in his.

'Good,' he said. 'Good. It has been a long bloody war. Let us, for God's sweet sake, be happy while we can.'

Sarah dressed slowly after they had gone, enjoying her big quiet room and pausing often to look at the view. Ayesha, her new servant, came just as she finished dressing, to tell her that the Nawab Sahib would like to see her and was awaiting her pleasure in the garden.

She found him at the edge of the lake, helping Penelope to sail a little model boat. David was clasped closely in his free arm, his turban was on the ground and the lake wind had ruffled his dark hair. Gone was the polished, urbane ruler. He was absorbed in the safe launching of the boat – not until it was sailing did he turn to Sarah, handing David to the Ayah.

'You are fortunate in your children, Khanum, they are beautiful,' he said, and his eyes were clear and smiling as he watched David's efforts to outwit the Ayah and get back to the water.

'Thank you, Nawab Sahib,' she said, and to herself thought, And what were you doing, intruding into my dreams last night, with that beguiling seducing smile?

As if he could read her thoughts, he asked her how she had slept, was her house comfortable for her and was there anything he could do. They sat together under the trees and she asked about all the extra servants. 'They are of my household, and are included in the rent for the house which you so proudly insist on paying – imagine paying rent for your own house!'

'But there are so many servants – and the house is not mine, Nawab Sahib.'

'Those servants would have nothing to do if you were not here. It is not a question of payment or non-payment. It is my pleasure that they serve you, and they are happy to be able to do so. Please let there be no more talk about this, Khanum. All that I have is yours.'

'You put me under an obligation, Nawab Sahib.' Sarah decided that saying nothing more, she would pay each of the servants a small wage, because she did not wish to be under any obligation to the Nawab, however likeable she found him. He was certainly very easy to like. He obviously adored the children; he watched them all the time, his pleasure plain to see. Studying his face in the dappled shade of the trees, she decided that he was the most handsome man she had ever seen.

He turned his head unexpectedly, met her eyes, smiled an open, friendly smile and said, 'Well, Khanum, do I please you?' Sarah, completely taken by surprise, flushed scarlet, but the Nawab continued easily, 'I hope I do please you, Khanum, because now you see my true self, the face I can show to few people. I can only be at ease with my very close friends and family, those whom I love.' He waited for her to speak and then, while she still looked for words, he said sadly, 'But you are embarrassed. Do you not feel the tie of love between us?'

Sarah collected herself, tried to smile and said, 'But of course, there is friendship, a feeling of ease between us, Nawab Sahib. It is just that we Europeans take longer to put our feelings into words.'

He shook his head. 'Come, Khanum, "We Europeans". What are you saying? Do you forget that I have almost as much European blood in my veins as you have in yours? Do not try to be cold. You are as I am, and I am not cold, nor do I find it hard to put my feelings into words.' He looked at her, studying her face so closely that Sarah was forced to look down, feeling that every thought she had ever had was being laid bare. Then he sighed and looked at the children. 'Never mind, Khanum, I am riding too fast for you. But you will catch me up – very soon I think – very soon.'

He got up and went back to the children, where he received a vociferous welcome. 'The fourth generation is certainly making up for my cold half-European heart,' thought Sarah, grateful for the interruption. She called to

Dip Chand to bring coffee.

The Nawab spoke no more of love and friendship. They sat in silence, drinking their coffee, looking over the lake. The Nawab's white house reminded Sarah of Richard's visit there the night before. Finding the silence between them beginning to hang heavily, she said, 'I saw my husband go past to visit you yesterday evening – he did not have time to stop and see us. He is, as I expect you know, very busy getting his battalion into permanent camp.' The Nawab's blank stare halted her words.

'But Khanum, your husband did not come and see me yesterday evening.'

'But I saw him.' Sarah was beginning to feel foolish. 'I saw him quite clearly. He drove very fast over to your house, and left again about twenty minutes later.' The Nawab shook his head.

'Not possible, I assure you, Khanum. I was not in my house last night, I had to pay a visit to Madore, and I cannot believe in any case that your husband would not have stopped to see his family, if he passed so close to your house. No, he did not come. I think you saw my supply jeep, and distance and dust confused you.' Either he believed what he was saying, or he was trying to make her believe him. His calm insistence made her suddenly sure that if Richard had called at the house – and she was certain that he had – the Nawab himself knew nothing about it.

There were many reasons why Richard should call at an Indian household when the head of the house was out, thought Sarah, her mouth twisting. All the reasons would probably be connected with the *bibikhana*, the women's quarters. She changed the subject, and presently accepted an invitation for herself and Julia to go over to the Nawab's house for drinks that evening. Then he took his leave, and she saw that he had ridden over. She watched him ride away, down the shaded path round the lake, thinking again that he was magnificent to look at, and very attractive, more attractive than anyone she had ever met. She allowed herself to dwell on his eyes, and his shoulders, and his smile, because she was determined to keep her thoughts away from Richard. She knew, with a sinking heart, that Richard was very likely to be with her for the weekend, and thanked God that the move into the house had not been spoiled by his presence. The house seemed to offer warm protection, and even the thought of it drove her fears for the weekend away. She sat thinking and planning happily, for future pleasures, rides, and picnics for the children, while they played beside her and Ayah dozed under the trees.

Presently she heard Hans barking and the sounds of an arrival. Then Dip Chand came out, followed by Digby, Hans frisking at his heels. She asked where the others were. 'Oh, they will be along later. Alastair had transport of his own, so I suggested that he took Julia to see the silk market.'

He was so obviously delighted to be alone with her that it was impossible for her to hide her own pleasure in his company, but there was a shadow on her pleasure and Digby leaned close to look at her.

'What is it, Sarah?' The tenderness in his voice touched her and she gave him the honest answer he deserved.

'I seem suddenly to see where I could go with you, and I know that it is wrong for us both.'

She stopped because of the pain on his face, and after a silence he said, 'Sarah, this is a lovely day. Too good to spoil. I'll make a bargain with you – I'll say nothing that could not be howled from the housetops if you will promise to be happy and enjoy yourself. No worries. Promise?' He waited, saw that she was unable to speak, and bent and kissed her gently, saying, 'That seals the bargain. Now go and get that lovely body of yours into a swimsuit and we'll try the lake. I'll meet you at the diving-board.'

Ayesha, it seemed, had guessed that there was swimming in view, for she was waiting with Sarah's towelling wrap and green maillot. She helped Sarah undress and asked if she wished to be rubbed with oil. 'For the sun is hot and, Khanum, your skin is very pale.'

'My skin is fish-belly white,' said Sarah firmly, 'so no oil. I do not burn, I become brown. I will have my sandals and my wrap, thank you.'

Ayesha followed her out, carrying her towel, and Sarah wondered how many generations of service had been in her background, to make such an intuitive servant. She walked down to the lake where Digby waited, smoke from his cigarette coiling blue against the shade. 'You look like a water-nymph in that green thing. Thank God you don't wear a cap – they make women look scalped.'

Sarah was suddenly as shy and self-conscious as a girl. She gave her wrap to Ayesha and dived quickly into the clear topaz water, turning to float and watch Digby dive, a bronze arch against the sky. The water was icy and she was glad to swim hard to the raft where Digby waited to drag her up, dripping, beside him. The sun was hot and it was very pleasant to sit on the gently rocking raft, watching the water-birds dabbling in and out among the reeds and the reflections of the trees and the shrine on the island making another upside-down world under the lake.

Presently Penelope and David came shouting to the water's edge, wearing the smallest swimming trunks Digby had ever seen. Digby swam over and brought them one by one, screaming with delight, to the raft. Hans was running, frustrated, up and down on the shore which was more than Penelope could bear. 'Oh, that poor Hans. Oh, my Digby, please will you get Hans?'

'Oh, darling, he'll hate being stuck on the raft,' said Sarah. Hans settled the matter for himself by plunging bravely in and swimming towards them, his tail ruddering furiously. Digby swam out to him and dragged him on to the raft, where Hans rewarded him by shaking himself furiously, spattering them all with cold water. Watching Digby tirelessly teaching Penelope to dive, Sarah thought what a wonderful father he would be and hoped he would marry someone as kind and charming as himself; and he, seeing her dreaming in the sun with David leaning against her long slim legs, thought her unbearably beautiful, and was happy, forgetting everything but the present.

Penelope tired of diving at last and they all four sat quietly on the raft, almost asleep in the sun. Ayah appeared on the lake shore, calling the children to come for lunch. Digby ferried them over, swam back and looked threateningly at Hans. 'You can wait, my boy,' he said firmly, and Hans, sleeping in the sun, did not show the slightest sign of wishing to be elsewhere. Digby and Sarah watched the children go off, one on each side of Ayah, drowsy and happy with sun and exercise.

'They'll sleep well today,' said Digby.

'Heavens, yes. What a wonderful life this is for them! They'll remember this all their lives.'

And so shall I, thought Digby, and looked away from her; it was becoming difficult for him not to pull her into his arms. The sun, the light breeze that ruffled the water so that a thousand points of light sparked into their eyes, made a close circle of enchantment that neither wished to break with speech. Shoulder to shoulder they sat, and were lost in a dream of happiness in which they were alone together and yet completely apart. For Digby it was a permanent world, there would never be anyone else – in his mind, their love was real; there would be no parting nor misunderstandings, their path would be smooth and their lives would lie together. Sarah's dream was only one of companionship, the peace of the warm sun, and no fears or regrets to trouble her.

A water-bird cried loudly close by and there was a splashing in the reeds. Hans woke and stood up, looking over to the island, wagging his tail. Digby stirred and turned to look down at Sarah and she, seeing his expression, stood up and dived into the water. 'Race you to the island,' she called, and was off in a white lace of foam. Taken by surprise, Digby was easily beaten and she stood waiting for him, laughing, as he splashed up and scrambled on to the bank. Hans had elected to stay where he was, pacing backwards and forwards on the tilting raft, like the captain of a ship on the bridge in a rough sea.

The little shrine shone white in the sun and was doubled by reflection in the water. Trees, thick dark mango and the sacred banyan tree, threw a black shade behind them, and there were cannas and marigolds growing in the little garden in front, and a fountain, broken with age and choked with dead leaves and twigs, coughed and gurgled to itself in the sunlight. There was a small stone jetty to one side and below it, where the crumbling stone steps were overgrown with reeds and water-weeds, a white bird had settled.

'What a heavenly place! The children would love it. I suppose it would be sacrilege to have a picnic here.'

'Oh, I shouldn't think so. Indians see things differently for different people. They would know that you would not be desecrating the shrine – I imagine you would be welcome to picnic outside here. Anyway, the Nawab is a Muslim, isn't he? So he wouldn't mind, and he's the overlord round about here.'

'Yes, he's the Ruler. But he rules over Hindus and Muslims – they have equal rights in Lambagh.' Her hair gleamed in the sun like wet satin, her skin took reflections from the green stuff of her suit, and Digby could hear nothing she said.

'You are a water-nymph, I do believe, and you've come out of the water to enchant poor men into giving you their hearts.'

'*La belle Dame sans merci* – in that case, you had better stop palely loitering!' She refused to be serious, she laughed at him and walked over to the water's edge to have a closer look at the stone steps and the white bird resting there so quietly in the sun.

She stood so still that Digby, who had been examining the fountain, called to her and, getting no answer, hurried over, knowing something was wrong when she put one hand out as if groping for support. He took the seeking hand in his and held it tightly.

'What is it, Sarah?'

She turned a colourless face and, wordless, pointed.

The white bird? Bird? Too large, too still, this, to be a bird.

Mercifully face down in the reeds, long hair tangling with water-weed, white sari dabbled with blood, a woman lay, a woman who must have been young and beautiful before her throat had been cut, slit like a pig's throat from the lower angle of the jaw to the opposite ear. Digby, bending over her, found her still warm, the blood that spread on the water in dark oily streaks was still flowing from the wound, but she was dead – her head flopped back over his arm, the cut gaping wide, obviously only her spinal column held her head still attached to her body. Dead – quite gone.

But if she had gone, it was fairly certain that the killer had not. Digby put the woman's head and shoulders gently down, and straightened. His main thought was to get Sarah off the island. 'Sarah, go at once and get Dip Chand. He'd better send for the Nawab, and tell him to send the gardeners and any other men you have over here.' Hans, on the raft, suddenly gave a long shuddering howl, and then another. Sarah had turned so pale that he was afraid she was going to faint, but she turned immediately, dived in and began to swim strongly for the opposite shore. Hans, after a series of short sharp yelps, and another tearing, terrible howl, sat quietly on the raft, and Digby turned from the quiet, huddled figure on the steps and went quickly towards the shrine, cursing his lack of any kind of weapon. But he need not have worried. There was no one there, and no one in the shadows of the trees. The island was small – it was soon plain that there was no one else on it. A strong swimmer could have made his way to the shore and hidden himself while he and Sarah were on the raft. He remembered suddenly the cry of a bird, very loud, and the splashing in the reeds that had roused them from their happy dreaming. Had that been the woman's death cry, and had the splashing been the killer getting away from the island? The bright sun was not darkened, the lake sparkled and danced in the brilliant noon light, but Digby felt cold. He stood beside the fountain and found that the choked gurgling was getting on his nerves, and was glad when he saw a small boat put out from the shore in front of the Ruler's house.

12

The Nawab stood looking down at the woman's body with an expressionless face.

'She is the wife of one of my watchmen and came very recently from Lambagh. Now why? Jealousy, I expect.'

'Jealousy? You mean her husband killed her?'

'Yes, of course. Who else? No one else would have any reason to kill her, except her husband. It is always the husband in these cases when a married woman is killed. If the husband is killed, unless it is an inter-tribal killing, then it is usually by poison given to him by his wife.'

'Good God, Nawab Sahib, you cannot be so sure. It could have been anyone, a lover, a jealous woman, a thief.'

'Why would a lover kill her, when she is all the world to him? And a jealous woman would not kill by the knife. She would give poison. It is easy to get poison here. Do not forget the snake farm on the way from Madore, only about two miles from here, where they are working on snake-bite serum. Oh yes, a jealous woman could get poison easily. A thief? Well, yes, that is possible. It could have been a thief, but he was not trying to rob this girl – she has lost nothing but her life. See, her gold is still with her.'

Sure enough, Digby saw with a pang the gold earrings in the girl's ears, so like the ones that Sarah wore, and the gold bracelets on a slender outflung arm.

The Nawab leaned down and looked closely at the girl's arm. 'She was dragged here. See, her arm is bruised and the flesh is torn. I think she fought for her life. This was a brave girl. If it was a thief who killed her, then she was very brave. How much easier to let him steal the thing he wanted, and keep her life, especially as there is nothing on this island now to steal.'

He spoke, it seemed, to himself; Digby did not understand what he was saying. By this time the State Police had come, a Sikh inspector and two young constables. All three were obviously deeply in awe of the Ruler.

The body was moved, and now lay on the grass in front of the shrine. Turning his eyes from the pathetic tumbled figure, Digby saw Sarah standing with Alastair on the lake shore opposite the island. He waved to them and they waved back, and then the Nawab told him that the Inspector would like to take a statement from him. When he had finished telling the Inspector how the body of the girl had been found, Digby said, 'I looked, but I could find no one here. I suppose the murderer got away by swimming – we would not have heard him, as we were swimming ourselves.'

'We?'

'Yes, Mrs Longman and myself. We swam over from the raft.'

'But this woman did not get here by swimming. Her clothes are dry. She and her companion – or companions – must have come by boat. You see, there, on the other side, the island is nearer to the mainland. A man could row a boat over and back very easily, and quietly. But one thing –'

The Nawab paused, frowning, his gaze on the further shore. 'One thing I do not understand. Why bring her here and kill her in broad daylight? Very strange. It is years now since there was any reason for a thief to come to the shrine, and all my people know this.'

Digby saw the Inspector and the Nawab exchange a glance, and then the Inspector nodded. 'You are right, Lord of the Hills. No one but our own people knew – and therefore no outsider could ever know.'

The Nawab stood looking first at the woman and then at the shrine, with a frown that cut two deep lines on his forehead. 'That is no longer so certain, Inspector. These days are different, and money has great power.'

Watching the Nawab, Digby was unhappily certain that this murder was not going to be easily explained, and feared for Sarah and the complications it could bring for her – endless statements, and visits from the police.

'If there is nothing more I can do, Nawab Sahib?'

'But of course – I am so sorry, you must be getting cold. I'll send you back in the boat.'

Digby declined this offer, explaining that he preferred to swim, and dived into the lake, glad of the cold water and the swift hard movement of fast swimming. He collected the shivering Hans, and the Nawab watched him, his gaze turning from Digby swimming to Sarah waiting on the shore, and then thoughtfully back to Digby again.

Digby was glad of the dressing-gown Alastair held out for him, and of the mug of beer Sarah gave him. Sarah said quickly, 'Digby, Alastair and I both think that Julia had better have this played down – she gets so upset.'

'Yes, I remember her on the train. We won't tell her anything until we have to.'

Sarah hurried back to the house, and Digby told Alastair as much as he knew himself, while he towelled himself dry and dressed.

'Bloody unpleasant. I give Sarah full marks. She welcomed us back as if she had done nothing all morning but enjoy herself. Sent Julia up to change, and then told me what had happened. Of course she looked bad, but Julia wouldn't notice that as apparently Sarah hadn't been very well and gets over-tired. That is the story Julia's been told by her gallant brother, anyway. Digby, what do you make of all this?'

'All what?' Digby looked defensive, and Alastair could see he did not want to discuss Sarah so he smoothly changed direction.

'Well, this killing. Is it a family affair, husbandly jealousy, or what?'

'Or what, I should think,' said Digby slowly. 'I can't make anything out of anything at the moment, and that

Nawab fellow – apart from the fact that he has the State Police in his pocket, he's obviously very upset about the whole thing. I wish I could remember where I've seen him before, and what I heard about him.'

'Oh, my God, Digby, all this nearly put it out of my head. There is news – here's a chit from Battersby – he'd like to see you. I think there is a flap on, but I do not know what it is, or where.'

Digby read the note and put it away in his wallet. 'Well, this is, or looks like, good news.'

'Oh?'

'Yes. It isn't exactly what he says, it is more what he doesn't say. I doubt if we will be moving anywhere for a while. I think they want us here.'

They sat, discussing the future, until Dip Chand came to tell them that tiffin was ready.

Julia took all the strain from the conversation. She had enjoyed herself, and spread such an air of happiness around her that the horrible ending to their morning began to lift from Sarah and Digby. Digby, in any case, was happy to think that there was a chance that the battalion would not be leaving Madore. He told Sarah, and hoped that she was pleased. Julia broke into their conversation to tell Sarah about her visit to the silk bazaar.

'It was like Aladdin's cave, Sarah, silks and silks, all colours, piled up all over the floor on Persian carpets, and sandalwood chests full of those gauze scarves and rolls of brocade, and –'

'And I couldn't get Julia away, which is why we didn't swim today. I think she has ideas about going back there to live with the silk merchant. Very personable old gent he was, about ninety, but Julia wouldn't have minded being his fourth wife if she could have had all that silk, would you, Julia?'

'Oh you!' As Julia turned on him they all heard a jeep arrive, and a few seconds later Richard was smiling at them from the door.

Settled at the table, he looked about him and took a

long swallow of the beer Dip Chand had poured for him. 'Well, Sarah, this is certainly a beautiful place. But much too far from Madore. We won't be able to stay here, I am afraid.'

He paused, and started to eat, apparently unconscious of the dismay he had spread round the table. Even Dip Chand, pouring more beer into Richard's glass, paused for a second and steadied his hand. Consternation flooded into Julia's face. Then Richard looked blandly round the table and continued, 'However, it will work very well for a bit. I've come to say goodbye, darling. We're being sent to Ratna, and we'll be there for some time. Maddening really, you moving in here so quickly; you could have saved yourself a move, and come with me.'

'To Ratna?' Digby spoke involuntarily. 'Would you have taken the children there as well? I mean, the rioting there has been pretty unpleasant.'

'Oh, my dear chap! For once these riots are not directed against the British. They are just killing each other at the moment. Intercommunal.'

'Yes, but not a very pleasant atmosphere, and you never know which way a rioting crowd is going to turn.' Digby felt his eyes beginning to burn with rage, as Richard lounged back smiling at him.

'But my dear chap, I wouldn't take *my* wife and family into any danger, you know.' He let the possessive pronoun hang in the air for a second, and then said, 'In any case the situation does not arise, because Sarah has tied herself up with this place, and I'll just have to leave you here to get disentangled, darling. I'll be taking Kullunder Khan – you obviously don't need him here – and he can look after me in Ratna. I'll try and get back for weekends, and we can discuss where you want to live then.'

Sarah seemed to be watching herself and the others as if she was looking at a stage luncheon party, with actors. She waited, it seemed, like a prompter, for someone to make the wrong speech or forget their lines. But miraculously it became an easy time, with Julia and Alastair wrangling with each other, and Digby and Richard exchanging news about mutual acquaintances and regimental matters, with no appearance of strain. Slowly Sarah felt herself beginning to relax. Almost, she thought, almost, everything is normal. Julia, because Sarah had not protested about moving from the house, felt sure that it was just Richard being funny and did not worry. She began to tell her brother about her visit to the silk bazaar, but he interrupted her to say, 'Now there is a place I would not go to. Stay out of the walled city in future, Julie. Alastair, that was running rather a risk, wasn't it?'

Alastair and Digby both stared at him. 'A risk?'

'Yes. There may be trouble in Madore any day now, and that silk market is right in the middle of the hot spot.'

'But there hasn't been trouble in Madore since that rising in 1867.'

'Quite true. But that doesn't mean there will never be trouble there again, and I would prefer my family to stay out of that area.'

'Well, you were there yourself, this morning. I saw you. So there!' Julia glared at her brother defiantly. Alastair shifted uneasily. He had seen Richard too, in a taxi, with his girlfriend. He had hoped that Julia had not. Sarah thought No, Julia, leave it alone, but did not dare to say anything.

'My *dear* Julia! You sound as if you were back at school! ''So there'' indeed. Very civil. Of course I go to the silk bazaar. I frequently go into the walled city. After all, if I had to take the battalion in, I'd look a pretty good fool if I didn't know my way around, wouldn't I now?' His smile was quite unruffled. Sarah prayed that Julia would leave it at that, but Julia was really roused.

'Well, of course I can understand that. But one thing I do not understand is why you have to take a woman with you on your investigations.'

Heaven intervened, in the shape of Dip Chand, at Sarah's elbow, saying, 'Khanum, the Police Inspector is here, and says to tell you he will come tomorrow morning, for only a few minutes, with a paper for you to sign – no trouble for you, the Nawab Sahib has told him you are not to be troubled.'

Before Sarah could answer, Richard was on his feet. 'What is all this? Police? Thieves already? I told you this place was too far out. You are not even in British India – you are over the border and into Lambagh State, so you will probably be burgled every night.'

Dip Chand, his old face like a rock, said, 'Nay, Colonel Sahib. Not thieves. We have no thieves here. This is about a woman who was killed on the island of the shrine – perhaps the Colonel Sahib knows the island, where the Peacock Shrine is?'

Richard completely ignored the old servant. 'Murder, Sarah? Charming place you've picked to live in, if I may say so. Could you perhaps put me in the picture? And then I shall go and book your rooms again in Piri's – you are certainly not living here.'

For a minute Sarah looked straight into Richard's eyes, and when she spoke her voice was so low that only Richard and Digby, who was nearest to her, heard what she said. 'As long as I pay, I live where I choose. I am staying here, Richard.' They stared at each other and it was Richard who lowered his eyes.

'Put me in the picture, Sarah.' His voice had lost none of its confident arrogance, but Digby felt like cheering. That was one round Sarah had won.

But now the cat was out of the bag about the murder, and Julia forgot all about seeing Richard in the silk bazaar as she listened to the story of the killing on the island. She was beginning to stare across at the white shrine with horror-filled eyes, when Alastair said quietly, 'Julia, don't be an idiot. Imagine getting all worked up about one killing, when you have just lived through a most horrible war. It is sad, tragic, bad – but not to become neurotic about it, I think.'

'But it is murder.'

'So is war. So were the gas chambers, and the firing squads, and the Japs executing their prisoners. Sheer murder. Come on out, and let me chill your blood with some war stories, while we sunbathe in luxury.'

He dragged her up by the hand and she lost the frightened pinched look as she went, with his arm round her, down to the lake shore. Sarah and Digby were about to follow them out, but Richard stopped Sarah, saying, 'Darling, I haven't much time, and there are several things we ought to discuss before I leave.'

Sarah, back in her puppet state, went slowly towards the stairs with him, and Digby, watching them, made a sudden decision.

'Sarah, I must go back for an hour or two. I have to see the adjutant. I'll come later if I may, and see if there is anything I can do. Thank you for my very good lunch.'

It was Richard who answered. 'Not at all – very glad you were here to take the weight this morning. Horrible business for Sarah if she had been alone. See you again, perhaps, as you say, this evening.'

Richard, urbanely the host, saw him off and came back to Sarah. She went upstairs with him, hearing the sound of Digby's jeep gradually dying away in the distance.

13

Her woman, Ayesha, was at the top of the stairs and stood back, salaaming, and Sarah was shaken by a longing to take her hand, beg her to stay with her somehow. As the girl passed, their glances met. Ayesha paused and held open the door of one of the spare rooms, and Sarah went in with Richard behind her. At least her own bedroom in this house would have no memories of Richard in it to haunt her sleep. She saw that Richard's uniform case and leather-covered basin were on the floor and that a few of her own toilet articles were on the dressing-table. Ayah had obviously guessed that she would prefer to keep her bedroom to herself, and had so instructed Ayesha.

Richard had flung himself down on the bed, his hands tucked behind his head and his feet, still in chaplis, on the brocade bedcover where already a long smear of mud showed against the soft faded colours. 'Richard, do look at your feet – you've got mud all over your chaplis and it is coming off on to that bedcover.'

'My dear girl, you sound exactly like a seaside landlady – never mind the bedcover, for heaven's sake! Come and tell me all about your morning. At least we have a room to ourselves, not a caravanserai, as you so cleverly arranged in the hotel.' He held out his hand to her, but Sarah turned away.

'I think we've talked quite enough about my morning. I want to forget the whole thing. That poor girl –'

'Well then, forget all about the poor girl. Come here, I will help you to keep your mind on other things.'

The wooing voice played on her nerves, the tone of

voice that had fired her with trembling, aching passion when they were first together now merely made her set her teeth with distaste. She had heard that tone of voice used too often, to so many other women – it now sounded false and affected. She made no move towards him, thinking violently of some way of escape from the next few hours, something that would not involve her in a wordy battle. But it seemed there was no time to think. Richard had got up, moving with cat-like silence, and she was in his arms, held closely, before she could move. She said 'Let me go, Richard,' her revulsion so strong that her voice shook.

'Listen, Sarah. The children are next door. Julia is downstairs with her boyfriend. So scream, my girl, and bring the whole lot in on the run, and then what? What will you say? Or shall I do the talking? Shall I tell them that you have decided against going to bed with your husband, that my beautiful hot-blooded half-caste wife is as frigid to me as an iceberg, however many times she takes her clothes off for other men? Has Digby had you yet, little snowbird? Because if he hasn't, perhaps I can use a little of the heat he has generated, if he has managed to rouse you at all! But whether you are hot or cold, like it or not, I am going to have you now!'

As he spoke, Richard lifted her on to the bed, pushed her skirt up, and then paused and stared down at her. Looking into the pebble gaze of his blue eyes, Sarah realised that he was indeed furiously angry, that there was murder in his gaze. Very frightened, she began to fight him seriously, exerting all her power, but his superior weight and strength defeated her. She felt his cruel hands moving over her body, and then he struck her twice on the face, and as she wept in despair, he took her. She knew with sick horror that her struggles, her fears, her pain and dislike, made a higher ecstasy for him, and her fear was conquered by her loathing. 'This is rape,' she said, her eyes hard on his, and saw the flare that leapt behind his eyes. He took her brutally, making her cry out with pain, and then at last it was over, his hands loosened, and he slept, as he always did, his heavy body still covering her. With infinite care she slid away from him, and got up and went into the bathroom.

The shower turned on full, she stood wondering if she would have the willpower to breathe in the heavy rush of water and so drown. Then she thought of the children and knew she was trapped, and tears came at last, blessedly, and she could think normally again.

She was knotting up her long wet hair when a sound at the outer door made her turn, just in time to see the door open and Ayesha come in, holding a tray with tea and a silver flask.

'The Old One sent me with this and said you are to drink it.' Blessed Ayah. Sarah sat on the edge of the bath, drinking the hot tea laced with brandy, and Ayesha, her eyes compassionate, massaged her feet and legs.

'Does the lady require clothing? I can bring –'

'No!' The thought of Richard waking and demanding her presence before she could get away was more than she could bear. Her swimsuit and her long towelling wrap were hanging in the bathroom. She put them on quickly and decided to go down to the lake.

Once outside, she felt that she could not face Julia and Alastair. She took the left-hand path and went towards the Ruler's white house, stopping at last in the deep shade of a large mango tree. She sat, looking over to the white shrine on the island, finding it in her heart to envy the woman who had died there that morning. She knew that it was not only the poor dead woman's horrible death that had broken the peace of this beautiful place. Richard, his presence – it would not matter where she went, he would take all her pleasure and peace from her. She remembered that she had thought that there was no change in him when she met him in Madore Station. I was wrong, she thought. It seemed to her now that there was a terrible change in him. She felt something was very wrong; she feared him, not only for herself but as if he could bring some dreadful harm to all of them. She sat, trying to understand her fear and the change she could feel in Richard, and as she thought she moved her body and it hurt her, and she was sharply reminded of his brutal handling. A feeling of total despair came over her and she began to weep helplessly. She was broken by such a storm of tears that she did not hear the Nawab the first time he spoke, and did not know he was there until he bent and touched her shoulder.

'Khanum, what grief is this?' His face, close to hers, was horror-stricken when she raised her eyes. 'In the name of Allah, the compassionate, daughter of beauty, nothing can be so bad!'

He was near enough to smell the brandy on her breath and frowned. 'Is this grief from a bottle? Why have you taken drink so early in the day?'

Sarah, in the extremity of her misery, did not hear the proprietary admonishing note in his voice. 'I am not drunk. I wish I was. Or I wish I was dead like that woman this morning. I wish I was dead, and could feel nothing more, ever again.'

The authenticity of the pain in her cry brought him to his knees beside her, his arm behind her as if he would take her into his embrace, and then with an effort he drew back. 'What is it? Tell me who has done this to you, who has caused you such grief? That young bull you swam with this morning. Did he do or say anything that upset you? *Tell* me!'

Poor Digby! Young bull! Sarah began to laugh as well as cry and for a moment hysteria threatened her, but she managed by an effort of will that made her feel sick to control herself. 'No, no, of course not. No one has done anything to me, Nawab Sahib. I am sorry you see me like this. I am only unhappy, I feel sad. Women are like this sometimes.'

What on earth was she saying? Words pulled up from some well of courage she did not know she possessed, to form a curtain between her mind and his. He paid tribute to the courage he could sense, and said, 'Yes – I could see that you were not happy,' but asked her nothing more. He sat with her for a minute or two, while she tried to dry her eyes, and then took her hand.

'Come with me and see my house. You can bathe your eyes, we could have some tea, and then you will be rested and I will take you back. Will you come with me? I cannot bear to see you in such sorrow.'

His deep voice was full of tenderness and anger. Sarah came quickly to herself. 'Nawab Sahib, thank you, but I must go back. I have already had tea, with brandy in it,' she added with a smile so difficult that it pulled her beautiful mouth into a strange ugly shape. 'Ayah made it for me.'

'Ayesha, do you mean?'

'No, my own Ayah.'

'Ah, the Old One. She has been with you a long time.'

'She is my friend, and part of my family.'

'Yes. That is how our servants are. But you will not hear Europeans speak so of their servants.'

'Nawab Sahib, you know you are wrong. Many of us have servants who have been connected with our families down the years for three or four generations, and are beloved, as I love Ayah, who is my second mother.'

He nodded, considering her words. 'That is, I suppose, so. Perhaps I am thinking of the new Europeans, who came out here during the wars that we have also helped to win. These new Europeans had no roots and no traditions, either here or in their own country.'

'They helped to save the world, and indeed India, whatever their traditions were. In any case, you cannot judge the traditions of the British, Nawab Sahib.'

'Can I not, *Memsahib*? Why? And what was India saved from? And for what reason, indeed, for what future? You should ask yourself those questions, you who love India so much.'

Sarah glared at him. The title Memsahib addressed to her in that tone seemed like an insult. He smiled at her, almost laughing.

'So. That is very good. I have made you angry, and you forget sorrow. Your eyes are like swords, stabbing in battle.'

118

She could not help returning his smile, and he nodded with satisfaction. Then, suddenly serious, he turned to face her.

'You defend England very fiercely, Khanum. Do you really love such a cold country? You belong here, to this land. We are of one blood, Khanum.'

'My grandmother Muna was only adopted by your family. There is no blood tie.'

'There are ties that are stronger than blood, Khanum. Love is the strongest tie of all. Certainly your grand-mother knew that, even if it is a lesson you have not yet learned.'

'How did we begin to talk about my grandmother again? We were talking about my defence of England, I thought.'

'And you would rather talk about England than about your beautiful ancestor? Your English mother taught you to despise your Indian blood, I think.'

'No. Of course she did not. She loved my father very dearly, still does. They are very happy together.'

'Yes, living in England. She may have loved him, but she took him away from the country he loved, and before that she left him alone out here so that she could get you and your brother away before you in your turn grew too fond of this land. Your father could not live without her, so he retired too soon. I think he must often recall the State of Lambagh, the valley he loved so much. Even after he had left the valley, he loved to return and climb and shoot and fish amongst his old friends, and the first place your brother came to, when he joined his regiment, was Lambagh. He came on his first leave, and we climbed together, and trekked through the mountains just as our fathers had done. Ah, Khanum, I should not have spoken of your brother, but do not sorrow for him. He died very bravely.'

Sarah wiped her eyes and nodded and thought, Dear James, who loved life and his friends and India, and was so young! He died bravely, which made everything fine, and there must be no sorrow!

'I do not care how bravely he died. He was my brother, and I love him and miss him, and his death was a waste, he should be alive.'

'Yes, Khanum. War is terrible for women. But if he lived to be old and lonely and sick? I would rather die before old age takes the joy of life from me. My father and mother were fortunate. They died together, still young and very happy.'

'Your poor grandmother Sara.'

'Yes. Kassim Khan was already dead. She was very lonely. But not for long. She died within a year of their deaths. I was left. You do not say anything about being sorry for me.'

Sarah looked at the proud handsome face turned to hers.

'I do not think you would let grief get hold of you. You are, I think, a firm man.'

'Do you mean that you think I am a hard man, Khanum? Well, perhaps. But I can conceive of certain things that would crack my heart. However. We speak of death and disaster and grief. Against these things there are defences. It might be that your father is happier away from this present India. The India he knew will soon not exist. A new and strange country is growing up. Your brother might have been able to find something to like in this new land, he was young. But I do not think that your father, or indeed mine, would care for the new India, and the transition period will be unpleasant, I fear.' His voice was sombre, as if he were not looking forward to the new India either.

Sarah heard clearly from the house the sound of Penelope's laughter. The children's rest time was over, and Ayah was bringing them out for their afternoon walk. She got up, saying, 'Nawab Sahib, I must go. Dip Chand will be bringing tea. Will you come back with me and have some with us?'

'Thank you, Khanum, but I have arrangements to make for this evening.' The events of the day had driven his invitation from her memory. She wondered what

Richard was going to do; was he going to spend the night? Her companion said urgently, 'But you are coming tonight, Khanum? You said you would.'

'Nawab Sahib, that was this morning, which already seems a year ago. My husband has since told me that he is leaving for Ratna. I do not know if he is staying tonight.'

He saw and recognised the shiver of distaste on her face. A woman would look like that if she saw a snake or, putting her hand out in the dark, touched a rat or a lizard. He spoke quickly.

'Then, if he stays, of course he comes with you.'

'Thank you, Nawab Sahib. In that case, may I ask you a favour? Major Crombie and Major Lawton are coming to have a drink with me tonight. May I bring them too? I asked them last night, and I am afraid that I forgot.'

'That young bull' seemed to hover on the Nawab's lips, but he only smiled. 'Of course. I am delighted. Your friends are mine.'

They strolled together towards the house. As they walked she felt the breeze from the lake and shivered.

'You are cold?'

'No, but I think my bathing costume is still damp.'

He stared at her, saying nothing, and she was suddenly conscious that to him she was almost naked, and he found this unbearably exciting. His self-control was superb, but she was left in no doubt as to his feelings. She quickened her step, and he kept pace with her, then put out his hand.

'One moment, Khanum, I have a favour to ask of you.'

He stopped, and so she had to stop too, looking up at him, wondering what on earth he was going to do.

'I have a name, Khanum. You know it well. Can you call me by my name please?'

She felt at once relieved, and flattered – and excited.

'Of course. Sher Khan, and you will call me Sarah.'

'I will call you nothing of the sort. You were named for my mother – Sara. I will call you Sara, but only when we are alone. When we are in company, you are the Khanum.'

This whole episode, thought Sarah, has got so completely out of hand that I do not really know what to do.

Sher Khan looked down at her, then leaned closer to look at her face.

'Sara! Sarajan! What is this? And this? You have bruises coming on your face. Who –?' He stopped and caught his breath and then said in a voice as deep and rough as a growl, 'Who struck you?' Sarah shook her head. 'Please, Sher Khan. Leave it. I would rather you did not ask questions.'

He nodded slowly, his fierce eyes studying her face. Then he took her firmly into his arms, holding her very close, and said quietly in Urdu, 'Oh, rose of beauty. This will never happen again, I give you my word,' and released her, walking away without a backward look.

14

Sarah went back to the house, her thoughts as confused as her body. The Nawab Sahib was electric. No wonder he had found his way into her dreams!

The business of pouring out tea and talking to Alastair and Julia brought her back to normal life. Digby, she was relieved to see, had not returned. Richard appeared and sat down with them. Julia saw with rage Sarah's thickened eyelids and strained blanched face. For a moment she hated her brother, remembering how happy and peaceful Sarah had been that morning. She stared at Richard as he sat, enjoying his tea, immaculate in a clean uniform, the sun gilding his moustache. He saw her stare and smiled lazily at her, saying, 'Goodness, infant, what a glare. What *have* I done?'

'It is what you did not do. How could you drive all the way out here and not come near us, to see how we were, or if we needed help?'

The stillness that fell over the tea-table was like the stillness that comes when the wind drops, just before a storm. Even Alastair, who was almost asleep from sun and food and contentment, felt the tension and looked round him enquiringly. Sarah's toes curled and her muscles were tense with strain. Richard sat as he had before, lounging back, but Sarah saw that the pebble glare was back in his eyes and thought, Why – what is it?, for normally after making love to her he was relaxed and easy for hours. 'Making love'. What a phrase for a brutal sexual assault on her body and spirit, that left her bruised and destroyed but gave him great peace as a rule. Julia sensed now the rage in her brother, but she was angry too. And when he said, 'What on earth are you talking about, Julie? I've never been to this house in my life until today,' she turned on him at once.

'Well, you've been very near it! You drove out here yesterday to the Ruler's house and we all saw you! You could have come in here quite easily. Don't try and lie yourself out of this, Richard!'

'What charming manners you have, Julia. I think perhaps you should apologise. I repeat. This is my first visit. I do not know who you saw yesterday, but it was certainly not me.'

Julia was scarlet. 'But I saw you! We *all* did!'

Digby's arrival did nothing to break the strain. He looked at the embattled Julia in astonishment, then at Sarah's face, and was himself immediately enraged. Sarah looked at him appealingly, and he controlled himself and tried to change the subject. His remarks about the dusty drive from Madore were brushed aside by Julia.

'Digby, you saw Richard yesterday, didn't you? And Sarah?'

Digby took his cup from Sarah, saw her bruised face, and said slowly, 'Well, Julia, I thought I did. I saw a jeep, and was pretty sure I could see who was driving it.'

'It was really going too fast to see who was driving, Julie. I think it was the Nawab's supply jeep.' Sarah could not meet Julia's accusing eyes, but she sensed so much danger in the atmosphere that she was afraid. Julia looked from her to Digby and then got up and went into the house. Richard turned his head to watch her go, saying '*Well* what a tantrum! Too much sun and excitement. But I am sorry if I upset her.'

Alastair drank his tea and looked fixedly at the lake, and Digby and Sarah both talked at once with skill and determination, and then broke off saying, 'Sorry, what did you say?' and 'No, no, nothing, do go on –' and then lapsed into silence. Richard stubbed out his cigarette in his saucer, ignoring the ashtray, stretched, and stood up.

'Everything good comes to an end. I must go back. Pity this place is so far out, I won't be able to spend the night.'

He said goodbye to Digby and Alastair and raised his eyebrows at Sarah. 'Coming, darling? Just as far as the gate? Not too tired to walk back from there, are you? No? Quite sure?'

The fond tone, the secret look of the knowledge of pleasure shared – any loving husband trying to put off parting from a beloved and loving wife. It was a beautiful performance, thought Digby savagely as he watched them walk away together. The only thing that spoiled the scene was the flicker in Sarah's eyes, the pale strained look of her face.

Out of earshot, Richard stopped. 'Where is Julia? I do not like to leave her all upset.'

Sarah wondered, as she often did, whether this family feeling Richard displayed was genuine or just another of his disguises. She called to Julia and presently the girl came down, looking so like Penelope after tears, so near to being a little girl, that Sarah put an arm round her. 'Julia, Richard's just going.'

'Yes, Julie, I'm off. Goodbye, chicken, not still cross with me, are you?'

A kiss, a gentle squeeze, and Julia, her face happy again, saying 'Oh, darling Richard, I'm sorry I was rude. I truly thought –'

'Forget it, infant. Have a lovely time. See you very soon.'

Outside, tactfully left alone with Sarah, Richard said, 'Come with me to the end of the drive,' and got into the jeep without waiting to help her in. It was no longer a request but a cold, flat order. Driving, he said, 'How many of you imagined that you saw me? Just Julia, or all of you?'

'All of us, except Alastair. He wasn't there. But he saw you driving back.' Somehow it seemed safer that all of them should have seen him. Sarah had this extraordinary feeling of fear for Julia, irrational but enough to make her feel cold. Richard's voice reinforced her fear. It cracked with rage.

'I tell you, none of you saw me. I wasn't here. See? You had better go back and make bloody sure that they are all quite convinced that it was the Ruler's supply jeep you saw, understood?'

'Understood,' said Sarah quietly.

He said nothing more until they arrived at the big gate, and then he took his time, pulling out his cigarette case, lighting one for her and one for himself, blowing out a luxurious cloud of smoke before he spoke.

'You don't believe a word I say, do you, Sarah?'

The directness of the question surprised her, and she could find no answer other than 'No. I do not.' He nodded slowly.

'Not a word I say. That must be fairly obvious to everyone. Well, as a result, I tell you nothing that is important. You have never been interested enough in my job to even ask what I have done since I left Staff College, nor why I have returned to my battalion now. Well, there are many interesting things going on in India now, and a man with my experience and my knowledge of the language is a useful person for the government. But you, who could be a help, don't want to know, do you? So you won't know. However, you now understand this much. I was working yesterday, and none of you saw me. It was the Nawab's jeep, nothing else. Right?'

'I have already said that I will agree to whatever story you choose to tell – true or false – largely to console Julia.'

'Yes. Julia. You've even got her mistrusting me now. What a stinking thing to do.'

Sarah's cigarette went out as she was holding it so tightly in her fingers. She did not speak. Her straight gaze did not appear to upset him.

He returned her look, saying, 'I have no time to go into the rights and wrongs of our marriage now, Sarah. But one thing I do expect is loyalty. After all, I forgave you, and took you back.'

'Be careful, Richard. Don't push me too far. You forgave me because of my money. I realise now that you married me for my money. And that goes where I go. All *I* ask is peace. Otherwise –'

She did not finish her sentence. While he stared at her, for once silenced, she said, still using the same cold, steady voice, 'I have never discussed you with Julia. She loves and trusts you, as do your children. I have no intention of destroying that very misplaced trust, but do not push me too far, Richard. I would rather live without you. You only hold me because of the children. Incidentally, where were you yesterday, in case anyone asks?'

'Anywhere you like, but not round here. I am delighted to note that you understand that I will keep the children if you ever leave me again. Another thing. Kindly keep Julia and the children out of Madore City for the next few weeks. You should know well what the natives say about this place – balanced between heaven and hell, just on the borders of British India and Native India. Those borders will no longer exist of course, physically, in due course, but at the moment they still do, and Madore is a trouble centre, a focus for all sorts of turbulent elements. I do not want Julia or the children to run into any danger.'

'Nor, strangely enough, do I.' She climbed out of the jeep and stood looking at him. 'Just as a matter of interest, Richard, where were you at midday today?'

'Midday? Driving out here, of course. Why?'

'I just wondered. I'm going now, Richard. I'm getting very cold.' She turned and walked away, suddenly terrified by the silence behind her. But then she heard the jeep start, and looking back saw him driving away, a great cloud of dust rising to hide him.

She walked back between the trees, leaving the drive, and cutting down towards the lake. She wanted very much to think, but came on Digby, sitting alone at the lakeside. He had obviously been doing some deep thinking himself, and his thoughts had not been happy. He stood up with the evident intention of taking her in his arms, and she had to summon up the strength to stop him. He could hardly hear her voice, it was so faint.

'No, Digby. Please.'

'Sarah, I cannot go on like this. We must talk.'

'Digby, there is nothing for us to talk about. Nothing, ever. Please let me be now. I am so tired!'

He saw that she was very pale, and was shocked at the expression of total despair on her face. At once he put his arm gently round her and led her up towards the house. Julia came out to meet them, with Alastair, and Digby suggested that Sarah went straight to bed. 'We'll push off now, and perhaps see you tomorrow?'

At this, Sarah roused herself. 'Oh no, Digby, don't go. We've all been asked to go over the lake to the Nawab's house, and I am afraid I accepted for all of us. We can't let him down, he's been so good over the house. I shall be perfectly all right after I have had a rest. We'll have supper together here afterwards.'

There was no urging necessary. Both men wanted to stay, and Julia could not bear the thought of the evening being spoilt. Sarah went upstairs with her, Julia scolding her gently, saying, 'Sarah, what do you do to get so tired? You must rest more. Was it all that swimming, and then the shock of that poor woman? Let me help you get to bed, you'll have nearly two hours.'

'No, Julie, you go and entertain the men. I'll be fine. Ask Ayah to come to me, if she can leave the children for a minute or two.'

Julia went off and told Ayah that Sarah wanted her. The old woman went at once, and when she saw Sarah she muttered to herself. Then, lapsing into furious silence, she helped Sarah out of her bathing costume and the towelling wrap, and gave her a warm dressing-gown. She settled her on a long chair on the balcony, and covered her with a blanket.

'Now sleep. I will waken you in time for you to dress. Sleep, and dream of nothing but good.'

Left alone, Sarah lay looking up at the pale evening sky and the birds that scattered over it on their way to the lake and the trees. She was too tired for thought, too tired to worry. The peace and beauty all round her were healing.

Suddenly between a second and a second, she fell asleep.

15

Julia found Digby and Alastair in the old stables with a litter of puppies. They were fat and white and fluffy, some marked with gold and some with very dark brown. They had long soft fur and tightly curled tails, and they came from the hills beyond Lambagh.

'Oh, oh we must have one. No, all of them. Let us keep them all!' Julia was on her knees with a lapful of puppies.

'They belong to the Ruler.' Digby rolled one over and scratched its fat little stomach. 'You can ask him tonight. He'll probably sell you a couple at fifty pounds a pup. These dogs are very rare.'

'Oh, dear,' mourned Julia, 'I would so love to have them. Look, how tightly their tails are curled, like fluffy springs.'

'The Miss Sahib can surely have them.' The head syce was smiling at Julia and holding the bitch, who was anxiously watching her litter. 'These dogs come from our State. There are many, many, there, like stones in a river bed.'

'Digby! Oh, Digby, you fearful liar.'

'No, truly, I assure you. Worth enormous sums of money, especially in outer Patagonia, where they use them to smuggle gold over the border.'

'Round the bend, I should think, not over the border,' said Alastair, watching Julia who was hugging as many of the puppies as she could hold.

'What is the mother's name?' she asked.

'She is called Junta. She is mine, Miss Sahib. All her puppies are yours.' Julia made much of Junta and then watched her settle down with her voracious family.

Digby and Alastair, having detached Julia from the puppies at last, walked slowly down to the lake and watched the sun slipping behind the hills. Alastair and Julia were quiet, standing close together, and Digby felt in the way and went back to the house and out on to the verandah. He watched them pace up and down on the edge of the lake, envying them their companionship, their lovely careless happiness.

He was rewarded for his kindness in leaving them, because Sarah came down early and joined him, looking beautiful in spite of the dark shadows round her eyes and the growing bruise on her cheek. Dip Chand brought them drinks and, as soon as they were alone, Digby asked a question that had been worrying him. 'Sarah, why was Richard so determined that it was not him the other night, driving out to the Rajaghar?'

'I cannot imagine. But he was adamant that it wasn't him, and that therefore we hadn't seen him.'

'Yes, wasn't he adamant. I wonder –'

'Perhaps it was something secret. Something to do with Special Branch duties, do you think?'

'No, I don't. Special Branch does not operate like that. Very odd.'

Sarah felt the same cold chill of fear that she had felt before. 'Perhaps it wasn't him after all – The jeep was going very fast.'

Digby looked at her, saw the bruised cheek, and said no more. Presently Sarah said, 'Richard told me to keep out of Madore for the next few weeks. Said it could blow up, that Madore is balanced between heaven and hell and a focus for all sorts of turbulent elements.'

'Cheerful chap. Of course, he is right in a way. Madore has always had a tendency to blow up, but just at present everything seems peaceful, so I don't really know what he is talking about.' Privately he thought that Richard was probably anxious to keep his family out of Madore in case they heard of his activities. Sarah was also thinking along the same lines. They did not, however, exchange opinions on their ideas. Digby said again, 'Yes, I suppose he is right. Madore could blow.' He gestured towards the distant mountains. 'Up there, behind those mountains, the set-up is still feudal. I doubt if there has ever been a car or a bicycle in some of those valleys. Those people do not know anything about modern India, and they certainly do not know anything about this movement towards independence. They haven't really registered the British Raj yet! They are ruled by their own Rajas, and want nothing else. Madore is like a bridge between them and civilisation – if you can call what is going on in the world today civilisation! I think Sher Khan is a good ruler, but I'll bet he keeps his people pretty firmly behind their mountains.'

'I do not know about that. He took a good many of them to the war, didn't he?' Sarah felt an obscure desire to defend Sher Khan.

'Oh, by God, he did. First-class fighters, too. Yes, they certainly came out of the mountains, those chaps. But, you know, now that it is all over, they'll go back to their villages, and the war, and all that they saw and suffered, will be a story told round the fires at night. They'll go back to farming and hunting and riding those wild ponies of theirs, and forget everything they've learned, unless their Ruler calls them out again.'

He finished his drink and looked down at his beautiful companion. 'Sarah, I cannot discuss your husband with you. But quite apart from my feelings for you, why on earth do you stay with him?'

Sarah shook her head. 'Sorry, Digby, closed subject.'

'But darling, we must talk about it. Please, Sarah, I cannot stand this.'

'Digby. There is nothing to say. I am married, however unhappily. I must not let you imagine for one minute that there is anything for us to talk about. We have no future, Digby, you must know that.'

'Sarah, how can you say that? We – you and I –' He floundered into silence under her steady gaze.

'Digby, we kissed and enjoyed it. We are young, we are healthy, our bodies were hungry.' It was her turn to

132

fall silent as he looked at her. He walked away from her, to the edge of the verandah, fighting the urge to take her into his arms. Behind him she spoke, her voice firm again. 'Digby, nothing for us to discuss. But I love to have you here. I enjoy your company, as you enjoy mine. You are my friend. Please.'

He turned to face her again. 'Don't, I beg of you, Sarah, suggest that you will always be a sister to me! For God's sake, you sound like the heroine of a Victorian novel refusing her suitor. I am not your suitor. I love you with all my heart, and would marry you tomorrow. However, I will not annoy you by pressing my suit on you – provided you remember one thing. We have nothing to discuss, yet. Just remember that I am a man who loves you, and I am here when you need me, but I am only here because I hope one day that I shall possess you in every way. I am not, frankly, at all friendly towards you. So just think of that sometimes.'

He turned away from her again and looked down at the lake. He saw lights moving up from the lakeside, and in the last glimmer of the evening sky, the silhouette of a boat coming into shore. 'I think your princely landlord has sent his State barge for us.'

Julia and Alastair came rushing on to the verandah, Alastair saying, 'We've got a sort of Cleopatra's entourage, complete with peacock feathers and a band, waiting for us in a rather small type rowing-boat. I only hope we don't all end up in the lake.'

Dip Chand holding up an oil lamp to light their way, they went down to the lake where a long low boat, canopied and cushioned, was moored. There were six men with paddles, and on the prow flew a standard with a peacock with spread tail and an Arabic inscription embroidered on it.

They embarked, and settled themselves down on the cushions. Dip Chand came aboard and stood on the prow, and a small boy who had been sitting on the grass verge untied a rope and jumped aboard, and as the paddles hit the water he began to play softly on a flute.

'Well!' Alastair leaned forward. 'Julie, give me your hand. This romantic scene is completely unmanning me.'

Julia declined with a small scream. 'Alastair, keep still! Sarah, make him keep still! Oh, Sarah, make him lean back, or he will upset us. Anyway, we can't hold hands facing each other, we'll look as if we are being introduced.'

Alastair settled back and closed his eyes. 'Very well. Rather than waste this beautiful setting, and because of the singularly thoughtless way we have been seated, I shall hold your little foot.'

Slowly, accompanied by the lazy splash of the paddles and the tender dropping notes of the boy's flute, they moved over the lake. Dip Chand stood like a statue in the prow. Presently the rowers began to sing, a soft chant that lasted all the way to the landing below the Rajaghar.

The Ruler himself was waiting on the steps to welcome them. Julia, shyness forgotten, took his hand. 'That was the most beautiful journey.'

'I am glad that it gave you pleasure.'

'They sang! They sang beautifully. What were they singing? It was not at all the usual awful –' Julia stopped, appalled, and looked up at her host.

'The usual awful noise that Indian singers make? No, these boatmen come from the hills round my valley of Lambagh. Their type of singing is easier on Western ears than most Indian music.' He turned to Sarah. 'Khanum, I hope you are rested?'

'I am very well, Nawab Sahib. I have been looking forward to this visit, and the journey over the lake was a beautiful beginning.'

'I also was looking forward – come, Khanum, let me take you up.'

The stone steps led up to a house that was more a fort than a dwelling place. In fact, it was all fortified, the marble dais built out over the lake was obviously a later addition, much newer than the rest of the building. The walls were thick, and blind on the lake side. They entered by an arched door that opened into an enclosed court, from which steps led up to the dais. The court was paved, and a pool in the centre reflected the lights of oil lanterns hanging on hooks round the walls. There were several doors opening off the court, and their unlit black oblongs emphasised the feeling of age and desolation that brooded over the whole place. There were not enough oil lamps to disperse the darkness. Sher Khan apologised, saying, 'We have no electric light on this side of the lake.' A man with a flaming, smoking torch lit the steps for them, and on the dais were Persian carpets, piles of cushions and low tables, heavily ornamented with carving and ivory and brass inlay. The view by daylight must have been magnificent. To the north, the lake lay like a sheet of unbroken silver under the dark sky. Going to the edge of the dais, Sarah saw the glow of light from her house, and was able to pick out her balcony and her bedroom windows. Turning, she saw Sher Khan watching her, and was instantly made aware that he had often stood where she now stood, looking across at those windows.

The dais was better lit than the courtyard; ornamented oil lamps on stands were augmented by ordinary hurricane lamps. Three servants, dressed in white with enormous untidy emerald-green turbans, waited on them, passing round champagne in ordinary glass tumblers to everyone except Sarah. Her champagne was in a silver goblet, polished to glittering perfection although the tray was tarnished. There were plates of stuffed eggs, and nuts made pepper-hot with curry. As they were drinking their first drink, they heard a car drive up and stop, and Sher Khan, frowning a little, excused himself and left them.

They heard women's voices, and Sarah thought she heard Richard's name, a woman saying, 'But Richard? He is not here? I thought he would meet me here,' before Sher Khan's lowered voice answered. In a few minutes he returned, bringing with him two women and two men.

Sarah exchanged a rueful glance with Julia. She wore her usual casual evening attire of a silk shirt and slacks. Julia was wearing a long crimson skirt and a sleeveless blouse. The new arrivals were in very full evening dress. In fact, the two women could have attended a ball and their clothes would not have been out of place.

The woman in the very strapless black taffeta dress was, it appeared, married to one of the men, who was introduced as Colonel Nesbitt. The other woman, a splendid red-head, her creamy shoulders pushing out of a peacock-blue chiffon, was Mrs Nesbitt's sister. Both women were Polish. What Colonel Nesbitt did, or what he was colonel of, was not apparent. As he was in a black tie, and not in uniform, Digby and Alastair concluded that he was retired.

The second man was an Indian, as tall as Sher Khan and as good-looking. But some weakness in his face, something about his eyes and mouth, veiled and spoiled his looks. He was, however, very charming, his English was faultless, and he was introduced by Sher Khan as 'My cousin, his Highness of Sagpur'. After smiling and bowing, and saying a few words to Sarah, he seemed to have no desire for further conversation but sat, drinking steadily, and taking very little interest, it seemed, in the company or in anything that was being said. He was magnificently dressed; his grey satin coat, sewn with pearls, made him an Arabian Nights' figure, and Julia could not take her eyes off him. Alastair, after a comprehensive stare, turned away and said in an undertone to Digby, 'No competition there, old boy. More likely to make a pass at me, I fear.'

Sarah leaned back, sipping her drink, content to watch the others. Digby watched her, giving about a quarter of his attention to Colonel Nesbitt, who was turning out to be a first-class bore. Mrs Nesbitt and her sister were one on each side of Sher Khan, talking with vivacity, tossing the conversation from one to the other and smiling at their host with thrown back heads as if they were looking up at him, although they were both as tall as he. They are big women, thought Sarah idly – big, flat-faced peasant women – and wondered from what subconscious level her jealous observation came. Were all thin dark women automatically jealous of large blondes and red-heads? Sher Khan, from behind this barrage of female conversation, caught her eye and silently lifted both his glass and his eyebrows. She raised her glass in return, with a smile, met a sudden glare from Digby, and began to struggle with laughter. Certainly this dark woman, she thought, has no need to be jealous of anyone. On the heels of the thought she realised that champagne and fatigue were combining to give her a feeling of reckless unreality. She wanted to flirt, to laugh, to bask in male admiration, to forget everything. She looked across at Sher Khan again, and found he was looking at her. Digby was trying to break away from Colonel Nesbitt, who was telling him some endless story. Sarah settled more comfortably into her nest of cushions, and allowed one of the retainers to refill her goblet. The evening promised to be entertaining.

Then suddenly, for her, the climate of the evening changed. A bird called plaintively from the lake, and the breeze seemed to blow more coldly. To Sarah the lights and the laughter were all at once garish and noisy. She remembered the dead girl on the island. How could she have put that poor girl so heartlessly out of her mind? Just some young unknown Indian girl, but surely her death was worthy of thought and sorrow? How strangely detached we are, thought Sarah, twisting her goblet, and wondered if her Indian ancestors had put out a finger to touch her heart and remind her that she had the same blood in her veins as that girl. She put her glass down untouched and turned to look over the lake.

Sher Khan detached himself from his companions and came to stand beside her.

'Sara, what are you looking for, out there in the dark?' His voice was very low; it was as if for a few moments they were alone.

'Nothing, Sher Khan. Unless it is the spirit of that girl

who was killed this morning. I remembered her suddenly.'

'Her spirit would not stay here. She was a hill woman.
By now, her spirit is far away, over those mountains,
back in the valley she loved. Come, Sarajan, drink your
wine, and forget. It will not help her for you to brood
about her now.'

Sarajan! Ayah had called her that when she was a little
girl. It was strange to hear the name in Sher Khan's deep
voice.

She looked behind him at his guests and said, 'You did
not tell me it was to be a party –'

'It was not supposed to be a party. These people dropped in. They do so frequently. They have great hopes of
persuading me to engage Nesbitt as my military adviser.
The hopes are unfounded and I need hardly tell you, will
never be realised.'

'Sher Khan, the man you introduced as your cousin, is
he really a relative?'

'Very distant indeed. Three generations ago, or there-
abouts, his family intermarried with mine. There is no
blood relationship at all, but he is known as my cousin.'

'Hardyal. Is he a relation of the original Hardyal, the
murderer?'

'Yes. Great-grandson. But nothing like his forebear.
Just a very weak man who drinks too much.'

'I do not care for him.'

'Well, of course, how could you? With Muna's blood
rich in your veins! There is the voice of the past speaking to you. Ah, Sara, how like you are to the Rose. So
beautiful –' His voice had dropped, and she could not
turn the compliment aside gracefully, to hear herself
called beautiful in that tone was too much. It must be the
wine, she thought, and tried to change the subject quickly.

'Is the red-haired lady also trying for a job in your
state?' As a change of subject, it was a success. Sher Khan
frowned, and stared at her.

'Do you mean Leda?'

'Is that her name? She is a very magnificent creature. I feel that she also hopes to join your staff – in some capacity – or has she already joined?'

Sher Khan looked appalled, and embarrassed. 'Sara-jan, you must know who she is. Or have you not been told?'

She looked up at him, and then smiled wryly. 'No, I had not been told. Not until now.'

Sher Khan started to speak, but was interrupted by the arrival of both the ladies and Digby, followed by the determined Colonel Nesbitt. Digby looked belligerent.

'All right, Sarah?'

'Perfectly, thank you.' She smiled at him, but her eyes were on Leda. So that was the voice that she had heard asking for Richard when they had arrived. She knew, with no doubts, that she was looking at Richard's latest mistress.

Colonel Nesbitt was continuing his story, which appeared to be about a statue given to the Ruler's great great-grandfather by an Irish soldier. 'And that statue is still here,' he said impressively. Good manners alone prompted Sarah to say, 'And what statue is that, Colonel Nesbitt?' Her question started him off again, and he explained at length about a beautiful statue of Buddha which had brought from China by an Irishman who was military adviser to one of the previous Rulers of Lambagh. 'My great great-grandfather,' said Sher Khan. 'The Irishman was Colonel O'Neil, the father of the Begum Bianca.'

'Colonel O'Neil? He was killed, here in Madore during the Mutiny, was he not?' Sarah remembered the story of the massacre in the old palace of Madore.

The Nawab nodded, saying, 'He and his wife were both killed by my cousin's grandfather. Their daughter Bianca escaped because she had eloped to Lambagh with my grandfather.'

Killed by my cousin's grandfather – the words hung in the air, and after the silence that fell had lasted a few moments, the magnificent figure in the corner, his splen-

139

did coat gleaming in the lamplight, looked up and said, 'All a long time ago – all history now –,' his words very blurred. Meantime, the two Polish ladies were gushing about the romance of the elopement. 'An elopement is always very romantic. How I like to hear of these old love stories!' Mrs Nesbitt clasped her hands over the approximate region of her heart.

'Yes, we are a romantic family, we always have been.' Sher Khan's eyes rested briefly on Sarah. 'I have a picture of a lady I would like to show you, Khanum. She lived through one of the most romantic periods of our history. Would you care to see a picture of the most beautiful woman of her time?'

Before Sarah could answer, Mrs Nesbitt and her sister were both clamouring to be shown the picture. While their voices fluted round the Ruler like a whole treeful of birds, his cousin rose, and bowing in the general direction of the company made his unsteady way off the dais and down the stairs.

Sher Khan looked at Sarah across his two gushing companions. 'You would like to see, Khanum?'

'Thank you, Sher Khan. I would like to see your picture, and then I think we should go home. It has been a long day.'

'You live far from here?' asked Latta Nesbitt with determined affability. Her red-haired sister was not even trying to hide her pleasure in the fact that Sarah and her party were leaving.

'No, not far. Just over there, on the other side of the lake.'

'Over *there*? But surely not, that is the Ranighar.'

'Yes, are we not fortunate? We were able to rent that lovely house!'

The red-haired Leda was visibly swelling with indignation, and the peacock chiffon was becoming precarious.

'But I *understood*,' said Latta Nesbitt, 'I certainly understood that the Ranighar was not for renting. We have tried, you will recall, Nawab Sahib, how we have requested that you let us have it.'

Sher Khan bowed, limp with regret. 'Indeed I remember. But the house was in ruins, infested with rats – and damp. I could not let you have it. Also, for the Colonel Sahib it was too far out from the Cantonments.' He looked at Sarah. 'So, when it was repaired, and my dear friend and relative needed somewhere to live, of course, blood being thicker than water, where else would she live but in my house?'

'Relative?' said the two ladies together. Julia's eyes were round with astonishment, Digby and Alastair both turned to stare. Sarah lowered her eyes, and then looked up to meet Sher Khan's look, full on.

'A very tenuous relationship,' she said.

'But one that is important to me. My family owes yours a debt that can never be forgotten. Come, then. Let us see the picture.'

In an atmosphere that crackled with various feelings, he led his party downstairs into one of the rooms that opened off the court. This was well lit. Sarah saw the portrait in the alcove, and went over to it. She heard the voices of the others drop into silence one by one, and turned to look at them. So, as she turned, she and the pictured woman looked together at the faces that stared back in astonishment.

'Good God!' said Alastair. Julia said 'Sarah, it is you.' Digby said nothing; he was looking at Sher Khan, watching jealously the way he smiled at Sarah, standing beside her beautiful painted twin. The same delicately boned face, large tilted eyes, curved brow and wide mouth. The same expression – sad? mocking? what was it? The dark hair that fell so profusely over the slender shoulders in the portrait was the same that Sarah brushed and coiled on her small head, carried as proudly on its slender neck as the head of the painted girl. Sarah looked quietly at them, and at Sher Khan.

'So, there you stand beside your grandmother – and the likeness is unbelievable. Munabhen, the Rose of Madore, guarding my family as she did so long ago.'

Leda and Latta were rattling with questions. 'Relative – but this is fantastic! How you are related to the Nawab?'

'It is not quite as it seems. My grandmother was honoured by being adopted by the Lambagh Ruler of those days when she was very small.'

'And she grew up to be the most beautiful woman in Madore or Lambagh, and risked her life to save my grandmother's life.' Sher Khan spoke quietly. 'Now, I have something that I will show only to the Khanum. Please, will you have a drink while you wait for us. We will not keep you long. Come, Khanum.' There was no question of arguing with Sher Khan at that moment, however mutinous Leda and Latta felt. Sher Khan swept Sarah through into another room, leaving the others to be given refilled glasses by the three servants.

'Look,' said Sher Khan, 'Munabhen still guards the Lambagh Rulers.' They were standing directly behind the alcove where the portrait was hanging. Sher Khan put out his hand, pressed an unseen knob, and a panel slid open to show a small steel door. He opened this with a key from his pocket, and took out a delicately carved ivory box, creamy with age. When he opened the box, it was as if he released green fire into the room.

'The Emerald Peacock!'

'Yes, she guards it for me.'

Sarah put out her hand and touched the heavy gold chain, set with emeralds and diamonds, with a pendant which was one great emerald carved into the shape of the State emblem, a peacock with a spread tail.

'It is amazing – so beautiful. I have never seen anything like it. Sher Khan, is it safe here?'

'No one in my State would touch it. I thought of putting it here some years ago. Before, when the Ruler was down in Madore, it was kept on the island, beneath Shiva's statue. But when I brought the picture down from Lambagh, it seemed fitting to me that Munabhen should be the guardian. I am glad you have seen it.'

'Thank you, Sher Khan.' Sarah watched him lock the steel door and slide the panel closed, and then they went back to face the lively curiosity of the others. Sher Khan's face, however, did not invite questions.

Julia was still staring spellbound at the portrait. 'She is so lovely, but no one has told what she did.'

'To put it very shortly, she first gave up her life altogether, and went into the temple to save my grand-mother from going there. Then she again rescued my grandmother from death, and then she fell in love with an Englishman, Alan Reid. She went away to England with him, and here is her grand-daughter, standing beside her picture. A romantic ending to a romantic story – or a romantic beginning, perhaps, to the story of Munabhen's grand-daughter – what do you think?'

The romance appeared to be lost on the two Polish ladies. But Julia was enchanted. 'Oh, this is so incredible! Please tell me more, Sarah?'

Sarah, one eye on the sardonically smiling Sher Khan, said 'Yes, well I will, but it is a very long story and I think it is time we went back.'

Colonel Nesbitt had been out of things for too long to please him. 'And the statue? Are we not to see the statue that the Ruler's military adviser brought him from Peking?'

'But of course you will see the statue. Come, Khanum, it is on your way out; we will not delay you, if you are in such a hurry to leave.'

Sarah raised reproachful eyes but said nothing, and Sher Khan took her hand and led them out, through the main court and into a smaller one which was deserted. For a moment they were alone, and he had time to say, 'Forgive me – it is only that I hate to see you go,' and received a smile that maddened Digby, who was just behind them.

This courtyard was very small and the fountain in the centre, throwing a fine jet of water into the lamplight, reminded Digby of the choked fountain on the island. How quickly everyone seemed to have forgotten that poor woman. He decided that the Nawab did not care for his subjects at all, and that Sarah was obviously so flattered by his attentions that she was displaying all the symptoms of any spoiled beautiful woman, with no thought in her head but pleasure. Hot with rage, he turned his back on the company and went to a window in the courtyard, which opened on the lake. There was a fire burning at the village end of the lake, and he wondered if it was the unfortunate woman's funeral pyre. He turned back, and saw Sarah's expression as she looked at the fountain, and knew he was wrong. This was no heartless beauty. She had forgotten nothing.

They were led on by the Nawab, out of the small court by a carved arched doorway, and round to the front of the Rajaghar. The statue stood on a plinth of marble. Lamplight gleamed on carved features, calm, dreaming, looking with blind eyes down centuries of time.

The silence that fell on the company was distilled from that quiet figure. Invincible, untouched by all the years, it extracted worship from these alien people, just as it had from the priests in a temple hundreds of years before, and thousands of miles from its present home.

Flying foxes screamed in the trees and a little wind blew coldly off the lake. The company stirred, and conversation flowed again, all, except Sarah and Sher Khan, astonished at the spell that had for a moment fallen on them.

Sarah had walked a little part. Now she stood, looking down, almost as still as the stone god. Then, as if a spell had indeed held her, she moved suddenly, turned, and was thanking Sher Khan for his hospitality, insisting that they must go.

'Then go, Khanum, and sleep well. You are tired, I know. Thank you for bringing my picture to life for me. I have your portrait now, as well as Munabhen's.'

As they took their places in the little boat the two men in unspoken consent manoeuvred a change of partners. Digby sat beside Sarah, Julia with Alastair facing them. The farewells were said, the rowers sank their paddles into the water, and the boat moved smoothly away.

No one spoke on the way home. Digby sat beside

Sarah, not touching her, but feeling her closeness with every nerve in his body. Julia and Alastair held hands, leaning close together. Sarah lay back on the cushions and watched the lights of her house come nearer, and thought about nothing except the lights reflecting in the lake and the beauty of the night. She willed everything else from her mind. But a shadow kept falling between her eyes and the beauty of the night. A small shadow, shaped like the irregular black stain that she had noticed soaking into the sandy soil outside the Rajaghar. It was a twin to the stain she had noticed outside her own house. Richard's jeep was leaking oil badly and leaving tracks. The stain outside the Rajaghar was fresh. Richard must have driven up while they were there and then driven away again. Why?

The whole pointlessness of her life with Richard, all the lies he constantly told, all the humiliations both spiritual and physical that he put upon her had come crowding into her mind as she had stood looking down at that black stain. It could have been blood, it filled her with so much horror. She knew, with absolute certainty, that Richard must have been many times to the Rajaghar, and not as the Ruler's guest. Possibly he was fool enough to imagine that the Ruler did not know of his visits. Perhaps he had assignations with some woman there. Whatever he was doing, she was sure that Sher Khan knew all about it and was shielding her from the knowledge because it was something that was dishonourable.

Later, seated over supper, she thought over the evening. She tried to remember only the pleasure, and to laugh with the others about what Julia called 'The gaudy ladies', but behind her laughter she was seeing in memory Muna's pictured face looking down at her. Then she remembered the Ruler's words as he stood with her looking at the fabulous necklace that glittered in his hands. Was she really as beautiful as Muna? It suddenly seemed enough that he should think so – and then the gaudy ladies came back into her memory, and she laughed at herself for being flattered that a man as obviously experienced as Sher Khan could pay her a light compliment and she could take it seriously enough to hear, hours later, the very tones of his voice as he spoke.

The others were planning a picnic at Ramsaran Falls. Sarah put her thoughts away and joined in the conversation. There were to be two jeeps, and the men would come and pick them up at about four thirty in the morning, so that they could see the sun rise from Devighar. It was all to take place in a day's time.

The plans made to everyone's satisfaction, the men left, Alastair announcing that he did not know how he was going to live through the next day without seeing them. Digby was very quiet, and tried to look deeply and meaningly into Sarah's eyes, but failed because she studiously avoided meeting his look.

As the sound of their jeep, with Alastair singing 'I'll see you in my dreams,' died away, Julia turned to Sarah.

'Are you too tired to talk for a little while? I do not think that I shall sleep until you have explained about you being a relation of the Ruler of Lambagh. You did not tell me that when we came to the house!'

'Well –'

'Well, there are a lot of things you have not told me, Sarah. I know things have not been very easy for you, I see more than you think, and I hope so much that everything will grow better. I am sure it will. But please do not dislike me.' Julia spoke with her eyes raised appealingly to Sarah. 'Be my friend, as I am yours. I like you so much that it should make no difference that you and Richard are going through a difficult time. I can see you are, but people do sometimes, when they are married, don't they? Particularly when they are in a new place, and the man is working very hard. Richard always was inclined to be quick tempered, and I know he'll be sorry if he is upsetting you. But we can be friends, whatever happens. I always thought that when Richard married I would have a sister, and I was so delighted when I met you, I liked you at once –'

Going through a difficult time with Richard! What a

splendid understatement, thought Sarah, staring at her. But all she saw was sheer honesty and love smiling hopefully at her.

'Dear Julie, of course I am your friend. I do not mean to hold you away from me. It is just that so much about me seems to be odd that people expect me to behave in a certain way because of stories about my "unfortunate" background. I cannot see my background as unfortunate. I am very proud of my family, but I do not particularly want to discuss anything about it. I certainly don't want to distress or shock you.'

'In other words, my mother told you to respect my innocence!' Julia made her eyes big and astonished as she said this, her voice imitating her mother's voice perfectly.

'Yes, in a manner of speaking,' answered Sarah, laughing at her.

'Oh, I know my mother's manner of speaking.' Julia sighed, shaking her head. 'Oh, my mother, her rules and her beliefs! But she is not really bad – not as bad as she makes herself sound, Sarah, truly. She cannot help herself. She has not lived a very wide sort of life. She's terribly good and kind really, you must not mind her.'

Sarah privately thought that there was nothing good about her mother-in-law. How had that narrow-minded, hard-faced woman produced this kind honest little creature? She supposed it was easy enough to explain. All Mrs Longman's heart and interest had been devoted to Richard. Julia had grown up, therefore, with only her father's guidance. How fortunate for Julia! For old Colonel Longman was a charming man, kind, truthful and sincere.

Sarah felt a wave of affection for Julia, who was looking at her with big pleading eyes, so like Penelope asking for something. 'Please, Sarah, tell me about your grandmother? I long to know all about her.'

At eleven o'clock at night, after a punishing day? Sarah sighed deeply and resigned herself. The two girls went up to Julia's room, and Sarah talked as Julia got ready for bed.

16

'It is difficult to know where to start.'

Sitting on the edge of Julia's bed, Sarah wrinkled her forehead and spoke slowly.

'I do not know as much about my grandmother as I would like to know. My mother hated India, you see. She seemed to fear India as if it was her enemy. Talking about my grandmother seemed to make the feeling worse for her, although she did not hate Muna. She told me that Muna was a beautiful, charming person, loved by everyone; that was all she did tell me. My father did not talk about her at all once he saw that it upset my mother. They adore each other, those two. They are so close that there is no room in their lives for anyone else. And yet, loving him as she does, my mother cannot live in the country he loves so much. He retired very early and followed her back to England, because he could not bear to live without her. It was the same for her. She was never very interested in us children. Only in my father. It is still the same. They live for each other only.'

Sarah stopped, remembering how little she had seen of her beautiful mother. Ayah had been the central figure in her life. The break when her mother had taken her brother and herself back to England to school had been terrible. She remembered how she had hated the cold grey country, had seen nothing beautiful in the great trees, and the green neatness of meadow and hedge and garden. She had been sick with longing for the dusty plains, the smell of thorn twigs and cowdung burning, the early morning rides with her father, the warmth and the easy gentle life in their big bungalow in Ravipore. In

148

England there had been no loving Ayah. Lonely, the child Sarah had longed for India, and had hated the long grey-green summer twilights almost as much as she had loathed the frosts, snows and biting winds of winter, when her fingers swelled with chilblains and she had to wear the heavy hampering woollens of school uniform. She had made no friends among the daughters of her mother's friends; hockey, cricket, netball and tennis had seemed poor substitutes for riding, and she had been extremely unpopular at school, and very unhappy. 'Ugh!' said Sarah, 'how I *hated* England!'

Julia, who loved everything about England, could not understand but said nothing in case any word from her should stop Sarah talking. 'Your grandmother?' she prompted hopefully.

'Yes. Well, my grandmother can't have liked being uprooted to England either. She was twenty-one when she married my grandfather. What a flutteration there must have been in his mother's household when he took her home! She was a dancing girl, you know, a temple dancer.'

Julia knew all about temple dancers. They were prostitutes really, even if it was mixed up with their religion. Her astonished horror made Sarah laugh, but it was a rather bitter laugh. 'Julia, the temple dancers have an honourable profession. They are dedicated to the gods at birth, trained and groomed to a perfection that even a Queen could envy. Muna, my grandmother, was one of the most famous and respected dancers in these parts. She was also a harlot, of course. Julia, if your eyes get any bigger they'll fall out! Anyway, she met my grandfather when they were both helping the Begum Bianca and her daughter Sara to escape from a mob of rioters, here in Madore. She pretended to be Sara, and led the rioters off, while Sara and her mother escaped. The riot was organised, I think, by the grandfather of that rather effete-looking cousin of Sher Khan's – I'll have to get Sher Khan to tell you the story, Julie, I don't know much more.'

'I still don't see how you are related.'

'No, I do not either, really, but Ayah told me when I was a child that Munabhen was adopted by Begum Bianca's husband, the Ruler of Lambagh. There is no blood tie. Munabhen has an odd history, she was herself rescued during the Mutiny – picked up by an old servant of the Ruler of Lambagh and taken to Lambagh State. She was found beside the body of her dead mother who was, they say, an Indian girl married to an English soldier. So heaven knows who I am descended from! Poor Julie, what a sister Richard picked out for you!'

Julia, propped against pillows, and avidly listening, saw at last how exhausted Sarah looked.

'Oh, go to bed, Sarah. I feel awful, I've kept you up so late. But promise me you'll tell me more tomorrow. It is the most fascinating story I have ever heard.'

Sarah, going thankfully off to her own room, found Ayesha waiting up for her. The girl helped her to undress and taking up a brush, began to brush Sarah's hair with long slow strokes, infinitely soothing and relaxing.

Sarah, watching her still, brown face in the glass, saw that she had been weeping.

'Ayesha! What is it? Have you some trouble?' she asked gently in Urdu.

'Nay, Khanum. Not trouble, but grief. Lalani was my sister.'

'The girl – not the girl who was killed? Oh, Ayesha, why did you not tell me? Go now, I will finish my hair and go to bed. I am in sorrow for you, and your loss. I wish you had told me before; you should not have waited for me.'

'Khanum, I stay. Work is better than sitting and grieving. She has two children, sons, so she will not be altogether forgotten.'

'Ayesha, who do you think did this evil?'

Ayesha's face, with its thickened swollen eyelids, was without expression.

'Who can say, Khanum?' She finished brushing Sarah's hair and began to collect her clothes and put them away. 'Lalani was a good girl.' Her voice was very quiet. 'She was a good girl who loved her husband and her sons. Who did this killing? We all ask this. Whoever it was, time will discover him to us, and justice will lay her death at his door, and we her people will eat vengeance.' Her voice was a whisper as venomous as the hiss of a snake. She salaamed to Sarah and went out, her face looking like a mask.

Sarah, left alone, found that she could not sleep. She swallowed two of her pills and, taking a quilt from her bed, went out on to the verandah and lay on the long chair. She could see the lamps of the Rajaghar, and wondered if the party was still continuing. Leda and Latta – what strange names! – had looked as if they intended to stay all night. She heard the sound of a motor, and looking over the balcony saw lights going up the roads towards the Rajaghar. She could tell that it was a jeep because the headlamps were set high, and close together. The pills were beginning to work at last, and she could not keep her eyes open. She was still sound asleep in the long chair when Ayah brought her morning tea.

In the Rajaghar the party had broken up soon after Sarah and the others had left. As Sarah had sat on her balcony, looking over to his house, Sher Khan had been walking about on the dais, listening to one of the old boatmen who had been with him on the island that morning. As the old man sat on the floor, talking, he traced with one finger unseen patterns on the marble. Sher Khan said very little. He listened, and frowned, and when the old man was silent he called to a soldier who stood at the top of the steps, saying, 'Bring him.'

The man who came stumbling up the steps between two State Police was a hill man, a tall man in duffle robes whose slanted eyes were as blue as Sher Khan's own. There was a long scratch on his face and Sher Khan, seeing it, glared at the police. 'Who did that? I ordered no beating!'

'Lord of the Hills, that is an old cut – it must have happened yesterday. We have not touched him.'

Sher Khan looked at the man. 'Baldur, you have been in my service for how long?'

'Twenty-two years, lord.'

'You married your wife, Lalani, ten years ago?'

For the first time since he had come out on to the dais, Baldur lowered his eyes. As he answered Sher Khan he looked at the marble floor as if he could see there the patterns that the old man had traced with his fingertip. There was a short silence, then Sher Khan said, his voice sharp as a revolver shot, 'Why did you do it? Why did you sell Lalani to the white man?'

'He offered much money, lord.'

'You want for money?'

'Who has enough?'

'A man who can sell the mother of his sons for money, must indeed be hard pressed.'

Baldur made no reply. Sher Khan moved forward until he stood close in front of the hill man. 'Baldur, tell me, who bought *you*?'

'I do not know what you are saying, lord.'

'No? I think you do. I repeat, who bought you? You have served me long and very faithfully. Your wife and your sons were your pride. You did not come to the war with me, because of this –' Sher Khan touched one of Baldur's arms, and the man raised it, his dufflle sleeve falling back to show the withering of the arm, where an old scar puckered from wrist to elbow. 'You got that by saving me from a knife thrust that would have taken my life, and instead nearly took yours. So – who had the power to take you from me? Selling Lalani was the act of a man already lost. What did the Englishman pay you, Baldur? For your wife?'

'One thousand rupees.' Still Baldur traced with his eyes the unseen patterns on the marble floor.

'One thousand? A high price for goats, or a cow, but for the wife of your house, the mother of your sons?' Sher Khan paused. 'You have no more to tell me, Baldur?'

Sweat gleamed on the man's face. 'No more, Lord of

the Hills.'

'So. You still call me "Lord"?'

Briefly Baldur raised his eyes. 'You are my ruler, Lord of the Hills.'

'But you could not come and tell me that a snake had entered my house? Take him away, and keep him close. I want to make sure he did not kill his wife as well as sell her.'

Baldur went as quietly as he had come, and Sher Khan was left with the old boatman.

'A thousand rupees! The Baldur I knew would not have entered into such a transaction for a lakh of rupees. But I can guess what happened. Where are the sons?'

'They were here, lord. Then they went to stay with relatives in Meerut, and then yesterday they returned and have gone back to Lambagh, leaving early this morning with Baldur's mother. She left, weeping, and the boys were very thin, as if they had been ill, or starved.'

'Aye, as I thought. Baldur has no relatives in Meerut!' Sher Khan was looking over the lake to where a single window still glowed with light. Staring at the yellow square he said, 'No doubt the Government Police will be over tomorrow. Try to keep Baldur with our men if possible, Old One.'

'As you say, Lord of the Hills.'

It was the small hour of the night, when men's minds, if they are awake, are full of alarm and despair. A bat fluttered over the lamps, throwing a wild black shadow that danced as if of its own accord over the dais, Sher Khan's face and the carved tables. Saying nothing, the old man got up and extinguished the lamps one by one, and then went away, leaving Sher Khan to sit alone, looking over the lake to where the lamp burned for the rest of what was left of that night.

17

Sarah and Julia spent a peaceful pleasant day, reading and playing with the children and having all their meals down by the lake. By the time the children were taken off for their evening walk the two girls were almost asleep, drowsy with sun and relaxation.

'I should go and change, I'm filthy.' Julia stretched out her legs, plump and pretty in blue shirt and shorts, already growing tanned. 'Look how brown my legs are getting! Sarah, your hair has fallen down. I wish you'd always wear it down, you look fifty years younger, even if not so regal.'

'Thanks very much, that makes me about seventy-five normally! You look Penelope's age in those shorts, and your legs are certainly getting brown. We should both go and change – I have a shrewd suspicion that we probably smell, and the ends of my trousers are soaking wet after that last foray into the lake to rescue David's boat. But it is no good. I cannot move. Let us have tea first, no one is likely to come.'

Dip Chand brought the tea-tray, and Sarah was pouring the tea, when Julia gave a deep groan. 'Oh, I knew we should have changed, look!' There was a horse and rider coming down the road from the Rajaghar.

It was Sher Khan himself. He dismounted and joined them, dropping into a chair and accepting a cup of tea. 'I came to enquire after the health of my relative – you looked very tired last night, Khanum. But I can see you are rested now.' Sarah assured him that she was. She thought he looked tired himself, his handsome face blurred with fatigue, with dark lines under his eyes, and he sat listlessly. Too much of Leda's company? She asked if the party had gone on very late.

'No, they left soon after you did. But I was up all night with the enquiry into that woman's death. The police arrested the husband, and after questioning him took him back to his cell for the night. The Government Police came early this morning and when they opened the cell the man was dead. It appears he had been bitten by a krait, a very small, very poisonous snake. It must have got into the cell through the drain. He had been with me for twenty-two years, Baldur, and now we shall probably never know if he killed his wife or not.'

He refused another cup of tea and sat frowning at the lake. He was plainly worried and exasperated. Sarah imagined that the guards in charge of the cell would have had a very unpleasant day. She sat studying the strong handsome face, the face of a man used to getting his own way. Yet there was nothing soft or self-indulgent in his face. At that moment he looked up and saw her examining eyes, and stood abruptly.

'I must go. Thank you, Khanum, my kinswoman. Will you both please come to my house again soon? No party next time, just a family gathering. There is so much I would like to tell you, and learn from you –'

Sarah thanked him and Julia said 'Oh yes, please, Sarah seems to know nothing about her grandmother,' and he still stood, looking at Sarah with so much frank admiration in his slow travelling gaze that she flushed and looked away. He smiled then, as one who has won a contest, and turned to Julia. 'I will tell you everything you want to know. And I hear you now have seven puppies. Will not the brave Hans be jealous?'

'No, he loves them. The only person who does not like them is Bonnie Prince Charlie. He thinks they are cats, and screams every time he sees them.'

'I see,' said Sher Khan gravely. 'I see. Could you kind-ly tell me who this nervous prince is? I had no idea you were entertaining royalty.'

'Bonnie Prince Charlie is Penelope's parrot.'

'Yes. I see. Khanum, I will now take my horse, who is only called Rustom, and leave you to your growing family. Spare a thought for your lonely relative, please, and come soon?'

His Arab went into a flat run as soon as he settled himself into the saddle.

'He is a very dramatic gentleman, isn't he?' Julia was staring after the flying figure. She did not wait for Sarah's reply, but went off to look at the pups, taking Penelope and David, back from their walk, with her. Sarah sat on under the trees until the sun had gone, and Dip Chand came out to tell her that her bath was ready.

Ayah was waiting for her in her room. 'Is Ayesha off this evening?'

'Nay, I wanted to speak with thee, so Ayesha will put the babalog to bed. Sarajan, I am in great distress at what I must say to thee.'

'Ayah. What is it?'

'Thou knowest the cover on the bed in the spare room – the rose brocade?'

'Yes.'

'Sarajan, there is blood on it.'

'*Blood*?'

'Yea. Blood. I can see bruises on thy body, but no wounds. But, let me see thy feet.'

Ayah rose from inspecting Sarah's feet and legs, her face creased with worry. 'Nay. Thou hast no wounds. Sarajan, the stains were all mixed with mud, and at the foot of the cover – not much, but enough. Is it possible that thou stepped close to that poor girl's body?'

Sarah, her face paling so that the day's tan was like a stain over her pallor, shook her head. 'Nay, I was barefooted in any case, and I swam back from the island – so how –'

'Aye, how indeed. The Colonel Sahib was dressed as usual, and no doubt behaved as usual?'

Sarah recalled Richard lounging back, his feet still in chaplis, and the stain she had seen. She stared at the old woman in horror. 'Ayah! What are we thinking?'

It was a frightened cry, and the old woman put her arms round Sarah, and held her close. 'Nay, child, be still. We think nothing. I have taken the bedcover and cleaned it. No one knows anything but Pyari Lal and myself. But child, I fear for you. Thou hast suffered enough, and now – is it safe for you to be alone at any time with a madman? We your servants will wait and watch – but Sarajan, free yourself. Thou knowest I would die before I distressed thee, but this time it was needful.'

'Ayah, thou didst well, as always. I too think I must have my freedom.'

18

The whole house was awake and buzzing with activity at four the next morning. The children raced about, wild with excitement, Hans at their heels. Dip Chand and Pyari Lal carried an enormous tiffin basket to the outside steps, also several thermos flasks.

'He must think we are going away for *weeks*.' Julia was watching the preparations and admiring Dip Chand's attire. He was dressed in very clean khaki drill, even his turban was khaki, and he was full of bustle and importance. Julia, in shorts, was sent back by Sarah to change into trousers and a sweater. 'You'll freeze dressed like that. We shall be climbing, and it will be much colder than it is here.'

When she returned Sarah looked at her and nodded approvingly. 'Come on, let us get those children quietened down – they'll be exhausted before we start.'

Digby and Alastair arrived promptly at four thirty a.m., with two jeeps. The party embarked and started off, Ayah and Pyari Lal waving from the verandah and Hans barking hysterically from the back of Digby's jeep. Sarah and the two children travelled with Digby, and Alastair took Julia, Dip Chand and the food.

The air was fresh with the coming dawn, but the sky was still black and the jeep headlamps cut long paths of light ahead of them. Presently they began to climb, and soon the road was winding among rocky hillsides and the trees began to change to pine and oak instead of banyan and shisham.

The air grew colder. Once, a bear stood up, blinking in their headlights, and then ran with a peculiar shuffling scramble to the edge of the road and down out of sight.

'Oh, Mummy, I *want* that littley bear!' Penelope was trying to see through the darkness where the bear had vanished.

'Very well,' said Digby, 'I'll pick it up for you on the way back.'

'Digby, you'll be expected to do just that,' warned Sarah.

'Oh, dear. Well, Penelope, if the bear has waited, we'll collect it, but it may want to stay with its own family. See?'

'Yes.' Penelope nodded several times. 'Yes. I see.'

The hills closed in around them, barely seen shapes, black against the dark sky. They could smell the special mountain smell, pine and wood smoke and wet peaty soil. The road twisted round the steep shoulders of the hills, and at last petered out in a jumble of rocks and close-growing trees. Digby drew to one side and stopped.

'This is where we start climbing to see the sunrise.'

The other jeep came up and Dip Chand was left in charge of the children, who had both fallen asleep.

The climb began. They went in single file, brushing through thick fern and walking on a carpet of moss for the first short climb. Then they were on rock, and climbing steeply. The hillside fell away dizzily to a river far below. The river could be heard faintly, a rushing, splashing sound that would have been deafening if they had been closer to it. After a last scramble over piled boulders they came out on to a ridge and stopped. Digby opened his haversack and took out the big flask of coffee, and they stood drinking and watching the sky grow light. The mountains were there, close companions, range after range as far as they could see, stark, jagged giants, cutting into the sky, the high peaks blue-white and veiled in cloud at the summits. Like eternity, thought Sarah, staring at the ranged mountains. On and on for ever – no warmth, no life. She shuddered, and Digby put his arm round her and pulled her close. Leaning against his warmth, she saw the miracle. In a moment the mountains were warm with rosy colour, the clouds lifted from the peaks, and like a sword flash the sun was up and the snows were blazing white against a blue sky. For minutes the party stood and stared, stunned, before they were able to move and speak again. Digby got more coffee, and then stood peering over the valley to the opposite hillside.

'Alastair, come here a moment. Look over there. What do you make of that?'

Alastair, staring, saw that there were many men moving in an orderly fashion up the hill and out of sight round the curve of the mountain. 'What the devil, there must be hundreds of them! Here, give me those glasses. Yes, by God, they are in uniform. I thought they were. Digby, have they seen us?'

'No, I don't think so. We're below the hill here, and I think if they look this way the sun will be in their eyes. I'd give a lot to know who they are and what they are doing.'

They watched the stream of men a little longer, and Digby said, 'They look like Gurkhas, except for their headgear. Perhaps they *are* a Gurkha battalion on man-oeuvres.'

'Very odd uniform for Gurkhas – anyway, we know there aren't any manoeuvres going on at the moment. Who the hell goes on manoeuvres after a war? They go on leave, not scrambling about on mountains playing war games!'

Digby raised his glasses again. 'I thought so. There is the royal beast – look, on a horse.'

'*Who*?'

'The Nawab Sahib himself.'

'So it is. Very odd.'

'Not so very odd. I reckon those are his troops we are watching. State Forces, possibly going back to Lambagh Valley by some mountain route we don't know about. These mountains are pretty untrodden. I think Young-husband mapped them in about 1920, and they haven't been done since. I always wanted to go on trek here for that reason. On the other hand, perhaps they are not going on leave, in which case –'

As he talked, Digby was using the glasses. He put them down and said, 'Well, that's that. They've gone, vanished over the hills like a lot of ghosts.'

'I suppose the picnic is off.'

'Afraid so. Oh, hell, I don't know. I don't really see why we shouldn't have a shortened one, up where we left the jeeps, and then go back. I think we ought to report this movement of troops fairly rapidly – it is probably perfectly all right, and they are off on leave. But if it were anything else – well, it might be of interest to HQ in view of the situation in Ratna and Madore.'

'Not to mention the happy state of ferment all over India.' As they walked back to the jeeps they explained to Sarah and Julia why they would be cutting the picnic short. It was decided to have a breakfast picnic, and then go home.

'The children can have another picnic down by the lake. They'll enjoy that just as much!'

'I am so sorry! I hate like hell having to disappoint you, after all the trouble you took to get the picnic ready. I promise we'll do the whole thing again as soon as possible, only this time Alastair and I will bring everything – you won't have to do a thing.'

'I didn't do a thing anyway, Dip Chand did it all. I didn't even order anything. It was all organised for me, like magic.'

Digby, watching Dip Chand unloading the picnic basket and spreading rugs on the ground for them to sit on, wondered how much he knew about the Ruler's activities. Looking at the proud old face under the khaki turban, he knew that it would be useless to question him. He was Sher Khan's man, no doubt about that.

After they had breakfasted, Digby and Alastair climbed back up the path to fix a landmark so that they would know where they had seen the men. 'They came out at that rock there, and over that pass. Look, you can see the path quite clearly from here. Alastair, hang about up here, will you? I am just going down to have a look-see – there's a rope bridge down there that I can use.'

Digby scrambled down the hill and negotiated the rope bridge with a certain amount of trouble, as it was in a bad state of repair. Then he walked up the rough path to the pass.

He saw the path drop down below him, mile upon mile of twisting curves, to a valley misty with distance. He could see no moving thing anywhere, except an eagle swinging over the sky in searching arcs. Turning back, he looked down at the river, and a little to the left of the old rope bridge, almost hidden in the rocks, he saw a plank bridge. Strong, and obviously new, the planks were pale and gleaming against the dark rocks. 'Not very well hidden if it was meant to be hidden,' he thought, going down to it. Plainly only intended for foot passengers, the bridge was merely two tree trunks halved and lashed together with strips of hide. There was a hand rail made from thin branches. How Sher Khan had got his horse across it, Digby could not imagine.

He crossed the bridge and was climbing back up the hill path when he heard Sarah scream and Alastair shouting for him. Breathless, he finished the climb and rounded the curve of the hill, and Sarah ran sobbing into his arms. 'Oh, God, Digby, Julia's fallen – right over the waterfall. She's lying in one of the pools, on the edge. Digby, I think she's dead.

Sarah and Julia had watched the two men go out of sight, and had then turned and followed the goat track to the edge of the ravine. They stood looking down at the falls, misted with spray, dropping into a pool that reflected back the green of the trees and the blue sky.

'That looks a heavenly place to swim, what a pity we cannot go today. What do you suppose those men were doing, Sarah? Digby and Alastair seem so worried.'

'Goodness knows. Nothing probably. Just State Forces going on leave. But these days everything has to be watched. It is so important for India that the handover goes smoothly when we leave them after all these years.'

Julia did not appear to be listening to the latter part of her speech, so Sarah stopped talking. Presently Julia said slowly, 'Sarah, is Digby in love with you?'

Sarah turned and looked at her down-bent face. 'Why, Julia?'

'Well, all the things he does for us, and the way he looks at you, and then, this morning, he put his arm round you right there in front of us all! I think – well, you are married to Richard, and Richard is – I don't mean to be horrid and interfering, but –' She stumbled into silence under Sarah's quiet considering gaze.

'Julie, whatever Digby's feelings are for me, do you feel it is any of your business?'

The words were gently spoken, with no anger behind them, and Julia could think of no answer, but she felt so strongly that she tried again. 'Sarah, *don't* be angry, I can't help feeling it is my business. Richard is my brother, and I know you are not happy together.'

'Richard and I are both adult and, Julie darling, you were brought out here to enjoy yourself, not to be a guardian of my morals – or *did* your mother tell you to watch me?'

Julia turned away, furious. Most of the fury was directed at herself, for of course Sarah was right. It was none of her business. She valued the friendship that had been growing between them, and now it was all spoiled. Her eyes filled with tears and she walked a few steps blindly, trying to pull herself together. She was nearer the edge of the ravine than she realised. A stone turned under her sandalled foot, she lost her balance and, with Sarah's scream ringing in her ears, she plunged over the lip of the ravine and into the cold rushing darkness of the falls.

19

Digby held Sarah, saying 'Hush, don't be silly! The water will have broken her fall. Where is Alastair?'

'He went over the khud, climbing down to get to her.'

They heard Alastair calling, and Digby ran to the edge of the ravine.

'Digby, I'm almost down to her. Can you get a jeep as far down as possible? Dip Chand will probably know a way.'

Sarah wiped her eyes as they ran for the jeeps. Dip Chand had taken the children up under the shade of a stand of pines. They were happily building a stone fort with his help. He was horrified when Digby told him what had happened, and at once directed Digby's attention to a narrow path. 'This will lead directly to the pool, Sahib. There is brandy in that basket, and rugs are already in the jeep.'

As they drove slowly down the rocky path, Sarah sat silent beside Digby. All she could see as she stared ahead was Julia's body, tossed in the falls and then lying spread-eagled on the flat rock at the edge of the pool, like a broken doll, her red scarf a bright line at her throat. Poor Julia, so anxious to do the right thing – begging for her friendship, starry-eyed over the house, obviously falling in love with Alastair, and desperately anxious about Sarah and her beloved brother. Sarah had begun to think of her, not as Richard's sister, but as her own. Pretty Julia, lying dead in a rocky pool. Sarah felt wildly that she carried doom about with her, that she brought disaster to anyone who came close to her.

Digby looked down at her white face. 'Sarah, she may

be perfectly all right. The water will have broken her fall. Come *on*, darling, don't look like that!'

But Sarah did not answer, and when he put his hand over hers she moved her hand and shook her head.

When at last they rounded the curve of the ravine and came in sight of the pool, they saw that Alastair had lifted Julia out of the water and was bending over her. Sarah jumped out of the jeep before it stopped moving and ran over to them. Alastair looked up.

'This girl is an india-rubber *doll*! She is stunned, and I think her arm is broken, but she is all right. Oh, my God, Digby, *catch* Sarah!' But in the end Sarah did not faint. Ash pale, swaying on her feet, she leaned against Digby for a moment and then went to kneel beside Julia, murmuring to her and holding her hand, while the two men found the blankets in the jeep.

With the blankets wrapped closely round her, Julia was put lying in the back of the jeep with Sarah and Alastair to hold her steady against the jolting journey.

It was then decided that Alastair should drive the children and Dip Chand back to the house, and go on to brigade headquarters to make his report, and alert the hospital that Julia would be coming in. If it was possible, he would bring an ambulance back with him to make the journey easier for Julia. Digby would drive Sarah and Julia back very slowly and then, having collected clothes and necessities for Julia, she would be all ready for her journey to the hospital.

'Hospital?' Julia, at last safely in her own bed, flushed and brilliant-eyed with excitement and, Sarah feared, fever, watched Sarah packing a nightdress and her sponge bag, and begged not to be sent to hospital. 'Please, Sarah, oh please! I can't bear it. Don't make me go and lie in bed in a great ward with bedpans and things – please.'

'Well, sweetie, of course not, if you feel like that about it. I'll try and get a doctor to come out here. But Julia, if Alastair brings the ambulance I think you'll have to go. I doubt very much if they will force you on to a bedpan for a broken arm, you know, and there are private rooms. I am sure Richard will have met most of the sisters, and you will get the very best attention from them as a result, once they discover that you are related to him.'

There was a wry twist to her lips as she spoke, the almost sneer that Julia had noticed before when Richard's name was mentioned. But now Julia did not think of that. All her energy was spent on begging to stay away from hospital, and in disguising the fact that she felt very ill indeed. Her head felt hot and like a balloon, inclined to float off her shoulders, and her whole side throbbed with pain, not only her arm. Ayah brought her a hot milky drink, and after thought, Sarah brought one of her sleeping pills and Julia fell into an uneasy doze.

Digby, whose main object was to ensure that Sarah had a rest, took the children down to the lake, while Sarah moved from the drawing room to Julia's room, and did not rest at all.

Teatime came, and still no Alastair. The sun was low in the sky when the Ayah came down to take the children off for their baths, and Sarah went up with her, and found Julia awake, definitely very feverish, and complaining that her bandage was too tight. Sarah did what she could to ease her and went down to Digby.

'What on earth can have happened to Alastair, Digby? He's been gone ages. Do you suppose he couldn't find a doctor or get an ambulance? But in any case he would have come back to tell us, wouldn't he?'

'Yes, of course he would. I think I had better go off, Sarah. I will go to the first house in the Cantonments and telephone.'

'Oh, Digby, what a fool I am! There is a phone in the Ruler's house, he told me the first night we were here that I could use it. I'll send a message over at once.'

'No, I will go. I'll drive over and do the telephoning myself.' Sarah watched him go, and then hurried back upstairs. She heard the children laughing as she went past the nursery. Thank God they were well and happy!

She sat beside Julia's bed, and presently the girl seemed easier, and fell into a light sleep, while Sarah sat and wondered at her foolishness in forgetting that the Ruler had a telephone. It was the whole strange atmosphere of his ruined old palace, it had not seemed possible that anything as modern as a telephone could be installed in a place that breathed of age and the past.

20

When Digby drove up to the Rajaghar his first thought
was that his journey was fruitless, for the place seemed
deserted. He walked round to the back, and into the
courtyard through the unguarded door, before he heard
any sounds of life. But when he was inside the court he
could hear a hum of voices coming from a room the
window of which opened on to the steps up to the dais.
He walked to the window and looked in, ready to call,
and the words died on his lips as he saw the men in the
room.

There were only eight, apart from the Nawab. Of these
eight, six were the most important and deadly of the
many enemies of the British Raj, men who preferred
terrorism and anarchy to any form of lawful government, whether it was government by the British or by
politically mature Indian leaders. There was Hardyal,
the Ruler's cousin, and a European who was unknown to
Digby, but he could imagine what his race might be and
what his business might be with terrorist leaders, and
the Ruler of a hill state conveniently situated between
India and her far northern borders.

Digby dropped below the level of the window and,
moving as silently as he could, backed down the way he
had come. Speed and silence were all he could think of.
Why were there no sentries? He realised why almost as
his mind formed the question. All the people around, the
servants in both houses, the villagers, were the Ruler's
people. The Ruler had nothing to fear in this part of the
country. The mountains were full of his men, and the
audacity of holding a meeting at which these notorious

men were present, so close to the Cantonments, showed how sure he was of his surroundings.

The noise of the jeep starting was so loud! Digby sat sweating for a second, waiting to be shot, knowing that they could not afford to let him leave alive. But nothing happened. He drove away, expecting to be fired at even as he turned the corner of the drive, and having got safely out of sight of the house he was still waiting for annihilation, the bullet from behind, or from the side of the road.

When he got back to the house, Sarah was waiting for him outside. 'Julia is asleep at last.'

'Sarah, listen.' He told her as quickly as he could, grateful that she listened without interrupting him. Then, furious at the necessity, he said, 'I shall have to leave you Sarah. I *must* go and report this. If we could get those men, it would scotch a lot of trouble. They are the ringleaders of the terrorist movement in this part of India – nothing can come before the chance of getting them. I cannot think what the Ruler of Lambagh is doing. These men are poison, he must be mad to be mixed up with them. What can he be doing?'

Sarah could not imagine. They both stood frowning at different thoughts. Digby spoke first. 'It would be hopeless for me to try to get to Madore in the jeep, otherwise I would suggest taking all of you with me. But that would be no good, I'd never get through, they'll have their men out guarding the road. I wonder if Alastair got through.'

She waited quietly while he thought. He decided that he would have to go back through the fields, cutting round the road and the villages. 'I know this part of the country – I can be back in Madore, using short-cuts, in under an hour. Have you any idea if any of the syces are on duty? If they are, I'll have to ask you to get me one of the horses. That big Waler would be the best.'

They went carefully towards the stables, but there was no one there. The Waler was brought out, saddled and bridled, and Digby swung himself up. He told Sarah to get Julia and the children into the jeep and drive them to

Madore. 'It isn't safe for you to stay here – quite apart from Julia's condition. Things must be at boiling-point for all those chaps to be together in one place, and I do not like the smell of it, though I don't think they'll stop you getting through to the hospital. Take Dip Chand with you. After all, everyone round here knows you are related to the Ruler, and Julia is obviously very ill. No, I'm sure you'll have no trouble.'

He was talking to comfort himself, it was so terrible to have to leave her behind. He was very distressed. Sarah saw his trouble and said, 'Digby, don't worry. You get on – after all, as you say, everyone knows us round here, we'll be perfectly all right.'

She went to get him a flask of cold water, and coming back without it, said, 'Digby, don't say goodbye, and keep to the grass verges as you go. There is a man outside the dining room, and two more by the lake – strangers to me. Could you get off very quietly, and I will stay here, talking as if you were still with me, so that anyone interested won't realise you've gone. Don't worry – Dip Chand and the syces are all Ayah's relatives. Whatever happens, they will look after us.'

His last sight of her was the fluid grace of her body, leaning against one of the pillars of the verandah, and he knew that she would stay there talking until she was sure he was safely away.

He put her out of his mind and, keeping to the grass verges of the road, kicked the Waler into a swift canter, all his thoughts given to the necessity of getting to Madore with his news.

He was never to forget that journey. All his life, the smell of dust or the sudden crack of a dry branch breaking under his horse's foot as he rode in quiet woodlands of the future, would send his mind back to that night. Hurrying through the rakh, through small leafy bushes and pipul trees, skirting the thorn fences that divided the fields, he saw no one, except, in the distance, a farmer with his bullocks, turning over the soil with a plough in the last of the evening light, and once a herd boy sat up to stare at him, wide-eyed, as he threaded his way through a herd of great sleepy-eyed buffalo, twitching grey skins in a mud wallow.

It was quite dark when he finally reached the first bungalow in the Cantonments and, dismounting, stumbled in, exhausted and dirty. The people who lived in the bungalow were already alerted.

'Riots have started in the walled city, and everyone seems to be on standby, except two British regiments who have already gone in. Here, have a drink – and don't worry about your animal, my syce will see to him.'

Digby asked if the telephone lines were cut. 'Not yet – at least, they were all right ten minutes ago.' But when Digby tried, the telephone was dead. His host had got the car out, and Digby was driven off, still holding his untouched glass of whisky, while his horse was being led away to the stables at the back of the house.

Sarah waited until Digby had been gone ten minutes and then hurried into the house. She called the Ayah and said quietly, 'Tell me, is Dip Chand to be trusted?'

Ayah was affronted. 'With your life, Huzoor. Why do you ask?'

As quickly as she could, Sarah told her what Digby had seen at the Rajaghar and what she was going to do. Ayah shook her head.

'The Major Sahib is mistaken. The Ruler is not one who joins in plots and murderous things. Never mind, time will prove that what I say is true. Whatever else happens, it is better that we go to the hospital with the Miss Sahiba. I will get the children. Dip Chand will help me, and Pyari Lal. If the Miss Sahiba cannot walk, call me and we will carry her down.' Ayah hurried off, and Sarah set herself to the task of waking and moving Julia.

Julia was in great pain and very feverish, and was still much against going into hospital. She argued and wept, and Sarah, finally desperate, had to explain to her that troops were coming, and that there would very likely be shooting and she wanted to get the children away. Then indeed Julia tried to help herself and to hurry, but she was very confused and ill. Sarah was horrified to see how ill she was, and doubted very much the wisdom of moving her, but knew that she must. The silence that had fallen on the house was ominous. Normally there was a constant undercurrent of sound, the gardeners talking as they worked, the women in the house moving about, accompanied by the inevitable ringing of their bracelets. There were always voices calling from the stables and quarters. Now there was nothing, nothing but silence.

Ayah came to say that Pyari Lal was not to be found, and that Dip Chand had gone to the stables and the quarters to see if he was there. She hurried off to put the children into the jeep, and Sarah had to deal with Julia alone. As she made her slow way down the stairs, supporting Julia, Sarah felt a desperate impatience to get out of the place and away. There was suddenly something malignant in the house, a chill which made her shiver, an expectant silence as if invisible crowds were awaiting an inevitable catastrophe. Everything seemed to threaten her.

At last she was out in the darkening garden, and helped Julia into the jeep, making her lie down on a mattress in the back. Penelope and David were already there, David sound asleep, Penelope too drowsy to be curious. Hans' bright eyes peered at her from beside the Ayah. Sarah went round to the driver's seat, and was just climbing in when Julia asked weakly for a glass of water. 'I feel very odd, Sarah.' She looked dreadful, and Sarah rushed back to the house for the flask of iced water that always stood in the dining room for the children. Snatching up the flask, she remembered that there was no blanket for Julia, and ran upstairs to get one from the first room she came to – the spare room, with the rose brocade curtains and bedspread.

The room was dark, and as she ran to the bed she stumbled over something on the floor and almost fell. She clicked on the light switch and stopped, staring, her breath catching in her throat.

It was, she found, Pyari Lal who lay, horribly dead, his head lolling on one side, his turban at a drunken angle, his tongue sticking out of his puffed and swollen lips, while his eyes stared back at her, scarlet and terrifying, blood trickling from their corners. She forced herself to touch him, to feel for his heartbeat, but he was quite dead. A wire had been tied so tightly round his throat that it was almost invisible in the ring of proud flesh that had risen round it. He was cold, cold like ice. Sarah stood up, and backed away from that terrible staring face, and turned to run – but where? For a moment she was too confused to think clearly. Then her brain began to function again, and she put off the light and shut the spare-room door on its terrible occupant, moving very quietly.

Whatever the Ruler was doing, she knew with complete certainty that he would not have had anything to do with what was happening in the house. Dip Chand must go for him at once. She remembered her revolver, locked in the bottom drawer of her dressing-table, and went quickly down the passage to her room. She saw that the door on to the balcony was open, but did not have time to worry about that. She was intent on getting the gun out of the drawer, and knelt down, her keys in her hand.

21

'Where are you off to in such a hurry, Sarah?' Richard was standing in the open door, his blue eyes crinkling against the smoke of his cigarette.

She looked at his reflection in the mirror, and then stood up and turned to face him. Here was the focus of all the terrors and uncertainties of the day. She forced herself to move slowly, and to speak quietly.

'Richard! Where on earth have you come from? I didn't hear you arrive!'

'I imagine you were too busy to hear anything. Where are you off to? Is this a rather crowded elopement? I see it is Digby's jeep that is crammed with our family and retainers. The only missing object, apart from the kitchen stove, is Digby himself. Where is he?' The last three words cracked like a whip.

'Who? Digby?' Sarah was playing for time. She knew with terrible certainty that Richard had killed Pyari Lal – and that it was in some way connected with the men that Digby had seen in the Rajaghar. Pyari Lal must have seen too much.

'Yes – who else? Sarah, where is Digby?'

'He went back to Madore some time ago.'

'*How*, for God's sake? Leaving his jeep here?'

'He went back with Alastair. They've gone to alert the hospital. He left the jeep with me because Julia is badly hurt and I have to take her in.' She stopped speaking, because Richard was not listening to her.

'Stranger and stranger by the minute –' said Richard. 'Digby bogs off, leaving a Command jeep to be used by a motley selection of civilians and animals. He'll get a hell of a reprimand for that, if not a court martial. He must have completely lost his head. What an effect you have on the male sex. Come and sit here, on this rather lasciviously painted bed, and tell me exactly what is going on.'

Sarah kept herself from shuddering, held herself still, and said calmly, 'Richard, you didn't hear what I said – I've got to get Julia into hospital, she's hurt herself – broken her arm, I think and perhaps some ribs. She seems very ill.'

'Broken her *arm*? Ribs? How on earth?'

'She fell.' Again Sarah stopped herself. She did not want to say anything about the picnic, and the Nawab's troops in the mountains. Why? She did not know, only a warning voice seemed to say 'Don't talk.' She turned for the door and Richard followed her. They passed the spare-room door without a glance, Richard talking all the time.

'Poor little Julia – but I doubt if you will get her into Madore now. The hospital is just within the walls, and the city is in an uproar of the most magnificent type. Rioting broke out this morning in a big way, which makes me wonder how Digby and Alastair got here in the first place. There were barriers up on the roads by nine this morning, and all leave was stopped. Don't tell me the virtuous baronets spent the night here, plus army transport – very naughty of them, in more ways than one. Have you been having an orgy, sweetheart? With poor Julia breaking her arm in her efforts to escape from the brutal and licentious Alastair? And why are you dragging the children off in a jeep at this time of night?'

'Oh, Richard, don't be ridiculous! I didn't want to leave them alone!'

'Leave them alone? Why, is the Ayah drunk or something?'

Sarah ignored him. 'If there is rioting, and the barriers are up, how did you get here?'

'Oh, ways and means, my dearest girl – ways and means. Well, now, let us see what is best to be done about Julia.'

He walked forward to the jeep and Sarah saw Ayah's face contract with alarm at the sight of him. Warning bells began to ring in Sarah's head as Richard bent over Julia, kindly and gentle now, but completely ignoring his children.

'Well, Julia poppet, you are in a state, aren't you? How did you do this? Falling down stairs?'

Julia's voice was the high uncertain voice of fever. 'Oh, Richard, I feel so bad. I hurt all over. I expect, in the end, I shall have to go to hospital.'

'Never mind, Julie, the matron is an old friend of mine in the hospital you will be going to. You'll be very comfortable.'

'Oh, but I hate hospitals. What a horrible day this has been, and it started off so well. We were having a lovely picnic, but it all got spoiled.'

'Yes, I can imagine, breaking your wrist would spoil a picnic.'

'Oh, but we never had the proper picnic. When Digby saw all those soldiers in the mountains, he said we'd have to come back and tell somebody.'

The intensity with which Richard listened made his face a rigid mask, in which his lips hardly moved. 'Soldiers, Julia? Where were you when you saw all these soldiers?'

'We were above the Rama Falls.'

Sarah knew what she had forgotten to do, and knew too that it would have been no use. Julia in any case would not have believed anything against Richard, and would not have understood why he was not to be told everything. In fact she would have expected Sarah to tell him. Sarah listened, helpless, while Julia rambled on, telling Richard that Digby had seen terrorist leaders in the Nawab's house and had gone to warn someone in Madore. 'And we have to get out of here, because if they try and capture the terrorists there might be fighting. What a good thing you are here, Richard, to help us.'

Richard's voice was very soft. 'Yes, Julia, what a good

thing. Tell me, what time did Digby leave?' But Julia did not reply, she was lying with her eyes closed. He turned to Sarah. 'What time, Sarah?'

'Oh, about two hours ago.'

'Now I know you are lying.'

'What do you mean? Richard, I must go, I must get Julia to a hospital – look at her.'

'Shut up, Sarah! I'm trying to think.' He stood frowning for a few minutes, and then seemed to make up his mind. 'Yes. A doctor. No earthly good trying for Madore, though. She'll have to go to Ramchandra. Dassu!' He beckoned, and a dark-skinned Southern Indian came softly forward. Richard spoke to him in an undertone, and the man got into the jeep and turned it round. To Sarah's horror, he did not stop then – he accelerated away down the drive and through the gates. She saw David in Ayah's arms, Penelope's big startled eyes, a cloud of dust blowing back behind the jeep, and she could see no more.

'Richard!' Sarah felt as if her throat was closing. 'Richard, I should have gone too, they can't manage without me. Or are you taking me in your jeep. Where is it?'

'Oh, around,' said Richard vaguely. 'I shouldn't worry about them. Dassu is very competent. They'll be in Ramchandra Hospital in no time. They don't need you. Which is, considering all things, just as well.' He took her elbow and turned her towards the house.

As she went, obedient to his hand, Sarah felt how the atmosphere of the house and garden had changed. There was a feeling of waiting, the sense of impending disaster she had noticed earlier. A miasma of terror seemed to be seeping into the house like an evil fog. Sarah became terribly afraid, so afraid that a scream kept rising in her throat, and the effort of not screaming took all her strength.

At first she did not hear Richard speak, she was concentrating so hard on not screaming that he had to repeat himself.

'Why didn't you tell me about the men in the hills or, for that matter, the meeting in the Rajaghar, and why imply that Digby went back hours ago with Alastair?' His eyes were dull, she noticed, as they always were when he had been drinking or when he was excited. Other men's eyes sparkled and lit with pleasure or anger, but Richard's eyes went dull, flat blue, like wet slate. She stood silent, staring at him, and he answered his own question.

'Because you know a bit too much – or suspect too much, I reckon. And I would give a lot to know why.'

The drawing room was dusky with shadows and she had to strain her eyes to see his expression. He appeared calm and smiling, but her heart sank and fluttered at the tone of his voice. Excitement had given way to fury, naked, and all the more dangerous because it was controlled. He told her to sit down, offered her a cigarette, and sat on the window seat, looking out into the garden while he talked.

'Digby told you, I suppose, that I was at the Rajaghar too. Is that why you were rushing off?'

Sarah's complete astonishment made him nod his head in satisfaction. 'Yes, I thought he hadn't seen me. Very unobservant fellow. I could have shot him easily, but I hoped his arrival might cause a diversion so that I could get on with my business. However, it is just as well he didn't see me. He might have wondered what I was doing there, and passed his wonderings on.' He stared out of the window towards Madore, as if he could pierce the distance with his eyes and see the walled city. 'Those stupid bastards!' His teeth gritted with rage through the words.

'Who?' Sarah tore her mind from her despairing thoughts about the children and tried to listen to him.

'Oh, these fools! Freedom fighters, agitators, agents provocateurs – political idiots. The great Indian nation in fact. Screaming for independence, but can't wait as they were told until the time is right. Oh, no. Drama is all – so they jump the gun, and start the disturbances, without waiting for the signal. General rioting, organised properly, all over India, breaking out at the same time and in the right places – that is power. But little stupid clashes, easily contained! Oh, the fools. When I think of the money that has been wasted!' He stopped, and lit himself another cigarette, his hands shaking. 'All the money that was spent, bribing, buying arms, all thrown away! *When I think* what could have been done with a few properly trained men – these bazaar sweepings are useless.'

Gradually, as he talked disjointedly, Sarah began, with growing horror, to understand what had made him so angry. He was, it seemed, in the pay of Guntha Singh, the leader of the Sangha Singh sect, a band of terrorists, men who were against any form of law and order, anarchists and murderers. Richard was being paid to build a Freedom Army, and had been training a motley band of insurgents ever since he had arrived in Madore.

'Richard, how on earth did you get mixed up with anything so terrible?'

'Terrible? Nothing terrible about it. It was a job, and a very well-paid job too. It was tailor-made for me. I've always been able to train men. If things had gone well, I would have been on the way at last. No more hanging about waiting to see what the government would decide to do about the Army. No risk of a ghastly transfer to a peacetime British Army life. No, my life would have been good! I would have lived like those old Nabobs in the days of John Company. Well, it just didn't come off. I did everything I could to hold them, but these blasted politicians and their stupid oratory – the whole thing blown by a collection of disaffected babus, who like the sound of their own voices and harangue the crowds whenever possible, and off go the gangs, ripe for murder, and far too soon. These Madore riots will be over by tomorrow, and most of the leaders will be in jail, and the whole thing will be put back by a year, if not more.'

Sarah stared at him, unable to hide her disgust, and he saw her face and said, 'Why the haughty glare? If I'd been successful I would have been one of the most important people in India – and one of the richest.'

'On money earned by treachery to your own people.'

'Oh, don't talk like that, Sarah! For God's sake, what have my own people ever done for me? Paid me a pittance, and now the Army I was trained to serve in is going to be handed over to India, and who cares what happens to me?'

'But you are not the only British officer in the Indian Army in that position, Richard.'

'No, I am not, am I? But I happen to be the only one I am interested in. Easy for you to be superior, Sarah. You've always had all the money you wanted, inherited from *your* own people. Tell me, did you know, when you took this house, that the Royal Beast was a relative of yours?'

'No, I didn't register the name of the state, or I would have known of course. But it is a very distant connection, as you know. Why do you ask?'

'Oh, it might have helped if I had known – in one way or another. Have a drink?' He poured out two whiskies, added water and, giving her one, returned to his seat in the window, looking out over the lake. They drank in silence, and Sarah thought how pleasant and normal the evening seemed. The beautiful shadowy room was full of the scent of roses and jasmine drifting in from the garden, and here they were, husband and wife, sharing a drink at the end of the day. What could be more perfect? Or more false, she thought bitterly, as Richard lifted his glass to her; false, the whole picture, as false as her whole life with him. But the children, she thought in agony, what is happening to the children and Julia, where has he sent them? Surely he would not harm them? Through the shadows she stared at him, trying to see his expression, but it was getting too dark. He seemed to be lost in thought, and the room grew so quiet that when he spoke Sarah started nervously, and had to ask him what he had said.

'I said I hear you had a jolly time the other night with

the Royal Beast, and saw your grandmother's portrait.'

'How did you hear?'

'Oh, the lovely Leda is a friend of mine, in a manner of speaking. She told me that you had a private view of the Peacock chain, too. Very striking, isn't it?' He turned to face her. 'Where does he keep it? Leda was curious. She said you were the only person shown the hiding place. What a pity you are not a normal wife, Sarah, what a lot of trouble you could have saved me!'

Under his stare, Sarah's fear grew. She seemed to be coming to the reason for her fear, without being able to tell why she felt so afraid. She stared at Richard, her eyes so wide that the picture of him blurred, he seemed out of focus. He drank, finishing his drink in a long swallow, and came over to stand in front of her. 'Well, Sarah, going to tell me where?'

His cruel fingers found her breast and pinched and twisted viciously, while his other hand over her mouth stifled her cries. Then he moved his hand, and said, 'More of the same – or can you remember where the necklace is kept? Or would you care to have your face decorated a little – just here?' His cigarette on her cheek burned sharply, and she could smell her own flesh blistering. Shuddering and sick with pain she looked up into a face which wore no expression but determination.

'It is kept in an alcove cupboard in the wall of the inner room, behind the portrait. There is a locked panel and a locked steel door. Richard, what are you thinking of? Not stealing the Peacock?'

'You couldn't be more wrong. I am indeed thinking of stealing the Peacock. I have been trying to do just that for nearly a month, and a pretty penny it has cost me so far, too.'

'But it is as well known as the Koh-i-Noor. You could never sell it!'

'I wouldn't dream of selling it. It has other values. "Who wears the Peacock, holds the throne." Haven't you heard that? I know someone who would give a lot for the Peacock chain. Where is the key kept, Sarah?'

'He has it – Sher Khan.'

'What, all the time? No safe hiding place confided to you?'

'No, Richard, no. I have no idea where it is kept. Oh, for God's sake, stop!' Her trembling hands had no strength in them as she strove ineffectively to push him away. She was on the verge of unconsciousness when he let her go, and turned away to stare over the lake to the Rajaghar.

'The Peacock chain,' he said softly, 'the fabulous Peacock. I can pick up a lot of the pieces if I get hold of that.' He turned to look towards the island. 'I wonder when they moved it from the island. Did you know that it used to be kept, quite unguarded, under a loose stone in front of the statue of Kali in that shrine? Much more picturesque than keeping it in a cupboard, don't you think?' He did not wait for her to answer him, but continued, 'The Royal Beast is a very clever fellow. He moves the necklace in the nick of time, he sends his troops on leave just before harvest time – thereby ensuring that they are out of harm's way and no one can try and subvert them. No wonder Hardyal was in such a fury this afternoon.'

'Hardyal?' said Sarah with difficulty.

'Yes, Hardyal – the Contender. Sher Khan's cousin who has an eye to the Guddee. He has enough money to buy the whole state twice over, and yet he isn't content – or says he isn't – because he isn't the Ruler. He hoped to get Sher Khan embroiled in internal disturbances and, during the turmoil, step in and grab the throne – God, they are such fools, these people. He could have had a go at it any time during the war – the Royal Beast was off with his army – but Hardyal wouldn't even try, because the Peacock emblem wasn't in his possession and therefore, he says, the people wouldn't have listened to him.' His voice sank, and he sat thinking. Then, as if he had come to a decision about something long considered, he got up and poured out two more drinks and brought hers over to her. Sarah felt so ill that she could hardly hold her

182

glass, but she gulped the drink thirstily; her mouth and throat were dry and felt as if they were full of dust. The whisky was strong. Richard had not put enough water with it, it was fiery, and burned her mouth. By the time she realised that it tasted peculiar, it was too late, she had swallowed most of it.

Richard had turned away, and was staring over the lake to the Rajaghar again. 'Lights all over the place,' she heard him say, 'so the Royal Beast is still there.' His figure wavered in front of her, as if she were seeing him through water. Something he had said earlier came back to worry at her fogged mind. 'Richard,' – it was so difficult to speak, her tongue seemed too big for her mouth. 'Richard – the island. Did you kill Lalani?'

He turned and looked at her consideringly. 'Lalani? Was that her name? She was very foolish that girl, very stupid. Came with me to the island, pretending that she knew where the Peacock was – and expressed enormous surprise when she found it wasn't under the stone – and then gave herself away by trying to jump into the water and swim off. Pity about her, but she had to go. She would have told the Royal Beast everything if I had let her get away. Hardyal had her sons kidnapped, and then had to pay her husband a lot of money, and all for nothing. She was a pretty girl, too.' He sounded truly regretful, as he stood there sipping his drink and looking down at her.

As if someone had told her, Sarah knew that he was going to kill her. He was talking too much, too openly, hiding nothing. He could not intend to let her go, knowing all that she now knew.

Through the shadows she saw the glowing stub of his cigarette arch towards the fireplace.

'Well, another plan, another way – I shall make it yet. Now let us see about attracting the Royal Beast's attention.' He stood up, stretching. 'But first – how could I forget? First, our farewells, our long and tender, and possibly permanent farewells, my darling wife.'

As he bent over her, she tried again to hold him off, but

found to her horror that she could not move. Her brain still functioned and told her that she had been drugged. Richard was on her, and her helpless body was being mauled and used, while her mind stood aside, watching, untouched and unafraid. She heard him say, 'You have never been an enthusiastic partner, my dear, so really your present condition isn't noticeable,' and wondered if he would notice if she were dead. Suddenly, over his shoulder, she saw something move, and out of the shadows a pale face stared down at her, barely distinguishable, blurred – great tragic eyes looked into hers, stared for a second – and the face was gone. Who? The Begum Bianca, come back, and shocked at the happenings in her beautiful house? Wait for me, said Sarah's mind, wait for me, take me with you into your shadowland where you live. Wait for me! It will not be a long wait!

Richard had at last finished, was lifting off her, standing, and ordering his clothing, running a comb through his hair, whistling softly through his teeth as she had heard him do so many times before.

Now, Sarah's clear mind told her drugged body, now I think he is going to kill you. He looks quite mad. She waited, expecting a bullet, she could see his gun on the table beside her. But he did not shoot her. She could hear him moving about behind her, and then she heard him strike a match. His cigarette, in his ivory holder, was firmly clamped between his teeth when he came to her. He straightened her body on the sofa, and covered her with the light blanket she had been going to use for Julia. He tucked the blanket carefully round her, and bent over her, staring into her filmed eyes.

'What a pity about you, Sarah. It could have worked out so well. But a cold woman in a voluptuous body is really a dead loss, and you have never been very useful to me in any way. In fact, as I said. A dead loss. Yes, dead. But don't worry, you won't feel anything, the poison will see to that. Didn't you notice the stuff in the whisky? Well, goodbye, Sarah. I must go, and there are one or two things I have to do first.'

For a moment longer he stood, staring into her face, then he turned and left her to the shadows and the silence.

But the silence was not complete. There were little noises, cracklings and creakings, and a steady whisper like the sound of a tide coming in up a shingle beach.

Sarah lay quietly, unable to move a finger, while the noises grew, and became a steady roar, and she saw through blurring eyes the shadow of the flames on the wall, and knew what Richard had meant when he had said something about attracting attention.

Richard had set fire to the house.

22

On the other side of the lake, in the Rajaghar, the sunset was gilding the stone walls and laying long black shadows over the courtyards when the meeting broke up and the men came out. One of the Indians, his eyes deceptively sleepy in his soft, fat-jowled face, said 'Then, Sher Khan, this is your final decision?'

Sher Khan, leading the way out to where the long black cars were beginning to arrive, said firmly, 'Yes, Punditji. I have decided.'

'You have the right, of course. But you are making a mistake. You know Hardyal, the Claimant, is with us?'

'That is another excellent reason why I should not join you,' said Sher Khan, standing aside so that the other could enter his car.

'Your cousin is a man of wealth and influence. He sees our cause as just.'

'I have nothing against your cause, Punditji. You are welcome to it, and to the good opinion of my cousin. I do not change my allegiances so easily.'

'Oh, of course, you have English blood tainting your veins.'

'We are not discussing my ancestry. I repeat. I have nothing against your cause. All I want is to be allowed to run my own State and keep it as secure as it has always been.'

'You may have difficulty when your English friends leave.'

'I have never needed aid for my State from anyone – friend, or masquerading foe.' Sher Khan looked at the soft, flabby man and his eyes were not friendly. The man

186

shrugged.

'As you will. You could have kept your State, you know.'

'At what a price! No, thank you, Punditji. I *will* keep my State, but in my own way.' There was no reply this time. The big black cars roared away, disturbed water-birds rose from the lake and then settled again, like the dust in the courtyard. Sher Khan turned to go in, calling for his Dewan. 'Is everything ready? Good. I will collect the Peacock, and then we move – fast. Those men have not finished with me yet.' He turned, and the Dewan's hand came up with a revolver in it, as a figure ran out of the bushes on the drive.

'Maharaj – Ruler of the Hills! It is I, Ayesha, from the Ranighar. Heavenborn, there is bad trouble there –'

But Sher Khan had already looked over the lake, and was shouting to his men. There was a spreading rosy glow on the water, and he could see smoke rising in a straight dark column above the trees.

'Get over there fast –' To the Dewan he said, 'Kuda Bux, you go for the hills with some of my men, and wait for me at the first pass.'

He ran into the Rajaghar and came out seconds later and made for his jeep, calling over his shoulder to Ayesha to come with him. Seated in the jeep, driving like a madman towards the blaze he could now see clearly, he questioned Ayesha and got from her all the details he could.

'It is the devil's hand that I see in this. I must get away from here before the terrorist leaders come back for me. To hold me to ransom, to force their way on my State – either they will come, or the British Authorities will come asking for assistance which will involve the state – and I *will* keep my State free.' He was thinking aloud. Ayesha, hanging on in the seat beside him did not even hear what he was saying, until he asked, 'And the Khanum – where is she? My enemy knows me well. He knows that I could not leave her in any trouble or danger.'

They had arrived. His jeep screaming to a halt he

dashed up the steps and into the house.

The blaze was on the lake side of the house. The front was as yet untouched.

Sarah, in the Ranighar, had no way of knowing how much time had passed. The smoke in the room was thicker, and she had difficulty in breathing. The smoke smelt sweet and familiar, reminding her of days on trek, of camp fires, of happy childhood evenings in camp with her father. So long ago, and yet now those days seemed very close. Perhaps, she thought hazily, it was like drowning – all her past would pass before her eyes before she died in this burning, smoke-filled room.

Suddenly, over the crackling of the flames, she heard voices calling, distant at first, but coming nearer. Her efforts to call out tore her throat, and she choked miserably, achieving nothing but a faint croak. But it did not matter, she was found. Strong arms lifted her, there was a flurry of quick movement and then she was outside, gulping cool fresh air and gasping with pain as her lungs filled. Her sight cleared, and she saw Sher Khan's face above hers, his hands smoothed back her tangled hair. Sarah, her head raised from his arm with a superhuman effort, was mouthing at him and it was Ayesha who knew what she was trying to say.

'It is the children, Lord of the Hills. The Khanum asks for them.'

'Bring them.'

'Heavenborn, they are gone, also the Miss Sahiba. I saw the Colonel Sahib's driver take them away. Dip Chand says that he heard the order given to take them to Ratna, although the Colonel Sahib told the Khanum that he would send them to Ramchandra Hospital.'

'Ratna? A day's journey, and full of rioting mobs.' He turned to Sarah's terrified eyes.

'Be at peace, Khanum. I will send after them. My driver knows short ways. He will catch up with your family and bring them back. Do not be afraid. Ayesha, see to the Khanum.'

He went away quickly, and Ayesha took his place, kneeling by the bench on which Sarah lay. With gentle hands, she wrapped Sarah in a warm robe, pulling it closely round her. 'Khanum, I have hot tea here. Drink –'

The tea revived Sarah; she found that she could see more clearly, and feeling was coming back agonisingly into her arms and legs as Ayesha rubbed and kneaded with strong, clever fingers. She watched the saving of her possessions; men and women sprung, it seemed, out of the ground, were carrying furniture out of the house, and others had formed a chain and were passing vessels of water from one to another, up from the lake to the side of the Ranighar that was still burning fiercely. Beside her, she saw Julia's painted dressing-table. Julia!

'Oh, Ayesha, what has happened to my children and the Miss Sahiba?'

'I only know that the Old One is with them. She will not let harm come to them.'

But Ayah, however faithful and revered, was only an old woman and alone. Sarah thought with terror of Richard's lunatic eyes, and of the dark sneering face of his driver. Her thoughts were tormenting as she wondered what directions Richard had given to his driver. A tear slid slowly down her face, smarting on the place where Richard had burned her with his cigarette, and Ayesha saw the sore, and mopped gently at the little wound. Then she put her arm round Sarah and said, 'Khanum, now you must walk. I will help you, and Dip Chand. It will be hard, but it is necessary to get strength back into your legs. Call on your will, Khanum, and stand.'

Dip Chand on one side, Ayesha on the other, they got her to her feet. Her legs felt like boneless flesh. The sky whirled, and nausea dropped like a yellow veil between her and everything round her. Retching miserably, she hung helpless between them. It was like this that Sher Khan saw her as he came back, carrying her robe, and her handbag.

'Dip Chand, go and find some cases. Ayesha, go you

189

and help Dip Chand pack what is needful for the children and for the Khanum and the Miss Sahiba. Their rooms are not damaged. I will look after the Khanum.' He took her firmly into his grasp as he spoke. 'Come, Khanum, this will pass. Come with me to the water's edge, the air is fresher there.'

His arm strong behind her waist, he half carried her down to the lake and helped her to sit, sitting behind her so that she could lean on his shoulder. Once again he smoothed back her hair, and looked closely at her scratched, blistered face. Gentle as Ayesha, he pulled the robe closer round her, and feeling the warmth of the soft stuff against her flesh, Sarah realised that under the robe she wore nothing.

'My clothes?' Then she remembered Richard's cruel hands tearing at her garments and asked no more.

Sher Khan said, his voice very quiet and firm, 'You had nothing when we found you but a torn silk shirt and a blanket. Can you now tell me what happened here this evening?'

She could not see his face, it had grown too dark, but from his tone, this was not a request, it was an order. He reinforced his order by saying firmly, as she hesitated, 'It is necessary for me to know, Khanum. There will be great trouble over this, and we must be sure that the right people are punished.'

He was right. Leaning against his shoulder, she told him everything except that Digby had been to the Rajaghar. She found it impossible to suggest that she had, with Digby and Alastair, suspected him of treachery. He listened carefully to all that she had to say, and when she had finished, he said, half to himself, 'Thank God most of my men started on their way early. I think perhaps I am meant to be delayed here for some reason. To be accused of starting the riots, perhaps – I wonder. Well, we shall see.' As if he had come to a decision almost against his will, he stood up, saying, 'Khanum, rest here, for a little longer. I will send Ayesha to you, and when she comes, let her help you dress. I am going to take you away.'

'Away? Where? And my children? Julia?'

'Be still, Khanum. We are going to my valley, and the children and Miss Julia will be with us. Please do not distress yourself, Sarajan, trust me. Are you not my family? And your children are therefore as important to me as to you.'

'Sher Khan, you saved my life, of course I trust you. But my children! Where are they?'

'I promise you, they will be safe. Now, Sarajan, I said trust me!' He lifted her hand and kissed it, and went with no more words. Sarah lay, her thoughts moving like a kaleidoscope in her tired brain. She could not stop the terrible pictures that moved before her closed eyes, and presently found that she could no longer lie still, doing nothing. She forced herself to stand and walk a few steps, her head whirling, but relieved to find that she was growing steadier. She was standing, holding on to a tree, when Sher Khan came back with Ayesha.

'Here are some clothes for you, Khanum. When Ayesha has helped you to dress, do you think you can ride? I have sent my jeep to intercept the children and bring them to meet us, and my car is in Madore. In any case, after Safed we would have to ride, there is no motor road.'

Through her giddiness, Sarah managed to say that she would try to ride, and he went away, telling Ayesha to hurry. Ayesha had brought a towel, a basin of water and soap. She helped Sarah to wash, and combed and knotted up her hair. There was a long scratch down Sarah's face, as well as the cigarette blister, and her body, the white skin that Ayesha had so much admired, was blotched and streaked with bruises. The girl hissed through her teeth when, in the light of the hurricane lamp, she saw the marks. 'That man is a devil from hell.'

Sarah was too occupied in trying to keep herself upright and put on her clothes to reply. At last, exhausted, she was dressed, and Sher Khan came at Ayesha's call, with Dip Chand and a syce, leading two horses.

'You will ride Bedami, Khanum, she is very gentle.'

But it was immediately obvious that Sarah could not ride anything. As soon as he put her up, the giddy nausea intensified and she had to dismount. He stood, holding her, biting his lip.

'We must ride together,' he decided. 'Dip Chand, help the Khanum to stand, while I mount. Now, Khanum, put your foot on my foot. Can you? So, that is good.'

Sarah sat in front of him, leaning back, supported against his body. He held her firmly with his right arm, and turned to Dip Chand. 'You lead Bedami, and you, Ayesha, mount and lead the pack horse. We go.'

The servants mounted, and they all set off. The movement of the horse was terrible to Sarah at first. She dropped her head against Sher Khan's shoulder, and the darkness behind her closed eyelids reeled and staggered. Presently the air revived her, she began to feel better, and sat more upright.

'Good. You feel stronger, Sarajan. Then we will go more quickly. Do not fear, I will not let you fall.'

They seemed to move soundlessly at breathless speed through the darkness. The moon that had shone so brightly the night before was not yet risen and Sarah could not imagine how the horse could move so fast, so confidently. Shortly their progress became slower, they were climbing. The air grew keen and Sarah was glad of the sheepskin coat that Ayesha had made her wear. As they topped a steep incline and paused, the moon at last showed herself. Sarah caught her breath. Below them a valley lay, like a silver lake, and all round the mountains stood sentinel, their peaks as sharp and jagged as spears, shining and cold in the clear white light of the moon. Sher Khan heard her gasp, and said, 'Yes. Beautiful, is it not? We take the old road to Lambagh. We will thread our way through that barrier of mountains. You will understand, having seen this, why there is no motor road.'

23

The sky was growing lighter as they reached the first houses of Selimkot. Watchdogs gave warning of their approach, but no one challenged them. The houses were shuttered and silent. The whole village appeared to be deserted. They rode through the empty narrow street, their horses' hooves ringing on the stones, and stopped outside a house which was surrounded by a high white wall. There was a gate in the wall, and Sher Khan rapped smartly on it and shouted. There was an answering shout from within, and the gate was opened wide enough for a man with a lantern to slip through. His lantern threw a wavering light which showed nothing of his face, but did show he was holding a rifle. 'Who is it?' he said, holding the lantern high, 'who calls?'

'It is I, Sher Khan, you fool. If you hold the lantern so, had I been an enemy, what an excellent target you would have made, illuminated and ready for the killing. Where is the Hakim?'

'Oh, Maharaj! Wait, I open the gate.' He put down the lantern and the rifle, and fumbled at the gate, flinging it wide on creaking hinges, and standing back salaaming.

Sher Khan gave a growl of disgust. 'In the name of Allah the Merciful! What kind of a guard are you? Pick up that gun! Is there no one else here?'

'Maharaj, the Hakim is here, and two wounded English.'

Sarah's voice caught in her throat. 'Children. There are children?'

The man peered at her. 'There were children, but they have gone, I do not recall where.' Sarah could see that he was a very old man, the growing light showed his white hair and beard and skinny arms. Sher Khan dismounted, and reached up to lift Sarah down and set her on her feet, keeping his arm round her. They were standing in a small courtyard which was soon filled by Ayesha, her horse and the pack horse, Dip Chand and his horse and Bedami and the six soldiers who had ridden with them. When they were all inside, one of the soldiers closed the gate. There was a great deal of noise and shouted orders, and yet no one came. Sarah was shaking with apprehension.

'Now, fool,' said Sher Khan, 'where is the Hakim?'

'He is here, Maharaj, at the back, with the two English. Shall I call him?'

Sher Khan ignored him. Two of his men walked ahead of him, and holding Sarah, helping her to walk, Sher Khan went through an open door and into an enclosed back courtyard. There was a lighted window, and Sher Khan called, 'Andrej – are you there?'

A door opened, throwing a square of yellow light into the cold grey dawn light. A man in a white coat over native dress came out. He was very tall and thin, and he too carried a rifle.

'Andrej, is everything all right?'

'Yes, Highness, and if your companion is Madame Longman, I am to tell her that the children are safe, and that both patients are doing well.'

Sarah's knees almost gave way, her relief took all the strength from her legs. 'The doctor said "patients". Who is the second patient?'

'Me,' said Alastair from the verandah, where he stood looking down at her, his arm in a sling.

'Alastair! What on earth?' Sarah's voice was drowned by Sher Khan's astonished questions. Alastair came down into the courtyard and took Sarah's hand. 'Sarah, thank God you are safe. I didn't care for Julia's rather muddled description of what had happened to you after I left. Don't worry about the children. They've gone on to the next stopping place, with Kuda Bux and, of course,

194

the Ayah, and the doctor's wife. It was rather noisy here earlier on this evening.' He looked over at Sher Khan. 'I have a lot of questions to ask the Nawab, so would you go and see Julia, or she will fret herself into a fit?'

Sarah waited no longer; she turned and tried to walk up the steps to the verandah, staggered, and almost fell. The doctor and Alastair both moved quickly towards her but Sher Khan was there before them, and his arm supported her up the steps, and as she went through the door into the lighted room, the doctor asked if she had been wounded too.

'No. Worse. She was badly mauled and left tied in a burning house. When I got to her she was unconscious, but she revived in the fresh air, and was able to tell me what had happened. She thinks she was given some drug in a drink. I can imagine what the drug was – snake poison among other possibilities. Just enough to paralyse her, but for some fortunate reason it did not kill her.'

'But who? What on earth happened? Who did all this? Where did the poison come from?' Alastair stared in horror at Sher Khan, but it was the doctor who answered him.

'It is quite easy to get any type of poison here. There is an experimental chemical laboratory just outside Madore, where they are working on poisons and antidotes – including antidotes for snake bite and other poisons. If you have the antidotes, you also have the poisons. It is as simple as that.'

'As to the rest,' said Sher Khan, 'who but her natural protector treated her so brutally? Who else, but her husband? No doubt he got the poison from the lovely Leda. You will recall her, Alastair, you met her at the Rajaghar. She is, as I think you must know, Richard Longman's mistress, and she works at the chemical experimental laboratory. All so easy, no?'

He was interested to note that Alastair's face expressed horror but no surprise. He nodded grimly as Alastair said, 'That man is quite mad. We have been talking about him, Digby and I and one or two others. We reckon he is mad, and very dangerous.'

'Indeed. You thought so, but no one attempted to guard his wife. Not your business, no doubt. I do not always understand the English, even if I carry some of your chilled blood in my veins.' Sher Khan spoke in angry scorn, and turned away.

'We have not had very much time to do anything, and as you say – it was not our business. But other things that happened were.' Alastair sounded as angry as Sher Khan, who turned back to him, and saw that Alastair was very pale, and visibly in pain.

'I am sorry, Major Crombie. I should not have spoken like that. Now, can you tell me what happened to you? How did you get here? I know that you went to get a doctor for Miss Julia.' Alastair thought quickly. Sarah had obviously not mentioned the fact that he had really gone to report the sighting of the Nawab's men in the mountains. Therefore, he had better not mention it either until he saw which way things were going.

'I had just crossed the dry river bed about eight miles from Madore when I was stopped by a man in uniform. I thought he was one of the men from the camp in Namkum. I stopped, thinking he wanted a lift, but he called up several other men, and they hauled me out of the jeep. I tried to stay in the jeep and drive on, so the first chap shot me. The man in charge that was. He looked like a Tamil, or a Bengali, but I swear that the men with him were Punjabis. There was a furious argument, and I think that the leader was all for finishing me off, but the others were not keen on this, and thank God they won the argument. After a lot more talk, they loaded me back into the jeep, and drove me here. God knows why. They did not speak in front of me, and they've whipped the jeep.'

The doctor chimed in. 'Yes. They just threw the Major out of the jeep, shouted at the gatekeeper, and drove away. Of course their actions, after all the agitations of the news from Ratna about the riots there, started a panic. The villagers began to fire at anything that moved

196

once darkness fell; someone spread the story that Madore had fallen to the Hindus, and that they were coming to massacre all the Muslims here. Half the villagers ran away, and the rest are barricaded into their houses.'

'General upset and disorder, which is exactly what they wanted to cause,' said Sher Khan. 'Major Crombie, can you ride? Do you feel up to it?'

'Yes. I feel perfectly all right now, thanks to the good doctor here.'

The good doctor did not seem to agree with his patient. 'You can ride, certainly, but not for long. You lost a lot of blood, you know.'

Sher Khan nodded. 'Yes. I can see that he did. No, Major Crombie; you will have to come with us. I am returning to Lambagh, and I am taking the Khanum and her children and Miss Julia with me. This part of the world is not good for them at present. Do not worry. I will explain to your Colonel in due course.'

He walked away, leaving Alastair looking at the doctor in astonished disbelief. 'I would love to know how he is going to explain my departure into the hills without leave! Kidnapping perhaps?'

The doctor laughed. 'The Ruler is a law unto himself in these parts. You will find that he can arrange most things. It is in fact sensible that you do not go back. What good will you be with that arm? Relax, and enjoy your unexpected leave.'

'I do not think you can have met any of the senior officers at GHQ in Madore, Doctor. However, there seems very little that I can do, so I will take your advice. Relax and enjoy.'

Sarah had found Julia lying, her arm in plaster, in a clean comfortable bed. The girl herself, however, looked anything but comfortable. She burst into tears when she saw Sarah, and clung to her, and it was some minutes before Sarah could quieten her. At last she stopped crying, blew her nose, and apologised.

'Don't be silly, Julie, it must have been terrifying for you, not knowing where you were going, or what was happening. But tell me quickly, the children are all right?'

'Yes, perfectly. Ayah was wonderful with them. She was calm and paid no attention to the things that Richard's driver said. I think he was being very rude to Ayah, he was horrible, and I can't think why Richard sent us away with him. Anyway, when some men in uniform stopped him, by driving a jeep across the road in front of him, he pulled up quickly enough, and then two of them took him away, and we were brought here. Then of course, there was shooting here – and the doctor's wife, and the Ruler's Dewan, and the children went off at once, in those carrying-chairs, to the next stage. Sarah, I don't understand, where are we going?'

'To the valley. Lambagh. The Ruler's State of Lambagh.' Sarah spoke as if she was in some other age, in a day when it was perfectly normal for a family to set off by road for a valley set high among the mountains, a valley ruled by a powerful Prince. Julia's astonished face brought her back to the present.

'As long as the children are safe, then everything is fine, Julia. We can't stay in the Ranighar; it was set on fire, and quite a lot of the roof and several of the rooms were damaged.'

'Fire? How? And why did you take so long to come? Where is Richard? Is he coming too?'

'No. He went – he had to go back to Madore.'

'Oh dear, into those riots they were talking about? Poor Richard, how awful, I do hope he is safe. You heard what happened to Alastair? Wasn't it awful! But I am so glad he is with us. Sarah, you look terrible! What is it? And what are those marks on your face?'

'Nothing. I am just very tired. I had a fall. It was nothing.' Sarah was so relieved that Julia herself was still overtired and shocked and questioned her no further, but fell asleep before the doctor came in and demanded to examine Sarah. He felt her pulse, and looked at the pupils of her eyes, and tested her reflexes, and announced that the drug was wearing off. 'You will be

198

perfectly all right shortly, though a little stiff still tomorrow. The wound on your cheek is only superficial, though very painful, I can see. But you are fortunate. It will leave no scar. You and Miss Longman will be able to continue the journey in dandies.'

Ayesha then came in with a tray of tea. Sarah sat and drank tea thirstily, and watched Julia wake, and saw Alastair pour tea out for her and give it to her with his one good arm. They seemed very close; both being in pain and separated from everything they knew had speeded their friendship further along the road to love, she thought. She heard Sher Khan calling outside. It was time to go on with this strange journey.

Lying in her white canvas dandy, which was little more than a long carrying-chair with a hood, she felt isolated and sad as she lurched and jogged up the rough mountain paths. It was full daylight now and the scenery was magnificent, breathtaking mountains and valleys, and far glimpses of the plains, patterned like an embroidered map, brown and green and gold, veined with turquoise where the rivers ran. But she took no pleasure in the view. Ahead, she could see Julia's dandy, a more elaborate affair than hers, needing four men to carry it. Beside the dandy rode Alastair, his head turning constantly towards Julia. How fortunate they were, she thought, to be at the beginning of their story. Nothing really mattered to Julia at the moment – her broken arm, the riots, this journey, all were part of a magnificent adventure because Alastair was with her. There is no one any more for me, thought Sarah – nothing will ever soften the hard edges of life for me, no lover, no friend. From now on I shall have to face reality, cold and without any glamour to pull a veil over the harshness of everyday life. She felt very sorry for herself, and then was ashamed. How could she be so stupid! After all, thank God, the children were safe.

Sher Khan, riding up, saw her face and was alarmed. 'Khanum! Are you ill? Is the dandy not steady?'

Sarah made a sudden decision. 'Sher Khan, I feel better. I regret I have troubled you so much. May I ride now? Just for a little?'

'Khanum, of course you may, if you feel you are well enough. Oh, Dip Chand! Bring Bedami.'

He surrounded Sarah with attention, tightened her horse's girth himself, and gave her his linked hands to mount from. Mounted, she felt momentarily giddy again. His hands on her knee and waist were steady and supporting. 'Are you sure you are able to ride?'

She took up the reins, nodding. 'Yes. May I ride with you?' His flashing smile was her answer. He rode ahead of her, down the line of the escort, to the head of the cavalcade. Alastair and Julia were talking, and did not see them pass. Sarah made a face at Sher Khan, and he laughed. 'Love! It makes people deaf and blind to everything but the beloved,' he said.

'Young love, first love, maybe.'

'But Khanum, each love is the first love!' He was laughing, but his eyes were saying something else. Her lonely feelings not yet forgotten, she was grateful for his interest. She met his eyes and smiled in return, and his laughter stopped. 'Khanum, do not smile so at me, do not promise with your eyes. I keep my promises, and expect others to keep theirs.'

Sarah answered steadily, 'If I make a promise, I keep it, Sher Khan. But I make very few promises.' She looked away from him, saying, 'How long before we catch up with Ayah and the children?'

'By evening, certainly.'

'Sher Khan, what is happening? Is this a big uprising?'

'Who can say? As you know, I did not go into Madore. But my men, who went as far as the river, say that part of the walled city was burning, and they heard firing. Do not fret. You will be safe enough in Lambagh.'

'Yes, I am sure we will. But how long will we stay there?'

'As long as is needful. You have not reached Lambagh, and you are already speaking of leaving?'

Sarah shook her head. 'I only want to know what is

happening – if the newspapers make a big story out of the rioting in Madore, my mother and father will be worried. I should get word to them.'

'We are not savages in Lambagh State! There is a Post Office, and a dak runner goes down to Faridkote once a week – also we can send a wireless message to Madore, if you wish.' Sarah began to feel she was being foolish under Sher Khan's quizzical gaze.

It was a clear day and they made good time, stopping three times for tea and fruit. Sarah began to stare ahead as she rode, hoping to see the children's *dhoolie* and escort, but hours went by and there was no one in sight. Doctor Andrej came up and rode beside her. 'Katya will have made them hurry. She does not like to waste time on the road. Do not worry, Madame Longman, no harm will come to your children.' Sarah had to be content.

Sher Khan rode to the rear of the cavalcade, and came back to say, 'One of the pack horses has a bad saddle sore, the load should be shifted and the sore treated. Is there time?'

The doctor studied the sky and Sher Khan's face, and said, 'I imagine there is time. I will go and see if there is anything I can do.' He rode off smiling.

'Who is the Doctor?'

'Andrej Bukov? He is a White Russian. He came into Lambagh State about twenty years ago, with Katya, his wife. They have lived here ever since. He is a good man, and a very good doctor. He even knows a little about the ailments of the horse.' Sarah was suddenly convinced that Bukov had gone back because Sher Khan wanted to be alone with her. Her swift sidelong glance at him found him looking at her. He burst out laughing, and after a moment's surprise she laughed with him. 'He has no tact, the good doctor. On such a day, in such company, I do not need another man to share my companion. Let him go and talk to the Major.'

'That is unkind.'

'No, it is not. They have had hours together. I have had very little of your company. I want to talk to you

201

about many things.'

Sarah found him a fascinating companion. He reminded her of a boy going home, he was so delighted to be on the way to Lambagh. 'You will love the place,' he told her. 'It is the most beautiful place in the world. It has everything – lakes, mountains, rivers, and such flowers. The people are simple people – kind, cheerful, brave. They are wonderful soldiers.'

'You have a large army?'

'Yes. It is one of the largest private armies in India, my State Force.' He said it matter of factly, but his pride was obvious. 'We fought in the desert, from the beginning. We have two VCs. And now – now the war is over, and Britain is deserting her friends. Letting us all fall in the dust.'

'India has been demanding her independence for years.'

'No!' he said firmly. 'No. Not all of us want that kind of independence, to be ruled by a bunch of crooked, time-serving politicians. We have many splendid men, who would lead us well, but Britain does not wish to take the time to find them, to listen to them. She has not safe-guarded the Native Princes at all, in spite of their long loyalty, and their services through two world wars. No. We are being deserted, thrown to the dogs. What do you think will happen to the Princes when India is left to the Congress Wallahs? They are sitting waiting for our downfall, like vultures waiting beside a dying tiger.' His voice was low and angry. 'We can no longer trust to Britain. We must make our own arrangements.'

Sarah found herself afraid of the leashed power beside her. The man had become an angry stranger, and she and her family were entirely in his hands. She half turned her head, almost calling out to Julia and Alastair. Her movement jerked him out of his unhappy thoughts; he looked at her, and saw the fear on her face. Instantly he leaned to her, and covered her hands on her reins with one of his own. 'Do not look at me in fear! Would I harm one hair of your head? Khanum, this is love that you have beside you, a man so deep in love that he does none of the things he should do, but is idling here, talking to his beloved, and she gives him nothing but big eyes, and a frightened face! Sarajan, beloved Sarah, smile at me, tell me you know of my love, and that you feel love for me – Sarah!'

Sarah gasped at the heat and strength that he exuded as he leaned close, and she instinctively drew rein. With a muffled exclamation, he pulled her out of her saddle into his arms, and touching heels to his horse lifted it into a gallop, so that the company was left far behind and they were alone in the rush of air and swift movement. She could, for the moment, think of nothing but the ride, feel nothing but the air, his hard arms, and the steady drum of his heart under her head. Slowly a sort of unreasoning joy filled her, a crazy irresponsible pleasure. Let this ride go on for ever, like this, here was safety and peace, here in this circle – his arms, the air and the solitude.

But he drew rein at last, and as she pushed back her heavy tangled hair, there were other thoughts. Julia and Alastair – this, even their self-preoccupation would not be proof against. She reminded herself that she was not a girl to be swept off her feet, she was a woman with responsibilities.

Sher Khan had dismounted and, leaning against the horse, was watching her as she struggled with her hair, a half smile on his mouth. He looked so handsome, his attraction for her was suddenly so strong, that she drew a deep breath, trying to steady herself.

'Leave all that beautiful hair to fall to your waist. You look more beautiful than ever thus. Smile at me, Khanum – tell me you are no longer afraid of me.'

'I am not afraid,' said Sarah, and was appalled to hear how unsteady her voice sounded.

'Oh, Sarajan – come, get down from that animal! Your voice tells me all I need to hear. Come into my arms, kiss me!' His voice was triumphant, he was laughing with pleasure, he *knows* thought Sarah. She forced her voice to calmness. 'Sher Khan, please – there can be nothing like this between us! You know that. I am a married woman –.'

'Such a marriage! Do not speak to me of loyalty to such a man. He was almost your murderer!'

'Even so, I am still married. There are also other reasons.'

'Such as, for instance? Our different races? Your blood is the same as mine, Khanum, a richer brew than the pure English. Your children? They are now in my state, safe – no thanks to their father! They are your children, they are beautiful, and I love them. What else? Why do you waste precious time? The others will catch up with us soon, and even mad with love as I am, I should find it hard to make love to you before my entire entourage.'

'Thank God for that at any rate,' said Sarah, laughing in spite of herself, clinging to the pommel of his saddle against the pull of his importunate hands.

'Ho! You laugh, Khanum. Well, that is better than making those big terrified eyes.' His voice dropped. 'Never, Khanum, never look at me with fear. It kills me.'

He looked up at her, his whole face alight, every feature speaking of his love. She wavered, and then from behind heard the sound of the others.

'It is too late to continue our discussion now. They are almost here, alas Sarajan, for I think I saw victory almost in reach. Never mind, there are other days. But now –' With an adroit twist he loosened her grip and she fell into his arms. He kissed her slowly and with an experienced enjoyment that brought all the blood in her body to a sort of thundering turmoil. Then he put her back in the saddle and stood, holding the bridle of the horse and pointing out distant peaks, naming each one to her, while she tried to get her breath and order her face and hair before the others came up. At the last minute she whispered, 'You look *smug*,' and with a quick side glance he said 'I have good reason – and you? You look beautiful.'

Dip Chand led up Bedami, Sarah dismounted from Sher Khan's horse, and was given a leg up into her own saddle and, unbelieving, saw that Alastair and Julia were still deep in conversation and had noticed nothing. Others had. Several of the escort had broad smiles on their faces, but they were neither unpleasant smiles nor did they express disrespect. They were smiling with pleasure. It was right that their Ruler, a young strong man, should have chosen a beautiful woman for his pleasure. Their eyes were full of flattering admiration when they looked at her. Hot cheeked, her own eyes looking firmly at her horse's ears, she rode off again. Sher Khan was shaking with laughter.

As the day wore on, and the cavalcade stopped to rest, Julia spoke with Sarah. 'Sarah, aren't you tired? You've been riding for hours. I think Alastair is getting tired.'

'Julia! What an idiot I am! Alastair, you must take my dandy, I won't be using it. Just ride in it long enough to have a rest.' At first Alastair wouldn't hear of it, but he looked white and drawn, and when Doctor Bukov saw him, he added his commands to Sarah's and Julia's requests. 'Major Crombie, you must rest, otherwise you will be unable to do any riding at all.'

Alastair was glad to give in and climb into the dandy. 'I must say,' he said, leaning back with closed eyes, 'it is very good to sit on something soft. Very luxurious. I feel exactly like Cleopatra being carried in Caesar's triumph.' At that moment the two carriers raised their burden and started to walk at their usual fast uneven pace. Alastair put out his head. 'I now feel quite unlike Cleopatra. I feel seasick. I see why you prefer riding, Sarah.'

'Never mind, Alastair, stick it – then you will be able to ride tomorrow.'

'I doubt very much if I shall ride again after a spell of this. Nausea will be my permanent companion. Give my greetings to Julia, and tell her I died thinking of her, will you?'

Sarah rode away, laughing, to where Sher Khan waited for her. They rode together, talking easily, all restraint gone; they were close, and happy.

24

The sun set, darkness closed in, and the company rode more slowly, picking their way along the rocky path, the horses moving surefootedly, the carrying coolies slowing to a walk. Sher Khan, riding ahead of Sarah, dropped back to make sure she was not too tired.

'No, I am well. But I wish we could come up with the children.'

'Sarajan, they are now in bed in the Winter Palace. Please do not worry. They are perfectly safe. You trust me now, surely?'

'Sher Khan, you know I do. But they are my children, I long to see them.'

'I know. But you distress yourself too much. They travel light, so are faster than we are. They have already arrived and are safely asleep. See – the moon is rising. Now we start to climb. There, ahead, is the first pass. The peak of Tara Devi is above us. You will see how beautiful this is soon.'

They took a long lifting path up the slopes of Tara Devi. The valley and the shadowy forest fell away, and the ridged mountains came into view, the bare rocky hillside beautiful and strange under the light of the newly risen moon.

'Beautiful, no?'

'Yes – beautiful.'

Their voices were hushed. The climbing path narrowed, it was impossible to ride side by side. Sher Khan dismounted and came to Sarah. 'Khanum, you should ride with me, I am worried that you will fall, you are very tired.'

'But climbing like this – my weight will be too much for your animal.'

'Too much for Rustom? Never. Come, Khanum.'

Once again she was settled before him, the now familiar band of his arm held her steady and her head fell back into place on his shoulder. She felt him give a deep sigh, and then they rode on together.

She never forgot that night ride. There were clouds that drifted over the moon, so that the mountains were first seen clear and barbaric, the peaks a hedge of jagged silver, then clouded and softened, a strange misty landscape in which they seemed the only moving things. The rest of the company had fallen into silence, and they settled into a slow upward progress, at walking pace, up and up. Rustom moved easily, carrying her extra weight with no apparent discomfort. As they climbed, it grew colder, and the air seemed to sparkle. 'Like drinking champagne,' Sarah said, half whispering.

He heard her, and said, 'We will drink champagne together tonight you and I.'

'And Julia and Alastair?'

'Oh, my Queen! If you want me to provide champagne for the whole of this band, I will do so – say but a word.'

'I cannot speak. Look at that river, like burning silver on the mountain. I can hear it rushing, listen.'

'That is the Kanti, it runs through the valley, and you will be beside it soon.'

They mounted a steep incline, the road curved, with a sheer fall on one side, and then the mountains seemed to draw aside, and they looked down to a deep valley lost in shadows, where lights twinkled far below.

'Faridkote. We will be there by midnight, in the House of Paradise. I wish we could have approached by daylight, it is such a beautiful valley. I will bring you up here one day, so that you can see for yourself.'

'I can see now. It is fabulous by moonlight, look at that – white houses! And there, far ahead, that silver – is that a lake?'

'That is where we are going tomorrow, that is my

house, my home, the place where I was born.'

A man of the escort rode up, saluted and asked a question, to which Sher Khan nodded. The man went out on a rock that seemed to hang dizzily over the valley and, hand to mouth, sent a long high call out into the misty night. His voice resounded among the rocks, high, eerie. Far away, they heard the cry repeated like an echo.

'Was that an echo?'

'No, that is the watchman at Lungri, the first village. They know we are coming now.'

'Is this pass guarded?'

'Yes, indeed. You will see the men of the garrison in a minute.'

They climbed on, rounded a steep outcrop, and rode past a small stone hut, where lamplight shone on smartly saluting soldiers. Sher Khan drew rein to speak to the Guard Commander, then they rode on, the lights of the post out of sight immediately, as the path turned downwards. They dropped into the valley, moving from the heights, it seemed, as easily as bathers diving into a lake. On the floor of the valley it was darker; Sarah could hear the voice of the river but could not see it. She smelled pine and fern, and the horse trod easily and softly moving between dark trees.

They rounded a corner and saw lights ahead, a cluster of lights moving. Sher Khan drew rein. 'These are my people coming, Khanum, to welcome us and light our way. They are simple people, they will think nothing but good, but if you wish, you may ride alone.'

Something in his voice made Sarah say 'I am very well here.' She felt his arm tighten. He dropped his cheek to her head for a moment, then collected his horse, kicked him into a canter, and in a minute, from quiet darkness they were surrounded by shouting men holding torches, men who seemed delirious with joy. Hands reached up, eyes and teeth sparkled in torchlight – somewhere someone was beating a drum, and to Sarah's delighted astonishment she heard a bugle bravely essaying 'Highland Laddie'.

The crowds parted at a shout from Sher Khan, and they rode on, torches on either side lighting their way. The torches stopped at a gate in a white wall, and Sher Khan dismounted and held up his arms to her. As she slid into them, he leaned his head close to say, 'Khanum, the ride of my life.' The crowding men laughed and shouted, the gate swung open, and she went in, followed by the coolies carrying Julia's dandy. Dip Chand was there, calling out orders. There was thick turf under her feet, and there was a smell of roses.

Ahead was a lamp-lit verandah and on the steps, peering under her raised hand, was Ayah. Sarah almost fell into her welcoming arms. 'Ah, Sarajan, thanks be to God you are alive and well. Yes, yes, the children are well and asleep – or they were!'

A little nightgowned figure hurtled down the verandah. 'Mummy! You are a very naughty lady! Where have you been these long times? We've got a palace, and a tame cheetah, and four *bulbuls*, and Hans doesn't at all care for the cheetah. *Where* is the Bonnie bird?' Horrors! Kissing her daughter, Sarah foresaw tears and heartbreak. But Sher Khan at her elbow swung Penelope up into his arms.

'Oh, Moon of the Palace, how do you?'

'I do very well. Put me down, Nawab Sahib. You must not pick ladies up in their nightdresses.'

'Must I not? Oh, how sad!'

Penelope returned to the attack. 'Where *is* Bonnie Prince Charlie?'

Swiftly, Sher Khan knelt beside her. 'Thy parrot, oh Moon, is at home. He does not like riding.'

'He doesn't at all mind riding – he likes it.' Penelope's lower lip began to stick out dangerously.

'Moon of the Palace, someone had to stay to guard the house. So he, being a brave prince among parrots, stayed. However, if it will please you, I will send for him and bring him here – how about that, oh Moon of Joy?'

'Very well,' conceded Penelope, after a silent struggle with her feelings. 'But don't forget.'

'My precious Moon, I will not forget. Where does your beauty sleep tonight?'

'In a little bed. It is red, and has pictures of the Bonnie bird, and his brothers and sisters, all over it. Now, where is my aunt?'

'For heaven's sake!' said Alastair watching the progress of Sher Khan carrying Penelope down the steps to Julia's dandy, 'she has certainly tamed the Royal Beast. Julia incidentally is sound asleep. She is going to be furious that she missed our dramatic arrival.'

Julia, awakening to Penelope's kisses, could not be furious about anything. Presently they were all seated inside in a big room, where a fire crackled and leapt to take the cold from the air. A tray of glasses was brought in. 'Champagne *again*,' marvelled Julia.

'Julia, how blasé can you get?'

'I wasn't being blasé,' said Julia. 'I was being astonished.' She gave Alastair a wounded look that brought him to his knees beside her.

'Angel, of course you weren't being blasé – give me your little slipper so that I can drink your health.'

'You can't have her little slipper – her feet is all bare,' said Penelope. 'But you can have my little slipper, it is red, and it has a mouse's head – see?' She watched while Alastair poured some wine into her slipper and drank from it. 'Ugh, it's all *wet*,' she discovered afterwards.

'Yes, and my champagne was all woolly. Ah well, you can't have everything, can you?'

'Alastair, why are you and my aunt both wearing scarves on your arms?'

'Well, it is a long story.'

'Well, then, tell it.'

'Oh, well, you see, Julia started a fashion, and I followed it.'

'Because you like her?'

'Yes. Because I like her. Very much.'

Penelope found that the centre of interest had shifted. She made for Sher Khan, who had just come in. 'I am exhausted, extremely,' she said regally. 'Carry me to my little bed.'

'Please,' said Sarah firmly, but Penelope had the last word.

'Carry me to my red bed, Nawab Sahib, and please do not forget the Bonnie bird.'

Sher Khan lifted her, and held her close. 'Oh, Moon of Delight, I will forget nothing,' he promised, and carried her out of the room and down the passage. He stayed to watch her tucked into bed, asleep in the small red four-poster before her mother had finished arranging the bedclothes. David was sleeping soundly, his arms tossed up above his head, his lashes black on an apricot cheek. Ayah lowered the oil lamp, and they all three crept out.

'They are so beautiful, so charming, those little ones of yours.' In the lamplight his eyes were gentle, all the laughter gone from his expression. 'Did you see, she did not even ask for her father? It is said that children know. I am so happy that you are all safely here, in my State.'

Seated before the fire, long legs stretched out, a glass in his hand, Sher Khan was relaxed and easy, a delightful host, a man at home. Looking at him from time to time, Sarah found him charming. Her quickened blood told her that this was no casual interest. She found herself seeking his eyes, and her heart beat faster each time he looked at her. Exhaustion lowered her guard, and he knew it – all his conversation and his attention were directed at her.

Food was brought in on a trolley and they ate where they sat, plates on their knees. Then, with big cups of beautiful coffee, they stayed in front of the fire, half asleep, still feeling the swing and sway of the journey. Sarah roused herself at last. 'Julie! For heaven's sake, do you know what time it is? Nearly two! Come along, I'm sure the doctor would not approve of this. Incidentally, where is the doctor? How awful, I forgot all about him in all the excitement of getting here.'

'He is with his wife in their rooms on the other side of the courtyard. If you want him, I will have him called.'

'No, no, I am sure we are all well enough to get

211

ourselves to bed. Are you all right, Julia?'

'Miss Julia, if you feel you cannot walk, I will carry you to bed.'

Before Julia could thank Sher Khan and refuse his offer, Alastair was on his feet. 'I will carry Julia. You have already carried one lady to bed, Nawab Sahib – now it is my turn.'

'*Don't* be ridiculous, Alastair. I can walk. And in any case, you could not carry me with that arm.'

'Scorned,' mourned Alastair sadly. 'Poor me. Scorned. Would you care to carry me instead? No? Oh well then, Julia, take my arm. We can lean on each other down the passage.'

Their departure left Sher Khan and Sarah alone. 'Bird of my heart – I dare not carry you to bed, I would not be able to leave you. But one day soon –' His eyes brought the blood flaming to her cheeks and, watching her, he took her hand and kissed it. 'Go away, Khanum, go to bed and sleep. Tomorrow is another day, and I shall see you in it. Good night.'

Sarah's room opened on to a balcony, and beneath it she heard the river. Ayesha came in, and helped her undress, but Sarah was too tired for the nightly hair-brushing ritual. She fell on to her bed and, like Penelope, was sound asleep before Ayesha had covered her and left the room.

25

Sarah awoke, stiff and aching; she felt all her bones had been broken. But after a hot bath, and Ayesha's skilful and gentle massage, she felt much better. She found the others seated round an enormous oval dining table, in a room opening off the drawing room. The chair at the head of the table was vacant, and Dip Chand pulled out a chair for her at the opposite end. Alastair was arguing fiercely with the doctor about riding. The small woman in silk robes was Mrs Bukov.

She smiled at Sarah, and introduced herself. 'I am Katya Bukova. How are you?' This appeared to be all the English she knew. She had very Chinese features, her hair was raven black, and in her brilliant blue and green silks she was like a gorgeous tropical bird. She talked to Sarah in Urdu. 'I have seen a picture of a woman who is so like to you, she is your twin – the dancing girl who saved the Begum Sara.'

'She was my grandmother,' said Sarah, certain that this was already known to this gaudy little woman. The narrow black eyes watching her sparkled. 'Yes, of course! Now I recall, the beautiful grand-daughter who inherited everything from her grandmother – looks, charm and money. You are very rich?' Sarah found that she could not take offence, this was such a smiling honest creature.

She laughed and said 'I have enough.'

'That is good. To be beautiful and poor, is terrible. But beautiful and rich – ah, what happiness! And also the fortunate mother of beautiful children. You are rich in everything. I like to see this. Like a storyteller's

213

Princess, you seem.'

Sarah was laughing when Sher Khan, his eyes seeking her, came in. He came down the room to where she was sitting. 'Khanum – how are you? I heard your laughter, how wonderful that was, first thing in the morning! You slept well, I can see.' Singled out so publicly, conscious of the others listening, and of Mrs Bukov's bright glance, Sarah was embarrassed.

'Yes, thank you, Sher Khan. I am stiff of course – I had not ridden for so long.'

'That will soon go. Is everybody rested? That is good.' He seated himself at the head of the table, opposite Sarah, and began to eat with enjoyment. 'I am glad you had good sleep on your first night in Lambagh Valley. Tonight you will sleep better still.'

'That sounds ominous, Nawab Sahib! If I sleep any better tonight than I did last night, I shall be dead!'

'Please, Major Crombie! Do not say such a thing! No, no, I mean you will sleep better because you will be in my proper home in Lambagh – on Tara Lake, in Lamba village, at the head of this valley.'

'You mean we travel again today?' Julia looked, and sounded, horrified.

'Oh, but only a short, gentle journey. No climbing, and no hurry – a walk through flowering meadows. You will enjoy it, I promise you. We will picnic on the way, and by teatime we will be home. And you, Miss Julia, do not frown! You will ride in a queen's palanquin, very beautiful. Major Crombie and the Khanum can take it in turns to share it with you. It will be a royal progress.'

There was no more to be said. Everything had been packed while they breakfasted. Ayah and the children had already started. Out in the courtyard, Mrs Bukov stepped nimbly into a carrying-chair, raised a splendid scarlet parasol, and bobbed off in the wake of the children's more sober *dhoolie*. Julia's equipage was a magnificent wood and basketwork palanquin, cushioned and hooded, with eight carriers. Sher Khan handed her in, and then turned to Sarah.

'Do you ride, Khanum, or will you be carried?' In spite of stiff muscles, Sarah longed to ride.

Julia made the decision for her by saying, 'Oh Sarah, do come with me, I haven't seen you to talk to since all this began.'

If Sher Khan was disappointed, he hid it. He helped Sarah into the palanquin's rather musty splendour, and said to her uplifted eyes, 'Khanum, Bedami is being led behind you. When you are ready to ride, tell the *jimpanis*. In any case, Major Crombie should not ride for too long, I think.'

The movement of the palanquin was smooth. 'Imagine – eight carriers for us! Sarah, this is an experience, isn't it? Tell me now, everything that happened after I drove away. I was so dopey that I did not realise that you and Richard were not with me until the Ruler's men stopped the jeep.'

'When was that?'

'Well, I can't be sure of time, but I think it was about an hour after we left you. These men stopped the jeep and took the driver away, and a new driver took us on. He was a much better driver than Richard's driver, and he was polite too. I didn't like that little dark driver of Richard's at all, and Ayah obviously hated him. She was frightened of him, I could see. But never mind that now. What happened to you? How did you come?'

'I rode. There was no other transport, and anyway we came across country, over some mountain passes.'

'Goodness, no wonder you are so stiff. But what happened first?'

'Oh, there was trouble – and someone tried to burn the house down. I must tell you, Julie, poor Pyari Lal is dead. He was – well, he got killed in the general rumpus. I was lucky, because Sher Khan saw the flames and came in the nick of time – like the American Cavalry again.'

'Oh, but poor Pyari Lal – how awful! But this thing about the American Cavalry, Sarah. What do you mean?' Safely diverted, Julia talked on, while Sarah thought about her dead servant, known to her since he was a small boy, and wondered how long it would be before Julia began to ask questions about Richard. She was glad to see the syce bringing Bedami up alongside, she was tired of the musty smell of the old palanquin and longed for fresh air and movement. So did Julia. She looked wistfully after Sarah's vanishing figure, and lay back, resigning herself to loneliness and boredom. But the carriers had stopped again – they lowered the palanquin and Alastair appeared on foot beside it.

'Julia, may I share your palanquin? My God, what on earth does that sound like! My old father must be turning in his grave. Try and imagine you are Cleopatra, and I am Marc Antony, wounded in battle for your sake – and move your lovely opulent hips a little to the left so that I can sink down in lustful luxury beside you. There. No good refusing to hold my hand now. Damn it, we're almost in a double bed together as it is!'

Sarah, riding back to check that Julia was all right, found them playing poker with a pack of cards borrowed from the doctor, and rode off again, relieved, to join Sher Khan. Alastair watched her go, frowning a little. 'Poor old Digby, the Royal Beast has certainly put his nose out of joint!'

Julia followed his eyes, and primmed her mouth. 'I should have thought you would say "Poor Richard". After all, he is her husband, not Digby.'

'What a husband, my God!'

'And he is also my brother,' said Julia, getting very pink.

'Yes, I know. Sorry, Julia.'

'Well, I should think so. Why don't you like Richard, Alastair?'

Alastair looked at her thoughtfully. 'Julia, may I talk to you seriously?' It is time, he thought, looking at her downcast face, it is high time someone put you in the picture. Otherwise you are going to be most bitterly disillusioned. He set out for her, in quiet incisive

216

phrases, exactly what Richard's activities had been, not only within his marriage, but during the last few weeks. He hesitated to tell her that her brother had tried to kill Sarah, but her mutinous face and disbelieving eyes forced him on. He added for good measure his own suspicions about Richard's loyalty.

When he finished, Julia said nothing for a few minutes. He saw that her face was very white and serious, and realised what this could mean for them both. He was not only attracted to her, it was a deeper feeling. He knew suddenly that he loved her, that she was the girl he wanted to marry, the one who would complete his life. Her extreme loyalty, her simple, trusting, loving nature were not faults. He took her hand, and found it was very cold. She faced him, and he saw that her young face had taken on dignity and beauty. Julia always looked pretty and childlike. Now she looked like a woman.

'Alastair, I know Richard. He has lived for the Army since he could think. He could no more be disloyal than – than I would have thought you could!' He noticed that she was not attempting to deny her brother's cruelty and unfaithfulness to Sarah.

'Darling Julia, I should not have discussed him with you, but I did not want you to hear about him from anyone else. But don't you see? Because he loves the Army so much, he might have got mixed up in this intercommunal business. When Britain hands over, heaven knows what will happen to the Indian Army. There will not be room for all of us.' It was no good talking, he was only upsetting her. 'Well, Julie, I'll say no more. Still friends?'

'Still friends,' she said slowly, and her eyes filled with tears. They had, she thought sadly, so nearly been more than friends. But she knew that for both of them there had been a break in their happy relationship. Her arm throbbed, as if her sore heart was affecting it. Alastair sat silent beside her, feeling as wretched as she did. The *jimpanis* ran on tirelessly, the scenery unrolled before

217

them, each turn of the road showing more beauty. It could have been empty desert; they saw none of it.

Sarah rode far ahead, stiffness forgotten, enjoying the beautiful ride, the clear blowing air, the mountains framing the golden meadows, and the streams of the valley. They followed the largest of the streams. Peacefully it meandered, almost silent except when the passage of the water was broken by great rocks, where water-birds rested. Sher Khan, riding beside her, his eyes watching her face, made all her pleasure keener.

The valley widened as they rode, green fields spread out on each side, sloping gently up to tree-covered summits. Behind, the mountains towered, all snow-capped and appearing to stretch, range after range, as far as the eye could see. The air was fresh and sunlight sparkled on streams that webbed down the green slopes and joined the river Kanti, that ran alongside the path.

The people of this valley lived in small slate-roofed white houses, clustered together into villages of twenty or so dwellings. The villages were not walled; the security of the land seemed assured. Alastair, noting that almost all the male population under a certain age seemed to wear the State Forces uniform, wondered if that was why. It was a prosperous valley, with fat cattle and sheep and fields of barley and maize. Every village that they rode through turned out to welcome their Ruler, and the welcome was real; faces smiled with pleasure, the women with their garlands, the children running forward to touch Sher Khan's stirrup, all were obviously delighted to have the Ruler back, and their welcome spilled over on to his companions. Alastair, holding a bunch of pink roses thrown by a smiling slant-eyed girl, said, 'I suppose Royalty enjoy this sort of thing all their lives. I must say it gives one a very inflated feeling.'

Julia did not reply. While all the laughter and joy washed round them like a rising tide of pleasure, she was struggling with a bleak misery, a terrible feeling of despair, so strong that she felt physically ill. She raised her eyes to the mountains. There, where the mist was still clinging in grey wreaths and nets about the high peaks, seemed a more suitable climate for her. She did not belong down here in the sunshine, the warmth and the singing.

Alastair, caught into the joy all round him, was laughing and waving. Turning to her, he saw her sad face with a pang. 'Julia, darling, forgive me. I've ruined everything, haven't I?' She nodded, her eyes filling with tears.

'Don't. Oh, don't cry, Julia! Listen, this must not come between us. I only talked to you, so that the truth would come from me.' The laughing crowds around them forgotten, he leaned towards her to catch her hands. 'Darling, I love you. I did not mean to fall in love when I met you, but you are so sweet. When I saw you lying in that pool, apparently dead – oh Julia, I felt such fear and misery, because I realised that if I lost you, I lost – not everything, it would be stupid to say that. But I would have lost all the zest, the thing that makes life worth living. Together we are something good. Oh, I cannot say what I mean!' He released her hands, and struggled with a signet ring on his little finger. Then he took her hands again.

'Julia, this ring is always worn by the wife of the eldest son in my family. Look, if you won't allow me to put it on your hand, it will go back on to my finger and stay there for ever, for I will never marry anyone else. Look at me, Julia – say yes. This is too important, this is for our whole lives. No quarrel must spoil this for us.' His urgent, pleading voice, his steady eyes, did their work. Julia looked at him, weeping, and was drawn close and kissed and comforted, and the ring was put on her finger. The forgotten crowds, delighted, cheered loudly and pelted them with flowers.

'Well! Really!' Sarah, riding up, was laughing at them. 'What a carry-on in a palanquin!'

'Oh, Sarah, I am going to marry Alastair – Sarah!'

The two girls, laughing, crying, looked at each other. Alastair shouted to the *jimpanis* and they lowered the palanquin. Sher Khan, coming back to find out what had happened, was immediately part of the family. His hand grip and smile for Alastair, his kiss on Julia's cheek – 'We must celebrate. This is a fortunate home-coming! Dip Chand, come, we will lunch here.'

The crowd dispersed to a decent distance, rugs and cushions were arranged on a little rise above the river, shaded by the shivering leaves of silver birch and willow. Soon they were seated, drinking from the silver goblets. The sun was catching sparkles of light from the river and the silver, the air seemed to be full of splinters of light. It was like sitting at the heart of a diamond thought Sarah. She was quietly happy for Julia, and envious of her, but there was no bitterness in her envy. Sher Khan sought her eyes frequently, all his words were slanted towards her. He lounged back on his cushions, looking impossibly handsome, toasting Julia and Alastair, whom he insisted on calling 'the happy couple'.

'It sounds as if we are married already,' said Alastair.

'When will you marry?' asked Sher Khan.

'Well, we will want to marry soon. But I suppose, Julia, your parents will want to come? Mine are watching me from heaven, very pleased no doubt. But yours, Julia they will want us to go home, I suppose?'

Julia doubted if her mother would care very much where she married as long as she married well. Her father would want her to be happy. But as for the wedding ceremony – a great distaste for all the waiting and drama that would surround the wedding if her mother ran it came over Julia. She immediately decided that she would be married as soon as possible. 'I would like a quiet wedding – very soon,' she said firmly.

'A quiet wedding very soon! That's my girl. I knew I loved you, but I did not know how much until now. Julia, you are a miracle, a dream. Give me your hand,

and sit here close to me, so that I know you are real.'

Presently the picnic and the laughter were over and they started on their journey again. This time Sarah joined Julia in the palanquin. Julia had so much to say. 'Sarah, isn't it odd – I am so happy? I know so little about him and yet I know we are right. My mother will be pleased after all – did you know Alastair was a baronet? I didn't.'

Sarah said, 'Well, yes I did. You know they were known as the wicked barons in their regiment, don't you?'

'You mean Digby is a baronet too? Sir Digby?'

'No, but he will be. His father is still alive.' A shade had fallen on Sarah's face.

'Where is Digby, Sarah?'

'I do not know, Julie. I wish I did. It is so horrible not being able to find out, but if something had happened to him, news would have got to us, wouldn't it?'

'It is only four days, of course. Heavens, it seems much more! So much has happened!'

'Yes, hasn't it just,' said Sarah slowly.

Julia, confident in her great happiness, said, 'Sarah, I nearly didn't get engaged to Alastair.' Her eyes rounded with horror at the thought. She went on, 'We quarrelled badly this morning. You see, Sarah, he said some terrible things about Richard.' She looked anxiously into the beautiful face beside her, noticing suddenly how fine-drawn it was. Sarah's eyes were shadowed, her beautiful bones, the structure that would be her beauty in age, showed too clearly in her young face. Sarah, looked at closely, showed what she had suffered. Julia began to have terrible doubts. There were those dreadful bruises and scratches, hidden now, and the burn on her face. Staring at the river, Julia saw none of the beauty around her. Her mind ranged back in time to incidents in her childhood that had been either glossed over or quickly forgotten because of the pain they had caused. She remembered her mother and father enraged with each other, her father saying, 'That boy is mad. He has a power complex. If it is not taken in time, God knows what damage he may do when he is older.' And her mother's swift, biting reply, 'You are jealous of your own son, my dear', and she remembered the despair on her father's face.

With these thoughts in her mind, Julia turned again to Sarah. 'Sarah, Alastair told me that Richard tried to kill you – and that he thought that Richard is very dishonest and even disloyal. I could not understand all of what he said.' Sarah's silence, her firmly set mouth and steady eyes, made Julia falter. She said desperately, 'Sarah, it isn't true, is it?' and fell silent herself, too horrified to weep.

The two girls sat looking at each other in a sort of misery that could not find words. All the fears and despairs and uncertainties that Sarah had been pressing back into her subconscious rose and confronted her, a many-headed monster so horribly real it was as if there was a third person in the palanquin with them. She bowed her head into her hands and sat, face hidden, without replying. Julia, for the first time, found herself the comforter.

Presently Sarah was able to speak. 'Julia, forgive me. I cannot talk about Richard. But I do not think he is very well at the moment.'

'I cannot believe he'd do anything disloyal.'

Sarah looked sadly down at the girl. 'No, I couldn't either. But out of his own mouth – he said he was against the government, and had helped the terrorists.'

Julia, looking away, said, 'Sarah, he was a very jealous person. You don't think that he got jealous of you?'

'Jealous?'

Julia flushed, but struggled on. 'Yes, you know Digby showed how attracted he was to you.' She looked unhappily at Sarah, afraid to say all she was thinking. For surely Richard had reason for jealousy. Had there not been that affair before, with some other man?

But Sarah shook her head firmly. 'Richard is mixed

up in something too bad to be caused by jealousy of me, Julie.'

Julia looked at her, searching her face for signs of guilt or shame or indeed any kind of feeling of dismay over Richard having had cause for jealousy, either in the past, or over Digby. But she saw nothing in Sarah's face but anxiety and strain. Nothing more was said about Digby. Sarah sat frowning, deep in thought.

Finally Julia said, 'Does Sher Khan know about Richard? What does he think, which side is he on?'

'He suspects Richard. How could he do anything else after what happened? But I have not discussed it with him very much – it is not an easy matter to discuss,' Sarah said suddenly hardening her tone, sick of this verbal fencing, this apparent defence of Richard. 'Not very easy to discuss the fact that your husband tied you up and left you drugged in a burning house, Julie!'

She was remorseful when she saw Julia's stricken face, heard her say brokenly, 'But he was never unkind to me, Sarah, and I thought he loved you –'

'I am sorry, Julia. Look, this is your engagement day! Do not think about anything but yourself and Alastair. Forget Richard for today. I told you I thought his sanity had gone. He is sick – think of him as a man with an illness, and for today, think of nothing but your life. And speaking of Alastair, I think he has ridden far enough. I shall ride again, and let him have a rest.'

But Julia was not finished with her questioning. 'If he is sick, then that is different, isn't it? A man who is mentally ill cannot be blamed for anything. It was probably the strain of the war, Sarah. Like shell-shock. He could be cured, there are special places –'

Sarah drew a deep noiseless sigh, and nodded. If it comforted Julia to imagine that her brother was anything but a homicidal maniac, then on this day, which should be so happy for her, let her think that all could be made right again for Richard. 'Yes, Julia. There are special places. Look, here comes Alastair.'

The palanquin was stopped, and the exchange

effected. Julia sat beside Alastair and held his hand, and watched Sarah ride up to the head of the column.

'She looks terrible,' said Alastair. 'Absolutely strung to breaking point.'

'Yes. But it will all be all right, I hope, Alastair. I know that she thinks Richard is mixed up in something very bad, and that he tried to kill her, but she thinks he may be insane, and of course that would explain everything.' Blithely unconscious of Alastair's amazed eyes, she continued, 'You see, it is probably the strain of the war years, and these days, things like shell-shock and so forth can be cured. So once he has been taken to a good doctor, he will probably have to go into a hospital for a while, and then he will be himself again.'

Alastair, like Sarah, was content that his Julia should, with all her love for her brother so plainly displayed, be comforted. He said nothing about his own opinions about Richard, but gently turned his girl's thoughts to other things, and Julia's face was soon as clear of worry as her heart was content and happy.

Sarah rode up to Sher Khan and was welcomed with a wide white smile. The riding in the clear mountain air was turning his face darker, his eyes seemed a brighter blue by contrast. Sarah, looking at him, was astonished at his looks. He laughed at her.

'Sarajan, you stare at me as if you have never seen me before! What is it?'

Confused, she laughed too, and said, 'You are getting very brown!'

'So are you. You are turning a beautiful colour, like honey. Have you looked at yourself lately? So beautiful, but much too thin. Your eyes – are you worried, Sarajan?'

Thus easily, Sarah was presented with the opening for all the questions that she wished to ask, and yet did not know how to begin. Under his blue, laughing gaze, she found it difficult, and finally said, 'Well, one thing that worries me is, what is happening in Madore? And why have you brought us to Lambagh?'

'But you know why I have brought you to Lambagh. Would you have preferred to stay in a burning house? Come, Sarajan, by bringing you here, I have avoided for you a great deal of unpleasantness. A police investigation of two murders, Lalani and your servant Pyari Lal. You would have been alone there, to manage that, for it was necessary for me to get up here as quickly as possible. I could not have left you behind, ill and in danger, so this seemed best, to bring you all to safety. Does this not seem right to you?'

It seemed very right and very sensible. But why was he in such a hurry to get to Lambagh, wondered Sarah? Sher Khan, looking at her creased brow, continued, 'As for Madore, I am not sure of what is happening there. But we will have news soon. One thing I am sure of. The Indian Army will have stayed loyal, the rats of subversion will have had no success there. Your husband should have known better than to have imagined treason and disloyalty among the soldiers, even if he has spent most of his time as a staff officer. No doubt some of those bastard plotters will have worn Army uniform to put the forces into disrepute. Indeed, Alastair's experience proves that. But do not worry about what is happening in Madore, Sarajan, you can do nothing about it, and you are safe here.'

'How long will you keep us here?'

'*Keep*, Sarajan? You are not prisoners, you are my guests! You will stay as long as you wish. This is your valley too, Sarajan, you are returning to the place that your grandmother loved more than any place on earth. Do you not wish to be in Lambagh?'

'Of course I do!' Sarah was finding it harder and harder to ask her questions. Sher Khan looked as if he might be not only offended, but angry as well, but she forced herself on, although the feeling of ease between them had gone.

'I cannot help wondering – what *is* the trouble in Madore? Alastair said that it had been quiet for some time, although Richard told us not to go into the walled city because there might be trouble there. Is it the usual intercommunal trouble?'

'I have said, I do not know yet, Sarajan. We will have news soon. Leave these hard questions now.'

His eyes had grown remote, his face looked cold and stern. They rode in silence for a little while, approaching another small village, a welcoming party coming out to meet them with drums and flutes and smiling people with flowers. Sher Khan was offered a reed basket full of garlands. He took up a heavy circle of roses and jasmine, and put it carefully over Sarah's head, leaning from his saddle to do so.

'There,' he said. 'Come garlanded into your own country, take that frown from your beautiful face, and leave me to do all the worrying.'

So simple! Sarah smiled in spite of herself and they rode on through the little crowd. Looking about her at the laughing, welcoming faces, she saw a group of men standing on one side who were conspicuous by their silence and stillness in the noisy, enthusiastic crowd. Dressed in dark coats and tight, wrinkling white trousers, with small black pill-box hats on their heads, these men seemed to have nothing in common with the happy people surging round Sher Khan. He had also seen the group, and his forehead creased into a formidable frown. They rode on, and out of the village, and then Sher Khan turned in his saddle and called up the Guard Commander, and spoke to him. When the man had dropped back again, Sarah asked who the dark watching men had been.

'They are from outside, not men of the hills. Up till now I have let them come and go. But not any more. I do not want such men here. Agitators, paid disrupters of the peace.'

'Sher Khan, it is so sad that after such a long war there should begin to be so much trouble in India.'

'Sarajan, Britain is now leaving India. This is going to be a very bad time. Everyone is jockeying for position, trying for the rich prizes that they think will be left

226

unguarded. I am determined to keep my State out of the maelstrom that will follow the coming of Independence. I will keep my people and their way of life safe for as long as I can. We have never been dependent on Britain, nor on any other nation. I have inherited a free country. I intend to keep it so as long as I can.'

His eyes were hard, his expression cold, and Sarah asked no more questions. They rode on in silence, and looking at him, she felt that he could be a terrible enemy. Then she remembered his gentleness and obvious love for her children, his kindness when he had found her in the burning Ranighar, and the joy expressed by his people now that he had returned to them. It was hard to think anything bad about him. Not only because of what she saw, but also because of what her own heart was telling her, and the pleasure and excitement that she felt in his presence. Sarah tried to put all thoughts from her, striving to enjoy the ride and the glorious day.

And then, with no warning, she found herself thinking of her grandmother who had loved the valley so much, and had left it for ever because there was no place for her in Kassim Khan's life. Kassim Khan, Sher Khan's grandfather. She wondered if Sher Khan was like his grandfather, and like a raven's wing an old sorrow seemed to shadow the bright day. To love a man like Sher Khan and lose him, never see him again! Already her heart told her, already you are in jeopardy! How unwise to even think of love, but how wonderful. To be free to love and to trust; the mere thought of such freedom lifted the shadow from her mind. As if he had felt something of her thoughts, Sher Khan turned to look at her, and then smiled, and with that smile Sarah found it impossible to think of anything but the moment's pleasure, the warm sun, and the scent of the roses that garlanded her shoulders.

They came in the late afternoon to the largest village Sarah had seen so far. It was a walled village, the stout walls pierced by an arched gate guarded by troopers of the State Forces, who turned out smartly to salute Sher Khan, big smiles breaking their disciplined gravity. Sher Khan spoke briefly to them, and then the cavalcade clattered through the gate into an eruption of welcome that made all the previous demonstrations seem nothing. Laughing, dodging the rain of flowers that fell from the little wooden balconies that fringed the close-packed houses, Sher Khan looked like the young man he was, instead of the stern Ruler.

'This is the heart of the state, Khanum,' he called to her, 'this is my village of Lamba. Soon we will be home.'

They rode past a temple where drums throbbed and the conch shell brayed to welcome them. Further on, Sher Khan dismounted at the gate of a mosque to receive the blessing of the robed and turbaned Moulvi. Then they were through the village and riding out through another high arched gate with more uniformed guards. Ahead, Sarah could see the river had widened into a lake and on a rise beside the lake stood a large white house, domed and walled and set about with trees.

'There,' said Sher Khan, deep satisfaction in his voice, 'there is the Mhormahal. The Peacock Palace. We have come home.'

26

Entirely surrounded by wide verandahs, the house sprawled comfortably round a central courtyard where roses and jasmine competed for the air, and where peacocks stepped and postured round a splashing fountain.

The room they entered was large and high ceilinged. To Sarah the furnishings were a wonderful surprise; good old furniture, polished and clean, chintzes and velvets in gentle faded colours, everything spotless, sparkling with attention. Sinking into a comfortable chair, she sighed with pleasure, watching while Julia was helped in and seated. To them then came the children.

'You take so long, Mummy! Where have you been? This is a beauty house, and we can go on the water in a boat, but we must not go without Hyder Ali. Do you know what?'

'No, my little love, I do not know what!'

'Well, Hyder Ali is like Ayah's child. He will help to look after us because Pyari Lal has gone to his home, where Ayah says he is more happy. And something else. We've got two ponies and some little noisy hens with spots that lay littley littley eggs, and there are fifty million peacocks in the trees in the garden.'

'That is going to be nice,' said Alastair coming in. 'Have any of you heard a disturbed peacock? I wonder if anyone has any earplugs.'

Sher Khan came in, and looked at his guests.

'Well. You like?'

'We *like*,' said Sarah. 'It is beautiful. Everything is

perfect.'

'This used to be the Begum Bianca's home; she came here as a bride. The old Palace is down in the village. That palace was smaller, and was called the Chotamahal, but now – were you speaking about the peacocks? We are proud of them. They are the emblem of the state, and are protected. They were not native to this valley, but the Begum Bianca brought two pairs up here once, and they survived, and now look at them.'

He looked sternly at Alastair who said, 'Delightful birds. Have they all lost their voices, I trust?'

Sher Khan relaxed into laughter. 'Alastair, they cry in warning or when alarmed. You will become used to them. Now, Khanum, come, I wish to show you your rooms.'

With Penelope and David running ahead, they went out to the courtyard, past the fountain, and into rooms that delighted them all. The children had a night nursery and a day nursery, and their own bathroom. For Sarah there was a dressing room, a magnificently gleaming Victorian-type bathroom and a large bedroom. This room appeared to be older than the others. The whole of one wall was a big, alcoved window, filled with a cushion-heaped window seat. The view from this window was the lake, and beyond, mountains. There was a large bed, some small tables, and some beautiful silver lamps. Roses, white roses, grew in big white pottery jars, and the whole room seemed to glow softly, like the inside of a shell. Standing in the window alcove, Sarah seemed to glow like the room; her ivory skin and dark hair made her a portrait figure as she stood looking out at the lake, lost in admiration of the view.

'This room is a perfect frame, as it was intended to be, for a beautiful woman. May you be happy here, Khanum.'

Sher Khan seemed to have forgotten Julia and Alastair, and finally, Sarah blushing under his steady gaze, said, 'And for Julia and Alastair?'

'Of course. Come and see your rooms. They are just

across the courtyard.'

Julia was delighted with her room and dressing room and bathroom, saying, 'Oh, how perfect! Thank you, Sher Khan. But where do you sleep?'

'I will live in the old Palace. It is now my army's barracks and stables, and I have kept some rooms there. You will see them another day. But I shall, I hope, spend a great deal of my time here in the Mhormahal, with your permission of course, Khanum. This is your home now. You must ask for anything you want. I would like to dine here tonight, if you are not too tired? Good. Then we will have our drinks on the *chibutra*, that big open verandah outside the drawing room. I will come at sunset. Sunset on the lake you will like.'

He went away smiling, and Julia, watching him go, said, 'He has dropped years since we came here.'

'Yes, he has. I think I have picked up all the years he has dropped,' said Alastair, yawning widely. 'If you two incipient Begums will excuse me, I will retire across the courtyard where I understand my palatial quarters await me. I am going to sleep for hours. Julia, my only love, only the proprieties, my exhaustion and the presence of Sarah prevent me from begging you to come with me.'

After he had gone, the two girls decided to rest too. Julia found an Ayah waiting for her in her room, and Sarah stayed to see her undressed, wrapped in a cashmere robe, and lying on her bed, almost asleep, before going back to her own rooms where Ayah was waiting for her.

'Ayah, are you comfortable? Have you good quarters?'

'How not? This is my home, as it is yours. Come, you must bathe and wash your hair, it is grey with dust. The children are with Hyder Ali, who is the son of my daughter. They will be well guarded from trouble until I have finished caring for my dearest child.'

She removed Sarah's clothes, and then bathed her and washed her hair as if she was indeed a child, and Sarah submitted, her aching muscles relaxing under Ayah's skilful hands.

Later, wrapped in a creamy robe of cashmere, while Ayah dried and combed her hair, Sarah said, 'Where is Ayesha? I do not remember seeing her on the road.'

'She comes,' said Ayah briefly. 'She had some tasks for her family. She will come, maybe tomorrow, maybe later. Meantime, make shift with me, and my poor care.'

'Oh, Ayah, such modesty! You can teach them all! Tell me, how long do you think we will stay here?'

'As long as you wish. This is your home. You will stay until the troubles are over.'

'The troubles in Madore? Riots?'

'Aye, riots maybe, and other things.' Ayah, brush in hand, looked into the glass and met Sarah's eyes. Her face was closed and forbidding. Then she said, 'There is, however, no mutiny, Sarajan. It is said that some tried, with bribes and speeches, to make trouble in the Army. But the soldiers themselves, the *jiwans*, reported these troublemakers, and they were taken and jailed. Enough. We do not talk of this now. Enjoy this place, grow a little fat – Come, now you will sleep, until I bring you your tea. Come!' Sarah, led to the big bed, covered, and tucked in like a child, found herself relaxed and sleepy. With a satisfied nod, Ayah went away to find her other precious charges.

Sarah woke to late sunlight gilding the wide window and Ayah coming in with her tea. The old woman smiled as Sarah moved easily to sit up against piled pillows.

'So, the aches and pains have gone, eh? These old hands still have skill. Now, my child, you dress, and I will arrange your hair.'

But there was suddenly trouble. After a short search of the cupboards in the dressing room, Ayah left Sarah drinking her tea and went out to find Dip Chand. She came back with her lips folded in displeasure, but Sarah detected a satisfied gleam in her eyes.

'This is what comes of travelling without me. Your baggage is all in Faridkote.'

'What – all my clothes? My make-up?'

'Yes. All. Your jewellery, and also, all the clothes of

232

Julia Miss Sahiba.'

'Oh, dear –' Sarah looked at the Ayah in dismay.

'And do not ask me for the clothes you took off before your bath. They are being washed. Well, well then, do not look so distressed! Your home is here, no doubt clothes will be found also.' Ayah went into the dressing room and, following her, Sarah found her bent double over a deep chest that overflowed with colour. Silks, brocades and chiffons, folded and laid away carefully, and as Ayah moved them the room filled with the sweet evocative scent of sandalwood and roses.

'Oh, how beautiful! What are those lovely things?'

'They are some of the robes of the Begum Bianca, but not what I want,' said Ayah. She went to another carved chest, opened it and sighed with satisfaction. The chest seemed to glimmer with pale light. It was full of silks, but these were either white, or shades of cream. Heavily embroidered brocades shining with silver, fine chiffons and satins the colour of ivory. Ayah chose what she wanted, and began to dress Sarah.

Robed in brocade and silk, Sarah turned to her mirror. She had never in her life looked like this. The ivory silk did something to her skin, the result glowed; shimmering fabric and firm young flesh complimented each other. Her eyes blazed with excitement as she looked at herself. Sarah had never been conscious of her own beauty. Now she looked, and looked again, astonished and delighted. Ayah brushed and coiled her hair high on her head, and then stood back, her lips stretching in a smile of pure pleasure.

'Now, indeed I see you as you should be! How beautiful you look my child, a Princess of moonlight! But you should have jewels.'

'Well, my jewels are all in Faridkote.'

'Not these jewels. You should have emeralds and pearls.'

'Oh, indeed,' said Sarah laughing. 'And no doubt rubies and diamonds as well!'

'No. Just emeralds and pearls,' said Ayah, disregard-

233

ing her mockery. 'But never mind. For now, we will have this.' She brought a budding white rose and tucked it into Sarah's coiled hair. 'There. That will do, until the jewels are given.'

'Jewels? Given? No one is going to give me jewels, Ayah!' But the Ayah did not appear to be listening, and after tucking the rose more securely into her hair, Sarah got up and went across the courtyard with its splashing fountain, and entered Julia's room.

Julia was standing before her looking-glass. She was dressed in Lambaghi robes, but hers were deep crimson. She glowed like a rose, and was enchanted with her reflection. The two girls stood side by side, looking into the glass.

'I hope they never find our luggage again. I would far rather dress like this for the rest of my life. Just look at us!'

'Yes,' agreed Sarah. 'Just look at us. Imagine running for a bus, Julie, in all this!'

'I don't want to imagine anything so prosaic. I want to go and show myself off to Alastair.'

They walked together to the *chibutra* where Alastair and Sher Khan were sitting, and were greeted by a moment of complete silence. Then Alastair, getting to his feet a second after Sher Khan, said, 'Good God, what a fantastic sight! Have you two any idea of how beautiful you look? Julia, come and sit here beside me and tell me you are real. I am afraid you'll suddenly take off like a beautiful bird of paradise.'

Sher Khan said nothing. He pulled forward a long chair for Sarah, heaped cushions behind her back and, waving Dip Chand away, brought her drink to her himself. Then he sat at her feet and raised his goblet.

'This is a very happy night for me, to see the Peacock Palace with lighted windows, and to know that beauty lives here again.' His eyes seemed to burn; Sarah could not look away from his fierce, possessive gaze.

She lifted her goblet and drank and could think of nothing to say, but Julia, basking in Alastair's admiration, said happily, breaking the silence, 'Aren't we lucky that all our baggage was left behind somewhere? Imagine not having an excuse to wear all these lovely things!'

'Your baggage will be here soon. But, to please me, wear these clothes while you are here. There are others for wearing during the day. You will find them easy and comfortable. Promise me – or I shall arrange that your baggage takes a very long time to come!'

'Who did the clothes belong to? The Begum Bianca? There are so many, the chests in my room are full.'

'Yes, Khanum. There are many. Some belonged to the Begum Bianca, and others, older still, belonged to other ladies of the older Rulers. Many of the robes have never been worn. You will see them; no doubt your women are already unpacking and sorting the clothes.'

It was so good to have reached the end of their journey! They sat enjoying their first drink and watching while the sun fell burning behind the mountains, leaving the whole sky on fire. The evening was full of laughter and inconsequential chatter. They all felt relaxed and at ease with each other. Sarah forgot all her troubles. She sat at the dining table after their dinner had been eaten, laughing at Sher Khan's stories, and twirling her white rose which had fallen from her hair. She looked as young as she was, and really impossibly beautiful thought Alastair, and spoke his thoughts.

'You do look extra special in those robes, Sarah.'

Julia was totally without envy or jealousy. 'Yes, doesn't she. Sarah, you look like a Queen of the East, a Maharani –' Oh dear, thought Alastair, oh dear, my little crazy love, how you do put your foot in things. Haven't you seen and understood the look in the Royal Beast's eyes? He got up, pushing back his chair.

'Come along, my crimson rose, come out to the *chibutra* and let me tell you in private how beautiful *you* look.'

Left alone, Sarah and Sher Khan were silent, looking out at the lake where the lights reflected and ran in golden streaks as the night wind ruffled the water. Sher Khan said, still looking out, as if the golden reflections had brought something to his mind, 'An Eastern Queen would be a drab compared to you. You are a spirit of moonlight and water.' Sarah, so calm and self possessed could not understand why this one man could destroy her poise and leave her wordless and shy just by looking at her. Eyes lowered, she sat, and he leaned forward and took her hand.

'I love you, Sarajan. How wonderful to have you here, in my valley! I cannot yet believe it is true. Safely in my valley.' He sat quiet holding her hand and looking at her.

Then, as if he too found silence dangerous, he said, 'You must have jewels. Not your English jewels which are in such good taste that no one can see them, but the jewels our women wear which are beautiful and large and can be seen.'

This brought Sarah's eyes up to meet his, and she managed to laugh.

'You and Ayah! She suggested emeralds and pearls, no less!'

'Emeralds and pearls? Did she, indeed! Of course she is right.'

He picked up her left hand, where her wedding ring encircled her finger and said, 'And this fetter? When will you take this off, I wonder? Do you feel happy wearing it, Sarajan? The chain that holds you to a murderer? No, never mind, do not look like that! Forgive me.' He bent and kissed her hand, and took the wilting white rose from her fingers and tucked it into the pocket of his *achkhan*.

'You shall have white roses and jasmine every day, Moon Queen. How right you are to choose these colours. The colours of pearls, of snow and of moonlight.'

Again silence fell between them. Sarah felt her blood throbbing with the quickening beat of her heart. Her breath catching, she looked at the man sitting so quietly beside her. If he had put out his hand and taken hers then, she would have been in his arms, all her scruples forgotten. But Julia and Alastair broke the moment, coming in because the breeze had turned cold.

Sher Khan got up then, and said that he would have to go. 'Khanum, I will tell Dip Chand that you must have a fire every night. The temperature does fall when the sun goes down. I hope you all sleep very well. Tomorrow, I thought we could have a picnic, go out and see more of the valley? Yes? Very well, I will arrange.'

He took Sarah's hand, leading her to the door with him, saying low, 'All my success was stolen from me! Victory was mine at that moment, Sarajan. I saw the look in your lovely eyes – and then they must come in, being cold! But there are all the days we want ahead of us. I can wait until the time matches our desires. Now I say goodnight, and must lose you until the morning. Sleep Sarajan, sleep, and if good fortune is with me, perhaps we will at least meet and be alone together in our dreams.'

27

Sarah woke the next day to a world full of blue light, the cry of water-birds and the distant sound of temple bells. She went to the deep window seat and curled up there, drawing her robe close about her; the air was fresh. It was very early and the sky and the water were of the same clear pale blue, the blue of a robin's egg, the lake joining the sky in an unbroken line, so that she seemed to be looking into a bowl of blue, except where the jagged peaks made a black ragged tear. As she watched, the sky began to flush, and the colours brightened and sparkled as the sun rose. There were fishermen in small boats on the lake, and women were washing clothes further up the shore. Their voices were high and clear, like the cries of the water-birds. She could smell wood smoke and roses, and incense – someone was at their prayers in one or other of the small shrines she could see on the lake shore.

The children came tiptoe with her tea. Seeing her awake, they forgot caution and flew to her, Hans leaping with them. Their day stretched ahead of them so full of excitements that their little bodies could hardly contain their joy. Sarah remembered the tired pale-faced children she had lifted from the train in Madore, and looking at them now, already seeming plumper, with their skin turning golden from the sun, she felt a lightening of heart that was almost physical. Nothing could be wrong with a series of events that made her children well and happy. Ayah, smiling behind them, shared her pleasure. 'See how fat my children grow – like two partridges. Would that their mother would also grow fatter!'

'Ayah, I do not wish to grow fat! Heaven forfend!'

'Aye, well, that is as you like. But no harm to a little flesh on your bones. You will grow old and dry soon enough. Enjoy your youth and keep your beauty while you may. Come, my darlings, let your mother have her tea. Hyder Ali waits to take you to see the ponies.' The children rushed out and Ayah returned to pour Sarah's tea, run her bath and potter in the dressing room.

After her bath, Sarah found that Ayah had laid out the day attire of a hill woman – trousers and loose over-shirt, and a black velvet waistcoat. The trousers and shirt were of heavy ivory silk, ribbed and corded, and as soft as wool. It was a comfortable and becoming costume, serviceable and easy to wear. As she was putting on her lipstick a voice called from the courtyard and Ayah went out to see what it was. She came back carrying a single white rose and a string of jasmine. 'This is to come twice a day, as long as there are flowers,' said Ayah and, giving Sarah the rose, she twisted the jasmine into the coils of her hair.

When she was ready, Sarah walked through the sunny courtyard to the dining room. Alastair and Julia were already there. 'This place has a lot to commend it,' said Alastair from the sideboard, where he was giving himself a lavish helping of scrambled eggs and mushrooms. 'Fresh eggs and mushrooms, for instance – and your beautiful costumes. It is like breakfasting with two of the *houris* from a Muslim paradise.'

The table was laid for three – Sher Khan was not expected. Her feeling of disappointment was so strong that she was shaken. How far had her heart and her mind wandered, that she should be so distressed by his absence! She sat drinking her coffee and listening to the other two, putting in a remark now and then in case they should notice her silence. Her second cup of coffee she took out on to the verandah and sat there to drink it. She looked towards the village and saw riders coming swiftly over the green meadows and up the road that climbed to the house. The leading horseman was Sher Khan, his emerald turban bent low over his horse's outstretched neck.

The riders drew near, and the noise of pounding hooves brought the others out to join her. 'By God! Look at that – the fellow can ride, the one in the green puggaree.' Strange, thought Sarah, that I saw so clearly who the rider was, but Alastair does not recognise him. Was this the eye of love? There was supposed to be a moment in an affair when it was possible to see the spell under which one was falling – and to draw back. Now Sarah felt that the moment had passed unnoticed, and she was already enthralled. She watched Sher Khan dismount and throw his reins to one of his companions, and called on all her self-control so that she could greet him casually and pleasantly when he came out to join them on the verandah. He looked first at her, smiling, and said, 'So, you did choose to wear the local dress. It is comfortable, no?'

It was Julia who answered, and Alastair who said, 'I am not sure it is not even more becoming than the evening robes. Do not worry about them being comfortable – it is their duty to look beautiful for their male companions!' Sarah, then, was able to laugh and join Julia in her condemnations of Alastair's conceit. Sher Khan's long stare at her had seemed to touch her physically; she had flushed and the white rose in her hand quivered.

The plans for the day were made. A picnic on the lake shore – Julia and Alastair and the children would go to the picnic spot by boat. Sher Khan turned to Sarah. 'Will you ride with me, Khanum, or are you too stiff?'

'I am not at all stiff, thank you. I would like to ride.'

'Good. Then in two hours we go. Is that suitable to you? Now, Julia and Major Crombie, Doctor Bukov would like to see you in his hospital. It is just inside the Pearl Gate. I will take you there – I have two carrying-chairs waiting. With your permission, Khanum?'

Sarah watched them leave, the small carrying-chairs bobbing down the hill at an impossible angle. Julia would be glad when she could ride again.

She was still sitting dreaming on the verandah when Ayah came out with two long chiffon scarves for Sarah and Julia to wear on their heads when they went out. 'Please tell Dip Chand to bring fresh coffee when the others come back.' But there was no need to tell Dip Chand. As she spoke, he appeared in the doorway, followed by a younger servant carrying a large silver tray. This was put on a table beside Sarah and as the coffee cups were set out, she heard the voices of the others. Where had the time gone?

Presently they joined her and sat drinking their coffee and telling her about the splendidly equipped little hospital they had just left. Alastair had a fresh bandage on his shoulder and his sling was more firmly tied. He looked pale and drawn; dressing had not been easy. Sher Khan looked at him. 'Major Sahib, are you sure you feel well enough to come today? There will be many other days, you know.'

Alastair stirred uneasily – how many days? 'I shall be shot for desertion, at this rate.'

Sher Khan smiled. 'Oh, I think not. Seriously do you feel able to come?'

Alastair said he felt perfectly fit, and added, 'It was painful, but that chap knows what he is doing. Look, do call me Alastair, Nawab Sahib, Major Crombie makes me feel as if I am on parade – and is a constant reminder of the fact that I should be.'

'But of course. And you will call me Sher Khan. As for being on parade – I repeat, please do not worry yourself.'

Sarah, head swathed and turbaned, stood by Sher Khan and the horses, watching the boating contingent set off. Penelope was firmly leading Hans, who was reluctant to leave dry land and eventually, squirming, had to be carried on board. The boat was pushed off, the sail set, and Sher Khan turned to Sarah. 'Khanum, you are ready?' He helped her to mount and stood beside her, looking up. 'You got my flowers. Thank you for wearing them. I do not have to tell you how beautiful you are.' He spoke with a new serious air; his hand lay for a

241

moment, pressing firmly on her knee, then he turned away and mounted, and they set off.

For the first time since they had ridden together, as if he had decided that she could ride well, he set a hard pace. Sarah, giving her horse his head, had no time to ponder Sher Khan's serious manner. She gave herself up to the sheer physical joy of swift movement, of the fresh sparkling air, and the sun. She was flushed and laughing when he finally drew rein and she came alongside him.

'Goodness! What a ride that was!' She was struggling with her scarf and her tumbling hair.

'Give me that –' Sher Khan took the scarf from her and sat watching her as she tried to order her hair, his eyes admiring, adoring. The boat was still some distance away; she saw Penelope waving and waved back, taking her scarf from Sher Khan. She then tied it firmly over her head, and he said, 'Even with no hair showing you are beautiful. Come, we ride on, but more slowly. We go through the trees.'

They rode through a thicket of pine and larch, and then out into the open again. She could see, on a headland, a small white shrine.

'That is where we are going. It is a very old shrine. There is an altar there that Sikunder's men set up.'

'Alexander the Great?'

'Yes. Sikunder. He came this way, they say, into India. Many of my people claim descent from his soldiers.'

They rode up to the headland and stopped beside the shrine. Inside there was an altar, without an image, swept and clean, overhung by a canopy of chipped marble supported by carved pillars. On the altar were bunches of peacock feathers, and bronze bells and cowrie shells. The marble basin, shaped like a lotus at the foot of the altar, was full of fresh roses. A little oil lamp winked and wavered before the altar.

'But who tends this, who comes all this way to light the lamp?'

'People who pass, herders, travellers from the North coming back to the valley, and priests from the temple in the village of Lamba. The place is sacred, it is said to cure the bite of the serpent.'

'I thought this was a Muslim state. I hear the call to prayers every evening, and at dawn.'

'Yes. *And* you hear the temple bells, and the priests blowing the conch shell, and Andrej Bukov and his wife are Russian Orthodox and worship as *they* please. We be all one people, and unlike the rest of this troubled land are able to live together in peace. Come, Sarajan, let us wait for the others outside. We have not been bitten by serpents and there is no need for us to pray for a cure – or do you think that love is a serpent's sting?'

In a complete turmoil, she followed him to a green hollow, sheltered from the breeze, and sat down where he indicated, leaning against a sloping bank. He stretched out at her feet. 'Sarajan, this is very pleasant, to be with you here, like this. Do you like it too?'

'Yes, yes, I do. It is a beautiful, peaceful place.'

'Never mind the place. Do you like to be with me alone?'

All Sarah's confused emotions showed on her face, and he took her hand.

'Do not look like that! Be at peace for a little while. Let my love touch your mind and your heart. Dream with me for a while, feel the sun, fill your eyes with the mountains and the lake, and enjoy them more because we are together. Sarajan, let time stop for us for a space.'

'But time won't stop – it rushes on.'

'So, let it rush! It moves from spring to warm summer, from innocence to happy knowledge, from friendship to liking, to love. Time is a friend in this place.'

'Oh, Sher Khan! Time is not a friend.' Sarah spoke from a heart that was suddenly filled with sad knowledge. 'Time rushes from spring to summer – and then to winter and the end of everything. There is always an end, and even then, when everything is over, is finished, time goes cruelly on.' Her tears brought him to his knees beside her, his arms drew her close into his shoulder.

'Oh, dear love, what are these tears on such a day?

What end is this you speak of? What kind of a life have you had, that you speak thus? Do not remember old pain here, where we should be so happy. This is a place of love fulfilled, of happy dreams brought to a happy awakening. Sarajan, dream a little, forget everything but me and this present time, and then you will be happy. Look at me, tell me you feel love for me. I know you do, but I want to hear you say the words.'

Sarah, lifted out of herself, turned to him, her heart in her eyes, words trembling on her lips. There was a scramble, a torrent of happy barking, and Hans joined them, the voices of the boating party sounding clear on the other side of the shrine.

Sher Khan stood up and laughed. 'Well, Sarajan, some fate attends me. All my moments of victory with you are broken. But I warn you, as you have said, time rushes on. I give you this to think about. Time hurries on, and will bring us to the moment when there will be no interruptions. I can wait.' Sarah, fending off Hans' delighted greeting, wondered wryly if she could.

The familiar silver goblets were unpacked from a hamper, filled, and passed round by Dip Chand. Champagne in the open seemed very potent. Sarah felt suddenly a lightness of spirit and a gaiety she had thought lost for ever. Everything seemed enchanted. The lake shone and glittered, the children ran about and played strange complicated games devised by Penelope. Dip Chand laid a cloth on the ground and put out a feast of curries and salads and cold meats. The children, fed, fell asleep and were carefully covered with a blanket each by Hyder Ali. All this time, all through the meal, Sarah was conscious of Sher Khan in a way that she had never been before. This was an uncontrollable urge, a longing to be close to him, and to be alone with him again. Unable to eat, she sat apart, sipping her wine, taking no part in the talk and laughter. Presently Alastair took Julia off to look at the shrine. Hyder Ali and Dip Chand folded the cloth and took the remnants of the feast back to the boat.

Sher Khan brought a bottle over to Sarah and filled her

goblet. 'You ate nothing, Sarajan, at least drink something. I was not hungry either. Never mind. Tonight we will feast. You will dine with me in my quarters in the old Palace? Oh, all of you, of course. The proprieties must be observed.' He smiled at her and put his hand to his breast pocket. 'Will you wear these for me tonight?' He put a packet into her hands, and watched while she unwrapped it.

'Oh, Sher Khan – how beautiful!' Sarah held a pair of earrings, peacocks with spread tails, fashioned from emeralds, sapphires and tiny seed pearls. 'But they are exquisite – of course I will wear them tonight.'

' – And whenever you like. They are yours, Sarajan. No one else will ever wear them.' She was overwhelmed, and stammered,

'But I cannot accept these – it is too much.'

'Too much? Too much for what? I give them to you. Of course you can accept them!'

'But – Sher Khan, surely they are part of the State Regalia?'

Sher Khan sat very still, the smile gone from his face. 'What do you mean?'

'Well, they are peacocks. Are they not part of the royal jewellery?'

'What if they are?'

'Can you give them away?'

'I do not understand you. Anything I own, I can give to anyone.' His voice was cold, and Sarah was shocked at the expression on his face. He was frowning at her, he looked furiously angry.

'I am sorry, Sher Khan. I did not mean to anger you.'

'I am not angry, but I do not understand you. Can you not accept a gift with grace? Or do the British find it hard to accept a present from a native, preferring to take it by force, perhaps? This must be your British side, the blood must be strong.'

Sarah got up and stood looking at him, bitterly hurt. 'I cannot accept a gift of such value, I fear. Thank you for the kind thought.' She rewrapped the beautiful baubles with trembling fingers, and put them down beside him. Then, her eyes full of tears, she walked away, not really able to see where she was going. She did not hear him move and did not know that he was beside her until he put his hand on her arm.

'Sarajan –'

'Go away,' was all she could find to say through her tears.

'Khanum, forgive me. A devil drove me, I can explain. Sarajan, you touched an old wound – forgive me. I cannot, damn everything, take you in my arms – there are, as usual, too many eyes about us – but turn to me, tell me you forgive me.'

She was as incapable of refusing him as she was of not breathing.

Her forgiving smile was beautiful, and he said, below his breath, 'I am punished enough by having made you weep in a place where I cannot stop your tears with kisses. Let me give you these again – keep them as a gift from one who loves you more than anything in this world.' They stood together, and as he put his present into her hand, Julia and Alastair came back, full of questions about the shrine, the children woke up, and Hans, with hysterical joy, found a water rat and filled the air with hunting cries. 'I swear no man has ever conducted a more disrupted courtship,' said Sher Khan through his teeth, as he turned to answer Julia's questions.

Julia's eager questions about the shrine were not the only interruption. Above the voices and the laughter came the sound of hoof beats. Sher Khan broke off his conversation and moved forward to meet a man who had ridden up from the direction of Lamba. The man saluted and dismounted and spoke quickly and quietly to Sher Khan, out of earshot of the party. Sher Khan listened to him intently, gave him what were obviously urgent orders, and the man remounted and rode back the way he had come, kicking his horse into a gallop. Sher Khan strode back to the others, and resumed his story of the shrine, and nothing was said about the messenger. Alastair would have liked to ask questions, but he had seen Sher Khan's expression, and decided against it at that moment. It would have been a pity to spoil a perfect day, and he let his mind think only of the sun and the soft sounds of the lake, and the stories of the shrine and the splendid past, when Alexander's warriors had paused to rest and had built the shrine.

The sun was laying long fingers of shadow across the lake when Sher Khan said it was time to return. Sarah felt herself as reluctant as the children; she did not want the day to end, and like her little daughter she comforted herself. 'There is still the boat to go home in,' said Penelope, preparing to leave the shore. There is still the ride home, thought Sarah, the ride home, and then this evening. She stood on the lake side with Sher Khan and watched the boating party set off, Hans barking hysterically in Penelope's loving clutches. Then she turned and mounted her horse and watched Sher Khan swing himself into his saddle, hoping that all her feelings did not show in her face, and they started their ride back along the shore and through the scattered, shadowing groups of trees.

Sher Khan's mood had changed. Now they rode slowly, and did not speak. He appeared withdrawn and thoughtful, and Sarah connected his silence with the messenger who had arrived in such a hurry. Suddenly she was watching him as if he were a stranger. What was he thinking, what had the message been, the message that seemed to have brought trouble with it, for a frown lay like a black bar across his forehead? Unbidden, thoughts of Madore came to her, and the trouble there, things that she had tried not to remember. That hasty departure from the Ranighar, such desperate haste that she had been forced to dress and leave like a fugitive. Had the Ranighar really been so badly burned, or had they indeed been escaping from some danger – what danger? Looking at him, she could not imagine anything that would make Sher Khan run from danger. There was no weakness in the face she covertly studied. Arrogance and determination and at that moment, something that looked like a killing rage. Then he turned his head, and she looked into eyes that were as fierce and wild as the eyes of a tiger. She could not meet that pitiless glare. She looked down and when she lifted her eyes again he was not looking at her, but at the walls of the white Palace, now in plain sight, and he still frowned. The ride was over and Sarah was glad. She had felt and shown fear and this time he had not tried to comfort her.

He did not come in with her, saying that he had things to do. 'I will send for you at sunset, Sarajan.' For a second his face looked relaxed and as she was used to seeing it, as he smiled and said, 'Goodbye. How easy to say these words when I know it is only goodbye for a few hours. I grudge every moment away from you, it is time wasted, Sarajan, soul of my soul. But at sunset I see you again.'

He had spoken in Urdu. What a beautiful language it is, thought Sarah, watching him ride away. In English it would not have sounded right. She went off to look for the children, her mind a jumble of pain and pleasure.

The children were still full of picnic spirits and Ayah had her hands full. Sarah watched, with Julia, their obstreperous bathing and then read to them while they had their supper and finally saw them nodding, poppy-headed with sleep, carried off to bed by Ayah and her grandson, Hyder Ali.

While she was dressing, after having a bath herself, Ayah came in and Sarah asked where Ayesha was. Ayah's reply seemed evasive. The children were safely in bed and asleep, so she herself could help Sarah to dress. There was no need to send for Ayesha.

'But where is she? I have not seen her since we left Faridkote.' Suddenly, for no reason that Sarah could explain to herself, it seemed important that she should know where Ayesha was.

Ayah looked wooden. 'I know not. She is not here. Who knows where she went? Back to Madore, perhaps?'

'Back to Madore? But why? What about the riots? How could she go back to Madore?'

'How can I say? I do not know where she went. Perhaps she was sent back to collect your baggage, which through her carelessness, no doubt, was left behind. Why do you worry about this girl, a new servant? Am I not your servant? Are these hands too old to serve you? Is your hair rough, or your dress badly arranged? Eh, who knows where Ayesha is. Let be now, and I will look after your dressing, or would you prefer that I sent out for another woman?'

Ayah's offended voice did not ring quite true. Was she trying to hide something, and if so, what? So many mysteries, thought Sarah, and then wondered what mystery there could be about Ayesha. She thought about the girl she had liked so much, seeing in her mind's eye the gentle, tranquil face of Ayesha, and even as she thought the face changed, and she seemed to be looking at the face of danger. This was the Ayesha she had glimpsed on the night when the girl had spoken of her sister's murder. Sarah shuddered. She did not want to think of that time, too much came back with it. The smell of burning, and pain, poor Pyari Lal's sprawled body, and the haste with which Sher Khan had set off for the hills, a haste that seemed so unlike her impressions of him. Another little thought came to her, creeping like a snake into her mind. Richard had so often visited the Rajaghar. Was Sher Khan truly unaware of his visits? Leda had made no secret of the fact that she had expected to meet Richard at the Rajaghar. Sarah could not bear to face her doubts. She was glad to submit to Ayah's ministrations, trying to fill her mind with small things, such as whether she should wear the cream silk or the grey, silver slippers or gold, have her hair coiled thus, or thus. Anything to drive away her doubts, save her from her thoughts.

Ayah finished doing Sarah's hair, and stood back in exaggerated admiration of her own skill.

'Eh, such beauty! Never has there been such beauty here!'

'Ayah, you speak foolishly. I come here to the valley

which saw the Begum Bianca, and the Rose, Muna, so do not speak to me of looking more beautiful than those two remembered ones!'

'Ah, but the Rose was your own grandmother, and you are her image. I have not seen her, but I saw the portrait. The Rose has come again in your person.'

'Did you ever see the Begum Bianca?'

'Yes. She was very old when I saw her. This was her Palace you know, long before the Ruler of those days, her husband, took her down to live in the Ranighar. She loved this place very much. This was where she spent her bridal night. There are stories here that she comes back, to stand out there, watching for the Ruler to return. So they say, as they say in the Ranighar in Madore, also. But I do not think Bianca comes back here. I think it is another.'

'What do you mean?'

'I think another comes back to stand and look for the return of another Ruler, a man who could never be hers. Her love was so great that it could easily bring her back, here to this place where the man she loved all her life lived. I think it is she who stands and looks at the lake and dreams still of earthly love, alone.'

Listening to Ayah's cracked old voice, Sarah forgot all her fears. Looking out of the glowing room into the dim, shifting shadows of the courtyard, Sarah understood what the old woman was telling her, knew who the other loving woman could be. As she watched the shadows drift and re-form she could almost see Muna. In her imagination, she saw her crossing the courtyard, her silks blowing about her, her step eternally free and young. Poor lovely Muna, to die so far from the man she loved and the place she loved. How sad to die! To be young, alive, loving and beloved seemed suddenly all that mattered. She searched for the little packet that Sher Khan had given her, and took out the earrings.

Ayah leaned over to look at them.

'Ai! The Peacock earrings. Sher Khan gave them to you?'

'The Peacock earrings?' Sarah spoke slowly, turning the earrings in her fingers. 'Of course. That is what they are. The Peacock earrings, and now I know why they seemed so familiar to me. My mother wears the Peacock ring, given to her by my father as her betrothal ring – and *that* came from Muna, having been given to her by Kassim Khan, Sher Khan's grandfather. What a chain there is, leading back so far –' She stopped speaking, looking down at the jewels.

'Indeed a chain! A chain of love. Put them on, child, and let me see.'

As she adjusted the earrings, Sarah thought about Sher Khan's anger when she had questioned his right to give away State jewellery, and his bitter question about the English being unable to accept gifts gracefully. No doubt Muna had accepted her ring as a gift of love, and now Sarah's mother wore it with pride; it seemed to be one of the things that had come from India that she did not dislike. Sarah felt ashamed of herself – she should have taken this lovely present with more grace. After all, Sher Khan was the Ruler, if he wished to give part of his jewellery away, there was no one with the right to stop him. In her heart a voice seemed to whisper, 'A gift of love'. She looked at her reflection and saw the earrings burn and glitter against her skin. Ayah watched, and sighed with satisfaction.

'Indeed, now I see a Queen!'

'Ayah! What dreams are you spinning? I am no Queen, and even though I wear a Begum's earrings, I am not a Begum.'

'Not yet, maybe.'

'Never. You know I can never be a Begum!'

'I know nothing so foolish. Do you then know what is written on your forehead? Fate will be fulfilled, the chain is a strong one. Wait, child of love, before you use such a long word as "Never".'

Ayah turned away, and began to tidy the room, and Sarah could find nothing more to say. She looked once more at her reflection, seeing nothing but the sparkle of the earrings, hearing nothing but Sher Khan's voice. 'Keep them as a gift from one who loves you more than anything in the world –' How could she doubt him, hearing the sincerity in that voice, how continue to think of him as a possible enemy? She got up and left her room and went out, crossing the shadow haunted courtyard, where the fountain whispered of other days, and the roses clustered, heavy with all the day's gathered warmth, which now seemed to be filling the evening with perfume. In the big drawing room Dip Chand waited with a silver goblet and a bottle. She took her champagne and went out to the *chibutra* where she found Alastair waiting alone.

'Champagne again!' said Sarah, lifting her goblet.

'Yes. And of course, nothing but silver to drink it from. We will be so corrupted by all this luxury. I do not know how we will ever settle down to ordinary life when we leave here. If we ever do leave here.'

'What on earth do you mean? Of course we will have to leave here! Are you in such a hurry to go, don't you enjoy it here?' Sarah's words sounded stupid in her own ears. She did not want to start thinking again. She wanted to push ordinary life, the waiting worries and anxieties, away and live only for this evening.

Alastair shook his head. 'Of course I like this valley. But I do wonder what is happening outside, beyond those mountains. Sher Khan sidesteps all my questions, and I wish that I knew a little more about him, and what he is doing here.'

'He is here, in his own State, minding his own business. And you sound a little ungrateful, Alastair. Perhaps we should just mind our own business too!' Sarah was surprised at her sudden anger; she did not know if she was angry with Alastair, or with herself because of her own hidden doubts.

'Please don't think I am criticising our host. But in fact this is not a time for a native Ruler to be sitting doing nothing in his State. India is on the verge of independence. I would have expected Sher Khan to be down in

Delhi. He does not strike me as being a man who would be out of the action normally. Also, he has a very large, well-trained and well-armed Force – very large for such a small peaceful State. As far as I can make out, every man in this state has done his time in the State Forces, and is a trained soldier. Why? What are they going to do, all these tough fighting men, now that there is no war?'

'Very much the same as all the other fighting men in other countries. Try to learn to live with peace for a change.'

'Hm. No doubt. All the same, I wish I knew what Sher Khan's politics are.'

'Why don't you ask *him*?'

'Because I have, and I don't get an answer. He changes the subject more cleverly than anyone else I know. I cannot believe he would take his army out against the British, if, God forbid, it ever came to that. He does not seem to me to be a man of treachery, and he fought alongside the British in the desert. Sarah, what do you think? You know all about him, don't you?'

For a moment Sarah felt all her own doubts and suspicions returning, flying about her like bats, driving all the happiness and pleasure of this gentle evening hour away with their black, shadowing wings. She managed to say, 'I don't know anything about him,' and then sat in silent misery, looking away from Alastair, and feeling like a traitor to Sher Khan.

'But you must know him,' persisted Alastair. 'Aren't you part of the family? Your father must have talked about him?'

'No. You know from Julia, I am sure, all that I told her about my mother's attitude to India. My father spoke about Lambagh of course, and about Jiwan Khan, Sher Khan's father. Jiwan Khan was my father's greatest friend, I think, but I never heard Sher Khan mentioned.' She sat thinking, going back in her memory to the things she had heard her father say, and like a gift from the past, she remembered a description of Kassim Khan, Sher Khan's grandfather.

Her face brightened, she turned to Alastair. 'One thing I do remember my father saying about Kassim Khan. He said that Kassim Khan was determined that no other country would have any rights in his State, that Lambagh would always be free – and that reminds me of something that Sher Khan said when we were riding up to Lambagh the first time. He said that he was determined to keep his people, and their way of life, safe for as long as he could. I am sure,' said Sarah, suddenly passionately sure, 'I am *certain* that is what he wants, and all he wants. He is going to keep his State free, as it always has been.'

'Well, I hope you are right. But he is going to have a tough time doing it, with the way politics in India are turning at the moment. The rich native states are bound to attract a great deal of attention from the new political rulers in Delhi when the time comes. All I hope is that Britain doesn't hand over in too much of a hurry, because the resulting bloodshed could be terrible. Sarah, what do you plan to do when we leave here?' Sarah looked away across the lake, too honest to pretend she did not understand his question.

'I don't know what I shall do. Go to England, start divorce proceedings. Oh, I don't *know*. It all seems so terrible that I don't want to think about it. Must we talk about it now?'

'No, of course not, if you don't want to. It is just that I worry about you. We have all grown very close, haven't we, Sarah?'

'Yes. Very close. A family.'

'Yes. In the words of the Royal Beast, slightly altered, you seem like my sister. So I cannot help worrying about you.'

Julia came out on to the *chibutra*, and Sarah just had time to say quickly, 'Don't worry about me, Alastair,' before Julia was beside them.

'Why are you worried about Sarah? Sarah, are you all right?'

'Perfectly. Come and drink your champagne.'

'I was just being given my goblet when I heard you talking. Alastair, why do you call him the Royal Beast?'

'Well, because Sher Khan means "The Tiger King".'

'So *that* is why you coined that name! I wondered too.'

'Sarah, I didn't coin it. He seems to have been called that years ago. So he told me, anyway.'

Sarah was glad to have the conversation about her future changed. By tacit consent, she and Alastair did not continue to discuss it in front of Julia, who was full of happy anticipation of the evening ahead.

They had just finished their drinks when they saw the lamps bobbing up the hill. Sarah hurried off to check that the children were asleep. David was soundly off, but Penelope sat up to stare at her mother.

'Mummy, you look a very beauty lady. Will you be bringing me back the Bonnie bird?'

'Well, not tonight, darling.'

'Well. Well, I shan't be happy, not really happy, until he is safely here.'

'Oh, darling, you were happy today? On the picnic?'

'Oh, yes. But not at the very bottom of my mind. I always miss my bird.'

Sarah laughed and kissed her and left her tucked up again and almost asleep. Riding down the hill in the swinging palanquin, she thought sadly that not once had either of the children enquired about their father, and wished that all she herself had 'at the very bottom of her mind' was a deserted green parrot.

Sher Khan was at the entrance to the old Palace to welcome them. Torches flared and flickered in iron sconces against the old walls, but the top of the arched door was lost in shadow. They crossed a large courtyard, patterned with light spilling out of open doors, where soldiers sprang to attention as they passed. The Ruler's quarters were reached through several dark empty rooms. Sarah was sure that she could smell bats and the air struck damp and chill. The large room into which he led them was marble floored, thickly covered with persian carpets. There were low couches round the walls, heaped with cushions, and there were more cushions on the floor. There were many small over-carved tables writhing with dragons and lotuses and peacocks, and the whole room had an air of magnificence gone to seed; velvet cushions with threadbare embroidery, tarnished silver lamps and pictures of Scottish moors with stags at bay fought for pride of place on the walls with priceless Persian paintings.

Sarah became certain that Sher Khan normally lived in the Peacock Palace, and that he had left it for them. Tonight, as if to prove something, he was dressed in a white brocade coat over tight white trousers, and in his emerald turban an emerald peacock flared and glittered, like the emeralds that she wore in her ears.

Alastair, wearing khaki slacks, a silk shirt and a scarf, sighed heavily. 'All this splendour, this Arabian night's finery, and here I am, clean admittedly, but far from fine. My luggage wasn't left behind anywhere. I just didn't happen to have any with me when I was kidnapped!' He laughed, but his laugh rang a little false and Sher Khan turned to stare at him with raised eyebrows.

'*Not* kidnapped, my dear Alastair, rescued! But I see I have been remiss. Of course, you must have clothes. We are about the same size, I think? You shall have a wardrobe tomorrow. In the meantime, let us get rid of some of the finery.' He removed his turban, putting it down as if the priceless jewel in it was so much glass. 'There. Now I am Sher Khan again, I only wished to be dressed up in order to welcome you suitably.' And to remind me that you are the Ruler of this state, thought Sarah looking at him, and then, meeting his eyes, blushed and looked away.

At that moment, the doctor and his wife were ushered into the room. Katya was most splendidly robed in stiff scarlet silks. She was delighted to see them all, and was very much at ease with Sher Khan, going up to him and kissing him affectionately. Dip Chand appeared with his tray of silver goblets and another servant brought round a large plate of samoosas, little curry puffs very highly spiced and fiery. A small boy came in with garlands of jasmine and big pink roses, and from somewhere outside a flute and a drum began to make music.

'We are to have entertainment tonight, before we eat,' said Sher Khan, and through the door swept a figure in crimson and gold. The drum beat quickened and the dancer glided and swirled in drifts of crimson veiling. She was, to their surprise, not a girl but a woman in her thirties. She danced briefly, with grace, her hand movements as supple and delicate as if birds were fluttering round her. She sank in a salutation with joined hands, palm to palm, before Sher Khan and Sarah, smiled with practised seduction at Alastair and drifted out, leaving the scent of sandalwood and attar of roses behind her. The liquid notes of the flute dropped one by one into silence after her departure.

'What a wonderful performance,' said Alastair. 'I have seen a great many dancing girls, but never one so elegant and graceful – or so brief.'

'That is Rhada, and she is very famous,' said Sher Khan.

Julia was obviously struggling with a question she wished to ask but did not quite dare. Sher Khan smiled at her, and taking courage she said, 'Tell me – is she a temple dancer?'

Sher Khan nodded. 'Yes. One of the best known dancers. She lives in Agra, but she is from this valley.'

'Then she is a *real* temple dancer?'

'A real one?' Sher Khan was puzzled.

'Yes. I mean, does she sleep with people?'

Sher Khan's eyebrows rose to his hairline. 'Well, I imagine that she does! Provided that they can afford her price. She is a very expensive lady.'

'Goodness!' said Julia, enthralled. 'Imagine, Sarah, that was a real pros –'

'Julia, *darling*,' interrupted Alastair desperately, but Julia swept on, regardless of the fascinated horror of most of her audience.

'Do you suppose your grandmother was like that,

Sarah?' Sarah was gathering herself for a reply, while Katya Bukova was obviously begging her husband for a translation of what was being said.

Sher Khan's voice was cool as he said, 'No, Julia. Munabhen was the most beautiful woman ever seen. More beautiful than the Begum Bianca. There has never been anyone else like her, except her grand-daughter.'

'And that should answer most of your questions, my little tactless *love*,' said Alastair and firmly took Julia to look at the carved stone peacocks that formed the door-posts. Sarah talked to Katya Bukova in her effortless Urdu, on which the other woman complimented her.

Then Katya, leaning closer, said, 'But Khanum! You are wearing the Begum's earrings. I must congratulate you. Indeed, this is good news!'

Confused, Sarah looked at her, seeing nothing but smiling goodwill in Katya's face. She was about to ask the woman what she meant, when Sher Khan came up, and with a word of excuse to Katya, took Sarah away to sit apart with him.

'Those jewels take their brilliance from your eyes tonight. May you wear them in good health, and happiness. I wore their companion in my turban. You saw it?'

'Yes. Was it meant to tell me that you are the Ruler?'

'It was to tell you that I have the right to give those jewels to anyone I please. I give them to you with love. The last woman to wear them was my mother, they were given to her with love by my father. She wore them with happiness.'

'I am proud to wear them, but I must return them when I go from the valley. I have no right to them.'

'I do not know what you mean. I tell you, those are a gift, from me, to the woman I love. You can never give them back. What is this talk of rights? I insist that you understand one thing. You are my love. Now, no more of this. Enjoy yourself, Sarajan. Not only are you my love, you are my guest.'

Whatever Sarah would have said in answer was interrupted as Julia came over with Katya. It was time for the ladies to retire, said Katya, to wash their hands while supper was being laid out.

With Dip Chand going ahead with a lantern, they stumbled into a smaller room which contained a camp bed, a folding table and a camp stool. Katya Bukova looked about her with interest and said to Sarah, 'The Ruler has learned to live hard on his campaigns. But I would have thought he had had enough discomfort! Why does he live here and not in the Peacock Palace? Nay, Khanum, do not look worried, there are many rooms up there, it cannot be that you are taking up rooms that he would use. Unless –' She paused and looked thoughtful, and then diabolically amused. 'Oh, of course – that is it. He does not trust himself too close to you. Khanum, can it be that you wear the earrings and still hold out? What more do you desire? You must be able to see how it is with him. He is a man overthrown by love. Do not strike too hard a bargain. Men are lovers for a very short time.'

The room was dim and cavernous with shadows. The bats that Sarah had smelt on her arrival were flying in soundless yet palpable flight, somewhere high above her head. Julia, coming out of a smaller room, said brightly, 'Is anyone else going to go?'

Katya removed her bright gaze from Sarah and said, 'She has finished, the little sister? Then I go and make water. These dinners of Sher Khan's can last for an age.'

Sarah, when she got back to the room where the men waited, could not look at Sher Khan. Did he too think that she was holding out against his love for any pecuniary reason? She felt soiled and cheap, and found herself disliking Katya. She sat as far from her as she could, but as the evening wore on she saw that she was being unjust. Katya was a peasant, who was judging her by her own standards; she meant no harm.

For once there were no servants. Alastair and Sher Khan and Doctor Bukov waited on the two girls, and Katya firmly waited on herself, flitting from dish to dish like the tropical bird she so much resembled. The evening gradually became what it had been intended to be, a meeting of friends enjoying themselves. The dancer came back and danced again, a strange dance that consisted mostly of neck and hand movements. Julia, studying her face, saw that she was not beautiful but she noticed that while she was in the room she held the attention of the two European men completely. Only Sher Khan was untouched by her seduction. His eyes were entirely for Sarah. When the dancer had gone again, Julia asked Alastair what it was about her that was so attractive.

'I do not know,' he said honestly. 'She means nothing to me and yet I cannot stop looking at her. She gives one the feeling that she is every woman, and everything that a woman can be to a man. She is Lilith.'

'Who is Lilith?'

'Well, she was Adam's mistress. Julia, I am only confusing you. I will explain it all another time.'

Sarah, leaning over, said, 'Put it away with the American Cavalry, Julie,' and they were still laughing when the first sounds of trouble outside came to them.

The flute kept up its gentle tune for a few minutes longer, but soon it could not be heard above the sound of raised voices, conflict, and trampling feet.

'What on earth is going on?' Alastair started for the door, but Sher Khan was there before him.

'Get back, Alastair, and keep the girls out of the way.' Sher Khan had his hand on the door when it was pulled sharply open, and two men came in, ordering their dress as they did so.

'Lord of the Hills. We have the Englishman you expected. He tried to fight his way into your room –'

As the man spoke, there was a furious upsurge of trampling and shouting from the darkness beyond the door. Struggling, several more men fell into the room, and from the mêlée rose Digby, his clothes torn, blood dripping down his face, to confront Sher Khan.

'A charming welcome, Sher Khan –' Digby staggered as he spoke, and Alastair hurried across the room to grab him, and keep him on his feet. Sher Khan barked orders, and most of the soldiers left, except for two, who came warily to help Digby to a chair. He lay back, his face very pale, and the cut above his eye bleeding profusely. Sarah snatched up a napkin and held it to his face, and the doctor nodded at Sher Khan who was holding up a bottle of Cognac.

'Major Lawton,' said Sher Khan, 'try and swallow some of this.'

'No difficulty, I assure you. My throat is full of dust, thanks to your rather overzealous guards. *Don't* do that, whoever you are!' Digby pushed the doctor's hand away. 'That hurts, but it is only a bump on the head. Nawab Sahib, I had five men with me.'

'Do not worry about them, Major Lawton, they are attended to.'

'Not dead, I trust? They were fighting rather well when I last saw them.'

'Don't be ridiculous, Digby. Of course they are not dead. Have some more brandy, and shut up.'

'It is no thanks to you that your men are not dead, Major Lawton.' Sher Khan's voice was very cold. 'Why did you try and get through the guards without sending me a message? Of course they thought you were someone else, about whom they had strict orders. If you had behaved in this foolish way at the frontier you would not have got into my state at all.'

'I did not realise that having once got in, I would be in difficulties if I did not identify myself to every guard I met! This place is guarded like a Turkish harem! Please tell this chap to leave me alone.'

But Doctor Bukov had had enough. 'Young man, be quiet. I am going to examine your head, it is necessary.'

'Oh, very well, if you feel you must,' said Digby, subsiding, but still holding off Bukov's hand. 'Wait though – Nawab Sahib, I have a great deal of news for you, and some letters.'

'They will have to wait for tomorrow,' said Doctor Bukov firmly.

'Now I am going to take you down to the hospital. Katya, go and tell them to prepare for me. I shall bring him down myself. Now, young man, you lie still, and be quiet.'

Digby's speech had begun to slur, and he suddenly seemed content to lie back with his eyes closed. Katya made her farewells; to Sarah's surprise she kissed her affectionately and said, 'Come and see me soon, Khanum,' before she left.

Digby was lifted, chair and all, by four soldiers, and carried out, apparently now unconscious. 'Good,' said Doctor Bukov. 'He is almost asleep. A most furious young man!' He said goodbye, and followed his patient, Alastair and Sher Khan going out with him.

'*Well*,' said Julia, round eyed, 'He didn't even see us! Was he very badly hurt, Sarah?'

'No, I don't think so. A bump on the head, and I imagine that cut will have to be stitched. He will be all right tomorrow, I expect, after a good night's sleep.'

Sarah spoke calmly but her thoughts were in turmoil. Who was the man the guards had been expecting, the Englishman about whom they had been given strict orders? And Digby: why had he fought his way in like a madman, what messages did he carry for Sher Khan? The peace of the valley seemed to have gone. Digby's arrival spoke of nothing to Sarah but more mystery, and trouble. She sat, answering Julia at random, until Sher Khan and Alastair came back.

'He's all right. Not wounded, just very roughly handled by my men. He was mistaken for someone else. If he had told them his name, and sent in a message, he would have had no trouble at all. As it was, he was very lucky. What an extraordinary man. He came by way of the old road, on foot, and using goat trails as short cuts. What a climber he must be. But I think, quite mad.'

'How did he get as far as this without being stopped?'

Sher Khan shook his head. 'This is why I say he is mad. When he got to the frontier, he behaved in a perfectly normal way. Gave his name, and showed the letters that

262

he was carrying for me, and had no trouble. But when he got here, to my Palace, he tries to break in, as if he is storming an enemy stronghold – with five men! He is lucky that his men were not killed. Most foolish.'

The evening had lost it gaiety. Like people leaving a theatre they were all suddenly confronted with reality. It was time to go home.

But Sarah had to ask one question. 'What news did he bring, Sher Khan?'

'Khanum, Bukov would not let us talk to him. We will hear his news tomorrow.'

The palanquins were waiting outside. Julia went first with Alastair, and then Sarah said her quiet good night. The others had already jogged away into the darkness, but when she turned to get into her equipage Sher Khan, who had taken her hand, began to draw her back towards the door.

'No, Sher Khan!'

'Come, Khanum, only for a minute. You will be back before them, I promise, they are being taken by a longer way.'

'Sher Khan, how could you?'

'Very easily. I only want to speak alone with you for a little while. I cannot let you go after such an ending to our evening.'

He led her into a small walled garden, where unseen plants breathed their scents into the night air. In the dusk and rustle of the garden he turned to face her.

'I have to be sure that you have forgiven me for being so rude to you today – have you?'

'There is nothing to forgive!'

'Good. Then there is something else I wished to tell you.'

The sky wheeled, stars fell, perhaps; for all Sarah knew, time stopped and the world waited while he kissed her.

Presently he said quietly, 'And is that love, my bird? Do not say yes. That is the outward showing, a little only of the showing. Deep within is the treasure of my love, beating with my blood, every beat timed by your closeness. Tell me, tell me you feel as I do, speak to me of your love now, let me hear your heart!' But Sarah could not speak. Shattered by her own feelings, she clung to him until he bent to kiss her again.

After a few minutes she said, 'You do not think me mercenary – that I hold you off so that you will buy my love with presents?'

Sher Khan's arms slackened on her body. 'Sarajan, I am, I think, made mad by your nearness. What you are saying makes no sense to me. What do you mean?'

Sarah looked up at him, trying to see his face in the darkness. 'I want you to know why I cannot tell you that I love you. It is because I have no right to do so yet. I am not free, and until I am I do not feel that I can tell you anything.'

Sher Khan took her close again. 'You are talking great nonsense, I think. Very well. Keep your fetters, Sarajan. Words have little importance. Your answer is already mine. I can wait for all the rest.'

A bird calling, disturbed, from the walls roused them. 'Sarajan, I must send you back. How foolish! Not for much longer will I put up with this foolishness. Come.'

They walked out of the little garden together, but when they came to the palanquin he said suddenly, 'No, I cannot bear it yet. Rama! Tell the syce to bring Rustom.' He looked smiling into her startled face. 'We will ride together once more, Sarajan, and I will hold you in my arms a little longer. We will tell the others how your palanquin broke.'

They rode slowly up the steep winding path to the Peacock Palace. It was very dark, a black windy night, with only a few stars wheeling in the sky. Wild geese flew high through the clouds that were blowing in ragged drifts before the wind. The call of the unseen birds was like the cry of the night itself. I shall remember this for ever, thought Sarah. No matter what happens.

The same thought came to Sher Khan. He bent his head close to hers, and said, 'These are the jewels we will

keep – these snatched moments that we spend together.'
She did not speak, but for the first time she kissed him
unasked. Rustom was surefooted and knew the way,
which was as well. The kiss was long. She felt afterwards
the deep thunder of his heart against her, and was
shaken at the strength of her own feelings.

The ride seemed to end too soon. They came round the
last curve in the road, and from the massive bulk of the
Peacock Palace a light streamed on to the steps in latticed
bars. There was the scent of wood smoke and roses –
they were home.

When Alastair and Julia jolted up in their palanquins,
Sarah and Sher Khan were waiting for them on the
verandah, steaming cups of coffee in their hands.

'My dear fellow, where did you go? I brought the
Khanum up, her palanquin was damaged. We were getting quite worried about you.'

'So was I,' said Alastair, briefly. 'Very worried. For
some strange reason our *jimpanis* got lost – took us quite a
different way.'

'I regret,' said Sher Khan. 'I will deal with them suitably.'

Sarah poured out hot coffee, not daring to look at
Alastair, and they all sat happily silent, Julia's hand held
close against Alastair's shoulder by his good arm. Sarah
and Sher Khan, decorously apart, met each other's eyes
and looked away quickly. Sher Khan cleared his throat
and said, 'Alastair, tomorrow we will go together to meet
Digby, you and I. Supposing I send a mount for you,
how do you feel about riding?'

'Yes, I would be delighted to ride. Palanquins are not
for me. They appear to get lost very easily, and also I am a
very bad sailor.'

Sher Khan held his expression of gravity. 'Very well,
and I will send up some clothes too; choose the garments
that fit you. I do not know if my boots will fit, but if you
can make shift for a few days, we can have some made by
my bootmaker in the village. Khanum, I think I shall be
able to bring Digby back for luncheon tomorrow, if the

doctor releases him. Now, if you will forgive me, I must go – I hope our next dinner party will not be so startling, but will end as happily.'

Sarah took a long time to go to sleep that night. The wind was stronger, and the waters of the lake beat like a sea below her window. Her room was full of the sound, and the smell of pines and clear water. Far above, as she leaned from her window, she heard the cry of the geese passing over, and knelt on the window seat to listen. When, chilled, she went to bed, she seemed to feel deep within her all the yearning loneliness of their wild crying.

28

The next morning seemed long. After breakfast Sarah and Julia walked down to the lake shore with the children and helped to sail a whole fleet of little boats, beautifully made in birchwood and reeds by Hyder Ali. This occupation ended when David overreached himself, fell into the lake and was hauled out dripping and carried home to Ayah. The children lunched, and went for their afternoon rest. Julia and Sarah sat out on the *chibutra* and Dip Chand brought them their pre-lunch drinks.

'Champagne, of course,' said Julia. 'Really, I wish I knew if Sher Khan always drinks it, or if he thinks the British are used to drinking it by the gallon, morning, noon and night.'

'I think you will find he always drinks it himself. And he knows British habits very well, you know, Julie. He is as English as I am!'

'Yes, of course he is. I keep forgetting about that. You seem so much more English than he does.'

'Or he seems more Indian than I do.' Sarah was watching the path from the village, where a group of riders was approaching. Her breath shortened, her heart thumped. This had been the focus of the day, not Digby's return, but Sher Khan's return to her. Everything else had faded into insignificance. All that mattered was the necessity of seeing Sher Khan, hearing his voice, meeting his admiring eyes. Angry with herself, Sarah felt suitably punished when she saw that he was not among the riders.

Presently Alastair joined them. When he had kissed

Julia, he said, 'Sher Khan has taken Digby off to see where his men are billeted. They will be along later.' He accepted a goblet of champagne and stretched with a groan. 'This luxurious living has done me no good. I could hardly stay on that animal this morning, and now I am as stiff as a board.' He drank thirstily, with the two girls poised over him 'Like terriers at a rat hole,' he said. 'Give me another drink, and sit down, and I will tell you my news.' Or some of it, he added to himself.

'Digby has not had much luxurious living. Not in the last few days, anyway. He came up by tracks that are used by the herders. No one seems to know how he found his way. He left Madore about five days after us. The rioting was grossly exaggerated. No question of the troops being mixed up in it at all. There were several agitators about, and some civil rioting, mostly intercommunal, in the walled city. Two British battalions went in to show the flag, but the whole thing was well contained by the police. Frankly, the most astonishing bit of news is this. Digby is on leave.'

'On *leave*?'

'Yes. On leave. Furthermore, I don't have to worry either. I have three months' leave too. He made out leave chits, told the C.O. what had happened, and here we are – perfectly legal.'

'Well! How on earth did he manage it?'

'We are entitled to leave – but we would not have got it, I don't imagine, unless Digby had used the magic words, "guests of the Ruler of Lambagh", and because of that, no problem. It appears that he went back to the Madoremahal, and the Ranighar, found a watchman who said you were all on your way to Lambagh, so he collected five of our men who were also due for leave, and are hill men, told his story about being invited up here, fixed leave for both of us, and for the men, and set off. Even the Ruler is lost in admiration!'

'Do I understand you to mean that he thought we were in trouble and came hot foot to the rescue?'

'No, Sarah, not by that time. You were right when you

said that you were sure that Sher Khan was incorruptible, and would have no dealings with revolutionaries. It seems that the only time Digby came close to trouble was when he reported his suspicions of the Ruler of Lambagh to GHQ. They fairly blasted him. Sher Khan is one of the most trusted of the Princes, will not have anything to do with politics and has returned to Lambagh with honours thick upon him, and the British Government is extremely anxious to keep on good terms with him. No, Digby didn't come to rescue us. I think he likes mountain climbing, fishing and hunting, all of which he hopes to get up here – among other things.' Alastair looked briefly at Sarah.

'Well, but if he knew we were all safe, what on earth made him behave like a lunatic last night?' Julia was looking from Sarah to Alastair as she asked her question.

Alastair hesitated, and then said, 'God knows. It seems he got put out when they started asking his business at the Palace, and he could hear a splendid party going on inside.' A lame excuse, he thought to himself. The truth was that Digby had heard Sarah's voice and Sher Khan's and had gone berserk with jealousy, but there was little point in saying that. He smiled at Sarah, saying, 'Well, there you are – all your instincts about the honesty of the Royal Beast were correct. Aren't you pleased?'

'Yes – but not surprised! Any other news?'

'Oh, bits and pieces. Letters for Sher Khan, news of the Ranighar, which should be habitable again in about three months. The roof on the lake side is the trouble. The whole of that side was gutted, including one of the rooms. Fortunately, Sarah, it was not your bedroom. Those wall paintings in there are priceless. But Sher Khan will tell you all about that.'

Sarah had unasked questions trembling on her lips. She was certain that Alastair was holding something back, but did not care to question him in front of Julia, because she was sure that the news she wanted concerned Richard.

269

They heard Digby's voice speaking to Sher Khan, and then they appeared, walking out onto the *chibutra*. No trace of the wild-eyed scarecrow of the night before! Digby was his usual immaculate self, except for various bruises and a dressing, taped over his left eyebrow. He kissed both girls with the casual affection of an old friend, and Sher Khan brought him a drink, and in minutes they were all talking as if they had never been apart.

Digby raised his goblet to Sher Khan. 'Mine host – here is gold dust in your eye! What splendid luxury you live in! You have no idea of the trouble I got into with the top brass when I rushed in and suggested that you were a traitor and a terrorist. I thought I was about to be court-martialled and shot. I think you might have put us in the picture.'

'*I* might have put you in the picture? I had no idea that I was an object of so much suspicion! Besides, I would have found it very difficult to say to you, "I am a loyal servant of the British Raj, I have no intention of joining any treacherous band of scheming Indians." I do not think that you would have believed me and in any case it would not have been the truth.'

Sher Khan drained his drink, and getting up, refilled his goblet. 'No,' he said, seating himself beside Sarah. 'It would not be strictly true. I served with your Army, bringing my troops with me, and I gave money for your war effort. *That* is true. But on the other hand I do not consider the Indian leaders who are preparing for independence to be traitors. Like them, I deplore terrorism and anarchy, and I will have nothing to do with violent action against law and order. I do not understand how you could so mistrust me.'

He turned to look at Sarah. 'Khanum, surely you should have known better! You know the story of my State; I do not believe that anything you ever heard about Lambagh State and its Rulers could have led you to imagine that we were revolutionaries! What made you so untrusting of me?'

Sarah could not answer him. It was impossible to say to him, I knew that my husband was a constant visitor to your Palace, you entertained his mistress, and therefore I found it hard to trust you, although everything I knew about you, and everything I felt in my heart told me that you are an honest man. Finally she said lamely, 'I think it must have been all those soldiers we saw in the hills. They looked so dangerous somehow –'

'They are very dangerous. They are highly trained fighting men. They fought bravely, and a great many of them died, both in the desert and in the jungles of Burma. What you saw were those that were left going home to their mountain villages. I think my soldiers deserved better thoughts in your mind. It was your country for which we fought.'

'That is not fair,' said Alastair. 'For one thing, Sarah defended you constantly when we voiced *our* doubts. For another, we had no way of knowing what your soldiers were doing. You know what the tensions are here in India now.'

Sher Khan bowed stiffly to Sarah.' I am grateful to the Khanum for defending me. But it would have been better if you had brought your suspicions to me. I have no record of double dealing.' He looked round at them all and his glance was not friendly.

Penelope and David, rushing on to the *chibutra* to see Digby, were a welcome diversion. Penelope ran into his arms with a shriek of delight.

'Oh, my own Digby! Where have you been?'

'Well, up to London to see the Queen, of course.'

'You did? And the King? And did you stop at Madore, and bring back the Bonnie bird?'

This needed explanations. Baulked of the parrot, Penelope sat on his lap and peered into his face.

'Very well,' she said. 'But I tell you something you forgot. You forgot my littley bear.' Digby, leaning his head back from her piercing close-up stare, demanded clarification from Sarah.

'You remember the bear on the way to the picnic? The

one you so rashly promised to collect on the way home?'
said Sarah.

'Oh, that littley bear!'

'Yes. You forgot it because of Julia's poor-sore-arm and
all the Nawab's men,' said Penelope, her lower lip jut-
ting.

Sher Khan leaned forward to look at her. 'Moon of the
Palace, what men of mine have annoyed you? Tell me,
and I will call a peacock to scream for thunder and lightning to frighten them.'

'Oh, no, don't do that,' said Penelope diverted. 'I
don't at all care for thunder and lightning. Besides, all
those men in the mountains who spoiled the picnic were
Ayah's friends. She told me.'

'What, all of them? My poor soldiers. What a lot of
trouble they have caused – even the Ayah had to defend
them.'

Penelope wriggled out of Digby's arms and went over
to stand before Sher Khan. 'Listen,' she said, on a high
note. Perforce, everyone listened. 'I want my Bonnie
bird. And I tell you something else. Julia wants her littley
puppies that you gave her. *Why* you don't send some of
your men to bring them up here? What do you think?'

'I think,' said Sher Khan kissing her, 'I think. What
girls this family breeds! Now my soldiers must be sent to
collect a bad-tempered green parrot and a litter of puppies – and green parrots hang on every tree like noisy
fruit, and the village streets are alive with small white
dogs.' He kissed her again, and was kissed enthusiasti-
cally in return, and his anger seemed to be forgotten.

'May I call you David, Penelope,' said Alastair.

She looked at him, laughing. 'Silly! He's David, I am
Penelope, a girl.' But the allusion was not lost on Sher
Khan.

'David, the sweet singer, who calmed King Saul. We
all need our sweet singers sometimes. Forgive me, my
friends. Yes, I lost my temper. I am sure you understand.
It is hard to be distrusted by those you love, but now it is
over. We have other things to discuss.'

Dip Chand, followed by innumerable helpers, brought luncheon out to the *chibutra*, and Ayah came for the children. The meal was a silent one for Sarah and Julia; the men were in close conversation and both girls were straining their ears to hear what was being said.

'Mountain passes – contingencies – small arms, boundaries and frontier posts; what on earth are they talking about? We might as well not be here,' said Julia finally.

'I don't know what they are discussing,' said Sarah, looking at Sher Khan's intent face, 'but whatever it is, it looks fairly important. Julia, how do you feel about trying to ride this afternoon? Just a little amble, nothing strenuous, to get you back into the saddle. You must be awfully tired of palanquins, however glamorous. Yes? Do you think you could, now that you are out of a sling?'

'Oh, yes, how lovely – but I have no riding kit here.'

'This local day attire is comfortable to ride in. All the women here ride, and very well too. After all, I wore it on the day of the picnic, remember?'

Sher Khan, told of the projected ride, thought it a good idea. 'Do not go too far. I would like us to meet at teatime, Khanum. I have various things I wish to tell you.' His eyes were telling her that he loved and wanted her. Nothing else seemed to matter, not even Digby's news which he had brought with him, and which they had not yet heard.

They rode along the lake shore. The sparkling water ran away in arrowheads from the busy fleets of moorhen and duck that lived along the reedy edge. They saw a kingfisher, an immobile blue and green shape on an old log. As they watched, he flashed into spearing life, and then returned to sit, a small fish crosswise in his beak. Parrots screamed and flung green arabeques from tree to tree, and sheep wandered ahead of them, pulling at the tufted grass. A small shepherd boy played his pipe to himself in a patch of shade. Women washing clothes waved and smiled, the gold on their arms and hands flashing back the sun.

'This place is too beautiful, like Eden before the serpent,' said Julia, reining up to watch another kingfisher hurl himself into the lake, brilliant blue against blue.

Sarah, watching too, said, 'Not before the serpent, Julie, look.' The tiny killer had returned successful, a fish the size of a sardine struggling in his bill. 'Before the serpent, he would have been eating grass, one presumes. But as you say, what a beautiful place.'

'Isn't it odd to think that you have come back to the country of your grandmother – she came from here, didn't she?'

'Yes, she was brought here, went away for her training, and then came back and met my grandfather, Alan Reid.'

'I wonder if they lived in the Peacock Palace. Perhaps they rode along here, as we are riding today.'

'I expect they did. This was the last of India for her. She married, and went to England almost at once, and never came back here.

Sarah looked at the glittering scene in front of them, at the soaring white-streaked mountains, felt the warm sun, heard the soft moan of wood doves echoed by the faltering notes of the pipe. It was as if she was hearing and seeing it on behalf of that other woman, who had left it all and gone to live far from her home.

Julia, unknowingly, echoed her thoughts. 'Could you bear to leave this for ever, Sarah? I don't think I could. I shall have to keep coming back.'

'You'll be far too busy with your duties as lady of the manor to come back – except perhaps for your golden wedding. Julie, we've ridden far enough, let us turn and go back. If we take it easily today, you will be able to ride tomorrow again.'

They separated to wash for tea. In her room, Sarah sat before the mirror, tidying her hair. The white rose and the jasmine garland on the table made her smile. Sher Khan's commands were certainly obeyed! She brushed her hair, pinned the rose into the dark coils, and went out, to cross the courtyard. Something about the fountain caught her eye and she stopped. What was that, lying in the clear water? Before she could stop herself, she cried out. Beady-eyed in death, as in life, staring up at her malevolently, was the green and blue shimmering head of a peacock, rudely torn from its body.

At Sarah's cry there was a movement on the far side of the court and a soldier appeared. 'Khanum?' He looked alarmed, and when she pointed a shaking finger at the fountain he hurried over.

'Hai. May Allah keep us from harm! This is the work of devils! Khanum, Khanum huzoor, you go!' The urgency in his voice and the horror on his face sent her hurrying across the courtyard and out to the verandah, where with a great lift of her heart she found Sher Khan alone.

'Sarajan! What is it?' Stumbling over her words, feeling that perhaps she was making a fuss over nothing, she told him, and saw his face darken. He went out, and Sarah sat and looked sadly at the lake. After the serpent indeed! Even in this lovely place there were horrors.

When Sher Khan came back, however, he made light of the whole affair. 'A hawk flying over dropped that trophy. Probably killed by a wild cat outside in the woods. I wish you had not seen the poor thing, knowing your family's affection for birds.' But Sarah could not laugh with him.

'Why was the soldier there, Sher Khan?'

'The Begum's rooms are always guarded, Sarajan. It is the custom. A ceremonial guard. Because you are there, the men have been told to be alert, but to keep out of your way.'

Sarah reflected that she had not seen any guards until this evening, after Digby's arrival. Was Sher Khan telling the truth?

'But how was the peacock's head put into the fountain if there was a guard on duty?'

Sher Khan sighed, with exaggerated patience that did not ring true. 'Sarajan, I told you, the bird must have been killed by a wild cat outside in the gardens. Then perhaps a hawk or a kite took the head and flew over, and dropped it, finding it too heavy. Please, light of my life, is such a small thing going to worry you?'

'A hawk with a good aim, to get that head into the fountain. Tell me, Sher Khan, are you sure that Digby did not bring bad news?'

'Nothing that we did not know already. In fact, his news was good. Alastair is on leave, the rioting in Madore well controlled; no, the news was not bad.'

'Then – why did you put a guard on my rooms?'

'Sarah, you show me plainly that you think I am a liar!'

Sarah shook her head at him. 'No. I do not think you are a liar. But I do not think that you are telling me the whole truth.'

'That is the same thing. Come, Sarajan, let us forget all this chit-chat about peacocks' heads and guards. We waste precious time. Come, sit close to me and let me look at you. That little pulse I see throbbing in your throat, does it beat so fast because I am near you?'

Sarah could find no way of making him tell her anything. He was charming, amorous, and she was convinced that he was hiding something important, that he had bad news, and that every word he said was designed to throw dust in her eyes and distract her from whatever it was that Digby had told him.

'Sarajan! You are not listening to me! I am telling you fascinating stories of Lambagh and you sit there with glass eyes, not hearing a word. Where have you gone, my love?'

'I am sorry, Sher Khan. Forgive me. But I am very worried. I wish you would tell me why I am guarded.'

Sher Khan became silent, looking at her. Then he said, all laughter gone from his face, 'Very well, Sarajan, I will tell you. When Richard Longman is dead, your quarters will be unguarded, if you so wish. But as long as he lives, you and the children are at risk.'

She stared at him, her face very white.

'Khanum, you know what that means. If you are in danger, so am I. You see, now look at you? The mention of his name makes you afraid. This is reason enough for me to wish him dead, no matter where he is. I sleep better because you are guarded by four of my men. So, does that answer your questions?'

As he finished speaking, the others came out to join them for tea and Sarah could say no more. She was desperately worried and very upset, but it seemed that no one noticed anything and she slowly collected herself. She wondered if Julia would notice the guard on her rooms in the Peacock Palace, and how she would feel if she knew they were there because of Richard.

During tea the two girls had the news broken to them that they would be alone most of the next two days. It appeared that Sher Khan was taking Digby and Alastair to see the border posts between Sabnattar and the valley of Lambagh. Sarah, looking at Sher Khan's face, thought, But there is something more. They wouldn't go now to look at border posts, there is no need. They are expecting something – or someone.

Underlining the unease she felt, Sher Khan turned to her and said, 'Stay close to the Peacock Mahal, and if you ride, ride towards the village rather than the mountains. Of course, you will not ride at all after sunset.'

Julia, listening, was immediately alarmed. 'I thought this valley was a haven of peace and safety – is there trouble up here?'

Alastair took her hand. 'Darling, of course not.'

Sarah, suddenly decided, said, 'That isn't good enough, Alastair. Sher Khan, you are keeping something from us, because you do not want to worry us. I am sure you would not tell us to stay close to the Palace and put a guard on us if everything was normal. You will have to tell us. I have my children to think of, as well as Julia. It worries me much more to sense something is wrong and not know what it is.'

Sher Khan raised his eyebrows at Alastair and Digby and said, 'Very well. I will tell you. You know that Hardyal, my cousin, is contesting my right to the *guddee* – the throne – of Lambagh State? Well, it seems that he is not only putting his case to the Viceroy and the Chamber of Princes. He is determined to come up here and put his case to the people. This is distressing, it could cause trouble among my people.'

'Is he here already?'

'Well, this I do not know yet. but Digby saw some travellers on the way to the valley, and he thinks they could have been Hardyal and his associates.'

Sarah stared at Digby, who avoided her eyes. Julia said, 'But that man Hardyal, we met him at your house, the night of your party. He seemed so quiet and gentle.'

Sher Khan's lips twitched. 'Oh, he is indeed quiet and gentle. Also that night he was exceedingly drunk. But however quiet and gentle he is, he has some unpleasant friends, and I prefer to know that you are protected against these men and their plans.'

'And why are you then going off and leaving us, going to the border posts?' Sarah spoke slowly. She was wondering if her suspicions about Hardyal's companions – or at least one of them – were correct.

A little shiver of fear chilled her as Sher Khan said, 'We are going to make sure that they do not get in easily. Now let us talk of other things. Give me another cup of tea, Khanum, and do not look so worried. Would I leave you in danger?'

Before Sarah could think of an answer that would not betray her deep disquiet, Julia said, 'Will you be a long time away, Alastair?'

'Julie, darling, two days. Which is an age, I know. But I will be back before you know that I have gone.'

'There is something wrong with that reasoning,' said Julia, inclined to be worried and therefore cross.

'Don't fret, pretty Julia. I have, assisted by Sher Khan who first suggested it, had an idea. Now that we are all gathered in one place, why shouldn't we have our wedding here? There is a Mission Padre at Pathanghar – we could have our quiet wedding beside the lake, and our honeymoon in fabulous surroundings in the House of Paradise. What do you think?'

'Oh, I think yes, what *heaven*,' said Julia rapturously,

278

and blushed to find them all listening and laughing.

Clever Alastair, thought Sarah – clever, kind and loving. Now Julia would have many plans and pleasures to think about, and would not worry for the next two days. The worrying would be all hers.

29

There was a new moon hanging like the tip of a finger in the light evening sky when they dispersed to change for dinner. Sarah stood at her window and watched the sky darken and the delicate crescent sink slowly down behind the mountains in the west. By the time that moon was full, where would they all be? A bird called from the lake and Sarah shivered suddenly and turned away from the window. She dressed in warmer clothes, soft ivory-coloured pushmina, a cashmere so fine that it was like cobwebbed lace, that clung and moved round her as airily as chiffon. She put the Peacock earrings in her ears and stood looking at herself. Riding in the sun had darkened her skin, and now she looked at a lovely Indian girl, dark eyes shining back at her from her mirror. She touched her lips with scarlet, smoothed her hair, and went out past her sentry through the lamplit drawing room and on to the verandah, knowing that she had hurried her dressing because Sher Khan might be waiting for her. But it was Digby who turned to greet her, and after a moment's blank disappointment she accepted that it was right that he should have the opportunity to speak to her alone if he wanted to.

He looked at her in silence, as if he could not believe his eyes. In those robes, he could see her beauty was Eastern. She would be a beautiful woman whatever she wore, but now, dressed in the local dress, she had an exotic beauty that made her a stranger. It was impossible to imagine this girl weeping in his arms. He got her a drink and sat beside her, looking withdrawn and sad.

'Digby, thank you. I cannot tell you how glad we all

were to see you. It was so worrying, not knowing what had happened to you. I had a terrible time after you left. You see, Richard was already in the house, and I am afraid that he killed poor Pyari Lal because he must have seen Richard and tried to tell me. Richard tried to kill me – well, I think he meant to kill me, but only so that enquiries into my death would delay Sher Khan, stop him leaving for Lambagh, or keep him away from the Rajaghar so that he could try and steal the Emerald Peacock. But there is something I must ask you. You thought you saw Hardyal coming up here. Was Richard with him?'

Digby frowned, shaking his head. 'I couldn't be sure – they were too far away. I don't think he was. He is in bad trouble, Sarah. There is a warrant out for his arrest. The Civil Police are after him now.'

'Is it because of that girl on the island, and Pyari Lal?'

'No, I'm afraid it is worse than that. You know he was living with that Polish girl, Leda? Well, I don't know what happened that day, he must have frightened her and she tried to get to the camp. She was found with her throat cut, and I am afraid they are pretty certain Richard did it.' Digby spoke with reluctance. He was very conscious that he was speaking of her children's father.

Sarah sat staring at him, her face all eyes and bones. When she spoke, it was in a whisper. 'Digby, he is quite, quite mad. Oh God, I knew he was going mad. He had changed so much. Digby, I was so frightened. Thank God we are safely up here and out of the way.'

Safe! She was not safe, thought Digby, not while that bastard was alive, and now it was fairly certain that he would try and get into the valley with Hardyal, full of God knows what fearful plots, thought Digby gloomily. If only Sarah and the children were in England! He turned to tell her so, and suddenly saw her clearly in the light from the big oil lamps that Dip Chand was setting around the verandah.

'But she's Indian – a lovely girl, but Indian,' he thought. But then she looked up at him, and it was Sarah again, the emeralds in her ears sparkling green light against her tanned skin.

'What happened to all your own clothes? Were they all burned?'

'No, but the clothes that we brought with us got left behind at Faridkote by mistake. However, we are delighted to have the excuse to wear these lovely things.'

'Did you need any excuse?' Implicit in his question was the suggestion that she obviously preferred her present mode of dress. Sarah looked at him without answering, knowing that he saw before him the Indian girl she had seen in her mirror, not Sarah Longman, and that he did not care for what he saw.

Digby said, out of a heavy silence. 'You look exactly like your grandmother's portrait now, only more beautiful. You've gone an awfully long way from me.'

Thankfully, Sarah heard Julia and Alastair coming out to join them. What could she say to Digby? It was true – she was far away from him now, she felt that he was someone from a distant past, someone she liked, but no longer knew very well. She drank her champagne quickly, and was ready for another while Alastair was pouring out Julia's first drink.

Sher Khan appeared, plainly dressed, his head bare. He went straight over to Sarah, sat down beside her and leaned back with a sigh. 'This is very good, to ride up the road from Lamba village and see the lights of the Peacock Palace, and to know that there is life and beauty here again, after so long.'

'We are the life,' said Alastair, clapping Digby on the back. 'I will not tell you who supplies the beauty. I'll let you guess. But seriously, are they not beautiful?'

Digby looked at the two girls in their graceful robes, the soft lamplight gleaming on hair and skin, and said shortly 'Yes – very beautiful,' and held out his glass for another drink.

'My God,' thought Alastair, 'we are all going to be rolling in the aisles in a very short time, if Dip Chand doesn't hurry up with dinner.' He moved away from

Digby to join Julia. At least she was drinking slowly and with enjoyment; her happiness made him feel proud, her welcoming smile was warm, and she had, at that moment, no worries. With a great sense of wonderment, he knew, that for the rest of their lives, as long as he was with her, Julia would be without worry, and would be happy – and then remembering Richard, he knew that there would be bound to be some grief he would not be able to protect her from. Richard was trouble for all of them.

But very shortly the men drew together to speak of their plans. The two girls tried not to listen, but it was impossible for them. Sarah finally made no pretence, but sat listening openly, and Julia did the same, a puzzled frown beginning to crease her young forehead.

They heard Sher Khan say quietly, with decision, 'We can make no real plans until we know what Hardyal will do.'

'It seems fairly obvious what he will do – come up here, and start creating trouble.'

'Not so. It is in fact anything but a foregone conclusion. You must understand one thing. Hardyal is not a bellicose man, not a very active man. He likes his comforts, and he is terrified of violence. Blood – Great God, a drop of blood would be enough to make him faint! He loves South India, and his great mansion down in Sagpur. He is the Nawab of Sagpur, you know. Really, he has no interest here at all. His grandfather was the one who wanted Lambagh. Once the old boy died, Hardyal was perfectly happy in his seaside Palace, with his – well, I think the best word for them is minions.'

'Minions?' said Julia. 'Minions? James the first had minions, didn't he – the Duke of Buckingham or someone. I've always wondered what it meant.'

'It means serving-men, darling,' said Alastair. He turned back to Sher Khan. 'If Hardyal isn't interested in Lambagh, then why all the plots and contrivances and general alarm? *Not* to mention visits to the Viceroy. Seems a great deal of trouble to take over something you don't really want, doesn't it?'

'Oh, he's being pushed now. I imagine the terrorists feel they want a native prince to lend them a bit of respectability. Also you've forgotten how splendidly Lambagh Valley is positioned from the point of view of our many friendly enemies – Russians and Chinese. It must be known that Lambagh State, under my control, is a very different affair from Lambagh State in the hands of an idiot like Hardyal.'

'It sounds as if there is no cause for alarm. If he is as uninterested as you say.'

'Well – yes and no. If he is being flattered and encouraged to see himself as the longed-for liberator of Lambagh, anything could happen. I do not think he will want to fight; a disturbed State, at this moment, is the last thing his friends and advisers want. No, I think he will try to get the people to back his claim to the *guddee*.'

'Well then, surely he has lost before he has begun? Your state isn't going to vote you off the throne!'

'Maybe not. But this is India, my friends. There are always agitators and dissatisfied younger sons, and place seekers, men open to bribery. Fewer here than in most States. But, none the less, here. And of course superstition plays a big part amongst such a simple sheltered people.'

'Superstition? You are surely not thinking of that peacock's head?'

Sarah, alerted, began to listen hard. So Sher Khan had thought that episode important enough to mention to Alastair and Digby.

'Not specifically. But all the same, you did not see that soldier's face. As far as he was concerned, my head might just as well have been lying in the fountain!'

'Oh, for heaven's sake, Sher Khan!'

'No, seriously. However, it was easy for me to reassure him. After all, here, what I say is important. I am the Ruler, I possess and wear the Peacock chain. Hardyal has never had it in his hands. Nor has any member of his line. But of course, he is of the family.' He paused, his face set in a scowl, then said, 'No one has ever seriously backed his family's claim. But there is always a first time.'

'Well, from what I have seen so far, I should say you are pretty solidly seated on your throne – *guddee*, call it what you will. I think you are unlikely to have any trouble.'

'You are right, of course. My people are – well, in every possible sense of the word, loyal. But as I say, this is India. There are many forms of treachery, and more ways of losing a throne than you could dream of.'

Julia said suddenly, 'I don't understand. I don't understand anything you are talking about, but you make me feel frightened. What is all this about treachery, and losing your throne? Sarah, do you understand?'

Digby, looking at Sarah, thought, oh yes, she understands all right. This is her country, and she accepts the possibilities that Sher Khan is trying to explain to us. He saw that Sarah, who looked so serene and beautiful, was in fact very worried and frightened. The wine was not affecting any of them; they had all stopped drinking as they talked. Alastair got up and went to sit beside Julia, taking her hand.

Sher Khan said, 'Julia, do not be distressed. We are talking about possible unrest in my state – possible, not probable.'

'But what is all this about the Peacock?'

'You know about the Emerald Peacock, the state emblem? Well, I was just saying that the Peacock has never been out of my family's hands, and over the years a superstition has grown up about it. As long as we hold the Peacock chain, we hold the State – it has become the luck of the State.'

By God, thought Alastair, watching Sher Khan, with all his civilised veneer, and after a truly active war, the Royal Beast more than half believes that himself.

Sher Khan stood up. 'Well, I hold the Peacock. So all is well. And if my evil relative appears, and tries to make trouble, we will throw him from the top of Tara Devi. Let us, for God's sake, have a drink.'

'Yes, do let us. Darling Julia, give me your glass. You are not worrying any more?' Kind Alastair, thought Sarah, but who is going to tell Julia that if Hardyal does come, he will probably be accompanied by her brother, my charming husband? Sher Khan was looking at Julia, and appeared to be about to say something!

Sarah said 'Sher Khan?' and shook her head, and he frowned but said nothing.

Dip Chand's announcement that dinner was ready was a relief.

The table was beautifully set, and sparkled with silver and crystal and candle-light. Digby, eating delicious food, and looking at the comfort around them, thought that Sher Khan had the most unusual court for a native Ruler that he had ever seen. This man lived like a rich and cultured European Prince; there was no comparison with the scruffy uncivilised palaces of a great many of the hill states, whose rulers had wealth but not the taste, or education, to enjoy it. Indeed, Sher Khan stood to lose a great deal if his cousin prevailed. Sher Khan, now talking to Alastair about fishing in the mountain streams, could not have looked less Eastern. His skin was no darker than Alastair's tanned face, his eyes sparkled frosty blue, the eyes of a northerner. Looking from Sarah to Sher Khan, he was by far the more Western looking of the two. Now, planning a fishing trip into the mountains, there was no sign of the Ruler who had made such careful plans that afternoon for the safety of the borders. Digby thought of the meticulously drafted orders, of the maps and dispositions. This was a man to be liked and admired and trusted: a splendid leader.

Jealousy twisted within Digby like a serpent as he saw Sarah's expression when Sher Khan turned to speak to her. 'You would like to come on a fishing trip. The children would love it, Khanum.'

Alastair said, 'Yes, and you would too, Julia. Shall we try and fit it in before the wedding, during it, or afterwards?' Julia laughed at him, and the serpent in Digby's mind twisted again as he saw their happiness. It seemed everyone was happy, only he was alone, with no one meeting his eyes with love and pleasure. Now they were speaking of the coming wedding, and Julia was telling him how glad she was that he would be there to be best man. With an effort that made him sweat, he forced himself to reply, to laugh and to appear cheerful.

Under cover of the conversation, Sher Khan leaned close to Sarah. 'Why did you stop me speaking to Julia, warning her about her brother? You protect her as if she was a little girl. It is not kind. You should tell her that Richard is a dangerous maniac and that you are going to divorce him as soon as possible. Do not pretend anything else. It is stupid.'

'I have not pretended anything. All I have done is allow her to think that he is sick – which he is – and also that –'

'That he is curable, and that you will remain his wife.' Sher Khan shook his head. 'Truly, Sarah, it is very silly. He is not curable. He is a murderer. It is dangerous to let her go on imagining that everything will be all right. She is not a fool; it is unfair to treat her as one. She should be told the entire truth and made to believe it. I say again, it is unwise to let her think anything else.'

He did not explain what he meant, but his words made Sarah very uneasy; she knew what was worrying Sher Khan. If Richard had entered the valley and came to the Palace, Julia, knowing nothing, thinking of her beloved brother as a sick man who needed help, might put them all in peril by letting him in, by not giving a warning. Sher Khan was right. She would have to tell Julia the complete truth about her brother.

She told Sher Khan that she would do this, and he said, 'Thank you, Sarajan. I know it is hard but it is wise.' He began then to speak of his departure in the morning.

'What time will you leave?'

'In about four hours' time. Perhaps we should break this up now. Khanum, are you tired?'

'No, not a bit, but you should sleep? You have so many things to do tomorrow.'

He shook his head, the candle-light making his face, with its ardent eyes and mouth, clear for her to see. 'I shall not sleep if I go, I shall lie and think of you. Much better if the others go, and you and I have the rest of the night and the dawn together. Do you remember the night rides we shared?'

'But of course I remember.'

'Night is for lovers – how much better if the others go,' he repeated, making her laugh with his vehemence.

But the others showed no signs of going. In the end, they all sat, bundled in furs and rugs, for the nights were getting colder, talking and watching the night sky slowly change until the streaks of a scarlet dawn reflected in the dark lake. Then Dip Chand brought out tea, and the men went off, Sarah and Julia standing together to watch them go. As the sound of the horses faded to a dull thudding, Julia said, 'What a nuisance this man Hardyal is – spoiling our lovely time here. He has no right to the *guddee*, has he?'

'No, none. His line is far from the ruling family. Julia – .' Sarah paused in the face of Julia's jaw-breaking yawns. This was no time to talk about Richard.

They parted, vowing to sleep until noon. 'It will make the time pass more quickly,' said Julia. 'After all, now we can say they are coming back tomorrow night!'

30

It was late when Sarah woke. Ayah had been in with her tea; it was cold on the table beside her. She got up and went to the window seat, huddling her robe round her, and sat looking out at the busy bird-infested lake. The children were down there, in their little boat, supervised by Ayah's grandson and a young boy, a *chokra*. They were playing at fishing. She heard Penelope's laughter, and smiled to hear it. What a perfect life this was for them, something they would never forget. She caught her breath on the thought. If she had to leave this valley, she would never forget a moment of her time here. Or was it the valley? Sher Khan's face was plain before her mind's eye, she heard his voice as if he was speaking beside her. In or out of the valley, wherever she went in the whole world, the home of her heart would be where he was; there was nothing else for her now, she could no longer hide from her love. It was not the valley she would miss. It was the man.

Thinking of him reminded her of her promise that she would make Julia understand the truth of her brother's total and disastrous insanity. The bright morning darkened at the thought. Penelope's laughter still rang like a bell of pleasure over the water, but Sarah no longer heard it. She bathed and dressed, trying in her mind to find an easy way to tell Julia all the terrible things that she had already been told once, but that she had glossed over because she loved her brother and could not imagine him to be treacherous, dangerous and a killer. There was no way to tell her gently, Sarah decided in the end. She would have to tell her the cold facts, including the news that Digby had brought; that Richard had killed not only Lalani on the island in the lake but that he had killed Leda. Poor Julia, but she must be told. Sarah went out to breakfast, dreading the coming interview, and could find no way to start it, with a Julia who was bubbling over with ideas about her wedding, and who had plainly no thoughts beyond Alastair's return. 'I hope they are not too long – I do not understand why they all had to go.'

'Julia, listen,' said Sarah, her courage finally gathered, but Julia jumped up at that moment and announced that she was going down to the lake to join the children. She went, and Sarah was left with her words unsaid, and Ayah arriving with a shoemaker, full of demands for new shoes for the children.

She had finished her interview with the Ayah, and was ready to go down to the lake, when she heard a horse coming fast up the road from the village. There was no reason to suppose that it could be Sher Khan, but nonetheless a wild hope sprang up in her heart, and she ran to the verandah.

But it was Digby who was dismounting at the foot of the steps.

'Digby! Has something happened?' It was an effort to keep her disappointment from sounding in her voice.

'Nothing happened. I had a lapse of memory, and forgot the map I made of my route over the mountains. Sher Khan particularly wants that map because it was while I was coming up by those paths that I thought I saw Hardyal, and it might give us some idea of where he is, or at least, where he was heading for.' Digby came slowly up the steps as he spoke, looking cross and disconsolate.

Sarah was afraid that he had sensed her lack of welcome, and tried to put more warmth into her voice. 'Digby, how maddening for you. Have a cup of coffee with me before you start back? I was just going down to join Julia and the children, but I know that there is some coffee ready. Come and sit down while I get Dip Chand.'

She had a cup of coffee with him for company, and while she was drinking it, saw that he was staring at her, and still looking very displeased. Presently he said, 'What a different welcome from the one you gave me when I came out to the Ranighar in Madore once. Do you remember, you were not expecting me, and you were so glad to see me that you glowed with welcome, like a lovely lighted lamp.'

'Oh, Digby, I am always glad to see you!'

'Well, you were glad to see me then. But not this time. You thought I was Sher Khan, Sarah, and you were bitterly disappointed to see me. You are in love with him, aren't you?'

She met his look steadily and answered honestly. 'Yes, Digby, I am.' She felt, as she said the words, a great wave of relief and happiness, and yet felt she should say she was sorry. Digby sat quiet for a few minutes, looking away from her towards the lake. When he turned back to her he still did not speak, but looked at her, frowning slightly, his eyes full of pain. Sarah felt terrible, full of regret and pity for him.

Presently he said, 'Sarah, I can understand any woman falling in love with Sher Khan. He is a charming fellow, and better looking than most. But I cannot quite understand you going overboard as you have. You must know most of the answers.'

'What do you mean, Digby?'

'Well, you are behaving as if this was the first time you had ever been in love.'

Sarah thought of Sher Khan saying, 'Every time you fall in love, it is the first time,' and smiled a little to herself, saying, 'Well, perhaps it is.'

'Don't be ridiculous, Sarah! Don't try to tell me you married Richard without falling in love with him. And what about Bruce? You didn't fall in love with him, I suppose?'

Sarah saw his blue eyes blazing with anger, and tried to keep her own temper. 'Digby, I do not see that this is doing any good –' but Digby swept on, his voice shaking. 'And what about me? Tell me, what about me?'

'Digby, I never told you, or let you think, that I was in

love with you.'

'You were on the verge of admitting that you were in love with me – only your stupid scruples stopped you. Where are your scruples now? They don't seem to have stood up to the blandishments of the Nawab Sahib very well!'

'I have not told him that I love him,' said Sarah very quietly. Her pity for Digby was fighting a losing battle with anger.

'You haven't told him? Well, he seems to have guessed! He is very full of himself, very much the master of all he surveys. My God, Sarah, what are you thinking of?'

'I'm not thinking of anything. Digby, don't you think you should go now?'

'I'm not going until I have said a few things – someone has got to make you see sense. Julia and Alastair are so lost in their own affairs that they can't think of anything else, and you – Look at you! You've gone back with a vengeance, haven't you? – right back to Munabhen. I am astonished every time I hear you speak English, because you look as if you have never heard of England!'

Sarah stared at him, horrified at the change in him. Digby was scarlet and shaking with rage. He looked at her as if he hated her.

'Digby!'

'Well, it is true. When you look at Sher Khan, your eyes are the eyes of an Indian woman looking at her master. I cannot bear it, Sarah, wake up! What do you think your mother and father would think of all this? Prancing about in fancy dress.'

'Fancy dress?'

'Yes – what else is it? All right, it is the dress of the valley, but you and Julia are English girls, so it is not your way of dressing.'

'Aren't you forgetting something?'

'What? Munabhen? No, I have not forgotten her. Look, Sarah, for God's sake, Munabhen was your grandmother. You never met her, and you were brought up in England. Until you came up here no one, looking at you, would have guessed anything about your background. Now look at you – you've gone native, taking Munabhen as an excuse, and Sher Khan has encouraged you for his own purposes.'

Sarah stood up, surprised to find how calm she felt. 'Digby, I've had enough of this. I'm going down to the children. Goodbye.'

'No, Sarah, you listen to me. You must, for your own sake.' His intensity held her beside him, and she slowly sat down again. 'Sarah – the children. Have you thought about them and their future? What do you suppose is going to happen to them if you carry this – this affair to its logical conclusion?'

'Sher Khan loves the children, and they love him.'

'Oh, Sarah, so he loves the children, and they love him! That's splendid. But what about their lives, their education, their whole future? What are they going to do? Get their education at some Mission school, and then stick around here in Lambagh in idleness, hangers-on in the state, because their mother is the Ruler's mistress?'

'I will never be Sher Khan's mistress!' Sarah's temper broke, her eyes blazed with fury and hurt. 'How dare you, Digby! You've said quite enough. I listened because I felt sorry for you, but I see there was no need. You are jealous, so you are trying to make me as miserable as you can.'

'You certainly do not have to be sorry for me – I am sorry for you. Sarah, you say you'll never be Sher Khan's mistress. Well, what in heaven's name do you think is going to happen? That man is not going to be satisfied with burning glances and a few kisses, or even a few nights in your bed. He'll want more than that – all your company, your thoughts and your body – for a few years, if you are lucky. What did you think? You surely weren't dreaming of marriage?' He stared at her, and she looked back proudly, her beautiful eyes still blazing defiance.

'Oh, my God, Sarah, you are thinking of marriage. You really are deluded.'

'There have been marriages like this before, Digby, you know. I think you are the deluded one!'

'Sarah, of course there have been marriages like this before.' Digby spoke quietly, and something about his quiet voice frightened Sarah. He leaned forward, looking steadily at her. 'Sarah, listen to me. Sher Khan is not going to marry you. He can't. He's got his precious State to think of – and you must know how precious this State is to him. His English blood doesn't mean a thing, will make no difference to him – the Indian side of him is far stronger. He will not do anything that is likely to harm Lambagh State, or put the succession in jeopardy.'

'I am afraid I do not see how marrying me will put his State in jeopardy. If you mean that he has to marry one of his own people – well, that is nonsense.'

'I mean that he has to have an heir, in fact, and if I recall things that were part of the gossip you hated correctly, you cannot produce one – right?'

'You are a bastard, aren't you, Digby?'

'No, in fact I am being extremely cruel to you because you have got to see sense before it is too late. As it happens, the succession is secure. How old do you think Sher Khan is, Sarah?'

'I do not know. About thirty, I should imagine.'

'And do you also imagine that an Indian Prince of thirty has stayed celibate to that age?'

'Don't be ridiculous, Digby. Of course I don't. But what has that got to do with anything?'

'Do you also imagine that Sher Khan stayed unmarried? Don't *you* be ridiculous, Sarah. If your dreams carried you as far as being the mother of an adopted heir, they lied as dreams always do. Sher Khan already has a son, Sarah – a legitimate son. Sher Khan married one of the Panch State daughters when he was eighteen. His son is now twelve and goes to Harrow. Something you didn't know? I suppose you thought that if you married Sher Khan, David might be adopted?'

The sneer sat oddly on Digby's normally kind face. Sarah looked at him. 'Digby – you hate me. Why?'

'Of course I do not hate you. Just because I'm being realistic, you say I hate you.'

'You are not being realistic, Digby, you are being cruel. But it really doesn't matter. I think I'll now go and brood over my awful future – if you'll excuse me.'

'Sarah, now don't go rushing off in a temper!' Digby, his rage leaving him, was beginning to feel worried.

'I am not rushing off – but I think you ought to. You'll never catch up with the others.' She spoke so calmly and walked away so steadily that Digby was deceived into thinking that she was unaffected.

As he rode away, he tried to justify himself. Sarah had to know that Sher Khan was married, had to see where she was going. He knew, miserably, that she could have been told more gently, and also knew that through jealousy he had interfered disgracefully in her private life and in Sher Khan's life. By the time he rode into the camp where Sher Khan and Alastair waited for him, he knew how dreadfully he must have upset Sarah, and that there was only one thing for him to do. He must tell Sher Khan at once what he had said to her.

31

Sarah sat in the window seat in her beautiful room and looked out at the lake, seeing nothing; not the lake, the mountains massed behind it, or her children. All she saw was herself. A foolish, posturing woman with a good opinion of herself, being manipulated by an Indian Prince who wanted to add her to his collection of women.

But Sher Khan would not fit into that picture. He was too much of a person, too well remembered as being a man of strength and integrity to fit the role of philandering villain. No, it was all her own doing. She recalled every moment of their time together, and through all her recollections could not find that she had not encouraged him. Like a schoolgirl she had stared and fawned and denied and trembled. Oh, how ghastly, thought Sarah numbly, even when I was saying no, he could see I meant yes. I flung myself at him, he only had to look at me.

All her pleasure in her lovely surroundings gone, she stood up, desperate to get away from herself – to get moving, anywhere, to stop thinking.

She went out and called to Dip Chand, telling him to take coffee down to the lake and to tell the syce to bring Bedami round.

'The Khanum will ride?' asked Dip Chand.

'Yes.' She looked at his face, and bit her lips, wondering how much he had seen, and imagining how he and the other servants must have smiled to themselves over this foolish woman who had thrown herself at the Ruler's feet. Before she could stop herself, she said, 'Did you know the Begum Sahiba?'

Dip Chand looked puzzled. 'The Begum Sahiba?'

'Yes, the Begum Sahiba – the wife of the Ruler.'

Dip Chand stared at her. 'No, Khanum. She did not come to Madore, where I usually stay.'

'Did she come here?'

'She came to Lambagh for the birth of her son.'

'Did she live here?' asked Sarah, despising herself.

'No, Khanum. She bore the Ruler's son in the old Palace, and when the baby was three months old she took him to England, and she never returned.' He looked at Sarah, and spoke gently. 'The Ruler has lived alone for many years now – this is not good for a man, Khanum.'

But Sarah missed the kindness in his voice and only heard his words, taking them to be a servant's reason for her presence in the Ruler's household – a woman to solace the Ruler's loneliness. 'Have Bedami brought round,' she said, speaking more roughly than she had ever spoken to a servant in her life.

He said, 'At once, Khanum,' and went quietly away.

Sarah, riding hard down the lake road towards the mountains, thought of nothing but her own stupidity, and how she could remedy it and get away. Tomorrow, she thought feverishly, tomorrow when he gets back, I'll tell him I must leave at once – I'll explain to Alastair –. Her thoughts whirled in her head, plans and ideas flashed and vanished, and all the time she was conscious of the pain of loss, a pain that burned and sickened.

When she saw the little shrine where they had picnicked, she realised how far she had come and drew rein. Bedami was blowing and was glad to stop. Sarah dismounted, loosened the girth, and left the horse to graze while she walked over to sit on the steps of the shrine, looking down over the lake. Slowly the place brought her a measure of peace. At last she was able to think calmly and plan sensibly.

If Julia and Alastair wanted to marry here, in Lambagh, then they would have the wedding without her. She must leave. She and the children would go straight to Bombay and back to England. At the thought of the journey, the trek back through the valley, the long train journey, the boat – Sarah gasped with pain and apprehension and buried her face in her hands. But with her eyes shut she could see Sher Khan's face clearly, every bone and angle, his eyes and his strong mouth. She lifted her head again and made a determined effort to look at her future. For the first time in her life she was glad of the solid fact of her wealth. Poverty and insecurity would not be added to her unhappiness. Her money protected her – money, she remembered, that came to her from Munabhen. For a moment it was as if a gentle hand had touched her soothingly. Munabhen had loved a man enough to leave everything for him, and go away and live in a bleak country. Pain came back – to have to leave this beautiful land she loved so much, not only the valley, but the whole country and its people, *her* people, of her blood. Digby was wrong; of course she had a place here, this was her home, her country, more than England had ever been. The children were happy here too. Then Digby's words came back to her, 'Hangers-on in a state where their mother was the Ruler's mistress.' Hadn't she vowed to herself that no stigma would ever attach itself to her children? Then what, indeed, was she thinking of? She dropped her head back into her hands with a groan.

Bedami was moving restlessly and suddenly whinnied. It was time to go. With an effort, moving as if she was an old woman, she got up and walked over to her horse.

Bedami was no longer alone. Another horse grazed beside her. Sarah looked about her, frowning. Where was the rider? She could see no one, and decided that somebody had come out to worship at the shrine and, seeing Bedami, had withdrawn to wait until she left. She caught Bedami's reins, and prepared to mount.

'In a hurry again, Sarah?'

Sarah stood rigid, disbelieving her own ears. Where was he? She turned slowly and saw Richard standing beside his horse, smiling at her. Her one thought was to get away, and she tried to mount, but her shaking legs would not support her, and she leaned against Bedami, sick and terrified, and watched Richard walk towards her.

'Well, isn't this a fortunate meeting! How are you, my dear? As beautiful as ever, I see, even if a trifle pale. Shocked you, did I? So sorry. I couldn't think of a gentle way of announcing my presence. I mean, let's face it, I was going to be a shock anyway, wasn't I?'

Sarah saw the slow swirl of the sky and the trees and knew that she was going to faint. Even as her grip on her saddle slackened and she began to fall, Richard was beside her and had lowered her to the ground, forcing her head between her knees. After a minute he let her sit up. 'All right? Look – lie down for a minute, that's the way.' He went to his horse and came back with a flask. 'Here, swallow this.'

Obediently she gulped the burning spirit, and in a few minutes the world had steadied again. Richard sat back. 'That's better. Can't have you passing out. I *was* a surprise, wasn't I? So were you – never thought I would have the luck to find you alone.' His steady blue eyes were as hard and cold as always; he spoke with nothing but calm friendliness, yet Sarah was cold with fear, and could do nothing but watch him as if he were a coiled cobra poised to strike.

He screwed the top back on to the flask and stood up. 'Are you steady enough to ride? Stand up, and let's see.' Under his cold gaze she got to her feet, and he said, 'Good. Now, up with you.' He helped her mount, and mounted himself. 'That way,' he said, pointing to the mountain. 'I'll lead, you follow. And Sarah, don't try anything, because I shall shoot you – and if I don't, Dilbanu will. So just do what you are told, like a good girl.'

A third horse had come from the trees behind the shrine; the rider, a small dark Indian, had a rifle slung on his back.

'Where are you taking me?'

'To meet a friend of mine – come on. We've got a long ride.' Richard swung his horse round and started off, and Sarah had no choice but to follow. She was not thinking of anything; shock and fear had numbed her and she rode like an automaton, following Richard, his henchman clattering into his place behind her.

They rode steadily, on a path that led up, away from the lake, a road that wound along beside the fast flowing little river. There were, it seemed, no villages along this way. They saw no one. The lake was soon left behind, hidden by a fold in the hills. They came to a bridge, so narrow and fragile that Sarah closed her eyes as her horse slipped and skittered over it while the river rushed and roared below. The path then turned away from the river, beginning to climb, gradually at first and then more steeply. Soon it grew colder and a fine rain began to fall. The horses stumbled over a path that was now no more than a goat track. Mist came down, in veils and drifting shreds at first, thickening to bring visibility down to a few yards. To one side, dark shapes loomed out of the mist, and Richard clattered and slithered to a halt. He called to his man, who pushed up past Sarah and peered ahead. 'It is here, Sahib, to the left. Here is the path.'

Once more they started off, Sarah wet and cold, riding in a misery too deep for thought. When they finally stopped, it was growing dark. She could not dismount properly, but managed to slip from the saddle, and Richard caught her and steadied her before she hit the ground. She saw Bedami led away, feeling that her last friend was going.

There were men with lanterns standing beside a ramshackle stone house. Obedient to Richard's order, she stooped under the low lintel of the door and entered a small square room, windowless and full of acrid smoke from a fire burning in a corner. There was no chimney. Sarah dropped to the floor to tired to care about anything. By the fitful light of a lantern she saw that there was another man in the room, and heard Richard saying something to him, words she did not catch, but his tone was jubilant. Sleep, or some other form of exhausted unconsciousness engulfed her, and she heard nothing more.

It seemed hours later that she was awakened by Richard's hand on her shoulder, shaking her. It was still night; the hurricane lamp still burned. She sat up, blinking, to find him kneeling beside her holding a steaming mug. It was greasy and really rather horrible, but Sarah gulped the soup down and it revived her considerably. She looked about her. Richard was talking quietly to a man who half sat, half lay, against the wall on the other side of the smoking fire. Through the smoke and the dim light it was hard to see, but Sarah thought his face was familiar to her. She peered, wiping her streaming eyes. At that moment the fire leapt up, fanned by a draught. The man was Sher Khan's cousin, Hardyal, whom she had last seen in the Rajaghar at Madore.

Her involuntary movement of surprise brought both men's attention. 'More soup?' asked Richard. The casual enquiry, in such surroundings, made Sarah choke on sudden hysterical laughter.

She shook her head and Hardyal said feelingly, 'I don't blame you – faugh, what disgusting fluid. How much longer do we stay in this awful place, Richard?'

'Not long now, Raja Sahib. Dilbanu says there is a better place a day's journey from here. So we'll push on and wait there.'

'Anywhere away from here.' Hardyal sounded fretful. Sarah had heard Richard's use of the title – so Hardyal was playing Ruler, was he? Not much royal state for him here, and apparently no other courtiers or entourage. The hot soup had done its work well and Sarah felt alert and rested. She was, however, devilishly uncomfortable; her clothes were still soaking wet, and her hair was matted and damply clinging to her neck and shoulders.

She shivered, and Richard said, 'Are you cold? Yes, I suppose you are. Not much sense putting on dry clothes now, we will be going off again in about an hour – once the horses are rested. If we leave now, we'll be in well before dark tomorrow, and then you can rest.'

'Where are you taking me?'

'To the frontier between Lambagh and the USSR – very dramatic,' said Richard.

'Why? Why do you want me?'

'My dear Sarah, what an extraordinary question for an attractive woman of your experience to ask! You surely do not want me to show you why here!' He smiled at her, and Sarah's heart was filled with fear. Hardyal was sitting forward, glancing from one to the other like a man expecting entertainment. But after a minute Richard said, 'But there are other reasons as well. Can't you guess these reasons?' Sarah was watching him, holding her breath, and this time her fear was great, and was not for herself. He smiled again and said, 'You can't guess? Well, our reasons are simple. You are the bait to bring the tiger. See?'

When Sarah still sat staring, without saying anything, he looked irritated. '*Don't* you see? You are the bait – Sher Khan is the tiger. As long as we have you we can be sure, sooner or later, of getting Sher Khan. Because from all accounts he is not going to leave you alone for long, and when he comes to get you, we get him. Simple.' His smile broadened, and Sarah was afraid that she was going to faint again, she felt so ill with fear and apprehension.

Of course, Richard was right. Sher Khan would try and rescue her – in spite of everything, she knew that he would not leave her in danger. He would try to rescue her, and would be either killed or captured in the attempt – killed, probably, because that would make Hardyal's path to the *guddee* smoother. And it would be entirely her fault. He had asked her not to go far from the Peacock Palace, and not to ride towards the mountains.

Richard, watching her face, said, 'Don't look so depressed. Don't you think he'll feel it is a fair exchange?'

'What?'

'Why, you in exchange for the Emerald Peacock – what

302

else? He gives Hardyal the Peacock – in other words, hands over the State – and you go free. Just as simple as that. You should be feeling very flattered. Very few women are exchanged for kingdoms in this present day.'

'Do you mean that if he gives you the Peacock chain, you will let me go, and won't harm him?'

'My dear girl, of course! What on earth did you think I meant? A dramatic killing? That would not do at all. Hardyal must not step to his throne on the dead body of the Ruler. Those days are over, aren't they, Hardyal Sahib?'

The two men looked at each other and Richard suddenly laughed. 'Well, over for a while – they could return!'

Hardyal pulled a face. 'But you promised me, Richard – no unpleasantness, no blood! I cannot have that sort of thing, I am not a man who cares for violence.'

'Now, now, Raja Sahib, be calm. Of course there will be no blood. Why should there be?'

Watching him, Sarah knew that if Sher Khan came into Richard's hands he would never get away alive; nor would she. The square smoky room was alive with evil and malice. She shuddered, and closed her eyes before Richard's bright menacing gaze.

Presently it was time to go. She stumbled out into the cold night, glad of the freshness of the air, and mounted Bedami. She rode behind Richard, with Hardyal, followed by Dilbanu.

Now they were climbing continuously, the horses picking their way on loose sliding shale. It was not raining, but the air was damp, and it grew colder the higher they climbed. It was near dawn when they stopped climbing and were riding on level ground. As the light strengthened, Sarah saw that they were winding along at the foot of a range of mountains that walled in the high valley in which they rode. Far ahead she saw a break in the wall of mountains. This seemed to be what they were heading for.

32

It was a terrible day. Sky and earth seemed to merge into one, nothing to catch the eye, no sign of civilisation, no tree or shelter, only the grey endless plain, rock-strewn and desolate, and the black glistening mountains. A wind rose and was soon blowing up a storm.

Richard stopped, undid a bundle from behind his saddle, and tossed her a thick felt-lined leather coat which she clasped round her. She no longer tried to watch for landmarks, or remember the route; all hope of escape or of rescue had left her. Frozen, exhausted, she sat on her horse, seeing nothing but the grey blowing mist and the black ridged mountains.

By afternoon, buffeted by winds that swept down from the mountains, they had changed direction again. Now they rode beside a frozen river, the ice thick and grey white. Muffled, ominous, the noise of the river could be heard as it flowed swiftly under its icy cover. They left the plain, and again began to climb towards the pass. The trail was steep and icy, and Dilbanu went ahead, sprinkling sand from a bag he carried on his saddle. The tired horses slipped and trembled, and had to be rested every hundred yards or so. At last they reached the pass and, yard by careful yard, crossed the snowy crest and began to descend. In the distance the river, free of ice, twisted and turned, wide and yellow in the grey stony valley. As dusk set in, the mountains seemed enormous; they appeared to come closer, overpowering and threatening. The gentle country of Lambagh Valley, the white houses and the blue lake, seemed to Sarah to belong to some other planet, now gone for ever.

It was quite dark when they saw lights ahead – lights in such desolation, it seemed like a miracle. So too did the stone house into which Sarah was led. It was warm and clean, with felt carpets and quilted over-stuffed pillows piled on the floor. There was a *bukhari*, a stove, in one corner, glowing with heat. There seemed to be servants – Sarah saw a woman outside the window, and there were several men. She sank to the floor, loosened her coat and, leaning back against one of the pillows, waited for Richard and Hardyal, too numb with cold and too exhausted to feel anything except physical relief at lying down.

Hardyal came and cast himself down, throwing off the coats and shawls he had wrapped round himself. Without his turban, she saw how much he resembled Sher Khan. His skin was much darker, his eyes were black, and his whole face was coarser, but the likeness was there, and caught at her heart.

'Oh God, what a fearful journey! For God's sake, Richard, where's the brandy and tea? Hot tea, for the love of God. I am dying, you have killed me with your accursed journeyings. If I had known what this expedition was going to be like, you would never have got me over the border.'

Richard, coming in, looked tired and bad-tempered. However, he made shift to be civil to Hardyal and calm him down. 'Tea and brandy coming up, and this is more comfortable, isn't it? As for all the journeying, you want Lambagh, don't you? Well, just hang about, and you shall have it.'

'I am not at all sure I want the bloody place – all mountains and stinking weather and stupid peasants, as far as I can see. I was better off in Sagpur. After all, I'm certainly not going to gain financially, when all is said – in fact, half the revenue from Sagpur has already gone, paying for all these lawyers and petitions, and you, and those damned terrorist sharks!' Hardyal was furious and shrill.

'Don't be silly, old chap,' said Richard, obviously hold-

305

ing on to his temper with difficulty. 'Of course you want Lambagh, your Highness! It is your State, after all, and you'll make a splendid Nawab, won't you?'

'Well, I do not know. Oh, where's the brandy? I don't want to talk about this bloody State any more.'

With a muttered expletive, Richard went out, leaving Sarah feeling almost sorry for him. 'Don't you agree today was terrible, Madame Longman?' Hardyal obviously felt the need of an audience. He went on crossly, 'I ask you – Lambagh! Ugh. You do not know Sagpur, do you?'

Sarah looked at him. Tired, dirty, kidnapped, and this man was trying to discuss his affairs with her as if they were chatting at a cocktail party. 'Yes, of course I know Sagpur,' said Sarah, feeling as if she was Alice through the Looking-Glass. 'I went down there two years ago, Calcutta was so hot.'

'Oh!' cried Hardyal in ecstasy. 'You know my Sagpur! Oh, how wonderful. You remember my white Palace? What a beautiful place when at night the sea sighs on the shore below my balconies, and the fishing boats put out to sea, each one carrying a lantern at the prow. You saw this? You remember?' He had tears in his eyes as he spoke. Sarah had to force herself to remember that this homesick man was Sher Khan's most bitter enemy. 'When you come again, as of course you will, I will give myself the pleasure of showing you over my Palace. I have so many things of great beauty there. I have one room' – Hardyal looked indescribably coy – 'well, it is quite a room. It is my special bedroom, you know? I have everything in it from France. It is the exact copy of a room I once had in Paris. The bed is circular, and the ceiling and the walls are all of mirror glass. Oh, what parties of various kinds I have enjoyed in that room! You will like to see it, being a woman of the world, as I understand.'

The woman servant that Sarah had seen outside now came in with a tray. She took it first to Hardyal, and he poured himself a generous slug of brandy and topped it up with steaming tea. Sarah stared at the girl and then ept her eyes down and her face expressionless. The girl was standing between her and Hardyal and, as she turned, Sarah looked up. Yes, she was right. The servant was Ayesha.

Not by a word or a look did Ayesha acknowledge her but Sarah, helping herself to tea laced with brandy, felt hope for the first time. Whatever else Ayesha was doing, she was not on Hardyal's side. Sarah was sure that she had a friend in this camp of enemies. This was one of Sher Khan's people.

Richard came in and, like the others, lay down on the floor among the pillows and Ayesha brought in more tea and brandy. Sarah saw Richard look at the girl in a way very familiar to her – that proud possessive look, the look of ownership. Ayesha's stance was submissive; she did not raise her eyes when Richard put his hand on her shoulder as she bent over him, pouring his tea and adding brandy. She gave Hardyal more brandy, offered the tray to Sarah, and went out of the room, her bracelets clinking as she moved her arm. Sarah felt her eyes fill with tears as she heard that familiar sound. Her tea and brandy only half finished, she fell into a deep solid sleep and did not wake until morning.

She woke to a brilliant dawn; she saw the sky flame red through the window, and felt the bitter cold of morning. The stove had gone out. Hardyal, a shapeless huddle of quilts and coats, was still asleep, but Richard was not in the room. She remembered his eyes on Ayesha the night before, and wondered. At that moment the girl came in, a teapot and bowls on a tray in her hands. She gave Sarah a bowl of steaming tea without meeting her eyes, though there was no one to see them. Sarah said, 'Ayesha.'

The girl, with a slight contraction of her brows, said, 'Lady?'

So. It was obviously not the time to try and speak to her.

Sarah said, speaking as if to a stranger, 'I am cold and stiff. Are there any dry clothes for me? And I shall want a bath.'

'I can bring dry clothes for the Lady, they are my clothes, but clean and warm. But a bath! The Colonel Sahib is bathing in the river, but that is very cold. We have very little wood here, we cannot heat water.'

'Never mind the cold. When the Colonel Sahib has finished bathing, show me where to go, and give me the clothes.' Ayesha bowed her head, put the tray beside Sarah and went out.

Sarah sat sipping the hot tea and reviewed her position which, on the face of it, seemed hopeless. Ayesha had so far given her no sign. Was the girl disloyal? She could not believe it. After all, Richard had murdered her own sister, the girl on the island. No, Ayesha had good reason for not acknowledging her. She heard Ayesha speaking to someone outside and then Richard came in, sleek, haired and glowing, in clean clothes.

'The girl says you want a bath. Well, the river is icy, but go ahead. I cannot imagine you wanting to stay as you are now, in any case.' Struggling to her feet, Sarah felt dirty and unsavoury before his newly bathed magnificence. Ayesha was waiting for her outside. She came out into bright sunshine and looked round her. The flat plain stretched to the black wall of mountains, but there were stunted trees and bushes, and the river flowed smoothly between low sandy banks.

The water was icy. Ayesha stood watching, holding towels, while Sarah splashed and soaped, shivering. But the girl made no effort to speak to Sarah, even when she was helping her to dry herself. She had brought dry clothes, a warm thick overshirt and trousers, and country slippers with turned-up toes, and a thick waistcoat and headcloth. Sarah dressed quickly and then sat on a flat rock in the sun, drying her hair.

'Will the Lady take tea?'

'Yes, if I can have it here.' The thought of going into the stuffy little room, where Hardyal still slept, was unbearable. Ayesha inclined her head and went silently away, and Sarah, combing her wet hair, looked around her. The plain stretched out before her, the wide, smooth-flowing river cutting it in half, flowing from one side of the mountain wall to the other. Sarah stared across the river and fancied she could see buildings on the other side and people moving about.

Ayesha came back with her tea, and two chapattis, and with her came Richard. 'Feeling better? Well, certainly looking better, quite your beautiful self again.' Sarah paid no attention to him, drinking her tea and eating her chapattis spread with honeycomb. This was how she always liked her chapattis. It was like a message from Ayesha, as if Ayesha was telling her that she had a friend who would help her.

Richard, undeterred by her silence, went on talking to her. He showed her a map, very old and yellow, and frayed at the edges.

'Sher Khan is not so popular up here, on this border, as he imagines he is. I got this map from one of his guards. They are very bribable here, which is why we have such comfortable quarters. We shall have no trouble getting this state on our side, once – well, once we have the Emerald Peacock, and things are organised.'

He shot a sideways glance at Sarah, and she was careful not to look at him, not to let him see the fear in her eyes. She was certain he had almost said, 'Once Sher Khan is dead.' She said, carefully casual, 'Why do you need the map?'

'So that I can work out how far we are from the nearest Russian post.'

'A *Russian* Post?'

'Yes. Over that river, and then a bit of no man's land, and then Soviet Russia. People there who will be glad to know that this state is on our side. This is one of the easiest routes down into India, but of course, the Lambagh Rulers have been a nuisance until now. But not for much longer.'

'But is Hardyal going to like handing his new state over to Soviet Russia?' She spoke as if she believed everything he said.

He laughed quietly. 'It won't really matter. He won't

want to stay up here. I shall run this state for him – or even for other people.' He spoke with perfect confidence, and Sarah was once more made certain that if Sher Khan came within his reach he would not get away alive – and nor would she. She wondered if Hardyal himself would be killed too, but did not care. She clung to her hope that Ayesha was not the only faithful person up here, that there were others. Ayesha came up to her to take her empty plate, and once again a proud possessive look flashed over Richard's face. He put out his hand and held Ayesha's arm. 'Ayesha. I left some clothes for you to wash. Did you see them?'

'Yes, lord, I will wash them now.'

'Good girl.' With a lingering caress of his hand on her arm, he let her go, watching her as she walked away. Then he turned back to Sarah. 'Fantastic girls, these hill girls,' he said. 'They love work, and like nothing better than making a man comfortable and happy. Their love making – my God, there isn't anything they won't do to please you. Trained to pleasure men from the time they are old enough to walk.' His voice was almost gentle, and Sarah looked at him amazed. Surely Richard was not being softened by love? He stood up as she stared at him, and looked down at her. 'I must say, those clothes become you, Sarah. You look exactly what you always were at heart. A native woman. Pity you didn't inherit their nature as well as their looks. Anyway, the looks are fantastic. I expect Sher Khan any day now, plus his emeralds.'

'You are quite mad.' Sarah spoke with all the hatred she felt for him in her voice. 'Quite insane. Sher Khan certainly will not come, unless he comes with an army, and he would never exchange the Emerald Peacock for me.'

'Oh, won't he? You haven't a very high opinion of your swain, if you think he'll leave you here in peril of your life, without attempting a rescue. You see, if he doesn't hurry, we'll send him something to speed him up, like a certain long slender-fingered hand, one he has robably kissed. He will come, don't worry. The neck-ce doesn't matter a damn, sweetie. You heard Hardyal st night. He doesn't want this place. But I know people ho do. The only thing I need is Sher Khan, and we shall ave him – today, tomorrow, it had better be fairly soon. hate the thought of taking one of your beautiful hands. Vell, I had better go and see if His Highness has sur-ced.' He strolled away, handsome, debonair and leased with himself, and Sarah sat on the flat rock and tared in horror at her hands. All her hope and con-dence had gone. Sher Khan would most certainly try to escue her, and he would do it with an army. The flat, eatureless plain, the wide, smooth flowing river, the lack wall of mountains, became a nightmare landscape, fit setting for the horrors she was picturing in her mind, nen fighting and dying, perhaps Sher Khan wounded or illed – she shuddered in the sun, and tried to think of ome way of escape.

She could see the further bank clearly now, but there vere no people there, only a huddle of low stone build-ngs, like the buildings on this side of the river. This was bviously the ford, the narrowest part of the river. She aw some inflated cow skins piled nearby, the means hat the hill people used to cross rivers when there were o bridges. Ayesha came down with her pile of clothes or washing and squatted on the bank, scrubbing. Sarah nade no effort to go over to her. She felt sure that Ayesha vould contact her in time.

A man came along the bank, carrying a kid. The animal bleated, and Ayesha looked up, and then stood, beckon-ng, and the man went over to her. There was some talk, ilver changed hands, and the shepherd wandered on, eaving the kid with Ayesha – no doubt the supper for hat night. Ayesha stopped her scrubbing and carried he little animal back to the huts. Then she returned and began to scrub again, but this time she brought the vashing much nearer to Sarah. Suddenly alert, Sarah vaited, and the girl, rinsing the clothes, moved closer still to the rocks where Sarah sat. Presently she was right

in front of Sarah, bending and swishing clothes in th
water. Sarah heard her low voice. 'Khanum, take dow
your hair and ask me for a comb – say you have droppe
yours.'

Sarah undid the coil of her hair with shaking finge
and, after looking among the rocks, said, 'Ayesha, I hav
dropped my comb. Get me one, please.'

'I have one here, lady. Let me comb your hair.' Ayesh
got up, dried her hands on her skirt and, kneeling besid
Sarah, began to comb her hair. The river murmured an
chuckled, birds called from the bushes, and the su
gained strength and lay like a warm hand on Sarah'
back. Ayesha's voice was so low she could barely hear i
'Tonight, Khanum. When Hardyal sleeps, come ou
Come here, and wait.'

'The guard on the door?'

'The guard will not stop you tonight. Just come. I ca
say no more now. Do not question me.' She coile
Sarah's hair up and left her, collected the clothes, an
went back to the huts.

The day was interminable. She stayed alone at th
water's edge, and at noon Ayesha came with food for he
but she did not meet Sarah's eyes and did not speak
During the afternoon Sarah got up and walked about, n
one paying any attention to her. She heard raised voice
from the hut – Richard and Hardyal arguing. It gre
colder, the sun took a downward swoop and vanishe
behind the mountains, and the plain filled with a col
grey light that made the mountains more black tha
ever. The voice of the river grew loud, and Ayesha cam
with a hurricane lamp to tell Sarah that she should com
in. She followed the bobbing lantern back, marking ev
ery foot of the way in her mind. Would it be possible t
move noiselessly down to the river, without falling ove
anything?

The interior of the hut, though stuffy, was warm an
seemed treacherously comfortable after the cold gre
evening outside. The stove glowed warmly, the lamp
threw a cheerful light. Hardyal was jovial, brandy glas

hand. 'Ah, Madame Longman, how beautiful you
ok after your day in the sunshine. Really you are a very
·autiful woman, a pearl. You will be an ornament at my
·urt, perhaps.' He frowned suddenly, and Sarah did
·ot know if it was doubts about his own future or hers
·at worried him.

Richard came in, smiling, smoothing back his hair. He
·oked sleek and contented, with a flare of excitement
·mewhere in his eyes. 'Well, good news. I have just
·een told that Sher Khan is on his way. He should be
·ere, one way or the other, by tomorrow night.'

'What do you mean, one way or the other?' asked
·arah, through stiff lips.

'Well, either as a prisoner, or of his own volition.
·hat else could I mean?' asked Richard, his bright cruel
·lance meeting hers.

Hardyal sighed, and said, 'Well, I hope you are right. I
·ill not stay here much longer, I am bored with this
·wful life. I am bored altogether. You might at least have
·t me bring Sona Singh with me.'

'Sona Singh would have died on the journey, and you
·now it. Can you see that young gentleman sitting on a
·orse on the roads we have travelled, or enduring this
·lace, or drinking soup, or putting up with a night spent
· soaking wet clothes?'

'Great Gods, what a terrible thought!' said Hardyal,
·iverted. Richard brought Sarah a brandy, and she
·rank it, watching the other two. Richard appeared
·uch more casual with Hardyal than he had been up to
·ow. Hardyal did not seem to care for Richard's attitude.
·he wondered if he had any idea of Richard's true plans,
·nd of the danger in which he stood himself, if he got in
·ichard's way. The news that Richard had brought made
·er more than ever determined to get away tonight.
·erhaps she would find Sher Khan and stop him coming
·nto danger. But it was not going to be easy. The servants
·ad lit a big fire of brushwood outside and the fire was
·nrowing more light than the lamps. It must be as light as
·ay outside, she thought, worried. Everything seemed

to be conspiring against her getting away unseen.

Ayesha brought in trays of food, and Sarah ate mech‑
nically, without knowing what she ate. Ayesha w
dressed in red and looked very attractive, her eyes fres
ly outlined with khol, her lips reddened. Richard, wh
had been drinking solidly, could not keep his eyes, or h
hands, from her. Ayesha seemed to return his interes
Her glances at him were provocative; she moved with a
indolent sway of her hips and lingered within touchir
distance of him. Hardyal watched them both with
smile; Sarah with hope. Richard was obviously going
be heavily engaged later in the evening. The only tri
would be Hardyal.

But whoever was planning her escape had thought
Hardyal, too. When Ayesha brought in bowls of drie
fruit, she was followed by a youth, barely out of chil
hood. Slender, golden skinned in the lamplight, h
bowed before Hardyal, holding a tray of little coffe
cups, his doe eyes resting submissively on the face of th
man before him.

Hardyal was enthralled; his eyes did not leave the bo
and when the coffee tray was carried out, he spoke
Ayesha. 'Who was that boy?'

'Lord, that is Sennabhai, a boy from the village. H
sings well. Would you be pleased to hear him?'

'Yes, indeed.'

Hardyal looked restive, and Ayesha said soothingl
'Some pleasures must be felt in private, lord. There is a
inner room here, see, behind these curtains. It is smal
but warm, and there are cushions. Sennabhai will brir
his sitar, if you wish, and you can listen to him withou
interruption.' By the merest flick of an eye in Sarah
direction, Ayesha let her know that her way would b
clear. Hardyal lumbered to his feet, and went throug
into the inner room, and presently Sennabhai came i
with his sitar, and went in after Hardyal. A thick curtai
of stitched skins fell across the door and shortly afte
wards Sennabhai's voice and the plucking of the sita
strings sounded, muffled by the heavy curtain.

Richard swallowed the last of his drink and stood up. 'Good night, Sarah. Sleep undisturbed. Tomorrow ill be an exciting day for us all, no doubt.' He flicked an onical salute at her and went out.

33

How long should she wait? At least until the servan
outside quietened down. The fire was still blazing, ar
the men talking. From the inner room came the plainti
sounds of Sennabhai's voice, singing softly. Sar
began, in spite of herself, to feel drowsy. She got up ar
stood by the window, then went and extinguishe
the one hurricane lamp that was left. The room was
darkness, the fire outside throwing leaping shadows
the walls.

Gradually it grew quiet. In the inner room, too, the
was silence, or partial silence. Still Sarah waited, hopir
the fire would die down, but it burned well; great flam
leapt up, fanned by a rising wind, and the logs crackle
and roared. At least her footsteps would not be hear
She decided to wait no longer. Drawing her headclo
over her face, she went to the door and raised the iro
latch.

The door was abominably noisy. Sarah waited besic
it, but no one seemed to pay any attention. She pushed
open and looked out, then, remembering the excuse sh
had decided on, went out boldly. If anyone challenge
her, she was on her way to relieve herself – but no or
stopped her. There was a guard on the door, but he wa
squatting, his back against the wall, his head dropped o
his breast, sound asleep. Sarah walked rapidly out of th
circle of light thrown by the fire and found herself i
black darkness. She closed her eyes for a minute and
when she opened them, could see dimly. She walked th
path she remembered and heard the river growing clo
er, then finally saw it, paler than the darkness, and fe

her way to the flat rocks where she had been sitting during the day. As she reached them, a darker patch of shadow moved up to her, and an arm she knew went round her in a fierce grip.

'Sher Khan!'

'Yes. Be quiet.' For a moment she was held close against him, and then he released her, his hand fell to her arm, and he tugged her into following him. He led her to the water's edge and, bending, felt about at his feet. She heard him give a grunt of satisfaction. Then he began to throw off his clothes. 'Take off your clothes – quickly!' His voice was only a thread of sound against the river noises. Shivering in the bitter night wind, she obeyed him, and he took her clothes from her and made a bundle of them. 'You can swim?'

She nodded, and then remembered that he could not see her, and said, 'Yes.'

'The current is strong. Hold the cow skin, and let the current take you. I am with you. Go now.'

Shivering with cold and fear, stark naked, Sarah launched herself into the river, the water warmer than the night air. In the blackness she felt the current seize her; the inflated cow skin swung round and, clutching it, she went bobbing into the centre of the swiftly flowing water. She saw a darker shape on the water's surface beside her, and heard Sher Khan say, 'Not long – and we will have to swim. I will tell you when.' Sarah hoped it would not be long. The cold was paralysing her arms and legs, she was afraid she would lose hold of her slimy, slippery craft. The light of the fire vanished; now there was nothing but the black night and the voice of the river and the feel of the water gripping her limbs, carrying her along. Panic began to rise in her. If her hands slipped and she lost her grip, the water would carry her away – where? Sher Khan's voice, steady and strong, saved her, 'Now, swim, Khanum, to your right. Swim hard, pushing the cow skin ahead of you and using your legs – *swim!*'

Kicking frantically with her stiffening legs, at first

Sarah made little progress. She saw Sher Khan's darke[r]
shape ahead of her, and was afraid she would be lef[t]
behind and so impede him. She made another franti[c]
effort and, heartbreakingly slowly, felt the current re[-]
lease its grip and felt that she was making progress. He[r]
legs touched bottom at the same time as she felt She[r]
Khan pulling her forward by tugging at the cow skin[.]
Then, staggering, she was able to walk through the las[t]
few feet of water and up the gently shelving bank. Th[e]
wind struck her wet body like a handful of throw[n]
knives. Sher Khan fumbled with something, and threw [a]
wet garment over her shoulders. 'Come,' he whispere[d]
and took her hand and led her inland, away from th[e]
river. A dark shape, a door, and they stumbled int[o]
warmth, out of the biting wind.

'Thank God! Sarah, you swam well. Are you ver[y]
cold?'

Through chattering teeth she tried to assure him tha[t]
she was all right.

'We cannot have a light, but there are some dry clothe[s]
somewhere here – ah, here they are. Now I will rub yo[u]
dry, Sarah, and you will afterwards do the same for me.[']
With hard swift hands he towelled her until she begge[d]
for mercy, her whole body on fire.

'Good. Now put these clothes on, and then help me[,]
for I die of cold!' Sarah flung on the clothes and then di[d]
her best to rub Sher Khan's shivering body into warmth[,]
until he said that he must dress. 'We must be quick[.]
There will be something hot for us to drink at our nex[t]
stop, but we must not wait here. Come.'

Out into the bitingly cold dark, slipping and stumblin[g]
behind him, Sarah moved in a dream, unable to believ[e]
any of this was happening. Presently Sher Khan stoppe[d]
and gave a low whistle. There was an immediate answer[,]
and Sarah heard the stamp and shake of harness, a voic[e]
spoke quietly out of the darkness, and guided by She[r]
Khan she stopped beside a man holding two horses[.]
Sarah heard Sher Khan speak quietly to him, and the[n]
felt his hand on her.

'Sarah, now we ride hard. You are fit?'

'Yes, Sher Khan, I am ready.' Indeed, suddenly, she was strong, nothing mattered. The dreamlike quality of the night had increased, and if it was a dream, then she could surely do anything. She mounted unaided, saw Sher Khan's shape in front of her and, settling herself in the saddle, gave herself up to swift hard riding.

As they rode it grew colder, and a light rain began to fall, rain which was freezing as it fell. She pulled up the collar of the poshteen she wore, and pulled down her headcloth until most of her face was covered. The sky began to grow lighter but, as dawn broke, the weather worsened, the track grew rough, and their pace slowed as the horses slipped and stumbled. The icy rain turned to snow and blew about them like spray on the ocean's face. Sarah began to feel she could go no further, and wondered how long it would be before she would have to call out to Sher Khan. Not long, she feared – and at that moment the mist swirled aside, and she saw ahead of them a cluster of *yurts* – skin tents – grey against the falling snow.

She saw camels kneeling near the round tents and a dog, tethered to a peg, leapt and barked furiously. Sher Khan drew rein and shouted. There was an answering shout, and a man came out of one of the *yurts* and ran to Sher Khan to help him down and kiss his hands in greeting. Two women came to Sarah and almost lifted her from her horse. She was so stiff and her body ached so much that tears of pain ran down her face although she was not weeping. Sher Khan came up, and with an arm round her led her to the door of the biggest *yurt*. 'Go, Khanum, with the women – they will get you warm. I will come later, I have something to arrange.' The two women, smiling slant-eyed women with rose cheeks, led Sarah to the fire in the centre of the *yurt* and began to undress her. Before they had finished she was asleep, and they took the last of her garments from her, exclaiming over her white skin and, covering her warmly, left her beside the fire.

She woke to see grey daylight filtering through a curtain of smoke in the circular opening of the roof of the *yurt*. On the floor a patch of the thick felt covering had been cut away and a fire of dried dung burned brightly. The place was clear of smoke, which all rose into the roof. All round her, pushed against the felt walls, were leather bags and boxes and baskets, tidily stacked and piled. She lay on thick quilts, and was covered by more. She was warm and comfortable, but as she moved she found she was so stiff and sore that she gasped with pain. Instantly a soft voice said 'Ah, Khanum, you are awake!' and, turning her head, Sarah saw the elder of the two women who had welcomed her the night before. 'You are stiff, Khanum? Wait, first you drink this, then we will take the pain from your bones.'

She gave Sarah a bowl of milk. It was very sweet, and Sarah gagged over it, but under the kind gaze of her hostess was forced to drink it all.

'Good. Now we will work.' She went to the door of the *yurt* and called. The younger woman came in, and both of them took the covers from Sarah's body, and the girl picked up a brass flask from close by the fire. Both women rolled back their wide, full sleeves and then started to rub the oil into Sarah's aching body. At first she cried out in agony, as the strong fingers kneaded and pulled at her muscles, but gradually it grew more and more soothing. The movement of their hands, the ringing of their many bracelets, and the feel of the warm oil, were soporific. Sarah felt her eyes closing, and although she fought desperately to stay awake it was no good. She tumbled suddenly into sleep again.

She woke hours later, feeling rested and moving with ease. How long had she slept? Where was Sher Khan? Sarah sat up, shedding quilts and furs, and found the two women sitting beside her, a brass tray full of lentils which they were cleaning between them. 'The Khanum is rested? Her bones are free of pain?' Sarah thanked them, and said 'Sher Khan?' 'He will return this evening, Insh'alla.'

'Return? Where has he gone?'

'He and the man of our house have gone back to the place of the ford on some business. He will return. Do not fret, Khanum. Now you will drink more milk and rest. Later we bring clothes.' The milk, sickly sweet, was brought and swallowed to the last drop. Her hostess was firm, with the gentle firmness of a matriarch. The girl was not her daughter, she was the youngest wife. 'She is a good girl,' said the woman, whose name was Jamal. 'She works hard, and will bear many sons for my husband. I myself had no sons, but my husband is a good man and did not put me away.' Both women admired Sarah's skin, and the length and luxuriousness of her hair. 'But you must grow more fat,' said Jamal. 'Fat is good, it keeps out the cold. Do you have children?'

'Yes, two, a son and a daughter,' said Sarah, and tears were suddenly in her eyes.

'Ah, may they prosper! Do not weep, Khanum, you will see them soon – and you will bear many more sons!'

Sarah, lying back, wondered exactly what the women would make of her story if she were to tell it. Looking at their strong calm faces, she felt that, outlandish as it would seem to them, they would accept it as part of life, something to talk about round the fire in the winter when they were unable to leave the shelter of the *yurt*. She fell asleep again, thinking with envy of their ordered lives, full of hardship though they were.

When she next woke the women brought a bowl of water, and she washed her face and then combed and rolled her hair up into a high coil. They brought her clean clothes, the usual full trousers and over-shirt and waistcoat. They rolled up the quilts and stacked them away, and brought in a big pot and set it, bubbling and steaming, on the fire. The younger one, Sherifa, went to the open door very often, and presently she called 'They come!' and Sarah heard the thump and clatter of the arrival.

Sher Khan pushed into the *yurt* and stood over the fire while the women removed his outer clothing. He looked down at Sarah, smiling. 'Rested?'

'Yes, thank you. You must be terribly tired. Did you have to go back?'

'Yes, to both questions.' Sher Khan, divested of bulky coats, came over and lay down beside her. 'Oh, Khanum, it would have done your heart good to see the chaos in that camp! They are searching the country for miles around. Richard has been out all day. They think you killed the sentry and ran away. A convenient villager saw you running back the way you had come. There will be others, who saw you in other places – the search will be a long one!'

'What will happen to Richard and Hardyal?'

'Nothing, unless they fall into the river and drown, or fall down a khud side, or have a fight. They cannot go anywhere, and they will just sit there until they are bored – which won't take long. And then they will go back.'

'Back?'

'Yes, back into India. No one will stop them. We certainly do not want them here.'

'Hardyal was speaking of going back the other night.'

'Yes. This is not his line of country at all. He has everything he wants in the South. He is a weak man, and not really evil. They must have played on his conceit, told him what a splendid Ruler he would make, because they needed his money.'

'They? Who?'

'The terrorists, men who dislike order and peace. Richard and his friends. Richard, now, he is a different thing. He can go back – but I wonder?' Sher Khan fell into silence, watching the women round the fire preparing the meal. Sarah looked at him, at his strong profile etched sharply by the firelight, seeing the marks of fatigue on his unshaven face. He felt her look and turned to smile at her, one hand going to his chin. 'Khanum, forgive me that I come before you so dirty – I have no razor with me here. I came in rather a hurry!'

In spite of his smile, his eyes seemed cold and considering. Now that she was rested and able to think

322

learly, she realised that apart from the moment when he had held her in his arms on the river bank, Sher Khan had shown her no sign of love. Don't be stupid, she told herself, one can't expect loving speeches and kisses in the middle of an escape. But however sensible she tried to be, she felt sad and chilled by his attitude. During the day she had looked round the *yurt*, and secretly, despite herself, wondered if here, in these bizarre surroundings, Sher Khan would at last make love to her. Her rested body lying close to him was suddenly alive, desiring him fiercely. Oh, never mind marriage, never mind anything – just love me, love me as you did, take me. To be his favourite, far from being a thing to avoid, seemed the most wonderful prize in the world. Red-faced, furious with her unruly mind and body, Sarah sat still and looked only at the fire, while Sher Khan talked.

The man of the house came in; his name was Wali Dad. He sat beside them, and the two women waited on them all. To Sarah's surprise, there was brandy to drink, and Wali Dad drank with them; his religion did not seem to trouble him. Sher Khan saw her surprised look and said, 'He has learned new ways. He was with me in the desert – Subedar Wali Dad, a brave soldier.' Wali Dad heard his name and turned smiling to talk to them. Watching them, Sarah thought of the two deserts this man knew – the faraway desert of battles and bravery, and this cold tundra, where every day was a different battle, a battle to live. They were so happy, this family, looked so contented with their hard life. Once again Sarah envied them.

After they had all eaten Wali Dad went out to see to his beasts and Sher Khan turned to Sarah. 'Sleep well tonight. We leave early in the morning, and tomorrow night you will not be so comfortable.'

'How long before we get back?'

'To Lamba? We should be there by nightfall the day after tomorrow.'

'One thing I do not understand,' said Sarah. 'How can we travel so freely in Russia?'

'In *Russia*?'

'Yes, Richard said this side of the river was in Russia.

'My *dear* Khanum. Richard must have lost all his maps.
He has got his rivers all wrong. That river was not the
Oxus – the Oxus is about four days' journey to the west.
No, we are still in my state. His information was not
really very good. Naturally, it would not be, he got most
of it from my people.' He got up, stretching, and said
'Khanum, I must go, and let you sleep. We will be up
before dawn. Wear very warm clothes.' He went out
leaving Sarah to a variety of feelings. There was obviously going to be no lovers' meeting about this journey.
Wear very warm clothes, he said – did he think she had
travelled with a wardrobe?

The women came in and rolled out the quilts and
helped her undress. There was the inevitable sweet hot
milk to drink, and then Sarah was left to look at the fire
making shadows on the felt walls until at last she fell
asleep.

34

Jamal woke her, with a bowl of water and a glass of steaming tea. Sarah splashed her face hurriedly and plaited her hair. While she was dressing Jamal brought a pair of fur-lined boots, knee high. 'Khanum, they will keep you warm. Are they a good size?' They fitted perfectly. Jamal also found her a pair of thick mittens.

Sarah was overwhelmed. 'You give me so much, and I have nothing to give you.'

'Please, Khanum, you are my sister. I am grieved that you do not stay longer with us.'

Sher Khan came in, tall and bulky in boots, poshteen and fur hat. 'It is terrible weather, I am afraid, but we must go. It is not right to stay with Wali Dad any longer; we are eating their winter stores and he will take no payment from me. Do you feel well enough to travel, Khanum? For if you do not, then of course we must stay.'

Sarah assured him that she was perfectly ready to go. He looked at her, attired in her bulky boots and coat, suggested that she pulled her headcloth still more over her face, and said, 'I hope you will be warm enough. Very well, Khanum, we go.'

Outside it was still completely dark, and a gusty wind tore at Sarah's coat as she mounted. Jamal took her bridle and walked with her to the path. 'Farewell, Khanum, God go with you. Oh, little sister, remember us with love – we will never forget you.' It was not only the wind that made Sarah's eyes sting as they rode away from that lonely little collection of *yurts*.

When a grey windy dawn broke, the dark plain stretched out all round them, marshy underfoot, making easier going for the horses. Ahead of them, the plain ended at the foot of snow-covered mountains, pushing jagged peaks into the sky. They stopped twice during the day, to brew tea and eat cold chapattis. By sunset the mountains were close above them and the path was stony and began to grow steeper. The wind was stronger, it was like riding into a solid wall, and Sarah bent almost to her horse's mane to avoid the stinging blast. Sher Khan rode ahead of her, apparently tireless. The evening grew darker and colder. Then, at last, Sarah saw Sher Khan draw rein. A rough lopsided hut, with a low slate roof, stood beside the path, and somewhere under the noise of the wind Sarah heard the sound of a river. Here, it seemed, they were to spend the night. Sher Khan lit a hurricane lamp and, holding it above his head, looked round the bare interior.

'Well, shelter at least.'

He brought their horses in, unsaddled and put their food bags on to them. The two horse blankets went down on what little space was left, and then from his saddle bag he produced a handful of dried yak dung chips and lit a fire. The windowless, chimney-less hut immediately filled with acrid smoke. 'The devil – we cannot sit in this!' Choking, he rushed for the door and went out, while Sarah tried to clear her streaming eyes. She was startled to hear movement on the roof, then with a resounding crack, which set the horses dancing with rolling white eyes, one of the slates fell in, and Sher Khan peered down at her. He came back into the hut a moment later and said, 'Is that better?' It was a little better. Most of the smoke went up through the hole, unless the wind changed direction.

The kettle boiled and they drank hot tea, well laced with brandy from Sher Khan's flask. Sarah felt warmth creeping back into her hands and feet. She looked at her companion, thinking of all the times when he had complained that they were never alone together. Well, they were alone now. But Sher Khan was not disposed to talk, it seemed. He sat, looking at the fire, and drinking his tea and brandy in silence.

Presently she said, 'Tell me, how were the children when you left?'

'They were well. I said you and I were going for a long ride, and would not be back for two or three days, so they were not worried.'

'That was kind of you, Sher Khan. And Julia?'

'Julia was out of her mind, of course. Not knowing how to tell her about Richard, I told her you had been kidnapped by Hardyal. I left Alastair to tell her whatever else he thought best. But Sarah, I am sure it is wrong to protect her from the knowledge that her brother is a villain.'

Sarah did not answer him. Julia's feelings seemed of little importance to her. The voice of the wind, the little fire, the hut – walled in together in complete solitude, she longed for him to take her in his arms, and it did not matter any longer that there would be no question of marriage for them, or that he had not been honest with her about the fact that he had a wife and child. Nothing mattered but this burning desire for his love. She wanted his embrace, his loving, as she had never wanted a man before. But he sat unmoving beside her, until the fire began to die down and he got up to throw on more twigs. Then he took one of the horse blankets and rolled himself up in it, and lay down as close to the fire as he could. 'Khanum, we should sleep. If you lie where you are, you will be sheltered.' It seemed he was asleep before he finished speaking.

It was a dreadful night. Sarah slept fitfully, but towards the dead heart of the night it grew so cold that all hope of sleep left her. The wind gusted and eddied through the hole in the roof, sending puffs of freezing fresh air into the stuffy atmosphere. The horses stamped and shifted restlessly, and Sarah felt her teeth beginning to chatter, try as she did to clench them. Sher Khan suddenly sat up and said 'Khanum? You sound like a handful of pebbles being rattled in a tin. I'll make you some tea.' He coaxed the fire into flame, boiled the kettle and helped her to sit up and drink the tea. Then he rubbed her arms and legs until she began to feel the blood running and was warm again.

'We would be better riding than freezing here. What do you think, Khanum?' She agreed, and they saddled up and set off in a cold gusting wind. Sarah found it hard to stay in her saddle, she was so tired. She swayed like a dummy and Sher Khan, looking back at her several times, stopped and waited until she drew level with him. 'Khanum, this will not do – you will fall. I do not like to tax the horses, but the path is easy here. Come, ride with me, your animal will follow.' He pulled her into his arms in front of him and, knotting her horse's reins on its neck, left it to make its own way. They set off, Sarah held firmly by his arm, her head on his shoulder.

Dawn was a cold grey light on the snow peaks. The path began to climb steeply, and Sher Khan drew rein and said, 'Now, are you warm, Khanum? Can you ride alone, do you think? I do not want to try this horse too hard, we have some steep ways ahead.' Sarah assured him that she could now ride alone. The wind on her back as she remounted her own beast was no colder than her heart. She remembered the other rides she had made, held in Sher Khan's arms, but how differently! Sad, feeling more lonely than she had ever felt in her life, Sarah followed Sher Khan up into the mist that wreathed the higher slopes of the mountains. It was, by this time, late afternoon, but the mist made everything dark and cold, and there was no view.

On the crest of the mountain, where the wind keened like a mourning woman, Sher Khan dismounted and led her horse and his, slipping and sliding down the path, a little way, to where two great rocks leaned together to make a shelter from the wind. He helped Sarah down, and made her sit with her back to the rocks while she drank hot tea. The tea was reviving, but she could not shake off the depression that clung to her like the mist clung to the mountains. Tea finished, they rode on down the mountains, and after an hour the mist was left behind and the sun grew warm, so that Sarah was glad to take off her poshteen and strap it behind her saddle. Far below, she saw the curve of the lake and the white shrine. The horses quickened their pace, and sooner than Sarah had thought it possible they were dismounting outside the shrine.

Sher Khan said, 'We have made good time – we are not expected for two or three hours. Men will come with fresh horses and something for us to eat and drink. We could rest here until they come, Khanum. I think we should, we are both very tired.'

Sarah agreed, and he turned the horses loose, throwing the saddles down on the steps of the shrine. Sarah longed to wash her face at least and comb her hair, hating the thought of what she must look like in the clear sunlight. Sher Khan saw her furtive efforts to tidy her hair and laughed. 'Khanum, please – look at your companion before you worry about yourself!' She looked at him, and saw the sunlight glinting on the fair stubble on his chin.

'Sher Khan, your beard is blond!'

'Yes, I would be a half and half indeed if I grew a beard. It would be golden, a fascinating sight with my black hair, yes?' She laughed with him, and he said 'Aha, that is good! I did not think I would ever see you laugh again.'

'I have not had very much to laugh at,' she said very low.

'No,' he agreed. 'That is true. But now you are safe, and in sight of home. See, far down the lake, you can see that patch of white? The Peacock Palace.' He looked with alarm at her sudden tears, saying, 'For God's sake – now must you weep? You are safe, and nearly home.'

'That is not what I meant,' said Sarah on a sob. 'Not why I am crying.'

Sher Khan stood very still for a minute. 'Khanum, we have much to say to each other, but not now, while we are so weary. Later we will talk.'

Suddenly Sarah was furious. 'No,' she said firmly. 'No. I cannot go on any longer, let us speak now.' Sobs overcame her again.

329

Almost in a whisper, Sher Khan said, 'This I cannot bear,' and tried at last to take her in his arms.

But Sarah, enraged, and exhausted to hysteria, said 'No' again, and beat at him with clenched fists.

'Khanum, do not flail about so, you will hurt someone – probably me.' Deftly he imprisoned her hands, and pulled her into his arms. 'There, Khanum, cry now if you must, and afterwards, if you insist, we will talk.'

It was impossible for Sarah to weep for long, held so closely, his chin on her head. She looked up at him.

'So,' he said. 'The floods are over and gone?'

'That is a quotation from the Bible.'

'Indeed?'

'Yes. The rest of it says something about singing birds, and "Awake my heart to be loved" – I think.'

Sher Khan raised his eyes to the sky. 'The ways of women are strange indeed. Now you choose to say such things to me, when we are both tired, dirty and, I fear, stinking fearsomely. This is the time you choose to suggest that I awake and be loved! Oh, I am awake, Sarajan, I am indeed awake.'

After a minute – or an hour? – he lifted his head to look at her transfigured face. 'What a filthy lover you are about to accept.'

'There is always the lake!'

'There is indeed the lake, but how chilling!'

'Chilling?' said Sarah with scorn. 'After that river we crossed, nothing could be chilling to me.'

'Oh, really, is that true? Also, come to think of it, after that river crossing, even in the dark, there is no need for hiding behind rocks to undress! Come, and let me see what I have only felt. Ah, Sarajan!'

35

When the men from Lamba village arrived, Sarah was not to be seen. Sher Khan accepted their welcome, assured them of her well-being and his, and sent them back with messages to Alastair. Then he returned to the hollow where Sarah lay, sound asleep, her slender arms over her face. He sat beside her, watching her while he drank, until, as if his look had touched her into wakefulness, she sat up.

'Thank God, Sarajan. I could not have woken you, but I am dying of hunger, and I want you to have a drink with me and watch the sunset before we dine. Look, I have prepared the feast.'

He had spread out a cloth and several covered containers and fruit and bottles and the familiar silver goblets. 'Champagne again,' said Sarah, a catch in her voice.

'Sarajan, please do not weep over the champagne. Instead, drink with me to the future, at last.'

'Never mind the future – the present is enough,' said Sarah, delighted to find she could say the words and really mean them. It did not matter what the future held for her, she could think of nothing but the man beside her, his fine sinewy hand holding hers, his shoulder firm behind her.

The sun did its usual vanishing trick behind the mountains and in the golden glow they began their supper. After a few minutes Sher Khan said, 'Among all the other things I shall always love about you is the way you eat. Women usually pick like hens, but you love your food. You enjoy it, and I enjoy admiring the beautiful results. Beloved, are you happy?'

'More than I can bear. And you?'

'Yes. We will now turn our minds to other things, or I shall lose my appetite – for food.'

After their supper, as it grew darker, Sher Khan lit a fire. Watching him, Sarah said, 'We do not return tonight?'

'No. I want this night. Tomorrow I will hand you over to your family again, but tonight we will have for ourselves.'

'But won't the fire attract attention?'

'Probably. But no one will come near us. There are guards. No, Sarajan, do not look around you so coyly. They are not in sight, and will not disturb us. No one will come near, I promise you.'

'Not even from the Peacock Palace? I was wondering if they would ride out.'

'They certainly will not. I sent Alastair a message,' said Sher Khan.

'Oh, did you? But then, they will know.'

'Know what, my bird? That we are here alone together, and making love? Well, why not? They will have to know soon. Do you think that we are going to remain at arm's length all the time when we get back, and that I will creep into your bedroom as if I was ashamed to be your lover? Or are you ashamed, Sarajan? Tell me.'

Ashamed of such a lover? Sarah gave him his answer, not in words. Presently she said, 'The only thing – Julia – and Digby –'

'Please, Sarajan. Julia is not a fool. She must have known for a long time that we loved each other, she has eyes! So she has this feeling for her brother, because no one will find courage to tell her he is a depraved villain. I wonder if she has not seen enough in the past to make her think deeply about his behaviour now? In any case, her heart and mind are too full of love and happiness for her to think too much of other things. As for Digby –' His voice changed, and his expression in the flickering firelight was suddenly hard and cruel. 'Digby has done enough. Through him, you rushed into Richard's hands, against my orders you put yourself in danger. Dip Chand told me that you rode off with devils after you. What did Digby say to make you lose your mind?'

'Oh, he said a great many things.'

'I understand that he did. I am sorry you saw fit to verify some of his facts by questioning my servant, Khanum.'

His voice was cold, and Sarah shivered suddenly and said, 'Don't speak to me like that, Sher Khan. I am sorry that I spoke with Dip Chand, I was nearly mad. If you had told me in the first place that you were married, none of this would have happened.'

Sher Khan's voice was kinder when he answered. 'Khanum, I suppose I should have unrolled all my past before you at our first meeting, but at the risk of sounding conceited, I did not imagine you had not heard of most of my doings. India is a very small place, and gossip rebounds from the mountains to the sea, and back. I knew all about you – your family background, naturally, but also your marriage, your affair with that man Whigmore. Why should I suppose that you knew less of me? In any case, I dislike discussing my past. I will not ask you again what Digby said, because he has already told me himself.'

'Oh, poor Digby – he was upset.'

'What a dreadful language is the English language – "upset",' snarled Sher Khan. 'He would have been upset permanently if I had my wish. I am very angry with Digby. The picture of your future life with me which he drew for you was very cruel, as he knew very well how unhappy your past has been. Your children turning into "poor whites" and you yourself an ageing favourite at my Oriental court. Khanum, I am also very angry with you. How could you be so foolish! After all, you have plenty of money of your own; if I had refused to pay for the children you could well afford to send them to good schools anywhere in the world – you are certainly not a pauper! What hysterical nonsense Digby managed to think up, and somehow force you into believing – and what a charming picture you drew of me between you Did you forget what I was really like so easily? Or is Digby so important to you that he can change your opinions so quickly? Beware of making me jealous, Khanum, for then I would be very Oriental.'

'I was too jealous myself to think clearly.'

'Jealous? Of what?'

'Of your wife – the mother of your son.'

Sher Khan put his hands on her shoulders and turned her to face him. 'Jealous of my wife? I have no wife, Khanum. My divorce from my son's mother took place when he was a year old. My marriage – suitably arranged for reasons of dynasty – was really a disaster. I was eighteen, my bride seventeen. I was arrogant, spoiled and innocent. She was arrogant, spoiled, very beautiful and, having lived for four years in France, very experienced. The boredom of our marriage drove us to excesses which astonish me now. Anyway, I last saw my wife on the day of our divorce – I am surprised you know nothing of this. The British and the French press had a splendid time.'

'I never read that sort of newspaper.' Sarah looked at him, suddenly remembered Dip Chand's words, 'The Ruler has lived alone for many years now.'

'Dip Chand in fact told me, but I did not understand.'

'I prefer not to hear about your discussions with my servant about my private life. And there is something else I have to say. I know, from Digby, that you can have no more children. It does not matter. My son is my heir. I want no children from you, Sarajan. I love you for yourself, not as a breeding machine. This state of mine – who knows if I will be able to hand on the *guddee* to my son? The Princedoms of India may be lost, along with many other things, good and bad, in the changes that are coming. But we will have, Insh'alla, a good life together, here in Lambagh Valley; and if I am driven from here, well the world is outside – there will be somewhere else.'

'So long as I am with you.'

'Sarajan, from now on, you will be with me. You

elong to me.'

Once, during the night when the fire, untended, was
urning low, Sher Khan drew his arm from under her
ead and got up to pull together the scattered logs. In the
eaping flame's light she saw him, a beautiful creature of
ard flesh and muscle. She put the image of his beauty
nto her heart to hold for ever, glad that her body could
natch his, that they were young together. Sher Khan left
he fire burning brightly and came back to her, drawing
er into his arms with a luxurious sigh.

In the morning, shivering, laughing, they bathed
gain in the lake and then sat close to the fire, drinking
heir tea, loath to break the spell and go back to the
everyday world that waited for them.

'Oh, this is so perfect!' Sarah looked around her. 'I hate
o leave here. I did not think anything like this would
ever happen.'

'Oh, come, Sarajan, how can you talk such nonsense?
Every move I made, every word I spoke, was leading us
o just such an ending – or beginning, rather. Certainly
on my part, I was sure of eventually taking you in love.'

'Well, yes, I suppose so, at first. But after I was kidnapped, you were horrible.'

'I was horrible!' said Sher Khan, outraged.

'Yes. Cold and withdrawn and hard. Not a word or a
ook. I thought you had stopped loving me.'

'Stopped – started – you make me sound like an in-
ferior engine. Love does not stop or start, it is there. I
love you. I will always love you.'

'We'll, you did not show it.'

'Khanum, you speak like a little girl. I did not show my
love? Listen to me. We were in great danger until we left
Wali Dad. He and I kept watch all the time we were
there, I did not sleep. I rode or walked many miles, killed
a man, swam that accursed river twice. I am, I know,'
said Sher Khan modestly, 'I am a King among men, my
Queen, but even I would have been hard-pressed to
have raised enough energy for a chaste kiss on your
forehead. And Khanum' – his voice grew grave – 'I put

335

myself at risk, which was wrong. I owe my people more than that; for their sake I must stay secure. I risked more than my own life. In my saddle bag I carried the Peacock – I would have even bartered that, if you had been in danger. So never doubt that you are valuable to me. You are the moon and the stars. Kiss me, Sarajan, kiss me with all your heart, and stop being a fool.'

It was so hard for them to leave that place! At last, with a sigh, Sher Khan said, 'We must go,' and getting up began to kick the fire out.

Sarah, watching him and combing her tangled hair, said thoughtfully, 'One thing – how shall I get divorced? Will I have to go back and live in England, or what happens?'

'I know about my own divorce,' said Sher Khan, 'but nothing about any others. We will make enquiries.' A shadow touched her bright happiness at the thought of all that lay ahead.

'Remember the toast you drank last night, "Never mind the future – the present is enough"? Do not worry about anything, Sarajan, it will all be made smooth. And come to think of it, there should be another bottle somewhere. Yes. Here it is. We can have a stirrup cup – not very cold, but strengthening.'

They were drinking when they heard a voice calling, 'Maharaj, may I approach?' Sarah could see no one, but Sher Khan called out, 'Dhanu – is that you? Come, then,' and a man came through the trees behind the shrine and walked towards them. He carried a small basket, and the sun being behind him his shadow was thrown, long and black, ahead of him. Sarah wanted to cry out, 'Keep away, go away.' Any other person was an intrusion. She moved closer to Sher Khan and felt his hand firm on her arm. 'Dhanu, what is it?'

The man stopped, holding out the basket, a small round reed basket, such as was used to send grapes from Kabul and Kashmir down to the plains. 'One told me to bring you this. He said to tell you, Ayesha sends greetings.'

'Ayesha!' said Sarah. Sher Khan stepped forward. Dhanu, tell the others to move nearer the road. We are leaving now. Give me that.' He took the basket gingerly, and as the man ran off Sher Khan took his knife and cut the string holding the lid of the basket.

'Why is Ayesha sending greetings?' asked Sarah, who was feeling unaccountably frightened and worried. Sher Khan! Please, what is it?' For Sher Khan, with an exclamation, had pressed the lid of the basket on again and was staring at it as if it was a nest of snakes. He put it down and stepped back, wiping his hands on the grass.

'Ugh! May Allah preserve us all! A rich gift indeed!' He was speaking to himself, and appeared to have forgotten Sarah completely; his frown made a black bar across his forehead and his mouth was twisted in a cruel snarl. Sarah drew back from him, and without a word to her he walked down to the water's edge and began to wash his hands.

Sarah stared fascinated at the basket and then, moving as if she walked in water, she went to where it lay and, stooping, raised the lid.

Sightless, pallid, marked with blood, two gaping holes where his blue eyes should have been, her husband's head grinned at her, his teeth bared in a terrible grimace. It seemed he had screamed when he died – Sarah could hear him screaming, shrill, terrible, tearing womanish screams. It was only when she felt the hard blow of Sher Khan's hand on her face that she realised that the grinning mouth was silent. It was she who screamed.

'Oh, God, Sarajan, I forgot. For a minute, I forgot. Come away, come to me here.' Soothing, stroking her head, kissing her gently, he carried her away from the terrible thing on the steps of the shrine. When she had swallowed brandy from his flask, and her rigid hard shuddering had changed to sobbing; he said, 'Beloved, do you mourn this man? Yes, of course you do, he took your young love, he fathered your beautiful children – weep for him, it is right that you should. But, Sarajan, remember the man as he was – do not make a new person

337

of him to pin unreal grief to. He has not changed, hi
actions and their results remain, even though he is now
dead.'

'But such a death!'

'Death is death, however it comes. He would have lef
you to burn alive.'

'But did Ayesha kill him?'

'Oh yes, I think so. In fact I am sure she did. Have you
forgotten Lalani? After all, this was how she died!'

'What will happen to Ayesha?'

'She will go back to her husband.'

'But murder – the police –'

'Murder? Who will cry murder? Sarajan, in a day o
two, runners will come with news of a sahib who fel
down a steep khud and was killed. He will be buried
there, and the villagers will raise a cairn of stones above
him. Another accident, a climbing fatality. So, you
would prefer a trial for murder, with all the publicity?'

Sarah thought of all that a murder trial would mean
this was surely a better way. 'But the – that –' she fal
tered. 'The head? That will vanish. Probably return to be
buried with the rest of him.'

'And Ayesha will go back to her husband, I did no
know she was married.'

'Of course she is married. She is Wali Dad's middle
wife.'

Sarah shook her head. 'This is all getting to be too
much for one day.'

'Sarajan, you were in that English atmosphere for too
long. This is still a native State, and many things happen
quietly, as I said, both good and bad. Are you going to
allow this to haunt you, or can you step over it and
continue your life – with me?'

As he spoke, a terrible suspicion began to form in
Sarah's mind. For a minute she could not speak, and her
hand fell away from his arm. Then she said with great
difficulty, trying to choose words that would not anger
him, 'I can forget this, but only if you swear –'

His eyes hard, his voice cold, Sher Khan interrupted

er. 'Khanum, we have, I hope, a long life ahead of us. Never ask me to swear anything. If I say a thing, you will find it true. I will never lie to you now, for any reason. I say to you that Ayesha killed this man of her own will, in revenge for her sister's murder, and her sister's husband's death. That must content you. I will tell you nothing but the truth, always. Now. Tell me, will this be between us, a shadow on our lives?'

Sarah, frowning, looked at him, his strong, stern face and firm mouth. Slowly her mind cleared. To be able to trust somebody – he was right. She had lived too long, not in an English atmosphere, but in total insecurity, with nothing to trust. Now she must learn to trust and believe, forgetting all the falseness she had known.

'Nothing lies between us, Sher Khan, and nothing ever will.'

'Sarajan, it is too much to hope that nothing ever will. We are not peaceful people, you and I. But I know that if you trust me, as I trust you, whatever battles we fight will end in happiness. There will be battles, because those who love as we do are bound to fight over certain things – the passion we bring to love, we will no doubt take into hate as well. And you are a very foolish girl. But I love you with all my heart, and I can say with knowledge, I always will. So, kiss me, my dear foolish love, and then we must go.'

They rode slowly back to Lambagh. It was sunset when they came in sight of the Peacock Palace, and heard, high and sweet like the calling of birds, the welcoming voices of Julia and the children. In tears, Julia held Sarah in her arms, and then she stooped to Penelope's embrace and David's smacking kisses.

Penelope looked all round her, when they were finally seated on the big verandah and the silver goblets were being filled by Dip Chand. Sarah had not taken her first sip, when she heard Penelope sob. 'Darling! My baby, what is it?'

'You've not brought him back – you went all that way, and didn't bring him. Oh, where is my Bonnie bird?'

Julia looked at Sarah, ashamed. 'I let her think tha[t] you'd gone to Madore, just to –'

'Bring back that parrot!' said Sher Khan. He knelt i[n] front of the loudly wailing Penelope, saying, 'Moon o[f] the Palace, listen to me. Please, you are cracking m[y] ear-drums, as well as breaking my heart. The Bonnie bir[d] is still guardian of your house in Madore. You *know* tha[t] every proper home has a guardian parrot. Well, you[r] bird, brave as his namesake, he is doing his duty. We wi[ll] find him a wife, and then he can raise a son to leave i[n] Madore and we will bring him back here. Will that be t[o] your liking?'

Penelope sobbed experimentally once or twice[,] allowed herself to be comforted, and was finally escorte[d] to bed by Alastair, Digby and Sher Khan, with David as [a] sort of outrider in Sher Khan's arms. Julia looked apo[-] logetically at Sarah. 'I am so sorry, but as time went on, [I] didn't know what to tell her.'

'Julie, for heaven's sake, don't apologise to me! Th[e] whole thing was my fault, in any case.'

'Well, I really don't know – Digby seems to think it wa[s] all his fault. Something he said. He's been like a wet do[g] all this time. It has been awful actually for both Digb[y] and Alastair, because Sher Khan told them that if the[y] tried to do anything, or help in any way, they'd quit[e] likely cause not only his death, but yours as well – and s[o] they have had to hang about doing nothing. I am so gla[d] you are back safely. I was desperate for you. That vil[e] man!'

Sarah looked at her questioningly 'Hardyal, I mean[.] What happened to him? Did Sher Khan kill him? H[e] looked as if he was going to kill someone when he wen[t] off.'

'No, nothing so dramatic. He has left Hardyal to hi[s] own devices.'

Julia's questions were beginning to worry Sarah. Th[e] memory of that terrible severed head rose before he[r] mind's eye. Julia looked at her paling face with alarm[.] 'Sarah, are you feeling faint? Here, put your feet up, an[d]

340

lie back. Never mind about a bath before dinner, you look much cleaner than I expected you to. Just rest, and never mind anything. You are safely back, that is enough.'

The others echoed her remarks when they returned from the nursery. 'Oh, I do so agree with you,' said Sher Khan, leaning back luxuriously. 'Let us by all means rest and relax. I feel as if I have been fighting through the whole desert war singlehanded.'

'You look as if you have, old boy – very exhausted and lethargic. Must be getting soft in your old age –' Under Alastair's bright, satiric gaze, Sarah began to blush. She instinctively put up her hand to pull her veil closer about her face.

'Oh, don't bother about your hair,' said the blissfully unconscious Julia, 'you look beautiful anyhow.'

'How true,' said Sher Khan, 'how very true. She looks beautiful, anyhow.'

Alastair favoured them both with a long considering stare, which ended in a sigh. 'Heigh-ho – the wind doth blow – how splendid to be young and in love.' Julia took this for herself, and sighed with pleasure, smiling at him. Digby said nothing, his eyes on Sarah's flushed face. He was very quiet all the evening, but seemed at ease and, on several occasions when Julia was about to ask questions, managed to turn her attention away from Sarah's experiences of the last five days.

They went to bed early, after Sher Khan had twice fallen asleep where he sat. 'You are not going all the way down to the village tonight, surely?' said Julia. 'There must be a room here ready for you.'

'Oh yes, there is, and I shall be glad to get into bed,' said Sher Khan, calling for Dip Chand.

Sarah fell into Ayah's arms in her big, quiet room, and told her everything. The old woman sat by her bed, listening and nodding her head. 'Eh, that is good,' she said at the end of the story. 'Now my children are safe. Ayesha is a good, brave girl. Do not be foolish and waste one thought on that man. I could tell you tales about the

Colonel Sahib – but not tonight. Now you sleep.'

Sarah said good night to her, and then got out of bed and stood by the window. A half moon dripped light on the roofs of the village and on the shifting rippling surface of the lake. So many thoughts and pictures formed and dissolved in her mind that she felt dizzy and, turning away, climbed into her big bed. But here, too, the moonlight disturbed her, coming in and lying in squares and patterns on the bed and on the floor. The curtains moved on a little wind that was like a sigh, and Sher Khan came in noiselessly and took her in his arms with a smothered laugh.

'Did you think I could stay away?'

'I hoped.'

'What, my bird?'

'That you could not stay away. But I was afraid – you were so tired.'

'Tired, yes, but not too tired. Also, there is time to rest, and time not to rest.'

The moonlight moved, and made different squares in different places, but now no one saw it.

36

Sarah woke slowly, with the delicious certainty that she was not alone and that all was very well with the world. Sher Khan lay beside her, raised on one elbow, watching her.

'Ayah will bring tea,' she reminded him.

'Ayah has brought tea. It is over in the window. Come and drink it with me, and see the morning on the lake.'

They drank their tea together, while they planned their day. The children, invading the room with shouts of pleasure and Hans in full cry, were not at all astonished to see Sher Khan. Though Penelope, looking at him narrowly, said, 'Why do you wear a sheet round your waist?'

'Because I don't wear clothes when I sleep, but I felt cold when I got up.'

'I see,' said Penelope. 'What about a lump of sugar? And one for David? Thank you. We are going out in our boat fishing now. If you care to, you may watch us, and I will wave to you. Will you wave back?'

'With alacrity,' said Sher Khan, kissing her.

'You are very prickly,' she discovered, one hand to her cheek. 'You have stung me.'

'Oh, dear,' said Sher Khan remorsefully. 'Yes, I can see, I have stung you. How are you?' he said to Sarah.

'Stung,' she replied, and Ayah arrived and took the children away.

After breakfast Sher Khan took Alastair and Digby aside, and when Alastair came back he looked very grave. 'Julie, darling, what are your plans for this morning?' he asked.

'Well, if Sarah is rested, I thought I would show her the design for my dress and tell her all about the wedding plans. We have a lot to talk about.'

'Yes, I can see – a full programme. Well, we are going down with Sher Khan to the old Palace, and we will be back for luncheon. Kiss me?' Over her head, his eyes met Sarah's, and he gave her a slight nod. Then he left, and Sarah knew that when he came back it would be to break the news of Richard's death to Julia.

Julia was talking about the Padre who was to perform the ceremony. 'He is called Guy. He is a French Canadian.'

'Guy what?'

'Just Guy. Padre Guy. That is his surname. He will come over the hills from Panulkutta. Will we be able to put him up?'

'Of course. But there isn't a church –'

'Oh, he'll sanctify the big drawing room, it is all arranged. They do it in Canada, I think. Sarah, could you sort of soothe Digby? We had an awful time keeping him here while you were away, he was desperate. So if you said something *kind* he might feel happier about staying for the wedding. You see he must be best man. Sher Khan will give me away, Penelope is my bridesmaid, of course, and David is my page. Ayah found some heavenly satin for his suit.'

'Julia, you are not planning to put David into satin knee breeches? Not really?'

'Why not? He'll look sweet.'

'He'll look like a little egg in satin knee breeches,' said Sarah, wondering what on earth she was talking about at such a time. Then she reminded herself that this was Julia's wedding they were discussing, that for Julia's sake she must try and hold her thoughts from the terrible news that was coming all too soon. Julia was now discussing her going away outfit. 'Lambaghi dress, bridal dress. Scarlet and gold. The veil is all covered with little gold stars, and the bodice is gold, and the skirt is like the veil, all gold stars and bands of gold at the bottom.'

'Very tasty. But where on earth are you going?'

'Down to Faridkote, to the House of Paradise. We'll have our honeymoon there. Only a week. Then we come back here for a week, and then off to Madore because Alastair's leave will be up, you see.'

'I see. It all sounds perfectly splendid.'

'Oh, Sarah, I am so glad that I have you, and the children. You are all the family I have now that Richard has gone.'

'Richard has gone?' said Sarah, a cold clutch at her heart.

'Yes. I imagine that after all that trouble, he will have been sent home to hospital, wouldn't you think? I know, Sarah, that you will be getting a divorce. I do know that. But it makes no difference to me, you could not stay married to him after – well, I do know now, what it must have been like. Alastair has explained much more. But you will be happy again, and I am sure that once Richard is given the proper treatment, he will be better, and happier as well.'

This was terrible. Sarah fought for the courage to tell Julia herself before the others came, but at that moment she heard the sound of horses on the road below.

'There,' said Julia with a satisfied sigh. 'Just at the right time. I was beginning to feel like a drink.'

Oh, poor Julia, poor love, thought Sarah, how cruel that this happy day should be ruined for her. Even dead, Richard had the power to spoil and lay waste.

Later, sitting in Julia's room and miserably listening to the girl's broken-hearted crying, Sarah could think of nothing to say. Presently Julia raised her head. 'Sarah, I know he was a cruel and wicked man. Everything I worried about in him was his true self. Alastair was right to tell me. But he was my brother. I can remember him going off to boarding school for the first time, very brave, but hating to go. I am crying for that little boy, as he was then. Sarah, you have less reason to weep for him, but you are weeping. Why?'

'I weep for my first lover, and the father of my children.' Julia nodded, and wiped her eyes. There was a knock on the door, and Alastair asked if he could come in. With him came Sher Khan.

'Julia? Come to me darling, I am lonely.'

Without a word, Julia went into Alastair's arms, and Sher Khan, with a backward shake of his head, drew Sarah from the room and closed the door.

37

That evening it was a subdued group on the verandah.
But the sunset was as glorious, the champagne as cold
and delicious as if no bad news had been heard. Ayah
came out with David, and Sarah said, 'But where is
Penelope?'

'Penelope baba cannot come she says.'

'Why on earth?'

'She cannot, she says, appear before you. She put oil
on her head – indeed, on her topi also.'

'Oil?' said Sher Khan. 'What oil?'

'Linseed oil, mixed with kerosene,' said Ayah flatly.

'Oh, for heaven's sake –' Sarah was on her feet.

'Wait,' said Sher Khan, and went off, returning shortly
with a subdued Penelope, her head tied turbanwise in a
white cloth.

'You smell *terrible*,' said Julia.

'Like a walking hurricane lamp,' added Alastair. 'Why
did you do this thing?'

'Because I want to grow quickly into a big lady,' said
Penelope, burying her face in her mother's breast.

Sarah held her smelly little daughter close. 'Why are
you in such a hurry to grow up my darling?'

'So that I can be a married lady.'

'But who will you marry?'

'Digby, of course. In ten years, Ayah said, I will be big
enough, but that is too long to wait. So I put the oil on to
hurry it up.'

'Well,' said Digby, 'that is very kind of you. Now let us
see – in ten years I will be forty-two. You will be fourteen.
Well –'

'Very suitable,' said Sher Khan lazily. 'In my country, as you well know, Digby, men of forty-two always marry girls of fourteen. Anything over fourteen is too old and doesn't appeal.'

There was suddenly a change of atmosphere, a feeling of tension where there had been nothing but friendliness. Sarah said hastily, 'But, my love, why did you put the oil on your topi as well?'

'That is my favourite topi. If I grow, I don't want to be too big for my topi – I want it to fit me.'

'I see.' The tension vanished.

'Give me my bride to be,' said Digby, 'and let me carry her off to bed. Oh, my dear little love, how you do pong – not altogether hurricane lamp. There seems to be an overtone of something else. *Don't* tell me – let me guess –'

'Well,' said Penelope, 'the mali puts donkey's big business on the flowers. So I –'

'Oh, *no*,' said Digby, and rushed his smelly burden off the verandah, and down to where Ayah waited in the nursery. He was some time returning, and was wearing a fresh shirt. 'Your daughter,' he said to Sarah, 'your daughter is going to be a handful. She offered me Hans, two newly-hatched peacocks and a share in the Bonnie bird if I would be willing to marry her immediately rather than wait for ten years. She fancies a joint wedding I think, Julia. I quietened her down by telling her that if we married she could not be bridesmaid and she changed her mind.'

'We will put a guard on her bedroom door, from her seventh birthday onwards,' said Sher Khan. Sarah bit her lip, but no one had noticed anything, it seemed, about his statement.

A few minutes later Julia said, as if it was the most natural thing in the world, 'Well, Padre Guy might as well build a church up here. There really should be a Christian church here, it is much handier than constantly blessing the drawing room, or whatever he is going to do.'

Sher Khan lifted laughing eyes to Sarah's scarlet face.

348

and said 'Julia, what an excellent idea. We will build a little white church, and ring the bell every hour. What shall we call it? Is there a Saint Julia?'

'I doubt it very much, but there should be,' said Alasair, toasting his laughing girl. 'But you could ask the Padre, though he might not be very interested as he is, after all, a Protestant. I have a strong feeling that he is a Baptist.'

'Oh, you terrible Christians! My little white church will be for everyone to worship in – no religious troubles here, not while I rule, anyway.'

It was dark, and Dip Chand came to say dinner was ready. Sher Khan took Sarah's hand and led her off the verandah to her place at the table. He spoke very low, for her ears alone. 'Church or no church, I have a wonderful thought in my head.'

'What?'

'There is a beautiful long night ahead of us, and we can discuss, and argue, and love each other. My love, your eyes are like lamps. Turn them away from me, unless you have lost your desire to be secret.'

38

Julia was married on a day of blowing sunlight, with the
lake whipped into blue and white movement by the
wind that scattered the rose petals into patterns as they
were thrown at her by the roaring villagers lining the
path to the waiting horses. In the end, Julia had changed
from her white satin and lace into trousers and shirt.
Riding in the scarlet and gold of a Lambaghi bride's
finery was not for her. The villagers took the wedding to
their hearts – for the last week the night had been full of
loud bangs and the falling stars of fireworks, and the
house was heaped with roses on the day itself.

The ceremony was performed in the flower-wreathed
drawing room. Dip Chand had produced a magnificent
three-tiered wedding cake and a banquet. The only
guests were the doctor and his little slant-eyed wife, and
four of the officers from the State Forces. Padre Guy, it
appeared, was not married. He was a tall thin Canadian,
who took everything in his stride and who fell completely
under the spell of Penelope. That young woman, enchanting in white satin and lace, a replica of the bride's
dress, was at ease with the whole proceeding. She
prompted Julia in a piercing whisper, and ordered the
page boy about until he retreated to Sher Khan's arms
for protection. In that safe haven, he raised appealing
eyes and plucked at his satin finery. 'You wish to have
this mummery removed? Your wish shall be granted,
my Prince. Come.' David finished the wedding comfortably dressed in his usual sweater and shorts.

When Julia and Alastair had thoroughly enjoyed their
wedding feast they went off to change, and then Julia
was held close for a moment by Sarah, kissed the chil-

ren, was firmly kissed by Sher Khan and Digby, and
anished with her bridegroom in a perfect hail of rose
petals and dried maze in lieu of rice.

After they had gone, Digby came to take his leave of
arah. Sher Khan had gone to see his officers away, so
arah and Digby were alone. Digby looked down at her
where she sat. There was a soft glow on her ivory skin in
he lamplight; the beautiful contours of her body, the
slim hips and swelling white breasts, were set in relief
against her dark draperies. For once, Sarah had forsaken
her cream-coloured silks and was wearing crimson, the
colour of a dark red rose. Her eyes flamed with the
excitement of the day, her dark hair was loose on her
shoulders. But it was her mouth and her eyes that he
looked at longest, that half-smiling mouth, red lipped,
wide to a point of ugliness and yet so beautiful – and her
dreaming, burning eyes. He stared, and stared again,
trying to engrave her beauty on his mind against the
empty days ahead.

'You are very lovely, Sarah. At least believe that I love
you – that anything I did was done for love's sake. I shall
carry the memory of you till I die.'

'Digby, you will not. There will be another woman,
and you will love her as you love me. You were wrong,
you know, in everything you said before.'

'I know,' he said briefly. 'But I am not wrong about
this. I shall always love you. And you almost loved me,
didn't you, Sarah – almost? I am going now. Don't
altogether forget me. If you ever need anything – Oh
God, Sarah, are you sure of what you are doing? Leave
now – with me. I'll make you happy! I can make you love
me, I proved it, you nearly loved me before!'

'No Digby.' Her beautiful deep voice was like a bell in
the silence. 'No. You see, Sher Khan did not make me
love him. I just do. Completely and for always.'

'You once said to me that nothing in love is for always.'

'Ah, but I did not know love then,' said Sarah with
finality, and Digby turned away and went without
another word.

351

39

Very early the next morning, Sarah woke. Cocks wer[e] crowing in Lambagh, sounding clear and loud as trum[pets], and behind them in diminishing rings of sound, th[e] cocks of every village in the valley crowed, so that the ai[r] was full of the sound of morning and the sky seemed t[o] hum with the sound. It hung in the ear like the note of [a] harp string, plucked and left, will hum and echo lon[g] after the trembling string is still.

As she listened, she saw the first streak of crimso[n] strike the mountain peaks.

Sher Khan spoke close to her ear. 'Your trumpeter[s] sound, my Queen. Are you happy? Did you sleep well?[']

'I slept well, and I am very happy. And you?'

For answer he pulled her close into his arms.

The light broadened, the snows caught fire, and lik[e] quicksilver daylight poured into the room.